BETWEEN THE BRIDGE AND THE RIVER

CRAIG FERGUSON

BETWEEN THE BRIDGE AND THE RIVER

A NOVEL

CHRONICLE BOOKS
SAN FRANCISCO

First Chronicle Books LLC paperback edition, published in 2007.

ISBN 10: 0-8118-5819-7
ISBN 13: 978-0-8118-5819-9

The Library of Congress has cataloged the previous edition as follows:
Ferguson, Craig, 1962–
Between the bridge and the river / by Craig Ferguson.
p. cm.

ISBN-13: 978-0-8118-5375-0
ISBN-10: 0-8118-5375-6

1. Psychological fiction. I. Title.
PR6106.E764B48 2006
823'.92–dc22

2005030673

Manufactured in Canada.

Cover design by Volume Design, Inc.
Designed by Brooke Johnson
Composition by Janis Reed

10 9 8 7

Chronicle Books LLC
680 Second Street
San Francisco, California 94107

www.chroniclebooks.com

This is for Milo.
A love so big I couldn't run.
And for his great-great-grandfather
Adam.

APOLOGIA

This story is true. Of course, there are many lies therein and most of it did not happen, but it's all true.

In that sense it is deeply religious, perhaps even biblical.

HISTORY

Nine of the first thirteen signatures on the American Declaration of Independence were from Scotsmen or men of Scottish descent.

CONFESSION

Is a sacred rite enhanced by allegory, exaggeration, and lies.

TIME

Is only linear for engineers and referees.

SCIENCE

The laws of physics state that given the mass-to-wingspan ratio of a bumblebee, it is impossible for the creature to fly. But it does.

ALPHA WOLVES

CLOVEN-HOOFED CREATURES passed this way.

They were never sure what kind. Some weird brainy kid like Gordy McFarlane or Freckle Machine might know but Fraser and George's limited information about wildlife came from children's television and the free posters that they got with their Pathfinder shoes. The ones with the little compass in the heels that they wouldn't be caught dead wearing now. Those were for kids. Thirteen isn't a kid anymore, you can't walk around with wee plastic compasses in your heels, not if you ever want to get off with Sharon Cameron and maybe feel her diddies.

No compass would point you in that direction; you have to do that kind of thing for yourself or get your friend to tell her you like her and see how that goes.

Toys, crying, and novelty footwear were definitely out.

Fishing was still okay, though, thank God.

They jumped over the muddy track where the cattle, unicorns, satyrs, and devils had trodden and headed down the shingle footpath to the canal.

The Forth and Clyde Canal connects the east and west coasts of Scotland and had, for a tiny moment in history, been used as a means of industrial and commercial transport. Horse-drawn barges carrying coal or machine parts or sheep.

The barges were long gone by the 1970s and the man-made waterway that cuts through the green valleys of the country's central belt had become a mecca for amateur anglers.

Professional anglers prefer a body of water that's stocked with more than a broken pram and some old tires.

The canal was reputed to contain two types of fish. Perch, a small, tasteless lump of tiny bones—a kind of aquatic hamster—and pike, a big, nasty, admittedly delicious freshwater shark that liked to eat perch.

It seemed to Fraser and George that both species were totally fictional; neither boy had seen or caught one of these elusive slitherers and they had never seen anyone else catch anything either.

The story went that when there was a pike about, the perch would all swim away, so that's why no one caught any, and that no one could catch a pike because they were super-intelligent and could spot a fishing hook underwater from fifty feet or hands or whatever fish measure distance in.

Fins, supposed Fraser.

George said that if the perch always buggered off to avoid the pike, then the pike would die of starvation and then the place would be teeming with perch.

The truth is both boys sort of knew there were no fish in the canal and they didn't care. The canal was a long way from their homes and school and church and all that trouble, so most weekends they took their fathers' neglected fishing rods and a few unfortunate earthworms and trudged five miles across the spongy green farmland to get away.

Fraser was Church of Scotland (Protestant).

George's father was a Protestant but his mother was a Catholic and she had insisted that he be raised Roman Catholic (Catholic).

The divisions between the two faiths are small and nitpicky at best.

Things like: "Take this, eat, this is the body of Christ" vs. "Take this, eat, this *represents* the body of Christ." (Millions all over Europe had died for that one.)

And: "We want to put up some nice pictures of Jesus in the church" vs. "A picture of Jesus in the church is idolatry and God will smite those who commit that heinous sin. And if God doesn't smite them it's probably because he wants us, his chosen ones, to do it for him." Etc. etc.

Neither Fraser nor George was in the least interested in the theological arguments of the two factions but they understood that they were expected to take sides and so when they had to, they did. They knew the rules, so they tried to avoid each other during the week, even though they attended the same school and were in many of the same classes. This was highly unusual because normally in Scotland, Catholics attend special Catholic schools and Protestants go to the nondenominational state schools, but a fire had burned down Our Lady's High a year ago and the papist pupils had to attend the regular school until further notice.

As a result they had to attend a Mass in the assembly hall every morning before their secular lessons.

Conspiracy-theorist Catholics (and if you are a Catholic, it certainly helps to be a conspiracy theorist) suspected that the fire was the result of arson by an extremist Protestant group (and if you are a Protestant, it certainly helps to be an extremist).

In fact the fire had been caused by Sadie Meeks, a twenty-year-old assistant lunch lady who had forgotten to turn off the deep-fat fryer in the school kitchen. The temperature had built up overnight and by three A.M. the heat from the machine had reached such an intensity that it melted the adhesive on the ceiling tiles above it. The fiberglass squares fell into the boiling, molten lard and ignited violently, shooting magnificent fountains of napalm all over the tubs of chicken morengo and vats of purple custard.

By morning light the place looked like a black Southern church after a visit from the demons in the white hoods. Sadie had been doped to the gills on mogadon, a powerful sedative given to restless geriatrics in nursing homes. She had gotten the drug from her mother's prescribed stash in the old biddy's bedside cabinet. Sadie suspected the fire was her fault but didn't mention it because she didn't want to get into trouble.

So no one except Sadie knew the truth. Everyone, Catholics and Protestants, presumed the flames were the fault of religious bigotry.

It certainly was the most feasible explanation.

So due to the combustible nature of cheap tiles and chip fat, Fraser and George were allowed to continue into their teens, in a slightly clandestine way, the relationship they had since they were infants living next door to each other.

This pleased them both.

But drugs, fire, and secrets won't keep the world away forever.

The boys had been sitting at the otherwise deserted canal bank not catching anything for about an hour before Willie Elmslie arrived. Willie was considered by the other kids to be "bugsy," which meant he was dirty and probably had head lice. He did not in fact have any parasites on his scalp but he had some nasty little critters grubbing around in his brain.

He was a tall blond boy of fifteen with vivid pocked acne on his white, white skin, which was irritated by his habit of picking and squeezing it for its precious creamy pus. He had the makings of a ruddy threadbare mustache that advertised the color of his pubes, and he smelled badly of Brut, the cheap aftershave that his stepfather wore.

He was carrying a plastic shopping bag and he approached the boys and asked them if they had had any luck. Fraser lied and said they had seen a pike jump out of the water and Willie told them that that was cool, man.

George and Fraser watched as Willie nonchalantly took a bottle of Eldorado from the bag, cracked the seal, and took a swig, grimacing as he had seen others do when ingesting alcohol.

Eldorado was an extremely inexpensive fortified wine from South Africa, a sweet, cloying, sickly brew that had enough alcohol in it to preserve a cadaver. It was famous as the rocket fuel preferred by street alcoholics. Willie had bought it from an Asian grocer in Abronhill who wasn't too tough on the age restrictions; plus, to Mr. Patel, Willie looked eighteen.

You can't really tell with white kids.

Willie offered the bottle to them. George declined but Fraser accepted. He retched when the noxious crap hit his taste buds but he forced it down.

Willie was impressed.

"Yer like an alky, man," he said.

"I know," said Fraser, trying not to sound too proud.

Again the bottle was offered to George but he declined once more, shaking off the derision from Willie.

Over the next hour Willie and Fraser drank the entire bottle, with Willie artfully making sure that Fraser took the lion's share. Both boys were drunk, but Fraser hideously so. He vomited cornflakes, eggs, and bacon into the canal and then passed out on the bank.

Willie laughed hysterically.

George, who had not touched a drop, pretended to concentrate on his fishing.

Willie told George he was a poof for not drinking. George ignored him. Willie told George he was a poof for being a Catholic and George let that one slide too. Then Willie decided he wanted to take off the comatose Fraser's trousers and underpants and throw them in the canal. He said that would be a great laugh.

Willie bent over Fraser and started to unbuckle his belt. He was salivating, his face near the unconscious boy's crotch.

He yelled in agony and surprise as he felt George's fishing rod strike the back of his neck like a cat-o'-nine tails.

George administered another fierce stroke of the fiberglass lash.

"Whit the fuck ur yae daen?" cried Willie.

"Leave him alone."

Willie stood and faced George. He swayed, trying to look as dangerous and unpredictable as his stepfather.

George stood his ground, ready to fight.

Willie saw that and backed down.

"You jealous ah wis gonnae see yer bumchum's tadger?"

George said nothing.

"Youse two are poofs, fuckin arsebandits, man. Ah'm tellin ivrybody."

He staggered off, pretending to be more drunk than he really was.

George rolled Fraser onto his side so that if he threw up in his sleep he wouldn't choke on it, then he went back to his fishing and waited for him to wake up. He had been around drunk people before; his father was Scottish and his mother was Irish.

He didn't wonder why he had attacked Willie, he sort of knew. He had sensed that Fraser and he himself were in danger, that if Willie had gotten away with taking off Fraser's clothes, that somehow things would have gotten worse and that he would be implicated too.

He had reacted instinctively in the presence of a predator.

Willie was later convicted of the rape of an eleven-year-old girl. He was sentenced to six years in a young offenders' institution, where eventually he hung himself in his cell.

The girl, Susan Bell, grew up to be the well-respected art critic on the *Glasgow Herald*. She had, predictably, trouble in her relationships with men and suffered periodically from deep depressions. At thirty-eight years old she finally entered psychotherapy and began to get some relief.

After two hours Fraser awoke feeling utterly miserable and sick. George told him what had happened and the boys were quiet on the long walk home.

George had been forced into a situation he didn't want by Fraser's stupidity and he resented that. Fraser was embarrassed and blamed George for his discomfort.

And it came to pass that the innocents were cast out of paradise.

Although they were always polite and they palled around for a few years to come, their friendship pretty much ended on that day.

HOLY FOOLS

IN THE BEGINNING, Saul took the worst of it, and in the end, Saul also took the worst of it. Leon was lucky, one lucky son of a bitch. An absolutely crazy bitch.

Leon always thought that his spectacular singing voice and incredible vocal timing were gifts from God. Sometimes, in an orthodox groove, maybe even from G-d. Praise God, Praise Jesus, Amen, Hallelujah, my friends, please send your donations to the number on the screen.

Saul, his younger brother, was less prone to preaching. He was the mystic, the brains, and plain grateful to be alive. He just ate, sat in his chair, and had hookers masturbate in front of him. He couldn't touch them anymore. Couldn't even jerk himself off anymore, no point anyway. Fuckin dead from the neck down, had to have staff just to wipe his ass.

He could count money, though, he still got a little solace out of that.

They weren't Jewish (Mom's family were Italian, originally from Rome) but she was a great admirer of the late Sammy Davis Jr. If Sammy had converted to Judaism, then surely there must be something in it. She gave the boys their names because she figured they would be helpful if the boys ever ended up in show business like their fathers.

Sophie, Saul and Leon's mother, had been a showgirl at the Sands Hotel in Las Vegas toward the end of an era when the Rat Pack were fatter and drunker and already halfway dead. Frankie banged her in the penthouse suite and even gave her a bracelet. "To Sophie, love Frank." She hocked it immediately.

Ring a ding ding.

Sophie thought about Frank's cock sometimes, how famous it was. Not as famous as his voice, sure, but famous in cock terms. Most cocks were seen by only a handful of people: Mom, Dad, creepy uncle, priest, bunkmates, and lovers. Frank's cock had been seen by thousands of showgirls. It was a well-known cock; more than well known, it was a star. Jesus, Frank's cock probably had anecdotes.

Sophie thought how ordinary Frank's cock looked, thought about the famous women it had been inside. (She fleetingly compared her pussy to Ava's but quickly came to the conclusion that that was a way to make her feel even more inferior. Ava's would be warmer, sexier.)

Like many of her sex, Sophie was fiercely competitive with other women, working on the crackpot theory that if she could be better in some way, men would like her more, respect her. Make her happy. She never cottoned on that the men she was attracted to, the men who found her attractive, didn't like women.

They liked variety. And fucking.

She never thought about Ava's dotage and death. She never thought how booze-sodden and miserable Ava had been at the end, hacking and shaking with DTs as she sat on the precious, much-envied cooze, now as dry and unused as an old hymnbook.

Sophie was too busy thinking about herself. Which was a major contributory factor in Leon's narcissism and Saul's staggering obesity.

By the time he was thirty, Leon had been variously diagnosed by a wide array of sources as talented, misogynistic, gay, straight, bi, a genius, a moron, sexy, shut-down, crazy, and cute. He was charismatic.

By the time Saul was thirty, he had been described as schizophrenic, manic depressive, bipolar, alcoholic, addictive, ADD, ADHD, sociopathic, deviant, sinful, and disgusting. He also weighed over three hundred pounds. He had a big appetite, it damn near killed him.

Their daddies weren't around to keep an eye on them.

They knew that the only person watching them was God. They knew God was on their side.

God saved them from their mother, Hollywood, and the killer ducks. What also saved Leon was his mother's belief that he was Frank's kid, and that if she harmed him in any way, Frank would somehow find out and would send the boys round, but Frank didn't even know Leon existed. It was never proven he was Frank's anyway.

There had been no DNA testing, no paternity suits. She was terrified of Frank being angry (she told him she was on the Pill), that he'd set his friends on her. That's why she moved back to Atlanta.

Leon had that wonderful voice and that incredible timing, so his mother steered clear of him. His mother concentrated on Saul, who was the result of a knee-trembler with Peter Lawford in the parking lot of "Love-it's" Frozen Custard. No one was afraid of that English pansy. He had lovely hands, though.

Munchausen by Proxy, the psychiatrist called it in court. The judge, a fat, old, pompous idiot used to dealing with drunks and winos, made him explain. Munchausen by Proxy was a condition that Sophie had: It meant she harmed Saul to get attention for herself. If he had mysterious stomach upsets (a little rat poison in his Cheerios) or strange episodes at school (LSD on rye with Oscar), then she would be a martyr. Long suffering, single parent, victim.

Special.

Helped.

This was before everyone in America became a victim.

The judge was appalled. This floozy had gone from Atlanta to Las Vegas and returned with two illegitimate children. Now she was physically hurting one of them and driving both of them crazy. He ordered Sophie placed in a mental institution and placed the boys in the custody of the state.

Saul was dismayed. He had resigned himself to the life of a gastrointestinally challenged mystic (LSD and rat poison), it was his identity, and now a court-ordered shrink told him he wasn't who he thought he was, that his mom was a fruitcake. He couldn't accept that, so he set out to become what he thought he was, as many do.

Leon felt guilty because Mom had gotten into trouble. Sophie died in the asylum. She was sitting on a deck chair in the grounds when she was stung by a bumblebee and had a massive allergic reaction. She had been slammed to the back teeth on Thorazine and no one even knew she was dead until it was time for round up and medicate. No one had noticed her. Most of the nurses had been in a meeting in the main building about the need for more nurses, as the hospital was hopelessly understaffed.

The boys lived in a state orphanage until their teens, then they ran away together.

The Lanky Crooner and Fat Rasputin in their own little road movie.

The Road to God.

PREPARATION

THE PROBLEM WITH SUICIDE is that it seems so flamboyant. It's camp. You have to be a bit of a drama queen to ever seriously consider it. Of course, George could make it look like an accident but that was inherently dishonest and he didn't want his last act on Earth to be a lie. He was very proud of how honest he was. He was glad that he had been a good man in life. He had been decent. A good egg.

Although maybe he hadn't been so good after all. Maybe that's what this was about. Maybe this was punishment. God knows he had a secret or three. Honest at work, honest in business, but not honest at home.

No, that's crazy thinking, just being emotional—understandable but not true. You could make yourself nuts that way.

He wasn't any worse than anyone else. Come on, he was a good man.

Although he wasn't that way to ward off juju. He wasn't a worker bee for Jesus. It wasn't that he wanted to store up karma for just such an occasion, like most people. He wasn't putting a little bit by for his miracle.

It was just his nature. Being a decent man just came naturally to him, it wasn't a struggle.

Consequently he had never really struggled. He hadn't had any practice, so he was in no condition for a lengthy, dramatic, painful fight that he was predestined to lose. He hadn't built any resistance.

He had worked hard and applied himself but he had never fought any inner demons. He didn't have any.

He did now.

A little dark inner demon sitting on his lungs.

Two times two is four, four times four is sixteen . . .

God, they grow so fast, don't they?

You have no fucking idea.

He didn't say that, of course.

No point in being rude just because you were dying. It's not as if it was going to change anything.

So he kissed Sheila and Nancy and patted Bruno and went out the door at half past eight as always, but when he got to the service station he filled the tank and took a left onto the M73 south.

George was never going to work again.

Fraser had a problem.

Fraser's problem was that he wanted people who didn't know him to like him, that's what made him bitter and desperate. When a person he didn't know didn't like him, as will happen eventually to anyone, he couldn't take it.

It made him furious.

Margaret, his agent, thought this was an example of just how arrogant and power crazy he really was.

"It's the nature of fame," she reassured him for the seven hundredth time. "Christ, Fraser! Some people didn't even like Jesus. He got killed for being famous. At least nowadays they just print a photograph of you looking fat in a supermarket."

Fraser would never discuss Jesus with Margaret.

"I won't discuss Jesus with you, Margaret," he told her. "It's inappropriate. You're an agent, which means you are in the employ of the Earl of Hell."

Margaret didn't really like Fraser but she thought she did. She tricked herself into believing he was complicated and artistic. That he was difficult because he was talented. She thought of herself as long-suffering and kind, which she was, as long as the money was coming in. Like most sharks, Margaret liked to think of herself as a victim of the cruel sea.

Becoming a television evangelist is not something that Fraser had even thought about before it happened to him. He had never been particularly religious, having been raised a Protestant. As a child he had gone to church with the other children at Christmastime and Easter and he had joined in as the other smelly little Scottish chubsters had mumbled their way through dreary English Victorian hymns that they had been forced to learn by Mrs. Hume, the highly caffeinated music teacher with the one vibrating eye.

Mrs. Hume's vibrating eye was a source of wonder to all the ten-year-olds in her charge. It danced from side to side as if she were watching a high-speed game of tennis on a very small court. The eye went faster the angrier she got, and of course, teaching a class of Scottish children how to sing "In the Bleak Midwinter" would make anyone tense.

George said that Mrs. Hume's eye vibrated because she was a witch.

Mrs. Hume spent her appendix years in a Kafkaesque prefab nursing home in Airdrie, watching TV all day and waiting for death to remember her. She became one of Fraser's biggest fans, watched his show every day. She even sent him a letter, a drooling warble of sycophancy on Hallmark pink.

She received a form letter and a head shot of Fraser looking pious and concerned in one of his trademark jumpers. One of the nurses Blu-Tacked it to the wall next to her bed and Fraser's face was the last thing she saw on this Earth. Her heart filled with love as the eye slowly ticked to a stop.

Neither one of them was aware of their history. She did not remember he was the tubby little fart-machine she had belted with a leather tawse in 1972 and he did not remember her at all.

Margaret dealt with his fan mail. Such as it was. The host of a five-minute religious segment late at night on Scottish Television was hardly in the Tom Jones league. His fans were gay men and old ladies. The old ladies loved his pithy wee stories that tried to put a positive spin on everything and the gays loved his jumpers, which ofttimes were sent in by the old ladies, who had knitted them themselves. After a while it became quite a craze among certain types of flamboyant Scottish homosexual men to knit jumpers and send them in to see if Fraser would wear them.

Fraser's photograph hung in gay bars.

He didn't know it but he was yet another unwitting icon.

Today his jumper had a creamy seagull with a red beak and a small black eye hovering fluffily over a pea-green sea. An inexplicable triangular pink mountain in the background a secret sign from the Knitter to the Queer Illuminati. The wardrobe lady, Daisy, had picked it out. Her long years of experience told her that it would have a high irritability and itchiness factor under the studio lights.

"Look at me. Who makes these things? I feel like a child's drawing."

Margaret sighed. "You need to do everything to keep your loyal viewers. In fact, keep it on for the meeting after the taping. It'll remind them of your cult status."

"What meeting?"

"With Gus, head of programming. It's renegotiation time. We're asking for a raise."

"Oh yeah. I forgot."

Fraser had a fantastic capacity for forgetting. It was a skill he had developed as a teenager in order to better lie to the teachers.

"Who else was there, boy?"

"I don't remember, sir."

"Right, boy, hands out."

But being physically abused by a well-equipped adult is better than being called a rat and despised by your fellow acne sufferers.

In 1979 the European Court of Human Rights banned corporal punishment in Scottish schools. A year too late for Fraser and George.

They grew up being whacked across their outstretched hands by state-endorsed bullies. The hands had to be placed up, in front, in supplication, to receive the Calvinist benediction of pain.

There is a town in Scotland called Lochgelly, which was badly affected by the court ruling. Lochgelly was the town that made the belts for teachers to use in schools. The "strap," as it was called by the children and teachers alike, was about eighteen inches long and an inch thick, with two or three strands on one end and a hole at the other, so it could be hung in the classroom as a deterrent to the unruly.

It came in three densities: the Lochgelly Hard, the Lochgelly Medium, and the Lochgelly Soft. There was some talk among the kids that there was such a thing as the Lochgelly Extra-Hard but most dismissed this as scaremongering. Actually, those in the know, and Fraser was certainly one of them, were acutely aware that the Lochgelly Soft was the one to be most feared. In the hands of a skilled thug like Mr. Weir (a.k.a. Le Merde), the French teacher, the softie inflicted a terrific shock of pain followed by a numbness and trembling that lasted for almost an hour.

It was the drama of the strap that really made it terrifying, though. The Ritual. The fact that a teacher, normally a sedate portly smoker with a disappointed air, would be so full of hate that he would shake off his torpor and use all that energy and a piece of expensive equipment to hurt a child was just awe inspiring to the victims. It really instilled terror, and that's the thing about terrorism—it works. Especially for the terrorists—they might not get what they want but it feels damn good trying.

For many terrorists, the means *is* the end.

Some of the sexier teachers really got off on the fear. Big Jim Sullivan (Assistant Headmaster—Lochgelly Soft—a.k.a. Big Jimmy, God, T.T.C. [The Total Cunt], and Skippy) used to carry his around with him in the inside pocket of his academic cloak. *A cloak*—in a comprehensive school in Scotland in the 1970s. Darth MacVader.

Miss Allen (History—Lochgelly Medium—a.k.a. Fannypad and Wonder Woman) kept hers in her handbag next to her sanitary towels and her dog-eared copy of *The Joy of Sex*. She was having an affair with

Mr. Stirling (English Lit.—no belt—beard, long hair, velvet jacket, a.k.a. Pretty Boy, Hippyshake, and Gilbert O'Sullivan). The pupils punished Mr. Stirling mercilessly for his nonviolent teaching methods until he started sending them to T.T.C. to be dealt with. It was, just as the children had supposed, not true that he was nonviolent. He was just a coward. A sneaky coward who got someone else to do his dirty work. Of course, Mr. Stirling was English.

Fraser and George and all the other children had to be ever vigilant in the face of such an intelligent, perverse, and cruel enemy. Sun Tzu wouldn't have lasted a fortnight.

Nowadays, Scottish kids are contained using the much more humane system of the X-box and heroin.

Fraser wasn't particularly badly behaved. He got into no more scrapes than anyone else, just the usual pranks and pushing matches with other boys. His curse was that he was charismatic and physically attractive. Tall, black hair, blue eyes, straight teeth—all present. All white.

Genetic luck is what made him stand out from the herd. A crime in itself. Not that it's unusual to be punished for your DNA. Millions were packed into the ovens for just that, so in many respects Fraser got off very lightly indeed.

It wasn't a case of why he was punished. It was a case of when.

So Fraser left school when he was sixteen. He wasn't stupid, or academically unsuccessful, but he couldn't take the fear and the constraint any longer. Mr. Tweed, his English teacher (Lochgelly Medium, a.k.a. Tweedy and Hammy Hamster), was terribly disappointed. He confronted Fraser through a nibbled Ritz cracker.

"Why? Your results are just getting good. You work hard for the next two years, you could go to university."

"I'm sixteen. I can leave. I'm going."

"You hate school so much, you want to throw the rest of your life away?"

"That's not how I see it, sir. I just don't like to be in an institution where they tell you where they would like you to be by ringing a bell. I feel like a lab rat."

"Don't be ridiculous."

The conversation would have gone on, perhaps Tweedy would have talked him out of it, but the bell rang and he had to go and force-feed Dickens to 4B.

It was at this point that Fraser's and George's roads took different directions. Fraser was leaving and George was staying on to take higher education. He wanted to be a criminal defense lawyer.

George had developed a thing about standing up for people he thought needed his help since the time he had whipped Willie Elmslie with a fishing rod on the canal bank; plus he thought it would be like on TV.

Different case every week with satisfying endings and lessons learned. Also—good money.

"It'll be like being an accountant without the fun," said Fraser.

"Thanks," said George.

"You are the wind beneath my wings," said Fraser.

"Fuck off," said George.

They had been drifting apart for a while.

Home was sanctuary, the only nonviolent place in Fraser's life in the 1970s. His father never hit his kids, really because of all the fuss it caused, not through any real philanthropic notion. Mr. Darby's fear of intimacy extended to not punishing his children. Mr. Darby liked order. Liked things neat. This is because, as a ten-year-old child in Glasgow, he had seen twenty-three of his classmates killed when a German bomb fell on his school. He never wanted to be around anything that untidy ever again. Any kind of untidiness made him nervous. He even thought of himself as Mr. Darby.

Fraser's mother, Janice, was actually quite a happy soul but she had to hide it because, like all pseudo-intellectuals, she thought being cheery made her look stupid, which of course she was for believing that rubbish in the first place.

She liked to talk about Sartre sometimes, just as insurance.

The fact that Fraser had left school without any academic qualifications or certificates was a source of worry for his parents. His mother was actually secretly grateful. She lived on worry and Fraser's behavior was a particularly nourishing source. That's why he was her favorite. She had another kid, Fraser's older sister by two years, Elizabeth. An attractive, well-adjusted young woman who excelled in school, so was of no real interest to her mother.

Actually, during Fraser's rise to fame, Elizabeth got a Ph.D. in chemistry, married her high-school boyfriend Duncan, had two children, adopted another, and became the head of research and development for a large pharmaceutical company, but she always thought her mother would have been more interested if she'd been an anorexic lesbian circus performer with an addiction to self-mutilation.

And she was right. It wasn't that her mother didn't love her, it's just that Janice could only express love through concern and interference, and you can't really apply that to someone who's doing fine.

Fraser's mother managed to love him a lot. Ever since he was a baby he had provided her with fuel. He got croup at an early age. He was late with potty training. He didn't speak until he was two, he had terrible tantrums. He wet the bed. He was her dream child.

The bed wetting was a godsend. She dragged Fraser to specialists, psychiatrists, psychologists, and therapists, none of whom seemed to think there was much wrong with him but a small and rather weak bladder. Janice was sure it ran deeper, it was in "his subcontinent." One therapist, a pale-skinned and freckly ginger quack with a hacking cough whom Janice had been referred to by her exasperated GP, actually prescribed a bed-wetting monitor for Fraser.

An experimental device being tested by the National Health Service at the time, it was an electric blanket that fitted under the regular sheet that when hit with urine would emit a blood-curdling siren that would wake the whole house. The idea being that the patient would learn to avoid setting off the siren by going to the bathroom.

It really worked in reverse; Fraser damn near shat himself the first time it went off, as did everybody else in the house. The device only lasted two nights, until Mr. Darby decided it was disrupting family life, but by then it was too late. Fraser had developed a problem with his subcontinent. That is to say, he became subcontinent. Peeing himself in moments of great stress or when standing too close to a passing fire engine.

His father always thought he was gay, which meant he didn't really count. His father preferred Elizabeth. Good, reliable, and hard-working, like a Volvo.

The real reason Fraser left school is that he knew sooner or later a teacher would give him the strap and he wouldn't be able to hold the pee till he got to the bathroom. He would pee himself in front of the entire class.

Like most teenagers, he couldn't have lived with that.

He left school to save his life.

Fraser sat in the leather armchair on the set decorated to look like the sitting room of a Scottish church minister's manse in the 1950s. A standard lamp next to him, a small table with prop books and a cheap print of *The Monarch of the Glen* on the cardboard wall behind him. A stuffed canary sat self-consciously on a wooden perch in a gilded cage.

The buxom new makeup woman, Paula, fussed with Fraser's eyebrows, her breasts inches from his face.

He whispered to her, "Come to my room later. I'm going to fuck you, you naughty minx."

She giggled. "You are so bad."

But she would be there.

High up in the sound gallery, Stevie Henderson and old Charlie MacDuff smiled at each other.

"I tell you," said Stevie, "if he forgets to take the microphone off again I'm recording it."

Charlie laughed. "I am way ahead of you, youngster."

Women liked Fraser. He was very happy about that because he liked them right back. He had been a tubby kid, so the primary girls hadn't noticed him at all, preferring the boys who looked like girls.

When puberty hit, he stretched, the puppy fat disappearing so fast that he didn't even notice. There was a day in school, though, when

Amy Harrison talked to him on the stairs, said he had nice shoes. Said he was funny. Asked if he had a girlfriend. She came on pretty strong. She made it very clear, as women do, what she thought.

Fraser was glad he had just come from the bathroom, although after she left he went back there anyway.

Amy Harrison was gorgeous, and had breasts. Unbelievable.

As soon as he got home Fraser went to the bathroom and masturbated, thinking about Amy.

He feigned illness the next day, and once everyone was out of the house, he went to Elizabeth's room and put on one of her skirts and her tights. Then, looking at his erection in the mirror, he jerked off again, imagining the image of women's underclothing; his hands and cock were really him fucking Amy.

The results were spectacularly pleasant for him. He vowed to do it again as much as possible. And he did. He was never caught, and when he actually started really having sex with Amy, he ended his little brush with transvestism. He didn't think about it much until years later when he mentioned it to Carl, his therapist, who as you can imagine was delighted.

No one actually came out and said it, but vis-à-vis sex the prevailing wisdom in the Darby household was that men were horny bastards and wanted sex all the time, and women didn't really like sex but would let men do it as a favor in return for curtains and furniture.

Maybe some women liked sex but they were bad and dirty and probably Catholics.

What amazed Fraser, as he thought about this years later, was how frighteningly accurate it was. He was very grateful that he hadn't been brought up to believe that sex was a natural expression of love between a man and a woman. It would have taken all the fun out of it.

"Coming to you in five, four, three, two . . ."

The floor manager mimed the "one" and swept his arm below camera two.

Fraser was looking skyward, a beatific smile on his face, as if Jesus had just told him a joke he had heard before but he wanted to be polite. After a short pause, he turned and looked directly into the camera and read from the TelePrompTer.

"Hello, everyone. When I was a wee boy I had a cairn terrier puppy—a cheeky wee thing with whiskers that made him look a bit like my grandpa. . . ."

In the sound gallery Charlie MacDuff pretended to vomit.

Fraser continued, "My father had gotten him from a man at work. He said that the owner was going to drown him because he had no room for a puppy, and would I look after him. Of course, like any little boy, I was delighted. I named him Blackie, because he was black. That dog followed me everywhere, to Mr. McMurtry's shop when my mother sent me for potatoes, to Stoorie Burn when I went fishing, and when we went to my granny's house on Sunday, Blackie would sit outside waiting patiently for us to come out. My granny was a proud woman and she didn't want dog hairs on her Axminster carpet.

"When you think about it, that wee dog was a little bit like Jesus, wasn't he? Waiting for you, a faithful, loyal, and true friend. Although you can't nourish Jesus on Boneos and Bacon Bits, he needs your love and faith. . . ."

As Fraser continued with his ridiculous allegory, a leathery blond woman crept in and stood next to Margaret. His agent tried to ignore the woman, who smelled dreadfully of nicotine and hairspray. Margaret assumed she was another of Fraser's "friends." She was wrong.

"Are you Margaret Bonaventura?" asked the woman in a consumptive, forty-Marlboro-Reds-a-day whisper.

Margaret nodded.

"I'm Tracy Flood from the Sunday *Recorder*. Can we talk?"

DEPARTURE

GEORGE FARTED and enjoyed the smell in his car.

Canned ham.

Strange his farts always smelled like canned ham, as he never ate it.

Better try it soon or not at all.

I'll miss farting, he thought.

Perhaps there's farting in the afterlife, although he doubted it. Doesn't really make sense, wouldn't need to be—unless there was food, which, if there's not, then that doesn't sound like much fun either.

At least he had stopped coughing. His persistent cold had gone away too. It was odd but the symptoms that had finally driven him into the hands of the doctors had disappeared now that he knew he was fucked. He felt fine physically. He wondered how long he'd have to wait for the pain. He wondered what it would be like. Like a toothache or a sprained ankle? What?

Maybe he would see his parents again.

He looked at himself in the rearview mirror. He didn't look sick.

Just looked like himself. Sheila used to say he was handsome, never to him but often to her friends. He thought about the skull under his skin, how he would look when he had been dead for a few months.

He decided to get cremated, then he laughed out loud at the fact that he could be so vain about his appearance after he died, especially given the fact that it was highly likely that no one would ever see him again. Except perhaps for an archaeologist or two a few thousand years in the future.

He conceded to himself that he was handsome; he had green eyes and brown hair and nice skin and good teeth and he was tall and not fat and looked a bit like that magician who was engaged to a supermodel and fucking fuck he should have gotten laid more.

What the hell had he been doing getting married to his high-school girlfriend? He wasn't sure if he'd ever even liked her. She was just persistent and wouldn't leave him alone. She determined they would get married—he never really questioned it at the time.

He supposed he was having a midlife crisis. Yes, dying in the middle of your life could definitely be classified as a crisis.

He thought, I have never known how to have any fun.

Fraser could always have fun, I never had any fun, and now I'm fucking dying and that's just about the least fun I've ever had.

He had had three affairs in the time he was married. All with other lawyers, all of whom were also married. None of them were fun. He just felt guilty.

He had made love to seven women in his life. Sheila, then Lorraine, Sophia, and Glenda, his affairs, there was Tricia Docherty during a period when he and Sheila had broken up for a while, Olivia the English girl on a boys' holiday in Spain when he was engaged to Sheila but they were not yet married, and the prostitute at his bachelor party. Daisy, he thought her name was but he couldn't be sure.

Fraser had also shagged the prostitute and he wasn't even getting married.

George thought about the things in life that had made him happy and so naturally he thought of his daughter, Nancy. She had been wonderful when she was a toddler and when she was a little girl. Being in her company was like mainlining joy directly into his system. But she was a teenager now, surly and bitchy, and didn't want him around.

Said he was no fun.

The whole bloody dying thing was no fun whatsoever, he just couldn't get a positive spin on it. He wasn't thinking like himself at all and he guessed that he was having some sort of breakdown, which, given the circumstances, etc. etc.

He thought about his mother and father, how the chemotherapy seemed to have ravaged them as much as the illness itself.

He wondered if what he was doing—running away—would be the sort of behavior that would keep him out of heaven, although now that he was facing the big sleep, he just couldn't force himself into believing in all that. He would have liked to. If he did, he would have stayed at home and gone through the dreadful treatment and the drugs and the weeping and teeth gnashing but he just couldn't force himself into that foolishness.

He had been around, he had seen too much, he was a criminal defense lawyer, for Christ's sake, he heard more lies on a daily basis than a politician's wife.

Or perhaps a lawyer's wife?

Afterlife—bollocks.

It was like when he was at university.

Every Saturday night, the students from his class would go drinking in the Ubiquitous Chip or the Cul de Sac in the West End of Glasgow. At eleven o'clock when the bars closed and the young still had an appetite to party, somebody would always claim to know that there was a party in Clouston Street—usually fucking Fraser, who would hang around the Uni to meet girls even though he didn't go there. He had some glorified tea-boy job on the *Evening Times* sports desk.

So they'd spend the rest of their money on tinned beer and bottles of cheap blended whisky and traipse through the bitter cold looking for the party but there never was one.

There never was one, so you might as well drink as much as you can in the pub 'cause when it closes it's just cold and dark outside.

There is no party in Clouston Street.

He thought about Fraser. Jeez, what an arse he had turned into. Actually he had turned into an arse when they were about thirteen or fourteen years old. He had been an arse at school, an arse when they left, and now he was a professional arse among his own kind in the media.

He always fell on his feet, though. There's no way he'd get cancer, and he smokes. Probably; he used to anyway. George had given it up years ago. He still missed it.

His father had given up smoking six months before he died. Seemed pointless to George.

His mother hadn't given up smoking before she died. She had just given up. Cancer had killed both his parents and now it was going to kill him. He was an only child, like his daughter. He hoped he hadn't passed some kind of cancer gene on to her.

He had no way of knowing.

There's no justice, thought George, which you'd think he would have worked out by now, given that he'd worked in the legal system for fifteen years.

Fraser dropped his cigarette butt over the side of the balcony and walked back into Gus's office.

Gus's office, in fact the whole building, was a smoke-free zone, which seemed horribly undemocratic given that most people who worked there smoked. At certain points, usually just after lunch, it seemed as though the entire workforce was huddled outside on the fire escapes or at the entrances, like little pockets of pickets for earlier death.

He listened as Gus droned on, ". . . blah blah . . . cutbacks . . . setbacks . . . national adverting versus regional viewing . . . percentage . . . demographics . . . ho hum bladdy . . . crappity bladdy crappity blah . . ."

Gus was technically his boss, so he had to look like he was listening, or at least look like he was trying to look like he was listening. Gus had worked in television for a long time and he knew the realities of star versus management but he was a traditionalist, and also his ego was so huge that he thought most people found him as fascinating as he found himself.

Fraser was thinking about the new makeup lady—Paula. He loved that when she sucked him off she made a little humming sound that seemed to vibrate right through him, just like Julie used to.

They probably both read the same edition of *Cosmo*. Unlike Julie, though, she let him come on her face. What a great girl.

She said she liked it, that it was good for her skin, and also that it was dirty.

Fraser presumed she was Catholic but he hadn't bothered to ask.

". . . in conclusion smaller raises performance related blah brub-badah team pull together loyalty one of the family badaadah pigity pop."

Fraser snapped into the present when he heard the cadence and timing indicate that Gus's monologue was over. He smiled at Gus. Then looked at Margaret.

Margaret smiled professionally at Gus.

"Well, you've been very clear and precise, and of course you are aware of Fraser's popularity. Why don't we think things over and come back to you with some real numbers?"

"Fine," said Gus. "Think it over but . . ."

And off he went again.

". . . bladdy back in the days of . . . live documentary . . . my early years . . . investigative journalism . . . bruuddding broagde . . . vargggy pladdy blop . . ."

By the time Margaret and Fraser left the meeting, they were almost ready to accept a pay cut just to get out. Meetings with Gus, particularly negotiation meetings, were just excruciating. Gus was very smart. He'd bore you to his will.

I hate that fucking cunt, thought Gus. You had to think *cunt* these days, there were not too many occasions when you could say it out loud. Gus longed for the old days when *cunt* was okay and you could drink at lunchtime without some mad cunt suggesting you had to go to cunting rehab for alcocuntyholism. Arse. Fucking arsey cunt.

It was Americans who'd ruined the word *cunt*. They thought it was some kind of derogatory term for a vagina, or someone who had a vagina, but it had never been that in Scotland.

In Scotland the word *cunt* was cheery, like *shite* or *shortbread*.

Fucking Global Village, everything got confused.

Deborah, Gus's secretary, who was one of the main people he never said the c-word (as it was now known) in front of, brought him in a cup of tea. Gus was terrified of her because she was very sexy, with her dyed blond hair and her zaftig body pushing at the little Chanel suits she wore. He was convinced she would file a sexual harassment suit against him if he even looked at her the wrong way.

He was wrong, though. Deborah secretly wanted Gus to grab her and kiss her hard on the mouth, his big jaggy mustache scratching her face. She wanted him to pull her hair and rip her tights off and plunge his big hard cock in her cunt.

She didn't say that out loud, of course. She said, "Do you want a chocolate digestive with your tea?"

Gus declined, as nonsexually as he could, and Deborah left slightly disappointed.

Gus sighed and looked out the window to the great damp city of Glasgow. Most of the buildings had been sandblasted in the last twenty years, which Gus, along with most Glaswegians, secretly detested. This town used to be black and sooty and smelly and terrifying; now it looked like Disneyland in the rain, sad and wrong.

It hadn't just been sandblasted, it had been disinfected.

Gus thought about a paper cover he had seen on a toilet seat on a business trip to America. It had written on it "Sanitized for your convenience" in pleasant and friendly writing, with a little drawing of a woman smiling and giving a thumbs-up.

The drawing of the woman wasn't very good. She looked like Paul McCartney.

People were frightened to bare their arses in anything less than laboratory conditions. Glasgow had been sanitized for your convenience, but then again, so had Gus.

He had started out his working life in one of the great shipyards of Glasgow (now riverside apartments). He became a left-wing union official, fighting for the rights of the workers. A charismatic young man, he was spotted by the BBC and asked on to political panel shows. From there he went on to investigative and front-line reporting, doing a lot of face time on camera during the rise of Solidarity and the collapse of the Soviet empire. That was when he grew the trademark mustache. Somehow it associated him with Lech Walesa. They were brothers in politics, heroism, and facial hair, although this was unknown to Mr. Walesa.

From producing his own segments he went on to producing his own show and when Margaret Thatcher created conditions that were advantageous he started his own production company, making local news programs and documentaries exposing the evils of Margaret Thatcher and the like. His company became successful and wealthy, as he did himself.

He eventually managed a takeover of the Scottish media giant he now controlled, and now he sat at the top of his own private modern republic. Havel of his private Czechoslovakia. He hadn't deserted socialism, he just liked money and power.

He saw himself as a great modern left-wing intellectual trapped in the body and job of a successful capitalist media giant.

Of course, he was, in truth, a cunt.

He didn't like Fraser, though. He hated his jumpers and his bourgeois religious phony baloney show (although the advertising rates were great, viewing figures were great, fuck, business is business) and he hated the fact that something this twee was one of his signature programs.

He'd get rid of Fraser given half a chance, although he couldn't just fire a star, the shareholders would kill him. They loved Fraser's homespun image, his family appeal, they'd go mad.

He hated answering to those morons.

Deborah beeped him. "Tracy Flood from the Sunday *Recorder* on line three."

"What can I do for you, Tracy? Don't tell me one of my newsreaders is a crack whore."

"Better, Gus. Much better."

He stuck his hand into his waistband and leaned back in his chair.

Oh fuck.

* * *

Margaret couldn't help herself, she kind of enjoyed the fact that Fraser was panicking.

"Shit, Margaret! Why didn't you tell me before we went in?"

"What good would it have done?"

"He'll fire me."

"No one is going to fire you. You're a star."

"Oh, wake up, Margaret. I'm not a star, I'm a celebrity, and when Sunday comes I won't even be that. I'll be a punch line."

"Hey, it didn't do Hugh Grant any harm. In fact, his career went from strength to strength."

"Margaret, Hugh Grant is upper class, which means everybody already knew he was sexually deviant. He also was not a religious broadcaster in a country of narrow-minded religious bigots."

"Oh, that's right, blame Scotland, not your own penis."

"I have nothing against Scotland or my penis, in fact I'm very fond of both of them, but the truth is I have been playing to the religious crowd and I've been caught, literally, with my pants down. It's over, Margaret. I'm finished. I won't even get *panto* when this shit comes out."

"What about forgiveness, those Americans do it all the time. We'll do a documentary piece, you cry, you say you were abused as a child—"

"I was not abused as a child!"

"Oh, come on, play the game."

But Fraser was right and Margaret knew it. She also knew that, if she played it smart, there would be cash and prizes for her before he finally sank beneath the surface.

She'd have him on talk shows, an exclusive with as many tabloids as will pay, maybe even a book.

When the time came, Margaret could even sell her story to the tabloids, getting yet another bite at Fraser's big cash cherry. This might go national, yes, why not? If it was a light news day on Monday, as it usually is, then the English tabloids might pick it up.

Shit, of course they would pick it up, it has everything—naughty sex, religion, TV, and laughing at foreigners, the stuff English newspapers are made of.

Margaret felt the back of her neck tingle.

This could be her ticket to London.

Oh my God.

Much later, when he lost his sight, Fraser thought how odd it was that Margaret never at any point asked if the allegations against him were true or not.

Tracy Flood had never slept with Fraser but she wanked him off one Christmas. It was back at the *Evening Times* when he was on the sports desk and she was Big Bruce Patterson's assistant. She'd been drunk, of course, everyone at the *Evening Times* was drunk all year. The Christmas party just meant they were slightly more drunk with paper hats on. Fraser had put his arm around her in the Press Bar, had called her doll and said that Big Bruce couldn't find his fucking jacket without her doing it for him.

He had talked her up in front of the nasty wee damp men of Scottish journalism as they stood in their coven in front of the bar clutching their lagers and whiskies (always two drinks—one for each face). He even stood up for her when Jack Trampas, a ridiculous old buffoon who wore a trilby and wrote a restaurant column in the style of Raymond Chandler, suggested that she was shagging Big Bruce and that's why she'd become the editor's assistant.

She'd been grateful, not grateful enough to blow him or fuck him, but she'd performed a perfectly adequate hand shandy in the back of a mini-cab and the deal seemed fine with Fraser, who had then stumbled off into the night, leaving her to pay her own fare home.

She held no grudge, this wasn't personal. It was nothing to do with back then. The only thing she had against Fraser was his success. He was ripe for cutting. That was her job. She filed her copy. She knew it would get page one.

THE LORD'S LAYER!

Horny Holyman in Sexy Backstage Rites

Exclusive by Tracy Flood

TV cleric Fraser Darby has been revealed as a sex-mad pervert by former Scottish Television makeup lady Julie McGrade. Julie, who worked at Scottish Television for five years before leaving last week due to personal problems, says the randy reverend forced his attentions on her and many of the other employees he worked with.

Animal

"He's an animal!" said Julie. "He liked me to pleasure him orally before he did his programme. As I was doing it, he liked me to hum Psalm twenty-three, 'The Lord Is My Shepherd.' He said it put him in the mood for God. At first I thought he wanted a relationship, but I realize now he was just using me for sex."

Endowed

According to Julie, the pervy priest, who is NOT EVEN a real clergyman, is endowed with more than a gift for gab. "When I first saw his manhood, I was afraid. It was so big, but he just laughed and told me the Lord would protect me. He is obviously a very sick man, but I still hope that we can work things out and maybe one day get together and have a relationship."

Jumpers

Julie is only one of the many women who have fallen victim to the Rasputin-like attentions of the lusty TV vicar, who hides his rampant desires beneath his trademark fluffy jumpers.

Charlotte Cameron, an innocent nineteen-year-old student who worked on Darby's programme during her summer break from university, where she is studying modeling and media studies (see pic on page 3), said she is considering filing a sexual harassment suit against the star, claiming that he FORCED her to bend over his desk when she was handing him his morning coffee so that he could look down her blouse. "He said Jesus could have done better feeding the five thousand with my boobies than using some old bread and stale fish. It was disgusting. I'm a Jehovah's Witness, so what he said really shocked me."

Investigation

The star was unavailable for comment last night, but TV boss Gus Magoogan said that an investigation into the allegations would begin immediately.

"We are a family network," said Magoogan. "If these allegations are true . . ."

More on pages 6, 7, 8, and 10.

* * *

They hadn't used any of his publicity shots. Instead there was an old picture of Fraser that had been taken by an amateur paparazzo as he was leaving his local supermarket. He looked fat.

George missed the whole scandal; by Sunday he was in London. He could have got the Scottish Sunday papers there, of course, but he would have to have gone to a big railway station or the airport or a Scottish pub, none of which he fancied. He thought he felt the first stab of the cancer but it was just the intestinal complications of having eaten a three-week-old meat pie at Watford Gap services. Old offal and nerves will play havoc with your system, although he couldn't imagine why he was so jumpy. Jumpy, ha-ha.

He had already established that there was no afterlife, at least he thought he had. He had already convinced himself that there was no hell to look forward to, and even if there was, they'd have to have a pretty fucking lax door policy to let him in.

He tried to figure out what was scaring him about his impending death. Was it pain? No, not really, he was fairly convinced that he'd pass out during the fall. He figured that maybe what really scared him about dying is that maybe he'd be missing something.

He'd already missed a healthy dose of Schadenfreude that would have warmed him to the core of his being. Reading about Fraser's humiliation and disgrace would have reached him like Karen Carpenter to a coma victim. But he didn't know that he had missed it, because he had missed it.

He parked the car on a double yellow in Soho and took a taxi to Tower Bridge.

Fraser got drunk on Saturday night. He bought the early edition of the newspaper and drank almost two liters of Russian vodka alone, sitting on his couch weeping in self-pity and shame.

He was asleep in a pool of his own urine when the postman slipped the golden embossed invitation envelope through his front door.

They don't normally deliver on a Sunday.

IN DREAMS

FRASER HAD NEVER LIKED FLYING but since September 11 it had gotten much worse. Obviously.

What the hell was wrong with these people anyway? Fucking Arabs, flying planes into buildings and strapping dynamite to their shoes. Fuck!

One night in the Press Bar, Jack Trampas put forward the theory that the reason the Arabs were so angry was because they were so ugly. Howls of derision from the left-wing politically correct alcoholics he drank with, including Fraser, but Trampas persisted.

"Look at that shoe bomber guy, he's a freak. The mug shots of these hijackers, they're like the fucking Addams family. They're mad because they see pictures of the beautiful people in Hollywood and they're jealous."

"Nobody looks good in a mug shot."

"What about Zsa Zsa Gabor? When she smacked that cop?"

"She was cheatin; she's almost 90 percent Teflon."

"Winona Ryder?"

"Och, she's just a ratty wee junkie. Anyway, she never hurt anyone, she just stole a cardigan or somethin."

"Jack, you are a hideous specimen of humanity and I don't see you blowing things up," squeaked Robbie, the camp barman, as he poured himself an Advocaat.

Fraser laughed. "That's because he attacks the West with his god-awful literary style. Restaurant critique as jihad."

"Say what you like, but if these guys had a decent dental plan and took a bath every now and then, they'd be less likely to commit mass murder."

"Wouldn't we all," Robbie agreed.

Ewan Grayston, the taciturn sports writer from the *Herald,* who was annoyed that the conversation had turned away from the intricacies of Scottish league division football, decided to end the conversation with the coup de grâce to Jack's theory.

"I can prove you wrong in three words, Jack."

"Go on, then."

"Andrew Lloyd Webber."

"Sorry?"

"Ugliest bastard that ever lived, never hurt a fly."

"Aye, but he's rich. Anyway, I would disagree that he never hurt anybody. I went to that fucking *Phantom of the Fucking Opera* when I was in London, and I felt a distinct pain in my wallet. Plus I was bored to death with that prick with the Halloween mask swinging on a light and singing the same song for three fucking hours, and my fucking ears were bleeding by the time I left. When I think about it now, I should report the cunt to Amnesty International."

And so they continued.

There was always someone who was being raked over the coals in the Press Bar. They would be laughing at him now, thought Fraser as he sat in the back of the rattly, cold taxi on the way to Glasgow Airport.

Bastards.

The taxi slowed to a halt in the damp, wet traffic jam that consistently clogged the Kingston Bridge. Fraser, hung over and achy, fell into a light sleep. A white-haired old man in a red Indian costume appeared as if by magic. He sat next to Fraser, unnoticed by the taxi driver, who had turned into a dog-headed minor ancient Egyptian deity. Fraser turned and saw the old man in the outfit of a Comanche shaman.

"Bloody hell, Carl, Halloween already?"

The dog-headed taxi driver turned around.

"What's that, pal?"

The old man disappeared. The taxi driver lost his beautiful canine head and returned to being a thick-necked Glaswegian. Fraser was awake.

"Nothing," he said. "Just thinking out loud."

Fraser had been undergoing psychoanalysis for nearly two years. He hadn't sought out his therapist, rather it was the other way around.

Frasier had climbed the journalistic ladder with some ease. From working on the sports desk at the *Times* he had gotten a job as an on-camera reporter for *Scottish Sports Roundup* on Saturday afternoons, covering such Earth-shattering events as a goalless draw between Partick Thistle and Albion Rovers in the second round of the Scottish Cup. The producers of the local sports show, who also covered the news, were impressed with his easy charm and cheeky way with the camera. Soon he was promoted to weatherman on the nightly news, and like all weathermen, he pretended he was responsible for the weather, apologizing when it was raining and taking credit for the occasional sunny spell. It was a strange conceit but an industry standard. All weathermen do it.

Usually the banter is helped along by the anchorman or -woman or both, who pretend to be angry if they're not getting nice weather from the weatherman. This, of course, is insanity but it's also the media, so it doesn't matter. It's all lunacy. Mob rule. Bread and circuses.

One night before Christmas, Fraser was in the Press Bar enjoying much drink and ferocious calumny when he got a call. All cell phones had to be turned off in the bar and it was a strict rule that no one received a call on the bar phone unless it was an emergency. This Christmas Eve Fraser got a call from Gus himself. He was panicked.

"Fraser, are you drunk?"

"Not yet. Why?"

"Get back to the studios. Morris has just had a heart attack, he's been carried off in an ambulance."

"Jesus, okay. I'll be right over."

"Fraser, not a word of this to those fucking hyenas in there."

"Of course, Gus, of course."

Fraser hung up and announced to the entire bar that he had to go because Old Morris had had a heart attack and had been carried off in an ambulance.

The hyenas who were sober enough rushed to file copy. Morris Cuskerton had been an institution in Scotland for decades. He presented a variety show called *The Three O'Clock Gang* on Scottish TV in the fifties, then news, then a talk show where he interviewed local celebs and the occasional movie star who was passing through on the way to St Andrews for the golf. He was Scotland's Ed Sullivan, Johnny Carson, and Dick Clark rolled into one. Real old-timey television. For the past ten years he had been farmed out to the late-night religious spot, which was meant to be a bridge to retirement, but it became popular because it was live (Morris insisted on working live—it was the only way to do TV, he said, like the old days) and he occasionally would make fantastic blunders or be tipsy as he delivered his "Thoughts for the Day." On one memorable occasion he made a reference to the Virgin Mabel. People loved this shit, and the Christmas Eve broadcast was the most popular because he would almost certainly be hammered and make a complete tit of himself. All of the country would be watching except the Diogenes club in the Press Bar, who had no festive spirit.

Fraser was being called to fill in for Morris. This was the call to glory. Sink or swim, live or die. Live TV, no script, no net.

Fraser, the charmed, the lucky boy, was in the right place at the right time with just the right amount of alcohol in his system. He was relaxed, sexy, and confident, so when the word came through, only seconds before Fraser went on air, that Old Morris had died on arrival at the hospital, he took command and broke the tragic news to a shocked nation.

He was magnificent, he spoke with reverence and just the right amount of sadness. He recalled Morris's glittering career on Scottish

Television, remembering shows that even Gus had forgotten, like *Cartoon Company,* which Morris had hosted in the sixties, a cheap throw-together using Hollywood animated shorts like Tom and Jerry or Woody Woodpecker, where Morris pretended he knew the cartoon characters and "talked" to them on the phone even though they were in America.

He would put his hand over the receiver and say, "Daffy Duck wants to wish Stewart MacDougal of Falkirk a happy eighth birthday and a big hello to his Grandpa Sneddon."

Fraser talked of Morris's love of the Glasgow Rangers Football Club, and steered clear of the dead man's reputed fanatical allegiance to the bigoted and medieval Orange Lodge, a band of über-Protestants who had a very confused allegiance to William of Orange, a noted pederast and Dutch monarch who had successfully suppressed Catholics some hundreds of years previously. He talked of Morris's charm, his wit, and hinted at his fondness for strong alcoholic beverages (which is seen as a great character asset in Scotland). And then, the stroke of genius.

He finished with—

"—so as we are hanging up our stockings tonight and leaving carrots and whisky out for Santa and his reindeer, Morris Cuskerton will be arriving at the pearly gates. A Christmas present for heaven."

A grieving country was grateful for his words.

Fraser had landed the God spot. The G spot.

It was about this time that the late Carl Gustav Jung started working with Fraser. Jung, of course, had died in 1961, which was the year before Fraser was born, so the conditions under which they met were slightly unconventional, but as Fraser had never had any form of treatment before, he had nothing to compare it to. It seemed normal to him and was certainly much cheaper than paying a living therapist, who, chances are, would be nowhere near as good as Carl.

Fraser had gotten drunk on fame and champagne after the broadcast of Morris's death. The next few days he was lauded in the Scottish press as a hero for capturing the mood of the nation. He was a star, and by the end of January the following year he had his own show. Every night. People wanted him to talk about God, so he did. For cash.

As it is with success, sometimes he got too excited to sleep. He thought about taking pills to help him but he didn't want to get hooked on anything, so he just drank whisky instead. One bright night in April, Fraser concluded that he was drinking too much. He had become a little concerned about how much he was throwing down, and the last thing he wanted to do was end up in some crappy rehab or "show business hospital," as Jack Trampas called it.

He decided that he would abstain for two nights a week. The first night, a Tuesday, was rough and he didn't drift off until seven A.M., when the sun was peeking in through the heavy crushed-velvet drapes of his West End flat. As soon as he was asleep he found himself in a lovely meadow in Switzerland. A round tower was off to his left and he felt an urge to walk toward it; as he did so he became aware that instead of getting nearer to the tower he was sinking underground.

He found himself in an underground chamber that had curtains not unlike the ones in his flat. He opened the curtains. But instead of sunlight behind them, he saw a giant penis, about the size and color of a bull African elephant, veiny and erect and pointing to the sky.

Carl appeared behind him.

"Do you mind?" said Carl in a deep voice, laced with a sweet accent.

"Mind what?" said Fraser, without talking. He just thought it but he knew the old man could hear him.

"Do you mind not looking at my penis!"

"This can't be your penis," Fraser thought.

"It bloody is," said Carl. "Stop staring at it."

"But it's about a hundred times the size of you, it'd never fit in your trousers."

"I don't want it in my trousers. I like it in this big hole in the ground."

"You're nuts!"

"No, just the penis. My nuts are in my underpants. Boom-boom!"

Fraser woke up in a flop sweat. He checked himself. He had a massive erection.

Jesus, thought Fraser, but he was wrong.

Fraser and Carl met in the oddest of places. Carl, being dead, didn't have an office and could only appear to Fraser in his dreams, which in itself was very Jungian. He would only appear if Fraser had taken the requisite break from alcohol, so in a way Fraser could control the visitations, drinking when he wanted peace and stopping when he felt like therapy.

Although the dreams were Fraser's, he got the distinct impression that the old man chose the venue and implanted it in his psyche. They met in ancient Greece, in Studio 54 at the height of the cocaine seventies. They chatted as they walked through no-man's-land between the besieged armies in Ypres in 1917 (Carl had a fondness for the years 1914 to 1918, as, during life, he had had a bit of a breakdown during this period and felt he had missed a lot of what was going on in the temporal world, although he had been extremely busy elsewhere). The collective unconsciousness was their oyster.

Jung took full advantage of living in dreamland to appear in any guise he wanted, because Fraser would always know it was him, although Fraser put his foot down when he appeared as a ferocious grizzly bear.

"I don't feel comfortable with you like this," said Fraser, using the language of analysis that Carl had taught him. "I find it difficult to confide in an entity that may rip my head off and drink my blood at any moment."

"Sorry," growled Carl through his massive saliva-dripping fangs, and promptly returned to the stately European gentleman he had been in the latter years of his life.

Carl slowly got to know Fraser and Fraser got to know Carl. Through the dream therapy, the two became rather friendly.

Carl explained to Fraser that, since he had died, his challenge had been to stop becoming extremely smug because he had guessed so much correctly during his lifetime. He told him that even Freud conceded that he had been on the money and, after death, the two men had rekindled their friendship, enjoying regular Pictionary evenings with Socrates and Tony Randall.

Fraser was curious as to why Jung had singled him out for treatment. One night, in a fitful sleep instigated by an excellent lamb pasanda from the Crème de la Crème Indian restaurant in Argyll Street, Fraser met him by the statue of Dostoyevsky outside the Lenin Library in Moscow.

"You are a perfect patient for me," said Jung, who had appeared this time as a beautiful young English actress named Emily. "You are the totally dual entity. You are an amoral boor with the potential for sainthood. An intellectual moron. An atheistic priest. Plus I don't really get to choose my patients these days. I can only treat people who dream about me. You seem to do so on a regular basis. Can you explain that?"

"Not really," shrugged Fraser. "Although I read about you a bit when I was shagging a psychology student at Glasgow University. The only books she had in the house were by you and Freud and Adler and all that bollocks. She said you were a bit of a Nazi."

"Oh dear, where do they get this nonsense? Freud was convinced I was anti-Semitic because I disagreed with him on certain theories, and also, I made a couple of mistakes politically in the thirties, but no, never a Nazi. Simply because they were spiritually dead. Of what possible interest could they be to me?"

"Point taken," Fraser concurred. "You know any Nazis? Must be a lot of dead Nazis around."

"No, not many. Like I say, they were spiritually dead, so when the body goes, well, that's kind of it."

"So there's only spiritual people in the afterlife?"

"Well, it's a bit more complicated than that but you're on the right track. If the spirit is the only thing that survives, then there's not going to be much left of you if you have no spirit."

"What about evil spirits?"

"You're not ready for all that yet. Let's talk about you."

Fraser couldn't resist Carl's beautiful blue eyes, his high cheekbones, his full breasts pushing at his bodice. He kissed him on his soft, womanly lips.

"Hey, it's still me," said Carl.

"I know, but you're so beautiful."

Fraser woke up embarrassed and guilty that morning. He took a long shower before going to work. Jung's appearance in the taxi to the airport was unusual. Fraser had not been abstemious for the required time and Carl had never appeared during a catnap. This was a change.

Fraser was unnerved, hung over, and anxious about the long flight ahead. He brought out the invitation and looked at it again, feeling the raised golden letters beneath his fingers. From the Holy United Church of America.

Dear Fraser Darby
Your name has been selected by the Lord.
Working through our committee, Our Heavenly Father
has chosen you as the top religious media figure in your region.
You are most cordially invited to a gathering of Christian
believers in Birmingham, Alabama. Christian Broadcasters will
come together in celebration and discussion of how better to serve
God through the media.
We pray that you will attend.
Pastors Leon and Saul Martini.

There was a 1-800 telephone number to make hotel and flight reservations at discount rates for the faithful. Fraser had already called. He had to get out of town for obvious reasons, and Birmingham, Alabama, although nobody's first vacation destination choice, was as good a place as any.

No one would have heard of him there, there would be no Press Bar or *Sunday Recorder,* and who knows, he might just be able to wrangle some kind of job in American TV. You never know. Fraser figured it was an investment in his future, if he had one.

SATORI

GEORGE MUST HAVE SAT LOOKING at Tower Bridge for four hours before he came to the conclusion that today was not the day he was going to jump. Today would not be the day that he offed himself, so he went for a beer instead. Actually he had three before he noticed that he felt pretty good. He felt amazingly good for a terminally ill suicidal vagrant, although he wasn't technically a vagrant, given the wads of cash he had secreted around his person. He had three hundred pounds sterling in fifties in each sock, five hundred in his wallet in twenties—he liked the way they made his wallet fat, like a Cockney gangster. He also had two thousand in an envelope in the zip-up pocket of his anorak.

He never thought he'd have time to spend it all but now he was beginning to wonder. But it wasn't the money that made him feel good. He had plenty more in his bank accounts and stock portfolio and time share in the Algarve.

It was the freedom. Sheila could keep the money now. Get a new car, get Nancy some ridiculously expensive girly shoes that tubby teenagers think make them look like anorexic television actresses.

He felt free, he was enjoying the absence of responsibility and routine. He liked being self-involved and thoughtful and alone. He felt honest. Totally honest.

This is what it must be like to be Holy, he thought.

It was very good beer.

He ordered a fourth from the red-faced, mutton-chopped barman, who looked like a drawing of an Englishman on a Napoleonic propaganda leaflet, or an early naturalist's drawing of an orangutan.

"You Scots love to drink, don't cha?" commented the Anglo gibbon as he poured George another pint of the warm, sudsy nectar.

"Yes we do," replied George.

"No offense, mate," mumbled the monkey.

"None taken," said George. "It's true. We're a bunch of backward inbred savages whose erroneous self-importance is matched only by our national obsession with intoxication."

It was very good beer.

"All right, mate, keep it down. We don't need any of that kind of talk," warned the Saxon simian.

George nodded, feigning contrition, a delicious tickle of rebellion and cheekiness pushing up his heart rate. He paid for his beer and sat down in the corner of the tacky pretend stabley/countryish, totally imitation pub.

What now? he thought.

He looked around at the other drinkers, fat, white men in suits and ties, their open pores oozing boozy heat like New York manhole covers. His eyes rested on the "salad bar" that offered baked beans and croissants.

Jesus, baked beans and croissants. No wonder the French hate the English.

That's it. The French.

The ghastly nature of English pub meals had delivered a kick in the eye to George and he hadn't even had to eat one. He suddenly knew, without a shadow of a doubt, that he couldn't take his life in this damp and grisly Germanic dump. Why on Earth would he want England to be the last thing he saw? France, the French, the frogs know a thing or two about romantic and tragic death and they have plenty of bridges in Paris, he thought, although for some reason he couldn't sufficiently explain to himself, he had never been there to see.

"A man should see Paris before he dies," George said out loud.

He drew a few suspicious glances from the surly Londoners around him but no one said anything. The gorilla stroked his facial hair, puffed his chest, and paced behind the bar.

George downed the rest of his beer and left. He would have liked another, it was very good beer, but now he had a mission.

Paris.

Like a lover in a movie, George hailed a hackney cab outside the pub.

"Waterloo Station please, the *Eurostar*!"

"Yes, mate," smiled the Sikh cabbie through excellent dentures. "What time's your train, guv'nor?"

"As soon as I can get it," said George.

Fuck, I hope this drunken Scottish prick doesn't throw up in the cab, thought the driver in Urdu.

THE ROAD TO GOD: ONE

WHITE AMERICANS HAVE A VERY UNUSUAL SENSE OF HISTORY. They make it up as they go along, constantly revising to suit their tastes in a manner that would make Stalin blush. Very few of them saw any irony in the fact that during a recent nasty Balkans conflict, when Uncle Sam intervened to stop the Serbs from ethnically cleansing the Bosnians, the military action was performed using Apache helicopter gunships. Helicopters named after a people that had been ethnically cleansed in the United States less than one hundred years previously. Sixteen-lane highways across the sacred burial grounds. Yee-hah.

I-40 runs all the way from Nashville, Tennessee, to Barstow in California, where it joins I-15, which can either take you north to Las Vegas and then on to Salt Lake City or south to Los Angeles and Mexico. For most of the way it follows old Route 66, a highway White America remembers fondly because for them it conjures up a time of innocence before cigarettes gave people cancer and gasoline fumes burned a hole in the sky. A time before homosexuality and drugs, a time when the only threats to the world were Soviet Russia, aggressive extraterrestrials, or perhaps the occasional mutant insect that had inadvertently fallen into a nuclear reactor and grown to five thousand times its original size and was intent on eating Chicago.

In short, Route 66 was a symbol of what White America is really nostalgic for: a time that never existed.

Saul and Leon were, of course, White American. They used history, their country's and their own, and any suitable religious doctrine to suit their own ends. They were survivors. Like roaches.

Saul and Leon were barkers at the carnival tent catering to the low-income end of America's spiritually disenfranchised. (Historically, it is better for religions to cater to the poor because there is always more of them. They are more desperate, so therefore will cough up as much money and devotion as they can, plus their life on Earth is unpleasant enough for them to buy the idea that things might actually improve after death.)

Saul and Leon fell into the arms of the Lord for the first time almost immediately on leaving the orphanage. They had traveled by night, south from Atlanta, through Macon County to northern Florida and the little town of Crawford's Creek.

This is true hillbilly country.

Hillbillies are much maligned, as most of them place hospitality and kindness above cynicism and wit and therefore are deemed intellectually inferior by the cynical and witty who occasionally pass through their domain on the way to somewhere noteworthy and sophisticated. Hillbillies don't mind this, of course, because they place hospitality and kindness above cynicism and wit and therefore the cynicism and wit of the cynical and witty is wasted on them. No real harm done.

However, the cynical and witty often think this is just ignorance and, as with all cynicism and wit, there is some truth in it.

There is a streak of anti-intellectualism, a deep mistrust of smart folks, running through America's rural population, which is understandable when you realize that intellectual capitalist scientists applied farming methods that led to horrid diseases in the livestock.

Diseases caused by animals eating reconstituted organ parts of their own parents in the name of smarter economics.

Therefore the country folks like to keep things simple, so they don't respond well to metaphor or allegory.

This can lead to problems when approaching ancient enigmatic scripture, which is almost entirely allegorical.

For example, in the Bible it says:

> And these signs shall follow them that believe; in my name they shall drive out demons; they shall speak with new tongues. They shall take up serpents and if they drink any deadly thing it shall not hurt them. They shall lay hands on the sick and they shall recover. (Mark, chapter 16, verses 17–18)

People who embrace the concept of allegory would argue that this passage means basically accept God—the notion of a benign spiritual entity that controls an essentially ordered and pragmatic Universe—and you'll feel a lot more comfortable, physically, spiritually, and emotionally. That you'll be in much better condition to help those around you, and by being of service to those others, not only will they be helped, but you will too. That faith is the lifeblood of the soul, and the world is a lot more dangerous and terrifying without it. Or something like that. What this passage is almost certainly *not* advocating is the handling of real poisonous snakes and drinking real poison, especially as it was written in a time and place where you could hardly walk a mile without tripping over a couple of utterly deadly toxin-injecting serpents.

Also, there was probably no talking snake in the Garden of Eden, and for that matter, the existence of an actual place called the Garden of Eden seems unlikely (this, of course, does not count the nightclub in Hoboken of the same name).

God is probably fine with people eating apples, Eve wasn't actually made from Adam's rib, and Jonah wasn't really eaten by an actual large fish. (Although it is probably true that the people of Sodom loved it in the pooper.)

It is worth noting that one of the most prominent snake-handling cults, the Church of God with Signs Following, was founded by George Went Hensley, a Pentecostal minister who died tragically, if predictably, from a snakebite.

This being said, the congregation of the Christian Reformed Fellowship of Born Again Snake Handling Pentecostal Baptists (not associated in any way with the Hensley group) were a godsend to Leon and Saul. It was from these snake handlers that Saul's true vision would eventually come. They would be his inspiration for the powerful moneymaking juggernaut the Holy United Church of America, where Leon's charisma and astonishing singing voice and Saul's duplicity and greed would finally be joined in a spectacular marriage of Religion and Show Business. Of course, churches don't spring up overnight.

It began like this.

After they left the orphanage, Saul and Leon were technically on the run. Not actually on the run because:

1. Saul was already too fat to move at anything more than an amble.

2. No one was really looking for them. Runaway teenagers are not a high priority for any law enforcement agency.

However, because they were under eighteen—Leon was seventeen, Saul sixteen—they were still wards of the state, so if they got into any kind of trouble, or were reported to the police by any well-meaning do-gooders, then they would be sent back immediately. Which, frankly, on a couple of dark nights, they both secretly wished for.

The orphanage they had escaped from was not in any way Dickensian, it was a rather sweet two-story Victorian house in Duluth, a middle-class suburb to the north of Atlanta. The home itself was comprised of twenty-three children who were separated into male and female dorms. The whole operation was run by a Mrs. Wolf, a kindly old gray beast who, due to a botched harelip surgery as a child (in an orphanage herself), had the rather alarming appearance of someone who was snarling all the time. In truth, she rarely snarled, she understood the fears of the youngsters in her charge, she had been through it herself. She was patience on a monument.

From the moment they arrived at Mrs. Wolf's house when they were eleven and twelve years old, Saul and Leon were inseparable. They had not been quite as close when they lived with their mad mother but when she was removed, and when she died, they clung to each other like never before.

Mrs. Wolf was sensitive to this and placed them in bunks together, Saul on the bottom for obvious reasons. The children were taken to school in a clapped-out yellow bus driven by Ted Casey, who made sure every child who got on his bus, from the youngest to the eldest, got a Tootsie Roll lollipop. The kids adored him. Tootsiepop Ted, they called him. A few years later, long after Saul and Leon had gone, he became famous as Atlanta's most notorious serial killer when his double life was exposed. Every two or three months, depending on the position of the constellation Orion in the night sky, Ted would rape and kill an African-American prostitute and eat her eyes.

Still, he was good with the kids.

High school is tough enough on anyone, an absolute rule of the Universe being that if high school is not a buttockclenchingly awkward, emotionally difficult, and unpleasant time of your life, then the rest of it will be a crushing disappointment. Academic success is desirable, popularity (the only thing that most students really desire) is not. Those who excel socially in high school are truly damned. The homecoming queen does indeed bear the mark of the beast.

The irony is, of course, that this information is generally not available to high-school students, and was certainly unknown to the kids on the orphanage bus. Called The Bastards by the rest of the student body, they were as popular as Jewish tailors in 1930s Hamburg.

There was no way that one of The Bastards could ever be popular. No amount of athletic prowess or street smarts could save you from this leper colony. It was worse than being retarded or having Jehovah's Witnesses for parents, or even having retarded Jehovah's Witnesses as parents.

The Bastards took this stoically, they knew their place, so they shuffled from class to class, heads down, eyes averted. Except Leon. Even then Leon knew what he had. He walked with his head up and looked other students in the eye, which got him beaten up a lot but he didn't care. He had a sense of destiny, he had a great schlong, and The Voice. But he kept his pants and his mouth shut, biding his time. The legendary timing of his father.

Saul, being fat and a Bastard, had the most horrendous time. His misery was compounded by alarming red acne that covered his face every few months. No one ever knew, not Ted, not Saul, not Leon, not Mrs. Wolf, no one, that Saul's acne attacks always coincided with one of Tootsiepop Ted's homicides. A coincidence that passed by the whole waking world.

With such a horrible high-school experience, the boys were set for greatness when Leon nearly blew the whole thing.

The Universe came to a fork in the road and for a second it was Saul's turn to drive.

Saul's Astronomy Club had been meeting in one of the classrooms off of the senior study hall for three months. The kids in the club were for the most part like Saul, outcasts in one way or another, either hideously disfigured by acne or extremely smelly, or had stutters or embarrassing parents. These were the kids on the outer rim of the high-school universe. The Plutos in the nerd galaxy. As most astronomy clubs are, this one was less about star gazing and more about solace and company for these poor souls who huddled in mutual consolation around high-powered optical equipment.

The Astronomy Club met in the evenings for obvious reasons. On one evening, as Saul was picking at a weeping doubleheader on his cheek and looking at Orion in Taurus through a Pathfinder 40x telescope and Lashanda Brightwell, Ted's fourth victim, lay cooling in a dumpster behind the International House of Pancakes in Buckhead, Leon was in detention in the senior study hall for failing to complete an essay on the American Civil War.

In a strange twist of fate, Deborah Thornhill and Julie Peters, the two most beautiful, most popular, and most desirable girls in school, had also received detention, for smoking in the girls' bathrooms. If that weren't enough, Django Ryerson, the beatnik muso kid who just oozed cool and even had a little soul patch beard, was also in lockdown for saying, "Because no one else gave a shit, man," when Mr. Hancock asked him why the Hittites had developed the world's first sophisticated metropolitan sewage system.

The other regulars of detention were also present: Geary McFarlane, a painfully thin young man with the body of a consumptive with rickets, who was always in trouble for his undiagnosed narcolepsy; Todd Bledsoe, the graffiti artist; and Millie Watson, who was forever writing articles in the school paper denouncing the fascist junta the teachers were part of.

Mrs. Cameron, who was meant to be supervising this punishment session, had left to take another long phone call from her hysterical sister in Des Moines, who had just broken up with her husband for the eighth time in two years. She told the students to continue to read quietly, and for the most part they did so apart from Django, who was noodling on the ancient upright piano that Mrs. Cameron used to murder Broadway standards for her drama group.

Django's genius transcended the old instrument's failings and he made it sound cool, like they were in a speakeasy or the lobby of the Waldorf-Astoria.

Leon, lost in the music, gazed out the window, across the soccer field to the school fence and the woods beyond. He watched a jet travel across the clear winter sky, and even though it was only six P.M., it felt like all the world was asleep but those in the room and the pilot of the jet. Leon thought of his mother, as he did often in quiet moments, his love for her still a pain in the pit of his stomach.

In the half-light bleeding out of the window, he watched a fat bee hover above a purple thistle underneath the sill.

Django's soft playing had a powerful impact on everyone there, everyone felt good. Cool. Relaxed. Somehow, air-conditioned. Before Leon knew it, his father stirred in his soul and the voice was out, unconsciously doo-be-doing over Django's tinkling.

The others looked over at Leon. He was still lost in reverie, not really aware he was singing out loud. He had forgotten where he was.

Django, with the ease of a born musician, played along instinctively, feeling that something weird and groovy was occurring.

Leon turned and looked directly into the eyes of Deborah Thornhill. He kept on singing, feeling the passion his father had felt for Ava when they first met.

Deborah flushed crimson. She felt an amyl nitrate–like rush. Her heart went boom boom. Leon almost buckled under his embarrassment, similar to the time he had inadvertently called Mrs. Cameron Mom when he had been asked a question in the middle of a daydream. He nearly stopped but he saw something in Deborah. The unattainable girl, especially to him, one of The Bastards, the outcasts.

He saw what his voice had done to her, he knew that it had gone to places on her body that he wanted to go with other parts of his body. He saw surprise and the beginning of something else.

Fuck it, he thought. Here goes nothing.

He opened up and Django went right along with him. An old standard about how champagne was no thrill and cocaine was boring.

This kind of song was not what most teenagers wanted to hear at that point in the history of popular music but the effect of the combined talents of Django and Leon knocked over that prejudice with ease. The sheer cool of what they were doing, the corniness of the number, made it even better.

Saul heard his brother singing from the room next door. So did the rest of the Astronomy Club. They left the telescope and walked cautiously as if toward a landed spacecraft, in the direction of the voice.

What he saw made Saul's blood run cold with terror.

The kids in detention were already under Leon's spell. By the time Mrs. Cameron came back from her phone call, the Astronomy Club, the detainees, and Mr. Petrov, the effete Russian janitor, had gathered round the piano where Leon stood next to Django.

Leon had moved through "It Happened in Monterey" and was on "Summer Wind," singing directly to Deborah, who was already wet.

Mrs. Cameron stood and listened. She didn't say anything, she looked like she might cry. Mr. Petrov actually was crying. The looks on the faces of the girls, Saul saw that. He knew that he'd better do something soon or he would lose his brother forever and he would be totally alone for the rest of his life.

ALTITUDE ATTITUDE

FRASER HAD BEEN WORRIED ABOUT FLYING long before the terrorist attacks on the World Trade Center in New York in 2001. In 1988, just before Christmas, he had been in London interviewing for a job as on-camera reporter for Thames Television. What they actually said they were looking for in the ad in *Media* magazine was a "Wacky Outside Broadcast Personality," which would mean he'd get to do the corny little news stories that went at the end of the local London broadcasts to cheer people up after the hatchet deaths in Peckham. The duties would involve interviewing "local eccentrics," which meant that Fraser would get to speak to syphilitic farmers who dressed their livestock as the Supremes etc. etc.

Thames, after seeing his demo reel, had offered to fly him there and back from Glasgow but he chose to drive the nine-hundred-mile round-trip for two reasons:

1. He had just purchased a new car—well, not exactly new, it was four years old with forty thousand miles on the clock but it had been well kept by an anally retentive cash-register salesman from Motherwell. It was a cream-colored Mercedes 200 that rattled a little but it made Fraser feel very successful and mysterious. He thought it looked like the kind of car that would belong to a highly paid assassin; in

reality it looked more like it belonged to an ambassador from a smallish African country, but Fraser loved it and wanted to take a road trip in it.

2. Jack Trampas had told him about a sensational massage parlor called Ladyfingers in Preston that he wanted to try out. Preston is situated halfway between Glasgow and London and therefore is the ideal spot to stop for a rub and a tug to alleviate the stiffness brought on by prolonged driving and a sporadically hyperactive libido. Fraser had resisted the temptation to stop in Preston on the way; he wanted to feel clean and virtuous for his big interview in London. As it turned out, he needn't have bothered. The interview was conducted by three ex-Cambridge television executives who had already agreed to give the job to an old friend of theirs from university, Richard Kelton-Peters, who had been a leading light in the Cambridge Footlights Review, the campus amateur dramatic society that put the children of the wealthy on the fast track to show business.

Fraser felt depressed after the interview; he knew it had gone badly. All three men kept pretending to not understand his accent.

Fucking English, thought Fraser as he walked out of the Thames building in Teddington. He wasn't the first Scotsman to think this.

Why the fuck would they bring me all the way here just to fuck with me?

He wasn't the first Scotsman to think this either.

The reason he had been brought to London was so that, if charged with nepotism, the executives could quite honestly point to the countrywide search for the ideal candidate before stating that "Dickie was simply, when all's said and done, the best chap for the gig."

Fraser walked across the car park and out onto the main street. He was headed toward the Underground station when he saw a middle-aged woman sitting by the doorway of an out-of-business fried-chicken franchise. The place could not have been closed for long, as it still smelled strongly of warm, dead poultry.

The woman was grubby and tubby and obviously had lost numerous rounds with extremely inexpensive alcohol products but she had a kind of matronly look about her even though she had been living on the street for no little while. She reminded Fraser of his mother and suddenly he felt very guilty indeed.

"Spare change?" the woman growled, her look more accusatory than pleading. There was no question in her voice; it was a statement of fact, monotone and aggressive.

"Spare change?"

Fraser walked quickly by, but the look of the woman, her predicament . . . Not only to be poor but to be a middle-aged woman and poor—Jesus!

He felt the wad of cash heavy in his wallet, which he had stuck in the arse pocket of his suit trousers. His Ladyfingers stash.

He only made it ten steps before he turned around and went back to the woman. He removed all the money from his wallet and handed it to her. Two hundred pounds.

"What's this?"

"It's money. For you."

The woman looked at him with utter contempt.

"Fack orf. Kint!"

This was not the tearful outpouring of gratitude that Fraser had expected.

"Don't you want money?"

"Fack orf. Kint!" explained the woman.

Fraser was mystified. What had he done? He had made a genuine attempt to be charitable, even though he'd just had an unpleasant experience.

"What is your problem?" he barked at her, a little more forcefully than he meant. He saw the tiniest glimmer of fear in the woman's eyes and he knew that that look would haunt him till his dying day. He took a breath and tried again.

"I'm just trying to help you. Why won't you take my money?"

She looked at him warily, then grumbled.

"Snot reel."

"Snot reel?" Fraser repeated, trying to make sense of the ludicrous exchange. Then it dawned on him. They were Scottish banknotes. The woman thought it wasn't real money. (Scottish notes, although legal tender in England, are sometimes not recognized by the uneducated or recent immigrants.)

"Oh no, it's real money. It's Scottish. If you take these notes to a bank, they'll give you English ones, if that's what you want."

"Leave me alone," she said.

"But—"

The woman started screaming, "Elp! Roip! Roip! Ee's gorris cack aht!"

Fraser judged it was time to go. He stuffed the money into his pocket and walked smartly away, not looking back as the woman kept up her yelling.

"Ee troid t' roip me! Ee troid t' roip me!"

She started crying, her heart breaking on every exhale.

Fraser elected to keep the money for a lucky employee of Ladyfingers in Preston. He assumed whoever she was, she would be more grateful for his largesse.

He was right. Sandra was another, different middle-aged woman, who worked in Ladyfingers on some evenings while Derek, her severely handicapped son, was at the community center Reach Out to the Disabled program. She was delighted when Fraser left her a hundred-pound tip after a truly breathtaking one-hour massage and French.

"That's for you," he said as he kissed her on the cheek. "Thank you."

"Bloody 'eckers, if I'd known you were so generous, I'd have put my finger up your bum, love," she purred.

"Another time," said Fraser as he left her in the semen-smelling cubicle and sauntered out of Ladyfingers and across the street, satisfyingly spent, to the assassinmobile.

It was late as he drove from Preston, and it was nearly ten P.M. by the time he got to the Scottish border. He ran into traffic. Not slow traffic, stopped traffic. No movement. A snake of stationary red taillights winding off into the distance as far as he could see. He sighed and ejected the cassette tape he was listening to, the BBC radio comedy *The Hitchhiker's Guide to the Galaxy.*

He flipped around for a radio station and finally found Borders Radio, where a shocked announcer who was more used to giving livestock reports told him that a plane, Pan Am 103, en route from London to New York, had crashed into the Scottish border town of Lockerbie and that a lot of people had just died.

The A74 is the main road between Scotland and England; it passes just east of Lockerbie. The town is clearly visible from the highway. Fraser guessed the traffic was stopped because of the crash. He didn't mind, though, because when he heard about it he didn't feel like going on.

He listened to the radio overnight. He slept fitfully in his car. He didn't dream.

He awoke as the traffic began to move in the early light. He drove bumper to bumper, at funeral speeds, until midmorning when, hungry and tired and desperate for a shite, he reached the crash site.

Angry, emotional policemen were waving the traffic through the one lane they had opened. They were shouting at the drivers, trying to get them to move faster.

"Come on, pick it up, don't look. Get a fucking move on."

Fraser felt his body contract, then flush hot with shock as he saw half of a plane cockpit sitting sideways in a sheep-grazing field. An image that was already becoming world famous. He drove on for ten miles before he became aware of his tears.

The traffic opened up but Fraser had to pull into a service station. In the car park he wept uncontrollably.

Huge tsunami sobs rolling in from his soul.

He gulped in air when he could but his heart was breaking on every exhale.

When he got back to Glasgow he went to the Press Bar to get drunk. Everybody got sad drunk for a while. After a few days some sick jokes started and people began to get normal drunk again but every time Fraser got on a plane he thought about Lockerbie. That's why he had already had four whiskies and a milligram of Xanax by the time his plane took off from Glasgow and headed southwest over the Atlantic.

* * *

Fear makes people unreasonable and unpleasant to deal with, and given that the flight attendants of American Airlines were unreasonable and unpleasant to deal with before that dreaded September 11, it would be silly to think they would be any better after it. Fraser knew this but the passenger seated next to him in the small first-class cabin (slightly bigger seat, different upholstery, cheesy nibbles on departure) did not. She was a professional of some sort, thought Fraser through his tranquil, boozy fog, perhaps a lawyer, all pens and gadgets and PowerBook and phone. A tiny phone the size of a small potato, to prove she meant business. Before the women's movement phones were large and obvious Bakelite gentlemanly affairs; now they were discreet and ruthless.

Like stilettos.

The flight attendant, a blond Gorgon, pounced on her like an alarmed cat.

"You can't make calls during the flight. Shut it off, now!"

The professional woman didn't look up. Didn't move. Did not engage with the bitter harpy in the nylon dress.

"I'm not making a call, I'm checking my schedule. It's also on my phone."

"Shut it off, now!"

The woman still didn't look up, or stop what she was doing.

"Please don't use that tone when you talk to me."

Furious, the Gorgon turned and stormed off to get her supervisor.

Fraser smiled at his fellow passenger's victory. He almost congratulated her but then remembered she might recognize him and know him to be a disgraced sexual deviant. He sunk further into his chair, guilty under his Lawson's Sausages baseball cap. Congratulations would have been premature anyway because the Gorgon returned a moment later with her supervisor, Colin. Colin was going to be fifty in two weeks, his lover Barry had just left him for a younger, prettier, richer man, he had hemorrhoids and an in-grown toenail. No bitch was going to back-talk him or any of his girls today.

"Excuse me, no phones are allowed during the flight. Please shut it off," spat Colin, the apoplectic Gorgon peeping over his shoulder.

"I explained to your colleague, although this *is* a phone, it is also a small personal computer and it is in that capacity that I am using it now."

Fraser pretended to be asleep.

"If you don't turn it off, I will inform the captain that we have an unruly passenger and he will make an unscheduled landing at the nearest airport."

"We're halfway across the Atlantic, the nearest airport is probably Miami, and we're going there anyway."

"That is up to the captain. If I make the report, you will be arrested upon arrival no matter where we land. Please turn off the phone."

The woman closed her phone and put it in her bag. Colin and the Gorgon inhaled their victory.

"If you use it again, I'll report you."

"All right," said the woman as she looked up and read his name tag. Colin and the Gorgon turned and walked away. The woman called after him.

"Colin?"

He turned.

"May I have some peanuts and a glass of Chardonnay?"

Colin thought for a moment, then nodded to the Gorgon and they both headed to the galley to fetch the nuts and wine before they did something really stupid.

The woman sighed and opened the in-flight magazine.

Fraser couldn't resist it. Without opening his eyes he said, "That was magnificent."

She smiled. "Thank you." She flitted through the magazine for a moment, then said, "I know who you are."

He didn't reply.

She unbuttoned her jacket. Her lacy bra was visible through her white shirt.

"My mother loves your show. I'm sorry about all your trouble. I don't think there is anything wrong with what you did. I like a man who enjoys sex."

Fraser missed all of this. After he heard "Thank you," the Xanax finally clashed with the whisky, and put him to the canvas. He was out.

The woman turned and looked at him. A little pool of spit that had been collecting in his mouth overflowed into a long, wet string that connected to his cardigan. She went back to the magazine, finally settling on a travel piece about the shopping delights of Old Town Helsinki.

The sun was a pale green as it dropped behind the northern horizon. Fraser sauntered across the medieval square in the center of the small Dutch town of Maastricht. He headed toward some little tables set outside a cutesy café. Jung was seated at a table on his own sipping a small lager and Fraser immediately recognized him even though he had taken the form of the late Jack Benny, an American entertainer who had been famous in his lifetime for his caustic wit, his meanness, and his comedic ineptitude on the violin.

"Fraser, what a charming spot, don't you think?" Jung beamed.

"I'm dreaming about you a lot right now, even in naps. Even when I'm drunk. What's going on?"

"I'm not sure," Jung said in Benny's burlesque American drawl. "I think you may be approaching some sort of crisis."

"I've already had a bloody crisis," snapped Fraser as he sat at the table, a little embarrassed to see he was wearing tight red panties and a peephole bra. "I've lost my job."

"I'm talking about a bigger crisis. A psychic event."

That's all I fucking need, Fraser thought.

"Nice outfit," smiled Jung, with a wink to a foot soldier from the army of Attila the Hun who had limped out of the café to serve them a generous salver of corpulent and glistening raw eel.

At the other side of the cobbled square was a magnificent Gothic cathedral. Unseen by Fraser and Jung, a man was trying, and failing, to open its large wooden doors by sticking his fingers in the giant keyholes and pulling. The man was deeply distressed, crying, his heart breaking on every exhale, tugging at the doors until his fingers started bleeding. He was so intent on his task that he noticed nothing and no one around him. He didn't even know what country he was in.

This was George, who was asleep in seat 16A of Coach 13 of the 1915 *Eurostar.* Waterloo to Gare du Nord.

PETIT MORT

GEORGE HAD TRAVELED ENOUGH TO KNOW that no town has its most interesting neighborhoods near its large railway stations, so when he got off the *Eurostar* at Gare du Nord, he thought about taking a taxi somewhere, but he knew he'd end up asking for something predictable like Notre Dame or the Eiffel Tower and he'd probably be ripped off by the driver, who would be able to tell he was from out of town by his Scottish high-school French.

He looked around the big station and saw a sign for the Metro. The Parisian underground rail system. He walked down to a ticket booth, bought a zone one fare that would allow him to go anywhere in central Paris, then walked to the platform. He got on a number four train and got off at the first stop he had heard of, St. Germain.

Directly opposite the St. Germain Metro entrance in the bustling, noisy square by the old church is a delightful café called Les Deux Magots (The Two Bigwigs), a busy bistro made famous by Jean-Paul Sartre and Simone de Beauvoir, who used to go there a lot for the delicious omelettes and furious debates on existentialism. Both of which are still available.

George sat at a tiny circular table outside. He sipped his coffee and nibbled his croque and watched people go by. He felt wonderful.

This is what dying too early is all about, he thought, feeling international and tragic all at the same time. For the first time in his life he knew he had become interesting. He had done something wildly interesting in that he had abandoned his dull, bovine wife in Scotland, he had left no note or clue to his whereabouts—that was interesting. He hadn't even told anyone he had cancer. Now he sat in a famous French bistro contemplating death and about to start smoking again. He was so interesting he could hardly stand it. He liked himself. It was a feeling he hadn't had in years. He couldn't remember when, if ever, he felt so fucking good.

He had bought a pack of Gaulois at the train station when he arrived, realizing that the health issue was no longer a problem for him. He had smoked Benson & Hedges at university but gave up when he got married. Sheila said it made the house smell like a saloon, and given that both his parents had smoked and had died of cancer, she said, he might want to pay attention to that.

Strangely enough it was not his parents' deaths that stopped him smoking, even though they were both fairly horrific and came within eighteen months of each other. It was Chippy Thomson, for some reason, that was the one that got to him. It was about two years after his mother's death. He had defended Chippy Thomson, a petty thief who was facing prison time for stealing two bags of frozen shrimp from the rear entrance of the Loon Fung Chinese restaurant on Sauchiehall Street. The crime itself was not considered particularly heinous but the court asked for seventy-four previous similar convictions to be brought into account. Chippy had cornered the illegal frozen shrimp market in Glasgow, and Dorothy Nardini, the public prosecutor, a bad-tempered middle-aged woman who had a secret penchant for watching rough gay anal-penetration videos, felt that this "mollusk Mafioso" (the term she actually used in court) be taught a lesson.

George's defense was that Chippy was dying of lung cancer (which he was) and that sending him to jail would be inhumane given the circumstances. The judge agreed. Chippy walked only to be arrested within two days for possession of stolen cod.

During the proceedings George had been obliged to interview Chippy, who had been remanded in custody at Barlinnie Prison. The prison itself is a big, dark Gothic Victorian nightmare, and the little smoky interview rooms where the prisoners meet their lawyers are hideously depressing and institutional. George half listened to Chippy's pathetic lies about extenuating circumstances and his rubbish about being an old soldier, but more than that, he watched him.

He watched Chippy smoke.

Chippy knew he was dying from inhaling the crap in cigarettes yet he smoked them constantly, he sucked in the poison with an alarming greed and passion that was inconsistent with everything else about him. Chippy was a sneaky little crook but the Tobacco Lords outfoxed him.

George determined there and then that he wasn't going to die like Chippy, sucking on a cancer stick like it was his mother's tit. George had not learned at that point that how and when he died was not necessarily his business. He gave up smoking after the interview. Chippy died in prison two months later. George secretly paid for the funeral. He told Sheila he lost the money betting on Betamax Pete, who came second to last in the 3:30 at Kempton Park. She didn't talk to him for a week.

She would have gone really nuts if she'd known the truth. Betting on the wrong horse is one thing, flogging a dead one is quite another.

George failed to realize at the time that paying for the funeral of an old villain he hardly knew and lying about it to his wife is actually rather interesting.

The waiter took George's plate and brought him another coffee. George took a sip, then he unwrapped the soft blue packet and drew out the unfiltered cigarette. He rolled it in his fingers, he smelled it, he put an end in his mouth. Heaven.

He cursed himself for not remembering to buy matches or a lighter.

He looked round for the waiter, who had disappeared.

Because of what happened immediately after, and because he didn't watch French TV or read French newspapers, George never knew that the waiter, Jean Luc DuCan, a thirty-eight-year-old former male prostitute from Marseilles, had at that moment actually disappeared and was never seen by anyone again. The French police launched a national manhunt in the hopes of solving this mystery but to no avail. To this day, the strange occurrence is fodder for furious and witty debate among the chic, wrinkly, chattering speculators of late-night discussion programs on French television.

But George never knew this. As he turned his head he came face-to-face with the woman who was sitting at the next table.

Claudette Bruchard.

ARRIVAL

DING AND SHAKE AND DING AND SHAKE and ding and shake and rattle rattle rattle bump. American Airlines Flight 112 Glasgow to Miami was heading into C.A.T.—Clear Air Turbulence.

Fraser was drinking mint tea in Tangier with a giant, hook-nosed Semitic carpet salesman who had skin the exact tone and consistency of Fraser's old schoolbag. The Arab had the unexpected name of Davy. Davy was explaining to Fraser that he was a Bedouin who spent half the year in the Sahara with his family and half the year in Tangier in his uncle's carpet store selling handmade rugs to American tourists. He said business had been very bad since the whole jihad thing and that he thought that fundamentalism was the scourge of decent people who were trying to live a good life and make an honest living. Fraser was surprised to find that Davy saw no difference between Christian fundamentalism and Islamic fundamentalism except that the Christians seemed to be rather more effective at killing large groups of people.

Fraser explained that the Christians weren't killing anyone. Davy asked who dropped the bombs on Iraq. Fraser explained it was the Coalition. Davy asked who the Coalition was, Fraser said it was a group of Western democracies, Davy asked who ran the democracies, Fraser said the governments. Davy asked who ran the governments and Fraser said the people. Davy asked what people and Fraser shut up and drank his tea.

Davy asked if Fraser would like some hashish. Fraser said okay, that would be nice. Davy put a little lump of sweaty Afghani black on a pin and set it alight using a *God Bless America* souvenir Zippo lighter that had a picture of an eagle with a Stars and Stripes flag in its talons.

Fraser noticed Davy's dirty fingernails.

Davy collected the smoke from the burning hash in an upturned glass vial shaped like a lightbulb. Fraser took a giant inhale of the hash and found it tasted and smelled like stale air, old farts, and microwaved bacon.

He was awake. Back in the plane.

At that same moment, in an old VW bus in the Northern Sahara, Mohammed Fisal awoke with a start and drew back the little purple curtain next to his bunk. It was still dark and the stars were crammed into the clear desert night sky. It never stopped being beautiful out here. Mohammed had been dreaming about smoking hashish in his uncle's shop in Tangier. He had been trying to stop smoking and he kept dreaming about it. He scratched his pubes—the sand always made him itch at night—and got up and walked over to the little portable fridge and got himself an ice-cold Orangina.

He opened the little lightbulb-shaped bottle and drank the fizzy mixture of orange juice and sparkling water. He gulped the whole bottle down and then gasped with delight.

"God is great," he cried out loud.

Fraser lifted the little window blind and looked out into the clear sky. The cabin lights had been dimmed and most of the passengers were asleep, including the sexy professional woman next to him.

A few seats over a man was watching a tiny television, his face lit from beneath. He looked slightly demonic. The plane banged and rattled a little more.

Fraser felt a rush of fear. He knew that turbulence was not dangerous but he just couldn't believe it.

He looked around. No one seemed nervous. He knew it would be no good taking any more Xanax, since the turbulence would have passed before he got any good out of it and he would arrive in America bombed and incoherent, not a good look for customs. The turbulence increased, the plane lurched up and then down, glasses rattling in the stewards' little area. The seat-belt light dinged on. Colin's unpleasant nasal drawl came over the P.A.

"Ladies and gentlemen, the captain has switched on the seat-belt sign. Please return to your seat and fasten your seat belt securely."

Fraser looked around for signs of unease in other passengers or in the cabin crew. There were none. A few sleepy passengers shifted in their seats and Colin and the Harpy came through the cabin making sure everyone was wearing their seat belt.

The turbulence took a real turn for the worse. The plane seemed to almost dive for two or three seconds before bouncing on some giant invisible trampoline.

Passengers paid more attention. People sat up. The woman sitting next to Fraser continued to sleep. Fraser felt angry at her, he was jealous.

The captain came on the P.A., talking in that lazy, relaxed drawl they use to try to make people feel secure.

"Hey, folks, as you can probably tell, we're running into a little bit of choppy air here, not in any way a safety problem, all perfectly normal, but I'm gonna ask you to make sure you're seated with the belt on and put your seat in the upright position. Cabin crew, take your seats as well, please. We're gonna bump around here for a few minutes but we'll get you back in the smooth stuff just as soon as we can."

The P.A. clicked off. Fraser was really terrified now. The cabin crew took away drinks and made sure everyone was sitting upright and had their belts on. They looked efficient but not scared in any way.

The plane continued to pitch and sway alarmingly. The cabin crew took their seats. The woman next to Fraser still slept, even though Colin had made her put the seat back in the upright position.

Fraser's heart was pounding, his palms sweating, a lump in his throat. Tears formed in his eyes. He stuck his face to the window looking for clouds. Normally, if he could see the source of turbulence, it somehow made it easier to bear, but now the sky was clear and starry as the Sahara at midnight.

He hated that something he couldn't see had the power of life or death over him. It terrified him.

Another bang. The plane bounced down hard and then shook up again. Fraser looked over at Colin and the Harpy, who were strapped into their jump seats. They were looking at something in *Peephole* magazine. They didn't even seem to notice the impending disaster.

Fraser was almost out of his skin. The cabin crew appeared to him the way normal people appear to Holy Ones.

He looked out the window again at the deadly air.

He prayed, from the pit of his soul, from the core of his being, he prayed. Muttering the words to the airtight Plexiglas porthole, his hermetically sealed, high-altitude confessional.

"God please help me, God please help me. I know I've been bad, I've been wicked and evil and wrong and bad and please help me God. I promise with all my heart to be good. I promise to be good. Please get me out of this and I'll do your work. I'll do whatever you want. I'll change please stop this please stop it *please please please please . . .*"

He continued to mutter the word *please* quietly as the turbulence threw the plane around the sky. It was part of Fraser's arrogance that he thought the turbulence affecting a plane carrying two hundred people was actually put there by a Supreme Being to directly threaten him. The God of Fraser's understanding, at this point of his journey, would bring down a planeload of innocent people just because Fraser liked to get drunk and fuck. Fraser's concept of God was still really that of his childhood. That God was a bad-tempered sociopath who you could placate with sycophancy and ritual. This would change later.

Fraser realized he was still muttering "please" when the turbulence had subsided and the seat-belt sign had been switched off. He hardly dared feel relieved but he couldn't help it.

"Thank you, God," he said. Friendly again with the Universal Bully.

The plane touched down on time at Miami International and Fraser quietly sent up another "Thank you" but it wasn't injected with anything like the energy of his earlier prayer. He was already looking forward to some fun in the big city.

FEMME FATALE

AT THE POINT AT WHICH SHE MET GEORGE, Claudette Bruchard had already had six Great Loves in her life. Six men she had adored, worshipped, and given her heart to, and all of them had died tragically, although very few people die any other way in Claudette's opinion.

Death had broken her heart six times and she felt she could never love again. This made her feel very French, which, of course, she was.

She was born in rural Normandy and her mother died of a brain hemorrhage before she was one year old, which was the beginning of the terrible relationship between Claudette and Death. Understandably, she grew into a gloomy child, and when she was ten years old her father, an apple farmer who drank consistently to overcome his chronic grief for the one true love he had lost, put her into a convent school where he said that the nuns would take better care of her, which was true.

What he didn't tell her was that she had become unbearably sexually attractive to him. Her eyes the color of polished chestnut and her skin milky white, her lips in a Gallic fellatio pout, and her long, dark, shining hair. He wanted to devour her, fuck her, split her open. He was disgusted by his desire but knew that if she stayed around and he was drinking he would eventually molest her and he wouldn't be able to live with himself if he did that. His choice was either to give up drinking a liter of Calvados every day or send his daughter away. He chose to abandon Petite Clau-Clau to the Brides of Christ.

It would have been too painful to stop drinking.

She entered the convent as a boarding apprentice. She wore an itchy novice gown that irritated her delicate skin, and as she got older she was punished more and more by the nuns for being too loud or impertinent or wicked. Truth is, she was none of these things but she did exude a smoldering sexuality that some of the holy virgins found threatening. She was one of God's greatest masterpieces and obviously built for sex. By the time she was fourteen she had to strap down her breasts, wrapping them in linen strips ripped from her bedsheet, so that they didn't annoy the sisters by their all-too-obvious struggle to escape the confines of the ill-fitting black habit.

By the time she was sixteen, she had become aware of the power of her beauty and no amount of threatening about lakes of fire and eternal damnation was enough to quell her growing desire for a man. A real, big, solid man to get her hands on. To feel the sex of herself and the shuddering excitement she imagined bringing to a creature much more physically powerful than her. She ached for sex. Not love. Sex.

She didn't need love because she was already in love with a man she could never have sex with, even with her magnificent body. She had loved him even before she had come to the convent. He had worked as a carpenter and rabbi two thousand years before she was born and had died tragically at an early age. The picture she had of him was from the stained-glass window in the convent chapel, nailed up on the cross, naked but for some kind of miraculous gravity-defying hankie covering his penis. He looked athletic, if you avoided the blood, and she thought he must have enjoyed sport or yoga. She liked his legs; they were long and brown, and as a teenager, she imagined him going for a swim with his girlfriend Mary in the Sea of Galilee, maybe having a picnic after, no problem if they forgot to bring wine.

She loved Jesus but she had needs that he just couldn't satisfy, so at the age of nineteen, she chose not to take her final vows and enter the cloisters but left the Catholic Church and headed for the civilization of

Paris. Her first dead lover, nailed to the cross, was left behind. Before she went, she knelt quietly in the little chapel and whispered that she would always love him alone.

Her second lover was an actor, and like many of his profession, he was pathologically self-obsessed. He thought about himself constantly, about his hair and if it was falling out, his weight, the bags under his eyes. His wrinkles, his career, his performance. He thought about himself so much, the only relief he ever felt was pretending to be someone else, which he did for a living and also in his private life, which wasn't particularly private.

His name was Guillame Maupassant, and when Claudette met him he was about to star in a musical version of Dante's *Inferno* that had been written by the horribly bourgeois but wildly popular English composer Anthony Boyd-Webster.

Guillame was to play the part of the poet Virgil, and during the show he would guide Dante (played by the great Parisian acting genius Gerard Reno before he got fat and crazy) through the different levels of hell by singing him catchy, middle-of-the-road pop songs.

In preparation for the role, Guillame had taken to walking the streets of Paris alone at night. He loved the feeling of being alone in the crowd. It made him feel like Virgil, above it all, a watcher without judgment.

From his apartment in the Sixth Arrondissement he would walk past St. Sulpice, through St. Germain and Opera and into the Latin Quarter, where the tourists sat shivering and eating crappy kebabs at the pavement tables. In truth, he liked to walk around at night anyway, preparing for a role or not, because he got recognized and laid from time to time, as he was still reasonably famous from his role as the brain surgeon Dr. François Villiers in the long-running television soap opera *L'Amour et Famille.*

On one autumn night, around midnight, as a light misty rain was smirring the air, putting the city into soft focus, Guillame was out walking. He had just had dinner with his friend Alain Pantelic, a doctor he had gone to school with. Alain told him he was getting engaged to a girl he had met working in the hospital and wanted to hear what Guillame thought. It turned out all Alain really wanted to do was talk about how great his fiancée was, which was also fine with Guillame, who was happy for his old pal. Alain had recently been promoted to head of cancer research at the university hospital and Guillame had teased him about that, saying he was too sentimental to be a scientist, he should be a country practitioner, delivering little fat babies somewhere like Normandy or the Loire Valley.

Alain had protested loudly but he suspected it was true. He felt he might be too emotional for the job. He hated cancer. Guillame walked alone along Rue de Vaugirard from the restaurant on Boulevard Saint Michel but he felt fat after the big dinner and thought a stroll might help him sleep. He walked past the big green doors at the entrance to his building and turned right up Rue de Rennes to Montparnasse. The rain got heavier suddenly and began to waterfall, so he sought sanctuary. He stumbled out of it into a giant empty brasserie for a brandy and a coffee. He sat down at a window table, took off his hat and scarf, joked politely about the weather to the aged waiter who, coincidentally, was called Virgil, and lit a cigarette. Then he looked across and saw Claudette, sitting alone at a table with a coffee and a book in front of her.

Her hair was wet and sticking to the side of her head and he almost gasped aloud at her beauty. She looked over at him and smiled. He smiled back. She looked away and then looked back at him and he was smitten. Claudette had been in town for only a few weeks and, after getting a job as an assistant in the bedding department at Bon Marché and finding a tiny room, had set out in pursuit of her lover. She had scores of offers from drooling youths and desperate older men but she just hadn't met anybody who made her want to be sinful. That changed when Guillame walked into the brasserie that she liked to read in. He was tall and strong looking with sandy-colored hair that was a little too long. He was slightly overweight and had kind eyes that were deep and blue. His clothes looked crumpled, as if he had been busy tickling someone or taking a nap on the floor. At fortysomething he was in his prime; he seemed confident and sexy and experienced and independent.

She put her hand inside her shirt and adjusted her bra strap.

Guillame looked over. He was already hard and his heart thumped in his chest. Boom boom.

Claudette knew what she wanted. She picked up her book and her cigarettes and walked over to his table. He looked up at her.

"May I sit?"

He nodded, afraid that he would squeak if he tried to talk.

They lived together for nine years in Guillame's large apartment at 66 Rue de Vaugirard, just next to the Luxembourg Gardens. She was his consolation in his career failures and his glamorous companion in his successes. When he won the Palm d'Or at the Cannes Film Festival for his portrayal of Hiendrich Schmidtennacht, the conflicted Nazi poetry teacher, in *Le Pamplemousse du L' Horreur,* she was by his side on the red carpet, drawing greedy snapping flashes from the ratty entertainment paparazzi. When his next film, *Big Friendly American Wedding Celebrity,* a ludicrous, formulaic American studio picture starring the lounge singer Leon Martini, was panned by critics and ignored by audiences, she took him on holiday to Corfu and eventually got him laughing about it.

It really was a stupid movie, as most of them are.

She learned social graces from him, how to be polite to The Evil in civilized society. He taught her how to dress and apply makeup, he bought her clothes, and she in turn loved him with her body and soul. She loved him because he was funny and sweet and other women desired him. She loved him because he was vulnerable and afraid of failure and she loved him because he was so grateful and indulgent of her sexual curiosity, which was boundless.

In their apartment they experimented with lotions and oils and devices and manuals and stimulants and aphrodisiacs. They laughed out loud at their efforts. Sometimes they brought in an extra participant, always female, but they only used this woman to enhance the lovemaking between themselves, like a tool. This would sometimes make the third party feel like a prostitute, which they occasionally were.

Claudette insisted that they never include a second man. She said that would be different. Guillame was relieved and delighted. They also celebrated the mundane in the way only the French and Italians truly can. Each meal was a delight, a walk in the park was a work of art, sitting in a café was a memorable experience. They truly lived and were blessed with unlimited happiness, which, of course, is limited.

One warm night as they fucked enthusiastically in their little kitchen, Guillame broke a little vial of amyl nitrate under his nose at the moment of orgasm and suffered a massive heart attack just as he ejaculated. Boom Boom.

He was dead before he lost his erection. He died inside her.

France mourned as it does when an artist dies.

She had to be heavily sedated the night of his funeral. She had a vivid dream.

She was walking in the garden of Gethsemane, dressed in the habit of her schooldays. She could hear music, and looked off to her left. Sitting under an olive tree at a harpsichord was a hideously ugly dwarf playing "The Girl from Ipanema." She recognized him as the composer Anthony Boyd-Webster. She smiled at him and he stopped playing and waved over at her and smiled back through a set of joke teeth, the type that can be bought at a party store. She walked on and then stopped as Lord Jesus stood in front of her, wearing a beautiful pinstripe suit by Hugo Boss.

"Hello," said Jesus.

"I'm angry with you," she said defiantly. "You took my man."

Jesus smiled patiently. "He wasn't yours."

"I loved him."

"I still do."

"Well, so do I, obviously, but he's dead."

"And what does that mean?" inquired Jesus, who was really beginning to irritate Claudette with his holier-than-thou manner although she was respectful of the fact that he actually was.

"Look," explained Christ, "I wanted to let you know, to perhaps lighten your load a little, that you are extremely important in God's plan."

"So He has a plan, then?"

"Oh yes, and your part in it is—you are His consolation to those about to fall, your beauty, charm, and sex are salve for the pain of passing. Claudette Bruchard is God's Gift to dying men."

"I don't want to be that."

"We all have our crosses to bear," said Jesus sadly.

Then she was awake. It took only a couple of seconds for her to completely forget the dream and remember that her heart was broken and she was in hell.

A string of lovers followed, all with the same horrifying results. Nigel, a dashing English Formula One Racing driver who hit a pillar in Monte Carlo at 170 miles an hour. The last thing to go through his mind was "Shi—" He didn't even have time for *t*.

Then there was Don, her American, who was electrocuted while changing a lightbulb in his office; Mikael, a Russian mobster who was assassinated as he left Kievskya Station on a business trip home to Moscow; and most recently, Bruce, an Australian diplomat at the embassy in Paris who had drunkenly stepped in front of a Metro train only six months previously.

Bruce had finally sent Claudette over the edge. She had told him that she was cursed, that men dropped like flies around her. He had laughed and said he was Australian and that flies didn't die over there, they just went to Brisbane. She didn't know what he meant but she felt comforted. She had been with him for a year and had started to believe that everything was going to be okay until that horrible night. She had hardly spoken since, shunning male company at all times, which was difficult for someone as beautiful and with such a large sexual appetite.

She walked from café to café. Drinking coffee, brooding, and trying to make herself feel better by reading infantile, optimistic pop-culture psychology books with titles like *Chicken Soup for the Newly Bereaved* and *Why Am I Afraid to Love?* She was rereading a book an American acquaintance had given her years ago, *Men Are Asteroids, Women Are Meteorites,* by Some Idiot, when she first made eye contact with George.

"Excuse me, do you have a light?" he asked.

She saw the desire in his eyes as he looked at her.

"Stay away from me, I am Death," she told him in perfect English.

George thought for a moment. "Then I'd expect you'd be more than happy to help me light a cigarette, Oh Dark One."

"I mean it," she snapped.

"So do I," said George. "If you are Death you could take me now and save me a lot of pain."

George was rapidly losing the ability to give a crap what anyone thought of him, even beautiful women.

Claudette felt terribly sorry for him because she sensed his sincerity and wildness, which had aroused her interest, and therefore she knew that his days were numbered. She lit his cigarette, allowing her hand to touch his.

THE ROAD TO GOD: TWO

SAUL SWEATED FOR A NIGHT OR TWO, anxiety/thinky sweat, not the normal fatty adolescent kind that he usually had going, although he was still pouring out that stuff too. In fact, his bedsheets were soaked in the morning with double the sweat output of a fat teenager combined with his nocturnal semen emissions, caused by dreams in which he imagined himself the Emperor Tiberius sitting in baths of tepid seawater as small carp nibbled at the savory bread crumbs he had sprinkled over his scrotum.

Mrs. Wolf never complained or embarrassed him but she was quietly astonished that the boy had any fluids left in him by morning.

Saul had to work fast. If Leon became popular in high school, he would never want to leave. He would want to stay in Duluth and be happy, have kids, vote. Saul couldn't allow this; he knew they were destined for greatness and huge cash rewards.

So Saul sweated over how to keep Leon from the damnation of high-school popularity until he remembered his dear mother and her Munchausen by Proxy. It was this that inspired him to embark on a short course of therapeutic poisoning.

Bad acid is like a taxi. You can never find it when you need it. For Saul to work his magic on his brother he needed some nasty, powerful, and dirty LSD. Not the kind of thing that you fall over at the Astronomy Club, although the Astronomy Club did have a resource that Saul knew would prove invaluable.

Science geeks.

Anyone who seeks true power needs science geeks. Guys who can drum up weird and noxious stuff that can scare the crap out of people. Stalin had the brilliant and troublesome Sakharov when the U.S. had Oppenheimer and his band of guilt-ridden geniuses. You need science geeks if you want control. This is, incidentally, where Hitler really messed up. He applied his ludicrous racial agenda to the universities before he even invaded Poland. He didn't want Jews running things in the places of learning. Too dangerous. He exiled Jewish academics. The trouble with this policy, however, is that whether you are anti-Semitic or not, you have to acknowledge that Jews tend to be clever, academic, and temporal successes. Success is not reviled in Jewish culture, there is no anti-intellectualism in mainstream Judaism like there is in the breakaway Jewish cults of Christianity and Islam. Therefore, Hitler lost some of his best geeks before the war started. Geeks who would later develop weapons for an enemy that would leave his nasty little dream a burned corpse in a Berlin bunker.

It should be said that Carl Jung accepted an academic post in Germany in the thirties, a post vacated by an exiled Jew. Freud saw this as proof of his anti-Semitism, although Jung hotly denied it. After his death he conceded to Freud that it had in fact been an error and he apologized unreservedly. The courtly Freud took the apology in good humor and nearly said, "No harm done," but then changed his mind, as that would, of course, have been wildly inaccurate.

Saul needed some bad acid. He needed to change his brother's mind, make him more malleable. He didn't know any drug dealers, nor was he likely to go unnoticed if he attempted to buy drugs anyway. This was before drugs became almost curricular in American high schools.

The preparation of the extremely powerful hallucinogen LSD (lysergic acid) is not a hugely demanding piece of lab work but it was beyond Saul's capability at that time. It was, however, a piece of cake to a compadre of his, Benny Alderton—or Nota Benny, as he was nicknamed by his fellow geeks, who prided themselves on their witty use of pidgin Latin.

He bribed Benny, a chemistry nut (who would go on to develop a topical cream that, when applied to the penis, acted as a stimulant, producing a thrilling erection, and a contraceptive, and made him five billion dollars before he died at the age of thirty-two in a microlite accident off the coast of Santa Barbara), with three back issues of the pornographic magazine *Hustler.*

Hustler should not be confused with *Playboy. Hustler* showed graphic pictures of women pulling their labial lips apart to show their red, fruity inner workings while pretending to be in ecstasy, whereas *Playboy* showed pictures of women pretending to be in ecstasy for no apparent reason whatsoever—perhaps they were excited sexually by being near a fake fur rug or a tennis racket. No fleshy, baboony hangings in the *Playboy* pictures. All the unpleasant nature of sex organs viewed at too close proximity was airbrushed away to make things neat. Nicely coiffured good-girl, All-American Vulvas—*sanitized for your convenience.*

Saul managed to get his hands on the goods. He had to feign interest when he took delivery from Benny.

"Be careful with this stuff, Saul, it's highly potent. Blah blah no alcohol blah blah induced psychosis blah blah."

Leon had a massive dose in his Cheerios the following morning. Saul waited as they boarded the Bastard bus to school. Leon didn't feel strange at all for about forty-five minutes and Saul was angry, contemplating his revenge on Benny, whom he feared had ripped him off, when the fun began.

Deborah Thornhill had taken to waiting for Leon in the schoolyard as the Bastard bus arrived. She loved him as only a teenage girl can love a singer. This had a startling effect on the rest of The Bastards.

Deborah's high-school kudos combined with her obsession with Leon made them much more acceptable. Deborah said she thought it was romantic that Leon lived in an orphanage, and Deborah's word had real weight with the other girls; therefore The Bastards became romantic. It became fashionable to be a Bastard. They were the outcasts. The awkward walking wounded. The personification of what all teenagers feel like. Punk rockers.

The Bastards loved this, of course, and were very grateful to Leon, who had become as a god among them.

He gave them coolness by proxy.

Leon got his bag from under his seat (he had taken to carrying his schoolbooks in an old sailor's tote, which gave him the air of his father in *Anchors Aweigh*—"Nu Yawk Nu Yawk id's a wunnafil down"), and walked down the aisle of the bus. Saul waddled behind him as usual.

As Leon got off the bus, Deborah began her showy *Wuthering Heights* run across the yard toward him. She did this every morning for two reasons: First, she knew it made her breasts bounce up and down and everyone wanted to look at that, and second, she loved the feeling of being breathless just as she grabbed Leon and kissed his lips. It made her feel romantic.

Leon looked and saw Deborah running just as the lysergic acid that had been prepared by the kid who would become the greatest pharmacologist in the world kicked in.

For the first time in his life, Leon felt real terror. He saw Deborah in a very different light. She was still Deborah but she was no longer the wildly desirable teenage princess. Her eyes had changed. Her irises, instead of being cobalt blue, were now yellowy white, the color of the urine stains on Saul's underwear. Her pupils were not black, they were red. Her perfect teeth were fangs and her skin like that of an albino turtle. She looked like a vampire squid in a summer dress, blue veins coursing black blood beneath the surface. Her breasts were moaning as they bounced in slow motion. They sang, in an exact impersonation of the New Zealand soprano Dame Kiri Ti Kanawa, "We Will, We Will Meet You" to the tune of the rock band Queen's "We Will Rock You."

Leon screamed and ran away from her as fast as he could, his heart thundering in his chest, the sound of a screaming waterfall in his ears.

The other kids laughed, as did Deborah, thinking Leon was pulling a joke. Playing a game. But Saul, the real Player of Games, knew what was going on and he felt a different rush.

The rush of directing the show.

Power.

Real power, the kind unseen by everyone but God.

The bell rang and the kids left for their classrooms. Everyone expected Leon to show up in a minute or two, but Leon was as gone to that high school as Jean Luc DuCan was to the city of Paris, and Saul was going with him.

Acid, even wild extra-weird acid prepared by Benny Alderton, wears off but it takes a while. As anyone who has taken acid knows, the trip always lasts much longer than you want it to, even if it's a good one. You can get really sick and tired of ecstasy. Many acid trippers have found themselves asking out loud at six A.M., "Oh, when will this fucking hilarity end?" Only to be taken again into another agonizing and exhausting wave of pleasure. It's torture, and that's if you're lucky, which Leon, on this occasion, was not.

Leon heard screaming bats as he ran. The purple pansies planted at the side of the school gate screamed, "Fuck you! Fuck you!" at him as he tore by them into the woods at the back of the school. He stumbled over a vine and tumbled, then fell and rolled down a steep embankment to an aboveground oil pipeline that ran alongside a railroad track at the bottom of a little valley. The dewy morning grass ripped blunt and dirty razors across his skin but he could not bleed because his blood had turned to hard rubber. His jaw and face had disappeared to him, he was neither in nor out of his body. He was in hell. Truly in hell. In a deep level reserved usually only for the schizophrenic, the bipolar, or the delirium tremens alcoholic.

Saul struggled down the embankment after him. He found him crouched under the pipeline trying to immerse himself in the small stones, broken glass, and dry white dogshit that was scattered around. He was clutching at his jaw and twitching and sobbing uncontrollably.

"Saul, fuck—are there ducks in these woods?"

"I don't think so," said Saul.

Leon had noticed that Saul kept turning into Billy Idol, a popular-music singer in the 1980s.

"Stop fucking doing that, man, it's freaking me out."

"Sorry, I can't help it," guessed Saul.

"Okay, okay, what the fuck are we going to do about the ducks? They'll fucking kill us if they find us."

"I can handle it. I'm not afraid of the ducks."

"They're killers, Saul."

"Fuck them. Don't you worry about it," said Saul, feeling like Bruce Willis, a movie actor who pretended to be very tough in his films. "I'll take care of you."

Leon wept with gratitude and crawled further beneath the oil pipe for safety.

Saul had been sitting sentinel for about an hour but luckily no killer ducks had descended on them. Leon was whimpering incoherently, crouched in the fetal position beneath the pipe. (Actually he was muttering the word "please" over and over again.)

Off in the distance, a horn sounded. Leon looked at Saul in panic.

"Don't worry. It's a train. It's come to rescue us from the ducks."

"Oh, thank you God, thank you God," intoned Leon as he rocked back and forth.

The train, one of the mile-long, slow-moving freighters that crisscross Georgia and the South, rumbled toward them at an agonizing twenty miles an hour. As the noise of the nearing train built, Saul kept softly telling Leon that it was all right, everything was fine, that the train was good and it was the ducks that were evil. Leon hyperventilated but didn't leave his crouch.

As the train was about to pass by them, it stopped, as they periodically do, waiting for a signal to proceed from further down the line.

Saul knew this was a decisive moment in his life.

"Shit!" he yelled. "Ducks, fucking ducks, Leon—run!"

Leon sprang up and ran in little circles like a mad whippet. Saul grabbed him, turned him to face the train.

"Quick, jump on. It's our only hope."

Leon bolted for the train, his brother struggling to keep up. They clambered aboard a giant rusting metal car that was laden with twenty tons of coal. Saul panted up the ladder behind Leon and collapsed next to him on the coal heap just as the train ground back into motion.

Saul laughed. "Fuck, we made it!"

Leon started laughing too, delighted to escape. "Thank you God, thank you Allah, thank you Buddha, thank you whoever you are!" he screamed, covering his options.

He lay back on the dirty black carbon and looked at the white-blue space of sky and laughed and laughed and laughed.

He was still laughing eight hours later after Saul had fallen asleep and the train passed over the state line into northern Florida.

The truth is that Leon, like a lot of those—maybe everyone—who trips on acid, never really came back. He recovered but he was never the same guy again. He had lost something—innocence of hell. Acid presses a little button in your mind that should never be pressed.

The coal train was stopped in some rural yard when Saul woke from his nap. Leon was gazing out into the sunset, which had turned the sky to the north an eerie pale green.

Saul looked at the back of Leon's head. He waited until his brother spoke first.

"Well . . . that happened."

"You okay?"

"Yeah," said Leon, sounding like himself again. "Man, that was fucking weird."

Saul was a little scared, he didn't know how to read this. "You remember everything?"

"Sort of. I think someone must have spiked me acid or something, some prick jealous I was boning Deborah."

"You wanna go back?" asked Saul.

"No fucking way. I'd be scared to even have a cup of coffee or a soda. Next time it might be rat poison or something. Mom isn't the only crazy person in the world, obviously."

"What'll we do?"

"Keep moving. I never liked it there anyway. It's best when it's just you and me. Blood is thicker than water."

Leon turned and looked at his brother with tears in his eyes.

"You're the only one I can trust," he said.

Saul smiled through his own tears and hugged the brother he loved more than anything in the world. He loved him even more now that he had broken him.

Leon eventually cried himself to sleep in Saul's arms and Saul held him until sunrise.

The boys felt that it was too risky to stay on the train. There were always rumors of mad psycho guards who would beat you to death for hitching a free ride, although in reality these bogeymen had disappeared in the 1930s. The boys didn't know that and what you don't know can hurt you. Beat you to death for dodging a fare.

They headed off into the woods with no idea of where they were going but with a certain faith that they would be provided for. A faith less to do with God and more to do with the fact that they were two white boys who grew up in the South. They knew, sooner or later, someone with old-time Dixie manners would offer them food or a bed or both.

Leon was still very jumpy and fragile from his trip and he almost fainted when a raccoon ran across their path, but Saul was there to soothe him and he listened to his fat brother coo in his ear as they both stumbled over bracken and roots on the forest floor.

They were in fact walking through the outskirts of the small town of Crawford's Creek, treading on a forgotten battle site from the Civil War. In a minor skirmish there toward the end of the conflict, after Sherman had burned Atlanta and was mopping up the South, a party of twenty-eight Union soldiers were ambushed by a gang of renegade Confederate troops who had been hiding out with the locals. All twenty-eight were killed (hence the forgotten battle—no survivors from the eventual winning side) and their heads were put on spikes in a giant circle in the forest.

The locals lit a bonfire in the center of the circle and everyone got drunk and danced, making believe that the South did indeed rise. The charred circle inside the severed heads became the clearing where the snake handlers eventually built their place of worship.

Critters and some starving, quiet, guilty rednecks from the town of Crawford's Creek stripped the burnt flesh from the bodies, and the bones sunk into the earth over time.

The Civil War was the bloodiest war in history, they say. Usually Americans say that but we have already examined the reliability of American popular history, although it cannot be denied that the American Civil War was a particularly gory and unpleasant affair. Brother against brother, and everyone knows how vicious that can be.

The woods got thicker and greener, the dense canopy of leaves allowing only shafts of light to stream to the ground. The boys walked on slowly and carefully. They looked like Grimm children in an El Greco.

And lo it was that they walked from the darkness into the light. The Christian Reformed Fellowship of Born Again Snake Handling Pentecostal Baptists has their place of worship in the heart of the woods, almost a mile from Crawford's Creek proper. A white wooden one-room structure by the side of a shiny bubbly stream. There is a little graveyard off to the side of the church where the faithful bury the finished.

Little bunches of purple pansies decorate the small whitewashed carved boulders that serve as headstones to mark the recent and the Confederate dead.

A fairytale church, but aren't they all.

MIAMI VICE

HOTEL ROOMS HAVE AN APHRODISIAC QUALITY. It doesn't matter how expensive the room is, it's just the fact that you are renting a room for a short period of time means you can do what you want. It suggests a lack of accountability, it promotes the desire for wantonness and abandon. No one would ever know—well, maybe the hotel staff, but they are sworn to secrecy in an occult brotherhood as dark and tight as a mulatto ladyboy. Hotel staff are pilot fish, cleaning the crap and crumbs from orifices of the sharks in their charge. A cheap hotel room gives the seedy, sleazy vibe that many, especially rich, deviants enjoy but Fraser personally preferred expensive hotels. To Fraser an expensive hotel room was a clean plate. A chance to start again, and God knows he wanted that more than anything.

When Fraser stepped into Room 113 of the Four Seasons Miami, he felt that little rush of adrenaline, he knew fun was on the way. He quickly dispensed with the porter, Steve, a worryingly tanned and shiny plastic queen, handing him twenty dollars in order to avoid listening to a lengthy and desperate, illiterate pitch about the benefits of the trouser press. There is just something thrilling about the full minibar and the military-style bed-making and the little soaps wrapped in cellophane and the jar of macadamia nuts. The only time in life Fraser ever ate macadamia nuts was when he was in a hotel. He wouldn't even know where to get macadamia nuts in the real world.

He opened his leather case and hung up his black Boss suit, a miracle of German efficiency—it would free itself of all wrinkles if hung properly on a hanger for an hour or two. He took off his trousers and threw them over the chair next to the bed, selected a small bottle of Stolichnaya vodka from the minibar, mixed it with fresh guava juice, opened the jar of macadamia nuts, and turned on the TV to CNN.

The Cable News Network promised up-to-the-minute news reports twenty-four hours a day but, of course, there isn't always news to report. So, in order to fill the airtime with something that felt like news, the Cable News people like to put on interview shows; after all, there are only so many human-interest "news" reports you can use to pad things out. Once you've seen one parrot that can ride a miniature bicycle, you've pretty much seen them all.

The interview show that was airing when Fraser turned on the television was hosted by a gentleman named Larry King, a pompous narcissist who thought he was a tough intellectual because he wore suspenders and had a voice that sounded like an aged camel in sexual ecstasy.

Larry was interviewing O.J. Simpson, who was complaining to Larry that people still were mean to him in airports and hotel lobbies, even though he had been cleared of the murder. Larry asked him if that was perhaps because they thought he was guilty. (Larry did, but he talked to politicians all the time, so dealing with self-justifying murderers came easy to him.) O.J. said that no, it was because they were jealous of his celebrity, and actually, in this case, O.J. was telling the truth, albeit unintentionally.

Most Americans are disappointed because they are not in show business. They're depressed because they are not famous. This is why "reality shows," i.e., shows where "real" people are the stars (the definition of *real* here is people who are ugly or poor or not famous), became so popular on American (and, of course, Britain is included in this, as it is now little more than an annexed colony) television.

Viewers want to believe that the fifteen minutes promised them in the famous sound bite by Mr. Warhol is just around the corner. The glorious day when they can Marry a Millionaire/Ordinary Guy/Beauty Queen/Midget and get front-row seats at the Golden Globes. Fraser watched Larry and O.J. blah for a few moments and became bored.

Fraser thought he should absorb some of the local culture and switched off the television. He reached across the bed and opened the nightstand. Inside was a Miami Yellow Pages, a telephone directory, which was a throwback to the days before the Internet. He looked up E for Escorts.

There is a language—perhaps not a language but a code—that goes with American prostitution. For example, in an advertisement for her services, an escort may offer a GFE, a Girl Friend Experience: This means the girl promises to kiss the client on the lips as well as the usual hooker stuff. You could also have a PSE, a Porn Star Experience: This means the girl will not kiss the client but she will have undergone an inexpensive and brutal-looking breast augmentation and she will allow him to ejaculate on her face.

Fraser noted with some mirth that no one ever promised a WE, a Wife Experience, presumably because most men who sought the services of prostitutes were already married and were already paying much more for their WE elsewhere. (Although Fraser had never been married, he had picked up a bitterness and cynicism about the whole thing from his angry drinking buddies in the Press Bar, many of whom had been divorced by their wives because they spent too much time drinking in the Press Bar with divorced guys.)

Even the term *escort* is important. *Escort* lets the prospective client know that he can expect intercourse, or Full Service, if he is willing to pay the requisite price. Hookers who advertise "Sensual Massage" will not allow clients to penetrate them but will perform hand jobs or fellatio.

Fraser was familiar with all this parlay, he was an old hand. He selected a full-page advertisement, a bad drawing of two women standing next to a stretched-out limousine with a private jet parked behind them. A giant champagne glass was also parked next to the jet, and at the top of the page, the name of the agency—Miami Platinum. (It is a common belief among workers in the sex industry that customers will pay more for sex if the word *platinum* is involved. This is not necessarily true but if you are in the sex trade you are already desperate, so what harm can it do to look a little foolish.)

For some reason he felt a little guilty, a little adrenal, which was unusual. He had done this many times before in hotels all over the U.K. Whenever he was away on business, in fact. He contemplated not dialing the number. Maybe just have a bath and watch TV.

"What's this about?" he said out loud to himself.

Thousands of miles away in Paris, even though it was getting very late, Claudette and George were still in conversation at Les Deux Magots. The mysterious intoxicating mist of human attraction had rolled in on them, causing them to stop and take stock of each other.

They were doing favorite authors. George said he'd read only one book by a Frenchman. Camus's *L'Étranger*. He'd had to study it at school. Didn't really get it.

Claudette said she thought it was a hateful piece of nihilism and that Camus wasn't even French, he was Algerian.

"A Frenchman would have written a nicer book?" asked George.

"Of course," smiled Claudette.

Fraser dialed the digits at the door of his undoing.

A woman answered. "Agency."

"Is this Miami Platinum?"

"Yes, sir. How may I help you this evening?"

"I'd like a girl to visit my room."

"Sure, honey."

Fraser put his hand down his Marks & Spencer's underpants. He was already a little turned on. By this time he had completely forgotten the deal he had made with God when his airplane was going through turbulence.

* * *

Fraser was disappointed when he looked through the peephole in the room door to see the girl from the agency. He had asked for a busty redhead and the agency suggested Tiffany. They had her call Fraser in his room—she sounded very sexy on the phone, although Fraser was long enough in the tooth to know that didn't mean much. He had a passing acquaintance with Senga Trotter, a sexy-voiced "phone hooker" who drank in the Press Bar. She charged men a fortune to talk filth to them on the telephone but she looked like a walrus—really like a walrus—same color, same weight, and a mustache.

Tiffany set a price (two hundred dollars to come over, plus tip, which meant probably another two, three hundred, depending on how much Fraser wanted) and Fraser had asked her to describe herself. She told him she was twenty-five years old, red hair and green eyes, with a 36DD-24-36 figure.

Fraser understood this description, bar a little salesmanship, to mean Tiffany was large breasted and young. When he looked through the peephole before he opened the door, he knew he'd been conned, but he went ahead and opened the door anyway.

The woman who stood before him was at least forty years old. She had a thin, undernourished look and hard eyes that were partially cataracted by cheap green contact lenses. Her mouth was lipsticked to a bloodred gash—it looked like a wound. Her hair, admittedly a reddish color, had been dyed badly some time ago and some white was showing among the dark roots. Her fingernails were angry and red and chipped. In fact, she was angry and red and chipped. Her skin looked slack.

She wore a cheap copy of a Chanel suit and white stilettos. She smelled of cigarettes and Listerine. She looked like a barmaid in a dockyard tavern who had gone to apply for a mortgage and been refused.

"Hey." She grimaced as Fraser opened the door.

"Hello," Fraser replied, trying not to sound too pissed off.

"Is that an accent?"

"Yes, I'm Scottish."

"Oooh, sexy," mumbled Tiffany halfheartedly.

Fraser guessed that would have been her reply no matter what nationality he'd said. He wished there was someone he could complain to.

He was relieved when she left. He had settled for an extra sixty bucks and a hand job, and he couldn't get her out of there fast enough. She offered to get naked but he talked her out of it, saying it was sexier with her clothes on, but the truth was he didn't think he would be able to maintain an erection if he saw her naked. She was the opposite of sexual. All the sex, all her joy, had been wrung out of her years ago, there was hardly even politeness left. She worked his juice into a little napkin she got from the bathroom, and he thanked her and almost bustled her away.

Annoyed, he got more vodka from the minibar. He didn't bother to mix it with anything this time. When the four little vodkas were finished he moved on to whisky. Fucking hell, what was he doing drinking vodka anyway, he was Scottish, fucking Scottish, pal, and don't you forget it, let's have a beer.

Fuck this TV, fucking Larry King with his fucking hair, fuck that nasty skinny hooker, I deserve better, he thought. Fuckit, I'm fucking going out.

And out he fucking went.

Miami was hot and clear like a movie. Pulsing gay techno beat from clubs and cars. Fraser, in his black Hugo Boss suit, wandered through the pasteled revelers like a nineteenth-century missionary. He was the anti-Presbyterian come on the quest for personal pleasure. He walked, walked and drank in bars, one, then another, always moving forward, always moving, always looking, he didn't know what for and he wouldn't have believed anyone if they had told him.

Fraser was so drunk he didn't even know he was in Boy Town. In a nightclub called Rage, among suspiciously big-handed women, he thought he saw Jung dancing. He approached him drunkenly, smiling and pushing. He hugged him ecstatically.

It wasn't Jung, it was Kenny Ipanez, a middle-aged orthodontist from Fort Lauderdale, who had driven to Miami for his monthly fix of crystal meth and raving. Kenny was friendly, friendlier than Jung had been recently, thought Fraser. Kenny and Fraser, unable to talk in the too-loud club, went to the toilets, where, in a stall, Kenny gave Fraser a line of crystal meth and tried to kiss him. Fraser felt the belt of the drug almost the second he snorted it. It cut through the alcohol and pushed him immediately to drink more. Kenny put his hand on Fraser's crotch.

Fraser head-butted Kenny, feeling no remorse, he was well out to sea now.

Kenny slumped in the cubicle, crying, as he did every month.

Fraser stumbled, spacey and whirring, back into the club. The crystal revved him much higher than any speed he had ever taken. He battered shots of vodka down his neck to keep from going completely psychotic. And he danced and danced and danced. Madness.

He was in a blackout when he staggered out of the club. His brain was capable of performing motor functions but nothing was being recorded. It was as if he had left the building with the lights burning.

That's when they saw him. They had been waiting for the best part of an hour for the right candidate and Fraser was just peachy. Prime. Out-of-towner, gotta be a fag in that suit, drunk, and probably stuffed with cash and traveler's checks. Couldn't be better.

BAD BOYS

T-BO'S REAL NAME WAS TOM BOSLEY, which is also the name of the actor who played Mr. Cunningham on the hit seventies situation comedy *Happy Days* on American television. The show also starred Henry Winkler as Arthur Fonzarelli, a.k.a. the Fonz—a cool character who wore a leather jacket and put up his thumbs and said "Hey" when anything good or bad happened. If T-Bo had been called Henry Winkler, he might have used the name, but Tom Bosley's character had not been cool, he was the stuffy dad who wore a cardigan. Luckily T-Bo was tough enough to make the other kids use the nickname of his choice, at least to his face.

T-Bo was tall. Tall and lean with a long, thin nose and almond-shaped dark brown eyes. This was because he was an almost pure-blooded Watusi warrior chief. If things had been different, then he almost certainly would have been a king and had many wives. Although if things had been different, Archduke Ferdinand would not have been assassinated in Sarajevo in 1914 and the First World War would never have happened, therefore the Second World War would have been the First, if it happened at all, which would seem unlikely. There would have been no treaty of Versailles to humiliate Germany into Evil and Nicholas II would not have been usurped by a desperate and panicky Russian mob. Therefore Europe would still be dominated by the Hapsburg, Ottoman, and Tsarist dynasties, and Hitler and Stalin would have been two forgettable serial killers in an industrialized society ruled by a slightly updated (minimum impact on the ruling classes, please) feudal government system.

T-Bo was unaware of his royal blood because two hundred years previously his great-great-great-great-great-grandfather Musinga had been captured and thrown into slavery during a raid by Portuguese brigands on his village. Musinga's ancestors had been related to the Pharaoh and had drifted south after the decline of Egypt. This is not the kind of information that would have shown up if T-Bo had ever tried to research his family tree on the Internet.

Musinga had fought the Portuguese fiercely but the Watusi were heavily outnumbered and their spears were just no match against muskets and steel. Of ninety-five people captured that day, he was the only one to reach America alive; his two wives, whom he adored, and the three children whom he loved beyond all reason died in the unbelievable squalor and misery of the slave ship.

The experience of the slave ship was so intense, so brutal and unjustified, so heartbreaking and agonizing that it was stored in Musinga's DNA as rage. Science has not yet identified that DNA can store rage or any other memory because the scientists, the grown-up geeks from the Astronomy Club, are too busy proving that genetics store really important stuff like the propensity to be overweight or lactose intolerant.

But in Musinga's DNA the rage was strong. It was there when he saw American children born from his new slave wife taken and sold off to God Knows Where. It was there the day he grabbed a fat white man's riding crop and pulled him from his horse and beat him to death with his bare hands. It was there the day he was hung, which was, of course, the same day he killed the boss.

Musinga's rage spread out through the slave population, mixing with the rage of other captured warriors, both male and female.

The rage fueled war, crime, and brilliance. In some descendants it produced a nobility and drive that beggars belief; in some descendants it produced the desire for justice and equality, for reparation and forgiveness. For other descendants it produced despair and self-hatred, alcoholism, addiction, and depression, the rage turning inward and killing the host body, as rage is wont to do. (It seems that alcoholism and addiction are highly present among present-day African-Americans, Native Americans, Aborigines, and Celts, people who are not without a certain amount of justified rage.)

Musinga's rage went forth and multiplied, and history piled injustice and denial on top, fueling the rage, making it stronger. Occasionally the rage would break out in an artistic movement or a riot, in the young the rage produced athletic prowess and strength, but the rage kept building. The intellectual and compassionate DNA battled the rage from within and movements were born, society changed, but only little by little, for there was fear and shame in the DNA of the descendants of those who had perpetrated the atrocities that had caused the rage.

They felt that if they allowed too much, those with the rage would consume them, so they gave only enough to keep the rage at an acceptable level to those in power. Like a pressure valve, let enough steam through from time to time to stop an explosion.

This worked for those who carried the fear and shame but it didn't do a whole lot of good for the individuals who carried the rage. Especially those individuals whose background or upbringing had not supplied them with enough tools to deal with the rage.

This was T-Bo. Born in the projects, never knew his father, mother had three low-paying jobs just to pay bills and feed her children. The state would not provide T-Bo with an education or discipline that he understood but the gang system would. Like most people would under the circumstances, he joined a gang, for protection and acceptance. The tragedy of this young black male was like that of many others, that in order to reach where most white kids start out he would have to be almost superhuman. But he wasn't, he was just human. Money is status. In the gang status is everything. You get a lot of money quickly from crime.

That's why T-Bo was standing outside a nightclub, coincidentally called Rage (although more like "It's all the . . ."), in Miami that night looking for a muggee.

With him were his friends Silky and Wilson, two young men whose stories were similar to T-Bo's, but the real difference was that T-Bo had big courage. He had a warrior spirit. Cajones. With T-Bo as their leader, the three boys had started robbing drunks coming out of gay clubs. This they did for a number of reasons: (1) Gay men tended to wear better clothes, which the boys stole and resold. (2) Many gay men mistrusted the authorities almost as much as the boys did themselves, so often the crime would go unreported. (3) T-Bo was homosexual and deeply ashamed of it, and although he never told his confederates this, he felt somehow better punishing men who openly lived the way he wanted to. And (4) even if the crime was reported, the cops were less interested because it was a fag who got rolled, and who fucking cares.

They followed Fraser along the street outside Rage to a blind alley that they knew well. Just as Fraser passed the alley mouth they rushed him, bundling him down toward the darkness and the trash and the vomit.

Fraser put up more of a fight than most of their victims and this adrenalized the teenagers—it was more like sport when the victim hit back. This, combined with the fact that up close T-Bo knew that Fraser was just the type of guy he was attracted to. He'd love to date him and go antiquing with him and kiss him on the mouth. With tongues. This meant that the violence that they meted out, especially as far as T-Bo was concerned, was far more horrific than anything they had previously committed. Although it had been escalating with every attack, as these things do.

Fraser lay in the filth, drunk as a lord, while T-Bo, Silky, and Wilson administered a beating so thunderously cruel and harsh that the blows and kicks rocketed him into a fourth dimension.

C'EST LA VIE

THE UNIVERSE IS VERY, VERY BIG.

It also loves a paradox. For example, it has some extremely strict rules.

Rule number one: Nothing lasts forever.

Not you or your family or your house or your planet or the sun. It is an absolute rule. Therefore when someone says that their love will never die, it means that their love is not real, for everything that is real dies.

Rule number two: Everything lasts forever.

For example, George was made up of billions of atoms, some of which had, at various times, been parts of, among other things, a Tyrannosaurus rex, a red felt hat, and some porridge.

In a staggering coincidence, Claudette had a few atoms of that same bowl of porridge in her system. It had been served to Alexander the Great during his campaign in Afghanistan. He loved porridge.

Perhaps that was the key to the attraction between George and Claudette—their shared porridge molecules. It makes as much sense as anything else that goes on between men and women.

Also they were in Paris.

Many people associate the city of Paris with romantic love, even if they have never been there. This is understandable. There is so much beauty and life and art and history in the city that to be there feels like being in love even if you are not. But there are many cities with art and beauty and history. Why, then, is Rome or Istanbul or Moscow or Williamsburg not Love's city? The answer is, of course, the French people and their language. The French understand that love, without cloying sentimentality—that irritating overfed cuckoo—is the meaning of life, and they celebrate and worship and laugh at it accordingly. French culture is extremely courtly and polite, as the French are themselves; they have a very delicate and beautiful manner, Parisians in particular. This is a fact that is hotly contested by boorish visitors to France who do not understand how it works.

For example, in Paris, if one desires to buy something, you enter the store and say, "Good morning, sir" or "madam," depending on what is appropriate, you wait until you are greeted, you make polite chitchat about the weather or some such, and when the salesperson asks what they can do for you, then and only then do you bring up the vulgar business of the transaction you require. To avoid this little exchange is to be extremely rude to the person working in the store and they are likely, at best, to be cold with you. To barge into a store and bellow, "Hey, buddy, any gum?" has almost the same effect as if you were to arrive and take a crap on the carpet.

The French, God bless them, also believe it is respectful that you make some form of an attempt to speak their language in their country, and contrary to the belief held by many American and British people, they don't all speak English and are just pretending not to understand to be mean.

So French, then, is the language of love. The only thing more alluring is English spoken with a French accent by a beautiful woman, and that is what George was listening to as he strolled down St. Germain at four A.M. with the remarkable Claudette.

Claudette told the story of her life and George listened, fascinated. The drunken father, the nuns, the movie star, the racecar driver, diplomats, and gangsters. It was so dramatic and urbane.

He forgot about himself for a while and Claudette noticed this and was intelligent enough to be flattered by it.

They reached an all-night bistro across the river from the dark Gothic dream of Notre Dame. George stared at its menacing silhouette as little thoughts of hell flitted across his consciousness, spurring flashes of adrenaline. Claudette noticed him worry, she put her hand on his arm and smiled at him, and he felt better. God's Gift to dying men, she ordered them coffee and pastries.

She lit two cigarettes, one for herself and one for George, a gesture he had only seen people do in old Hollywood movies. He drew the smoke deep into his lungs. It was his fourth of the night and he was already beginning to love them again although he had had to run downstairs to the tiny bathroom in Les Deux Magots and barf his croque after the first one. Luckily he had the perseverance required to re-ignite his addiction.

A few months later, for no explicable reason, the phrase *barfing your croque* became a slang term for ejaculation in the Australian sex industry.

It was unusual, the way that they took to each other, George and Claudette. Her terrible bereavements and his big news meant that they both had reached a place in their lives when anything rather than rigorous honesty seemed pointless, and because of this they were able to throw away a lot of the "getting to know you" rubbish required of strangers who find each other attractive. They were both acutely aware of the value of time, and they were both determined not to waste any that they might have. A real gift.

They cut to the chase. (The phrase *cut to the chase* has been attributed to the late Jack Warner, the demonic head of Warner Brothers Studios in Hollywood for many years. Supposedly, if he thought a movie that his studio was about to release was boring or too long, he would instruct the editor, regardless of the director's thoughts, to "cut to the chase," the inevitable climax to most movies. He damaged many movies this way but he also saved many movies this way. He was blamed when the movie was hurt and never praised if the movie was helped. He didn't care, he just liked money and broads. That was what made him so successful. He was like the vast majority of cinematic audiences and a prototype for every present-day Hollywood studio executive and agent. He didn't really give a rat's ass about films.)

Claudette asked George about his family and he told her. Of course, he now saw his life through a lens of recklessness, which allowed him to be more objective than he had ever been before. He told her about his parents, James and Susan, who had met each other in high school and had been in love until they died. His father first and then his mother, both of the same type of cancer that he now had himself. He told her that his father was a Protestant and his mother was a Catholic and she had felt guilty about not having more kids but she couldn't for some reason he wasn't sure of. He had a cousin, Sandra, who worked part time as a receptionist in his office. George wondered if his partners would keep her on now that he'd "copped a Stonehouse." (John Stonehouse was a British politician who faked his own death and disappeared in the 1970s, only to turn up later repentant and broke. George wished he was faking his death.)

He talked of his marriage, of how he had never loved his wife and suspected she wasn't desperately keen on him either but they had married because it seemed to be the path of least resistance. They had gotten engaged after his father died and squeezed the wedding in before his mother went. He thought they just got married to make his mother feel he'd be okay and that she could relax and expire. They had talked about getting a divorce when Nancy was little but neither one of them could bear the thought of spending time away from her. They hadn't had sex in nearly two years.

Claudette pursed her lips at this.

He talked of his teenage daughter, Nancy.

That was when Claudette first saw pain in his eyes. He didn't know what to do about Nancy, he loved her, genuinely and with all his heart. He knew that she would be okay financially and that her mother would take care of her but he hadn't said good-bye and he felt guilty as hell.

"That's because you are guilty. Being guilty tends to engender feelings of guilt," she pointed out helpfully.

George squirmed a little in his wood-and-plastic chair. "We've been kind of estranged recently. She'll hardly notice I'm gone. She's a teenager."

"You are her father. It is not her responsibility to maintain contact when she is this age, it is yours."

"Cut me some slack here, I'm dying."

"Ah yes, the victim excuse. Victim is where evil is born."

"Oh, for Christ's sake. I'm not evil."

"I know. You are beautiful but you are afraid. You are in danger of committing little acts of evil."

"Bloody hell," sighed George. He was beginning to wonder if he could handle this kind of scrutiny. He was just beginning to wonder if he should get away from Claudette—then she leaned over and kissed him on the lips.

It was the best kiss of his life.

Her lips were soft and warm and slightly parted. She put her hand at the back of his head and grabbed his hair, pushing his face deeper into hers. Her tongue touched his and she gave a little moan. Not only was it the best kiss of George's life (so far), it was in the top ten best kisses of anyone's life.

When they came up for air, she kept her face very close to his. She looked deep into his eyes, and he could feel blood rushing in his ears, actually for real hear his heart pounding. If he hadn't been sitting he would have had to.

She spoke very softly. "Evil does not question itself. Only Hope questions itself."

He suddenly felt a huge metal anchor of sadness dragging him down. "I have no hope. I'm dying."

"Nothing is written," she lied, and kissed him again, this time because she had noticed that actually it was the best kiss of her life.

"I've only known you for a few hours," he said, looking at her, genuinely mystified as to why anyone this beautiful would have anything but disdain for him.

"Courtship is bourgeois. It implies a lack of faith in yourself."

"What does that mean?"

"It means, when you know, you know."

And she was right.

Love at first sight is not rare, in fact it is extremely common, it happens to some people a few times a year. The feeling of "what if" when meeting the eyes of a stranger can be love unrecognized.

Social and safety concerns impose rules on human behavior that restrict people from listening to their instincts but George and Claudette lived very close to death and they heard themselves more acutely than the civilized and the safe. They heard nature the way an antelope does in the presence of a lion.

Also, the chemical and genetic structure imprinted on George and Claudette was so compatible that the Universe threw them at each other with all its might. Offspring of such a match would be extremely useful.

Love at first sight for George and Claudette was not romantic and whimsical. It was inevitable. The Universe wanted it.

And the Universe always gets what it wants.

It is, after all, very, very big.

THE ROAD TO GOD: THREE

POTTER TEMPLETON HAD NEVER been the sharpest tool in the shed but grief had cracked him so hard that he could barely function. It took him half an hour to brush his teeth, and putting his pants on could take all morning. He had lived in the woods for nearly twelve years before he met Leon and Saul.

He had moved into the little shack next to the church after Barbara (Babs, he called her), his wife, was killed just before their sixth wedding anniversary. He had been inconsolable, although no one really tried that hard to console him after a couple of weeks. It was too depressing; at least when smart people experienced grief you can distract them for a while, get them into another train of thought for a second or two, but Potter was too dumb to let his big slow-moving freighters interfere with his feelings. All he could do was cry and tell you how bad he felt. No matter what anyone said or did, no matter what cookies or platitudes were offered him, he just wept and complained, so people gave up, even though they sympathized. After a few years he stopped weeping but you still didn't want to get into too long a conversation with him; after the weather and sports he went straight to his dead family.

Potter and Babs had grown up in Crawford's Creek and had been best friends in kindergarten, through grade school, and had become high-school sweethearts. Babs was his intellectual equal. They had made sure they went to summer camps together and they always sat next to each other in Bible studies. Once they held hands and cried together at an Easter service when Babs was pregnant with their only child, an adorable little snaggletooth they had named Jamima.

Barbara had wept because she had been so deeply affected by the thought of Jesus' mom seeing him cruelly abused by the Roman soldiers who had beaten and crucified him. It was always a mystery to Babs as to why Mary hadn't done more to stop it. It wasn't like she wasn't connected. But Babs was a simple soul and the pregnancy hormones made her weepy. Potter couldn't stand to see her cry, so he had joined in. He had wished he could go back in time and kick the ass of everyone who had been mean to Jesus. He still did.

Babs had been driving Jamima back from choir practice when their station wagon was broadsided by an eighteen-wheeler big rig that ran a stop sign. It had been carrying frozen poultry north to Kentucky. The refrigeration unit on the truck had broken and the driver, Colin Sanders—his buddies called him Col—a twenty-year veteran of the road-haulage business, had been speeding, trying to reach his destination before his cargo spoiled. Col was also a good God-fearing man, and only two months after he killed Babs and Jamie in the truck accident, he put his handgun in his mouth and pulled the trigger. He didn't die but he became completely immobile, the brain damage so extensive that he couldn't move or speak or even hear. He was blind too. The only part of his brain that was left intact was that little piece that reminded him constantly that his impatience and greed had made him responsible for the deaths of a beautiful woman and her sweet daughter. That was all he remembered. He had even forgotten that one day he would die and be released.

It turns out that speeding irresponsibly in a large truck, placing personal wealth ahead of the welfare of others, is one of the greatest sins in the Universe, and Col Sanders' punishment was very severe. The kind of thing arms dealers and tobacconists can expect later.

Of course, Potter wasn't aware of any of this. He just knew his heart was broken and he was in hell.

Barbara's and Jamima's bodies were buried in the little churchyard next to the Confederate soldiers and Potter gave up his job selling industrial machine parts and slept in the shack to be near them.

Through time, the other parishioners grew to accept this and brought him food and blankets and whatever he needed. Potter kept busy by doing little odd jobs around the church, keeping the church and graveyard neat and tidy, and finding and capturing the occasional snake for services, although most of the local snakes were completely harmless, so were of no significant ceremonial use. The poisonous ones came from a specialty pet store in Tampa that the Reverend Pinkerton would occasionally visit. He had to get his snakes under the counter, you can't just buy a deadly snake in America, someone could get hurt. Anyway, if you really need something dangerous, get a gun. It's easy, it's cheap, and it's the American way.

By the time Saul and Leon came stumbling out of the forest, Potter was as much a fixture of the church as the snakes themselves; in fact, he was the Keeper of the Snakes. He kept them in an aquarium next to his bed. At night, alone, listening to the sounds of the trees bending and the crickets calling, he would watch the snakes move slowly under the dull red glow of the heat lamp.

Once a week he fed them a large live rat.

Potter was working on the church roof, plugging leaks, when he looked down and saw a fat, sweaty kid and a shifty-looking beanpole walking toward him.

The fat one spoke. "Pardon us, sir. We're lost."

"I was lost and now I'm found," replied Potter.

Leon, still a little spacey and weird, just sang out, "Was blind but now I see."

Potter had never heard such a beautiful voice in all his life. He looked at Leon, amazed.

Leon felt embarrassed, so he sang the song from the beginning, by way of an explanation.

"Amazing Grace/How sweet the sound/That saved a wretch like me."

Leon's unspeakably brilliant, clear voice filled the forest like the smell of fresh pine after the rain. What chance did Potter have? Even the snakes were charmed. Potter took the boys into his little shack. They sat on the upturned Bulgakov's Apricots boxes that Potter had converted into chairs (by upturning them—no fancy Catholic carpentry) and sipped the tepid, bitter sludge that Potter called coffee.

Leon, still "off world," was fascinated by the snakes. He couldn't take his eyes off them, they were so weird. So alien. Saul didn't like snakes. He made sure he sat furthest away from them. Potter fed the boys some grits he had made earlier, which they ate greedily. He listened to their tale, Saul doing all the talking, of how they had escaped the clutches of an atheistic orphanage where reading the Bible was forbidden.

"We were persecuted for loving the Lord," Saul told him.

"This country is turning to Satan. It's all a man can do to stand against the tide of the forces of evil," growled Potter.

"Amen," said Saul enthusiastically.

Potter eyed him for signs of irony, but finding none in the fat kid's clear-eyed expression, he mumbled an amen himself.

"Ma wife died. I miss her. Ma little girl too. Died for chicken parts."

Saul and Leon glanced at each other, confused. Saul took the reins.

"I'm sorry for your pain. They're with Jesus now."

Potter nodded. "You boys have been abused, like 'em poor Catholic kids—all those faggot priests. Evil, plain and simple. The Reverend Pinkerton will be happy I saved you."

And indeed he was.

The Reverend Alexander Pinkerton had been worried for some time. It was hard to be the minister of a snake-handling cult, after all. Other religions promised community and togetherness and the solace of communal worship, just like the snake handlers but without the rather unpleasant devotional duty of handling icky creatures that might well inject you with a highly toxic venom. He was beginning to feel that it was a tough sell; in his most secret of thoughts, he considered the idea of proposing that they handle other creatures from time to time, more people-friendly critters—puppies, a young goat, kittens—something that the kids could hold and enjoy. Maybe a cow—although that might be blasphemous because of the Hindu connection, you can't be too careful when it comes to Mighty Jehovah. (Coincidentally, Mighty Jehovah and the Hindu Connection is the name of a punk/jazz fusion band from Athens, Georgia. The drummer, Ricky, is a distant relative of Tootsiepop Ted, the notorious serial killer. Ricky has never killed anyone but he sometimes has an overwhelming urge to stab large mounds of cheese. To date he has never followed through with this. He'll be twenty-six in January and likes sincere girls, movies with robots, and walks on the beach.)

The Reverend Alexander Pinkerton wanted something that would bring people in. Crawford's Creek was a small town and had three churches, so the competition was fierce. He needed something that would allow his church to reach out to the community, plus he was getting bored with snakes. They don't do much, they just kind of exist. They're depressing animals, really. God made so many cheery, chirpy things, great and small—why must they specialize in the unpleasant, nasty ones? He never voiced these opinions, of course, he knew they were blasphemous, and he prayed that God remove his weak-minded liberalism.

He felt he was in a rut. Preaching about sin, handling snakes, preaching about hell, handling more snakes. Truth is, he was getting restless, and was goading the snakes to bite him just to break the routine. He got bitten a lot by snakes but it never seemed to have the slightest effect on him. He was a third-generation member of the Church; his parents and grandparents had been bitten hundreds of times before he was born.

Reverend Pinkerton's mother, Darlene, had been bitten by a black mamba, the world's deadliest snake, when she was pregnant with him. The snake had been brought to the church by Cletus Fairfield, an outlaw zookeeper from Tennessee, who had stolen the expensive African specimen from the Memphis Wildlife Park and was making a killing, often literally, touring the beast through the extreme serpentine cults of the South. People would pay a pretty penny to prove the strength of their faith by handling this deadly beauty.

Alexander Pinkerton's grandfather Abraham was a mad drunk who had emigrated to the South from Scotland when he was a boy. He paid five dollars for his pregnant daughter to hold the evil-looking killer. She knew better than to protest. Better to take your chances with the world's deadliest snake than a Scotsman drunk on moonshine and religion. Cletus didn't feel too good about it either but he could see a steely psychotic purpose in the old man's eyes and also witnessed the fearful acquiescence of the other parishioners. He took the snake from the basket using the little stick and lasso he used to protect himself from it.

Darlene stretched out her plump hand, ready to die if it be the wish of Jesus and her daddy, and the bored snake took a halfhearted stab at her wrist, more out of a sense of duty than any real snakiness. (He'd been biting his way around the Southern states and had figured out that biting was a way to avoid being prodded—rather like a Hollywood film star who finds out that bad behavior is rewarded in show business.)

Darlene didn't faint or feel any the worse for the bite, and her father proclaimed a miracle. It is true that the bite should have killed her and her unborn child within a few minutes but nothing happened, nothing visible anyway.

In reality, only the tiniest amount of venom reached Darlene's central nervous system. The poor snake was almost out—it was overmilked. The effect of the meager dose of poison was that it acted like a vaccination, rendering Darlene and her unborn clergyman completely immune to all snake venom.

This, of course, is impossible but it happened. Just like when a bumblebee flies or when Fraser's invitation was delivered on a Sunday.

Still, even this story did not help the Reverend Pinkerton in converting many new souls to his church, so when Potter presented him with Saul and Leon, two lost white boys who obviously needed to be shown the Way, he was indeed delighted.

He was appalled at the story of two young men being persecuted by heathens for their love of Christ, and he insisted that the boys come and live with him and his wife, where they would be safe from satanic governmental indoctrination.

He would regret that.

Reverend and Mrs. Alexander Pinkerton lived in a large white wooden house on the outskirts of Crawford's Creek. The house had been in the Pinkerton family for generations; in fact, it had been built by the Reverend's mad Scottish grandfather.

It was a beautiful big American house with a wraparound porch complete with rocking chairs, whitewashed fencing in the yard, and a covered well. It looked more New England than Old South. A Colonial masterpiece. Anyone would want to live there.

It was the main reason Sarah Pinkerton (née Muller) had married her husband. Sarah came from a family of Baptists, the tenth of thirteen children, and was hardly noticed by anyone until she hit puberty, when for some strange reason, her gawky bucktooth appearance was transformed. She filled out across the hips and lips and tits and became a pure corn-fed farmer's daughter fantasy girl. Had she not lived in such an out-of-the-way area, fashion vultures and show business hyenas would have swooped, snatching her for cash and prizes, mauling and pawing at her until they had drained her of all possibilities.

Her father noticed her beauty and sought to protect her by marrying her young to a good family. In Sarah Muller's father's bleak German eyes, a snake-handling family was mystic royalty. The offspring of snake handlers was as the Dalai Lama. Almost Jesus. A rock star. A great big celebrity worthy of his genetic treasure. Almost as good as a Baptist minister but he couldn't find one of those who wasn't obviously gay.

Alexander and Sarah's marriage was arranged by their parents. Neither one of them thought to protest, they had been in a vise since birth, they didn't really know that protest was an option.

Which it wasn't.

Also, when Sarah saw the beautiful house, she knew she wanted to live there and raise children and be happy.

But they had no kids.

Unfortunately, a side effect of all that serpent juice was that the Reverend Pinkerton's sperm was as dead as Claudette Bruchard's lovers. He had been firing blanks since he started firing and his libido was practically nonexistent, which he put down to piety and loving Jesus, but actually this was due to an almost complete absence of testosterone, which is also attacked and killed by snake venom.

They could have gotten help for this infertility but they believed that interfering with the reproductive process, even if it was faulty, was anti-God. It was against His plan. It never occurred to them that God may have provided the world with a vast array of very brainy medical types for the very reason of solving problems such as theirs. However, there is one thing that the medical profession cannot do and that is save people from being idiots.

Like many devout people, Alexander and Sarah saw God as a Great Big Luddite who didn't like smart-asses (and let's be honest, they're usually Jews or Japanese) messing with His stuff. So they lived functional, cold lives, doing church, doing the groceries, and doing each other every now and again but they didn't really click. They had no shared porridge atoms, so they made do. Tried not to get in each other's way.

Sarah hated snakes and hated that her husband, every week, would hold at least one in his hands and speak in tongues. (She didn't really get that either. She thought that her husband, when he did speak in tongues, sounded like an irate Norwegian who had inhaled helium.)

In the spirit of peace and to avoid a showdown, Alexander let her sit at the back of the church away from the snakes during services, which was a little unseemly for the minister's wife but was infinitely preferable to what Sarah wanted, which was not to attend at all.

They bored each other but didn't annoy each other, so it was a fairly comfortable marriage until Alexander brought the Martini boys home.

The problem was, as usual, Leon.

Saul noticed it from the moment they arrived. The way that women looked at Leon, they just couldn't help themselves, and the fact that Sarah, a healthy forty years old when the boys arrived, had never been decently fucked in her life definitely contributed to the situation.

Very quickly the boys were integrated into the life of the Pinkertons. They worked with Potter doing odd jobs and helping re-roof the old church in the woods. They slept in the Pinkerton home. They rose early and prayed with Alexander and Sarah. Alexander noted with satisfaction that since the boys had arrived, Sarah seemed to have gotten a new lease on life, joining in with morning devotions and checking on the repair work at the church every day, bringing the boys lemonade and sandwiches that they shared with the confused but grateful Potter.

Alexander thought that these boys were just what he'd been looking for.

It was just what any church needed. New blood. Young blood. Blood.

The boys shared a room across the upstairs landing from the Pinkertons, and when they knelt to say their prayers before sleeping, Sarah would watch them, her face full of what she thought looked like motherly love but what Saul could see was hunger. He could see the ache in her eyes. He knew she was hungry. Ravenous for his brother. He didn't condemn her for it, he'd grown resigned to the fact that this was the way things were going to be, but he knew it was dangerous and he didn't want to leave because Saul himself had fallen in love.

Not with Sarah, or with God, or with snakes, or even with Reverend Alexander Pinkerton, but with the Church.

The power and the theater and the thrill of the Church called to Saul like polyester to an Osmond. He could not resist it.

His first snake-handling service had been a revelation.

He and Leon had arrived with the Pinkertons early on Sunday morning for their first service. The Reverend said that they should sit at the back with Sarah, that perhaps it would be a little strange for them at first. So they sat on either side of Mrs. Pinkerton. Saul noted that she pushed her thigh against Leon's, he could almost smell her desire; he was actually a little surprised that the Reverend hadn't noticed it but then he didn't seem to notice his wife much at all, which was a crime given how sexy she was.

They watched as the parishioners arrived.

They came in ones and twos, mostly white but there were a few black faces, mostly elderly (more inclined to go to church as death becomes imminent, mused Saul logically), and mostly poor. Just boring, dusty, middle-of-the-road people. Plain folks. They sat on plain wooden pews and faced the pulpit, an oddly gothic dark wood platform reminiscent of a ship's bows. It was incongruous with the spartan nature of the rest of the church. It was high and grand and towered over the congregation. A harpoon could be thrown from it.

In the far right corner, away from the Pequod pulpit, an elderly woman played long wavery chords on a cheap electric organ as the faithful filed in. Next to her sat a ratty-looking kid at a drum kit, and Potter Templeton on a creaky plastic chair with a pedal steel guitar on his lap. Potter and the ratty kid didn't play. They waited.

When everyone was in and the ceremony was about to begin the doors closed.

Saul looked around. They were passing a bowl. People were putting money in it. A dollar each. Saul figured nearly fifty people. Fifty bucks. Not much. Not for the life he had planned.

The Reverend Pinkerton climbed into the control tower. Over his cheap dark suit he wore lush purple robes that Sarah had made from some old curtains. Saul was amazed by the transformation of the man. His dull and mousey features now looked dark and dramatic, his eyebrows were bushier, his nose was stronger and straighter, he seemed to have cheekbones. He no longer looked like the gaunt depressive who had taken them in, he looked like a fanatic, a dangerous, powerful fanatic. He looked like the man who put *mental* in fundamental.

He spread out his arms, gesturing to the harmless old biddies sitting in arthritic discomfort on the wooden pews, and yelled, "Sinners all!"

The elderly organist, the ratty kid, and Potter backed his exclamation with a crashing discord. Then the ratty kid hit an up-tempo 8/4 beat on the snare, hi-hat, and kick drum, and Potter danced a plectrum on a low E behind the organ noise. The music was basic but it did the job, provided a sense of drama, of anticipation.

Something real big was coming.

"Something real big is coming," cried Pinkerton. His voice in a vague impression of an enthusiastic Negro ringmaster.

"Something real big is coming!"

The congregation got on their feet. They raised their arms, they shouted amens. The whole place had sprung to life. Saul's penis went to DEFCON 2. Half-chub.

"Can you feel it?" yelled Pinkerton again.

The parishioners yelled their assents.

"I said CAN YOU FEEL IT!"

Saul could feel it. Full stiffy. Woah.

"Jesus is here. Right now. Welcome . . . welcome Jesus!"

Everybody welcomed Jesus. They yelled and waved and wept and rattled their walkers. Saul thought if the Holy Carpenter of Nazareth had walked in on this bunch of wailing nutjobs, he would have been terrified, but he kept his thoughts to himself and welcomed Jesus along with everyone else. Out of the corner of his eye he noticed that Sarah's welcome of Jesus was more muted. She had a little heretical restraint.

No wonder she stays at the back, he thought.

Leon was loving it, though. Jumping and singing and joining in. Saul hadn't seen his brother so animated since they fled the killer ducks.

This is it, thought Saul. This is how I save my brother from himself. This is how I keep him by me. This is how we shall live. Happy and together with Jesus.

But he saw Sarah look at his brother and smile. He had seen that smile before, the first night they had stayed at her house and her husband had placed her dessert in front of her at dinner.

The Reverend Pinkerton continued with the service. The music stopped while he berated his congregation for their wickedness.

These people are about as wicked as bunny rabbits, thought Leon, but he went with it. Pinkerton ranted about the evil in the world—evil governments, hippies, Muslims, evolutionists, abortionists, television, and homosexuals. He said that their only hope was to prove to Jesus that their faith was strong, that they loved him.

Loved him enough to handle the Deadly Things.

Then the music started again and the Reverend got down from on high and got a sleepy-looking snake out of a cardboard shoe box that had holes cut in it. He danced around, holding the snake in the air, trying to make it look more evil. (This was the snake's favorite part of the whole deal; if it had had vocal cords it would have gone "Wheeeeeeee," but like all good actors, it internalized the *wheeeee*. Less is more.)

A few worshippers danced forward and joined in, dancing next to Pinkerton, yelling their helium Norwegian gibberish. Saul saw his brother move to go forward but Sarah put her hand on him and held him back.

The dancers each got a turn to hold the snake but it didn't bite anyone, it was having too much of a good time. The snake was put back in the shoe box and everyone proclaimed a miracle and thanked Jesus.

Then the basket was passed again and Saul was amazed when he saw the mountain of cash that this bunch of dusty rednecks managed to fill it with. They had had their show, Jesus had turned up, and they were showing their gratitude by giving what they could.

Saul finally knew why he was on Earth. To rescue the lost—like his brother—and to be paid for doing it. God would provide.

Praise the Lord.

And so time passed.

The boys grew to manhood under the tutelage of the Pinkertons and the snake handlers. Saul stuck to the Reverend and watched him work. Watched him hustle for business, for converts, and for lower prices on deadly serpents. He learned the art of grifting from this sad shaman. Pinkerton had all the moves and was a terrific showman but he was just burdened with a terrible handicap. He was trying to sell a product he didn't really believe in. That, and he seemed a little too fond of the moonshine that he and Potter brewed in an illegal still behind the woods behind the church.

Leon and Sarah kept their affair quiet for years and Pinkerton was always delighted that he had brought the boys home because since they arrived his marriage had gotten much better.

She had needed a child to look after, he thought.

The boys were in their twenties when, one day, Saul and the Reverend Pinkerton returned home early from a snake-buying trip in Tampa and found Leon enthusiastically banging Sarah on top of the tumble dryer in the basement. Pinkerton was horrified. He had never seen his wife in such ecstasy. She was sitting on the dryer barking like a dog as the young man fucked her vigorously. They were both sweating and oblivious. Lost. Sinners.

What he found inexplicable, what confused and disgusted him—and the reason they hadn't heard him come in—was that the dryer was on.

She had been washing her husband's purple robes.

A terrible scene ensued with much weeping and wailing and gnashing of teeth—another little Greek tragedy in the boondocks, the stuff operas and talk shows thrive on. Sarah professed her love for Leon, said she wanted to marry him.

Leon was struck dumb and Saul had to stop the Reverend from fetching his rifle and killing them both. He did this by hitting the preacher over the head with a clothes iron he found next to the washing machine.

The boys hightailed it out of town. Sarah begged to come with them but Saul bopped her with the iron too. He was on a roll. He had been thinking for some time that he and Leon should get out of there and make some real money. He did what all big-timey businessmen do: He turned someone else's misery into his opportunity.

Saul and Leon stowed away in the back of a big rig that was carrying soft furnishings west from a discount warehouse in Orlando. They snuck aboard when the driver had stopped at a local gas station, just off the interstate, that was popular with truckers for its burgers and the amphetamines that the owner sold under the counter.

THE COLLECTIVE

FRASER WAS FALLING THROUGH SOLID ROCK. He felt surprised and surprisingly clearheaded. He noticed that his breathing was relaxed and normal. He didn't feel panicky or upset, which was not usual when he was emerging from a blackout. He felt fine, except that it was patently obvious that he was underground and descending at a rapid pace. Through gravel and granite, past bones and temples and broken pots. He wondered why archaeologists were always finding broken pots when they went digging; ancient folks must have been really clumsy or had a lot of Greek-style weddings.

Ancient Greeks—did they even have weddings? mused Fraser.

Weren't they all gay?

Down and down he went, each layer a civilization.

Millions dead.

Down through treacle-delicious puddingy peat, through hard black and blue coal, through blinding brilliant diamonds, and then the warm balm of white-hot molten lava, which didn't burn him but made him feel sexy and safe.

Then a breathtaking adrenaline rush as he burst through a rock crust into a sky above a vast subterranean sea. A world lit by the clear light of a full moon, which is impossible given the circumstances, but there it was, off to the north, shining like a fat white bride.

He fell through a cloud bank, tumbling toward the calm black surface of the water. As he neared the water he started to slow down. A wonderful sensation of floating above the surface.

He saw a small sailboat in the distance and he noticed he was headed toward it. As he approached it came into focus.

The boat was about twelve feet long with a wooden hull aged by countless storms and salt. The sail was probably white but seemed silver in the moonlight. At the tiller sat a rickety thin old man in a coarse brown monk's habit. He had a long beard and the bushiest eyebrows Fraser had ever seen. The eyebrows were so dense and bucolic that they hung down over the old man's piercing green eyes, giving him the air of a creature watching from behind a thicket.

Fraser wafted gently on the breeze and floated down on the bench in the middle of the boat facing the old man.

The two looked at each other for a moment.

"Hello," said Fraser.

"Hello," said the old man, and Fraser instantly knew that the old man was speaking Icelandic but he also knew he'd be able to understand it.

At last Fraser twigged. He must be dreaming.

"Carl, it's you, right?"

"No," said the old man. "My name is Saknussem. Arne Saknussem."

"Oh, sorry. I'm Fraser Darby. Nice to meet you."

He offered his hand for the old man to shake. Saknussem looked at it for a moment, then at Fraser, then back to the hand. He took his own hand from the tiller and the boat was adrift for a moment as he clutched Fraser's in his big skeletal claw. Fraser felt a chill shoot up his arm toward his throat. He pulled away quickly.

"Wow. You're cold."

The old man nodded.

"Still, cold hands, warm heart, right?"

The old man put his hand back on the tiller.

"No, cold hands, cold heart, cold teeth, cold hair, cold ears," he grumbled, his breath making his wispy mustache flutter up.

"Right-o," said Fraser. He was afraid of the old duffer. He was always excessively polite to people who freaked him out.

"So, where we headed?" he asked.

The old man gave him a look that told him their conversation was over. Fraser tried to fly away but found his bottom was stuck to the seat. The wind came up and Fraser had to duck as the old man swung the sail around and they tacked to the west.

The boat clipped along at a surprising speed and the old man's eyebrows were flattened by the breeze. He looked like a dog that had its head stuck out of a car window. Fraser found he could turn around and face in the direction they were traveling, and although he would rather not be in the boat at all, at least he didn't have to play jailhouse stare with the malevolent old collie at the helm.

Off on the horizon, a small island with three palm trees was silhouetted against the underground sky. Fraser couldn't help but laugh when he noticed it.

After a while, milky-white chalk cliffs began to loom up ahead of them and eventually the boat washed up on a shingle beach, the almost still sea lapping quietly at stones like an old cat drinking.

Fraser turned and looked at Saknussem, who pointed to a gray workman's porta cabin about two hundred yards up the beach next to the cliffs.

"On you go," he said.

"Right," said Fraser. He clambered out of the boat and started walking. Halfway up, he turned and saw that Saknussem was heading back out to sea. He shouted after him, "Thanks for the ride!"

The old man lifted his middle finger and gave Fraser a "Fuck you" gesture without even turning to look at him.

Charming, thought Fraser, and he headed toward the little hut.

A handwritten sign on the door of the hut read PLEASE KNOCK BEFORE ENTERING. Fraser tapped politely. No answer. He opened the door and walked in.

The interior of the cabin was set out in the style of a Beverly Hills dermatologist's waiting room. Comfortable soft furnishings from Z Gallerie or the Pottery Barn, in this case two large green sofas.

There was an aged pine coffee table with copies of *Architectural Digest* and *Golf Pro* magazines piled on top. Fresh flowers were arranged, hanging in little sconces. It was all very tasteful. Very nice. Relaxing.

A man sat on one of the sofas smoking a cigarette. He looked worried, his hand shaking with either nerves or the early stages of Parkinson's disease. He was a big man, handsome, very nice sandy-brown hair that he kept running his fingers through, about fifty years old.

Rakish, thought Fraser.

He wore a checked jacket and dark slacks with white loafers, and he wore a cravat. He looked up anxiously as Fraser entered.

"Carl?" asked Fraser.

"No, sorry," said the man in a soft Irish accent.

Fraser stood for a moment, then sat on the sofa opposite the worried man.

"I'm Fraser Darby." He put his hand out to shake. The man took it and shook it.

"Brinsley. Brinsley Sheridan. Nice to meet you."

"Nice to meet you too," said Fraser, happy to encounter someone friendly after the scary old boatman.

"I'm sorry, I'm a bit distracted, nervous, you know."

Fraser nodded. "Yeah, that old guy in the boat would rattle anybody's cage."

Brinsley looked at him, puzzled.

"The sailor, Saknussem—the guy who brought us here."

"I came in a Rolls-Royce. It was driven by a very nice Asian man called Tim. He made me a cup of tea."

Fraser chose a different tack. "So, what are you doing here?"

"Tim told me to wait for a Mr. Lovecraft. I've been here about fifteen minutes. How about you?"

"I don't really know but this is certainly one of the strangest dreams I've ever had," laughed Fraser. "Present company excepted, of course."

Brinsley gave him a sympathetic look. "You don't know, do you?"

"What?"

"I don't think this is a dream, Fraser," said the Irishman kindly.

"What are you talking about? I just fell through the ground, floated across the sky, and sailed a calm sea with a cranky pensioner. Granted it's not sexy or profound but it's hardly the kind of thing that happens when I'm awake."

"What were you doing before you got here?"

"Why?" demanded Fraser defensively. He still felt guilty about the ugly hooker.

"Look, before I came here I was in my bed in my house in London. My wife, Val, a lovely girl, love of my life, and my kids and my friends came to say good-bye to me. I had been in hospital with liver cancer but they said there was nothing more they could do. Val took me home. I fell asleep and woke up in the back of a Rolls-Royce with Tim making me a cup of tea. The pain of the cancer was gone and I had a full pack of cigarettes in my pocket. You see what I'm saying?"

Nothing.

Brinsley tried again. "I was losing my hair. I was going bald. Now look at it." He ran his hand through his unarguably gorgeous thick head of hair.

Silence as the penny slowly fell.

"I'm dead?" Fraser gasped.

"I don't know about you but I'm pretty sure I am."

"But I'm breathing. I can feel my pulse. I'm here."

"Yeah, that's all true for me too but I feel it. In my gut, which is probably an illusion."

"Are you a doctor or something?"

"No, I'm a used-car salesman but I'm also Irish and a poet."

"You're a car salesman and poet?"

"Not a lot of money in poetry, son. Mind you, the way things have been, there's not a hell of a lot in the car business either. You don't know anyone that would be interested in a Mercedes convertible? It's a real collector's item."

"No," said Fraser dumbly.

The men sat quietly for a moment.

"I play the harmonica too," offered Brinsley.

"And does being a poet and a car salesman and Irish and being able to play the harmonica make you any more knowledgeable about this than me? We might both be dreaming, in the same dream."

"Maybe that's what death is."

"Oh shit, you really are a poet. You really think we're dead?"

"Yup."

Fraser was thunderstruck. He thought for a moment. He thought about heading out into the Miami night, drunk and angry, he vaguely remembered head-butting someone in the men's bathroom, he got little flashes of dancing in the gay club, and then he got a few snapshots of himself fighting with T-Bo and Silky and Wilson.

"Holy fuck," he whispered.

"Jesus, be careful. Mind your language, we're dead here."

Fraser nodded. He started to cry. Fat, hot tears rolled down his cheeks. He felt about three years old. Brinsley smiled sadly at him.

"There, there, come on. It's all right. Everybody dies," he said.

"Oh no. I think I'm in big trouble."

"I think your trouble is over, my friend." The Irishman smiled softly.

"No, I mean with God and Jesus and everybody. I've been a bit of a lad in my life—scratch that, I've been a total prick. I always meant to clean up my act before I died. I think I'm going to hell."

"Yeah, I know what you mean. I'm worried about it too, I don't know what the rules are. I had some adventures myself when I was younger. We'll have to wait for this Mr. Lovecraft, I suppose."

Fraser nodded, very upset. He started weeping loudly, unable to help himself.

His heart breaking on every exhale.

Time passed slowly in the cabin for the two men. Eventually Fraser calmed down and sat staring into space, numb with shock, as Brinsley leafed through an *Architectural Digest*. Brinsley put down his magazine and looked at him.

"So what do you do, then, Fraser?"

"I'm sorry?"

"Your job, what do you do?"

"Oh, well. I'm unemployed right now."

"What did you do?"

"I was in television."

"Really? I have some friends in television."

"That's nice."

Brinsley could tell he didn't want to talk, so he kept quiet as long as he could, but he couldn't help himself. "Are you a celebrity?"

"No. I'm a disgrace," spat Fraser huffily.

Before Brinsley could ask why, the door was flung open by a tall, gangly customer, about forty-six years old, dressed in a black cape, black pants, and shiny black boots. He had a long dishlike face that ended in a big chin that was magnified by the smile on his strangely small mouth.

"Hello! Hello! Hello!" he bellowed cheerily in a robust New England accent. "I am so sorry I'm late. You won't believe the day I've had: gothic!"

Brinsley and Fraser stood up as he entered but the man ignored Fraser completely, strode over to the surprised Brinsley, and gave him an affectionate bear hug.

"Brinsley Sheridan, how wonderful to finally meet you."

Fraser looked at Brinsley questioningly. Brinsley shrugged.

"I'm Lovecraft," said the man. "Howard Phillips. Everyone calls me H.P. I'm a huge fan, Brinsley—may I call you Brinsley?"

Brinsley nodded.

"Did you bring your harmonica?"

Brinsley fished his mouth organ from his inside jacket pocket and held it up for Lovecraft to see.

"Oh, excellent! Absolutely spiffy! Like I say, I'm a huge fan. Let's head off, everyone is *dying* to meet you—well, perhaps not dying to meet you, if you know what I mean?" He laughed uproariously at his own joke.

"Are we dead?" said Brinsley.

"I am, you are." He glanced at Fraser. "I'm not sure about Laughing Boy here."

"What about my wife and kids?"

"They'll be fine. Miss you, of course, but All Is Well. C'mon, let's go. You're going to love this bunch of guys. They're loonies!"

"Am I going to hell?" asked Brinsley.

"Oh Brins, what are you talking about?" laughed H.P. Lovecraft. "You were finished with hell by the time you were in your thirties. All Is Well my friend, All Is Well."

The gentle Irishman couldn't help but smile and sigh with relief. He gestured toward Fraser.

"What about yer man here?"

"Someone will be along for him in a minute. Come on, come on. Let's go."

Brinsley could not help but be caught up in the enthusiasm and cheer of H.P., and he wished Fraser good-bye and good luck before he allowed himself to be hustled out the door. Fraser sat down again and waited.

L'AMOUR

RUE DE VAUGIRARD IS ONE OF THE LONGEST STREETS IN PARIS. It runs from the Boulevard Saint Michel, alongside the Palais de Luxembourg and its gardens, crosses Rue de Rennes, and heads out of the Sixth Arrondissement to the groovy wilds of the Fifteenth. It's a busy street during the day, lots of deliveries and the ubiquitous European buzzy moped funsters, but at night it is as quiet as the Pantheon.

Claudette and George, or Georges, as she called him (he loved it), had walked away from Notre Dame's gothic threat and seemed instinctively to be headed toward Claudette's apartment, the one she had inherited from her actor-lover. As they strolled by the dark palace, now a government building, Claudette told George how Hermann Göring had taken it as his personal residence during the Nazi occupation of the city. How he had looted the place of many art treasures, some of which were still missing.

It was a mystery to Claudette why the Nazis, who were so spiritually bankrupt, were such art lovers. She couldn't seem to equate the two, and why was it that their tastes ran to the flamboyant and expensive?

George said it was because they were criminals. He had seen the same thing with clients. Occasionally he would be called upon to defend successful career criminals. Ugly, brutish, greedy minds who would, when they had the funds, surround themselves with expensive and gaudy art. Art that the rest of the world, that history, had declared meaningful and beautiful.

They did this for two reasons, said George. One was that it showed everyone they were powerful and could acquire beautiful and expensive things, and the other was that they had no real idea of beauty, so they had to take everyone else's word for it. George said that it is impossible to see beauty unless you possess some yourself, but there is solace in this fact if it is examined.

Claudette agreed, delighted with the explanation. She said it was like when she had gone to Hollywood with Guillame, she had seen so many hideous men—Hollywood producers and executives, fat barrels of spite—who always had beautiful escorts with them. But the thing about the beautiful escorts was that they all sort of looked the same: big pouty collagen lips, large fake breasts, gym stomachs, and perfect round asses. They were like drawings of women done by a horny teenage boy.

"Exactly," said George.

The men have no idea what they want and the women cater to that. That same look is favored by criminals the world over. Big, noisy art in gilt frames. You won't see much Miró on the walls of the wicked.

"Does that mean the art is debased if it is owned by a philistine?" asked Claudette.

"*Oui,*" replied George, thrilled with his daring new controversial stance. "Just like the pouty Hollywood escorts."

"Are you sure you are not French?" laughed Claudette.

"I'm not." George smiled. "But I'm getting there."

And indeed he was. He thought about his abandoned wife, Sheila. He felt another stab of guilt but at the same time he could not remember when he had last had a discussion about art or Nazis or even Hollywood. He hadn't even been up this late in maybe five years. He wondered what the hell he had done with his life. He'd settled for less. Settled for the path of least resistance. Tried to be a good egg. Didn't want to hurt those he loved, which of course is impossible. If someone loves someone else it's going to hurt. That's part of it. He could see that now. He wasn't sure that he had ever loved Sheila, he thought probably not, and he didn't think Sheila had ever really loved him, it's just that he was convenient. She had acquired him like a big, gaudy painting, except he was more a kind of store-bought print.

Well, no more, he was getting French, *bébé*. Finding his inner Frenchman. He couldn't live for other people anymore, he was dying, and the road to hell is paved with good intentions.

As they walked under the covered arches on Rue de Vaugirard, opposite the Palais du Luxembourg, George turned and kissed Claudette again. He held her passionately and she returned his ardor with fire and enthusiasm. They were backlit with the light from a display in a clockmaker's window.

Across the street, guarding the palace gate, stood a gendarme who was in reality the angel Gabriel. He watched them from his little Perspex sentry box. He smiled approvingly and took a last drag on his cigarette. *L'amour.*

INFERNO

FRASER WAITED FOR FIFTEEN MINUTES or so after Brinsley left with H.P. Lovecraft before he thought of leaving himself. He tried to but found the door was locked from the outside—somehow he had expected that. He sat down and leafed through an *Architectural Digest,* finally getting interested in an article about the actor Robert Duvall, who liked to collect South American art and to dance the tango with his pretty young wife in their immaculate country home.

He heard a key in the lock and the door was opened by a short middle-aged man in a dark blue toga. He was red faced, chubby cheeked, and pudgy-fat. He held his hands up high in a rather effete affected manner and his tubby, sausagey fingers looked like they were being throttled by his many elaborate rings. Totally out of character with the rest of his outfit, he wore a JESUS IS MY HOMEBOY baseball cap. He spoke American-accented English, sounding almost exactly like Lee Liberace, the flamboyant homosexual concert pianist.

"Fraser Darby?"

"Yes, sir," said Fraser, standing. He threw in the "sir" just in case. You never knew what would keep you from the lake of fire.

"Oh, please. 'Sir' is my father. Call me V." He grabbed Fraser and gave him an affectionate but chaste little hug. "It's short for Virgil. I'm Roman originally."

"Okay . . . V," said Fraser.

"Sorry I'm late. I have a terrible time with directions, which is embarrassing really, given that I'm a senior guide here."

"Where are we, V? What is 'here'?"

"Ooh. Good question, smartyboots. All in good time. We've got a bit of a trek ahead of us, do you want to go to the bathroom or anything before we leave?"

"I don't think so."

"Course you don't, silly. It's just my little joke. Shall we?" He motioned to the open door and Fraser walked toward it. Virgil followed.

The landscape had completely changed.

The sea was gone and stretched out in front of, and indeed behind and to either side of, them was a vast, flat hardscrabble desert under a white sky. A couple of dowdy fake cacti were placed here and there, and about thirty feet in front of them was a large cardboard cutout of a camel that was smiling and wearing a pair of sunglasses. The earth was parched and devoid of all life, as if crossed by a retreating czar.

"Behold!" squeaked V.

Fraser turned and looked at him, mystified.

V apologized, then tried it again in a much more dramatic and appropriate tone.

"Behold!" he boomed theatrically.

There was silence for a long moment. V smiled awkwardly.

"Behold what?" asked Fraser.

"The Inferno," boomed V again, playing to the balcony. Fraser could not believe it.

"What, this is it? This is the lake of fire? This is hell?"

"Well, sort of." V shrugged. He had given up any pretence of sounding scary and prophetic. "Actually, I never really know what's going to appear until the client arrives. I had one guy, an Italian, few hundred years ago now, doesn't time fly—in both directions—you should have seen what he came up with. It was stupendous, although a bit over the top for me. We went on for days. All very allegorical and learned. A real masterpiece."

"Dante Alligersomething. That who you're talking about. Dante's *Inferno*?"

"Yes, that was him. Dante. Dan, I called him. 'Dan, Dan, the Renaissance man.' That's what I used to say, made him laugh. Sweet guy. Smelled a bit garlicky but, you know, Italian."

"You are the poet Virgil and you are going to guide me through *The Inferno*?"

"Exactly!" said V. "You're very quick."

"I did Dante's *Inferno* at school. It was nothing like this. Where're the levels and the wailing corpses and people frozen in ice and all that stuff?"

"You're talking about Dante's *Inferno*. This isn't Dante's, it's yours."

"What?" asked Fraser, genuinely puzzled.

"This is your soul, Fraser. It looks like this because this is the way you've made it."

"What do other people's souls look like?"

"Oh, it varies—some swampy, some dark, some cheery. I had a very nice lady from Toronto once, she had the whole thing covered in brightly patterned wool. Like a giant sweater. Very Canadian."

Fraser stepped forward and kicked a few pebbles toward the cut-out of the camel.

"So I'm dead, then?"

"I don't know, I'm just a guide. I don't get that sort of information."

"But I won't be going back to where I came from?"

"Dante did."

"Yes, I suppose he must have, to write about it. What do I do now?"

"It's your soul. We have to cross it."

"Why?"

"To get to the other side," said V smugly.

Fraser gave him a withering look.

"What I mean is, my job is to escort you across your soul to Your Solution, which lies"—Virgil built himself up for a dramatic finish—"BEYOND!" He gestured out across the arid plain.

"Oh, stop talking like that, you sound like a gay magician," grumbled Fraser.

"They have straight magicians?"

But Fraser wasn't listening. He started walking out across the desert to the eastern horizon.

V shouted after him. "You're going the wrong way!"

Fraser turned. "How do you know?"

Virgil smiled and held up a shiny golden compass that dangled at the end of a thick chain.

It glinted in the sunlight, momentarily blinding Fraser.

They headed west, as is traditional for Scotsmen in search of a solution.

The walk was dull. V made a few attempts at light conversation, complimenting Fraser on the tiny rock formations on the floor of his soul, but Fraser was too sad and angry to reply. He just grunted.

There was no sun in the sky, only the blank white light that seemed to have no definable source. It was neither too hot nor too cold but neither was it just right. It was empty, mile after mile of empty.

After three hours of walking Fraser eventually spoke.

"Jeez, it never ends. Are you sure we're going in the right direction?"

"Oh yes," said V.

"'Cause I don't get the impression we're moving at all."

"That's the soul for you. Infinite, you know—very big."

"If it's infinite, how can we possibly cross it?"

"Yes, it can take a while, no doubt about it, that's why the storytellers are the guides."

"Sorry?" said Fraser.

"Lovecraft, me, the new fellow, Brinsley—all the other guides of the soul. We're all storytellers."

"Why storytellers? Why not Indian scouts or Sherpas? People with a sense of direction?" whined Fraser pointedly, hinting at a suspected incompetence on the part of the ancient Roman.

Virgil didn't stoop to defend himself but good-naturedly offered an explanation.

"A good storyteller has an excellent sense of direction. Plus a good story helps pass the time crossing long distances. Wanna hear a story?"

"No!" Fraser snapped.

They walked on in silence for a while, V pouting a little at Fraser's brusque manner. The light didn't move or change, the temperature did not alter, Fraser felt no physical fatigue but he found himself sighing deeply, the old ennui needling at him.

"Who was your guide?" he asked eventually.

"John Lennon." V beamed proudly.

"That's impossible. John Lennon wasn't born until thousands of years after you died."

"Time is only linear for engineers and referees," said V.

They walked on in silence again, until again Fraser could no longer bear it.

"John Lennon wasn't a storyteller, he was a musician."

"He's an artist," said V. "All artists are storytellers."

"You make this crap up as you go along, don't you?" growled Fraser.

"I'm a storyteller." Virgil smiled infuriatingly. "I can't help myself."

And so they walked on. Fraser tried speeding up to put some distance between him and the portly poet but Virgil kept up with ease. On and on they walked.

"Oh, go on then," Fraser said after another six hours of silence.

"Go on then what?" asked V.

"Tell me a story."

"Hah!" said V. "I thought you'd never ask. This story is called 'The Midwife.' "

THE MIDWIFE

ONCE UPON A TIME there was a soldier who believed in God. The soldier, whose name was Joshua, was from the North of England, a town called Newcastle. He had grown up poor and took to soldiering as a way to escape the miserable life of a serf in his hometown. He had become, at first, a pikeman—that is, he carried a pike, a long stick with a pointed hook that looked a little like the vicious freshwater shark of the same name, into battle and tried to stab as many enemy combatants as he could. He was good at this because he had played a lot of darts growing up so had had a certain amount of training.

He stabbed horsemen, he stabbed horses, he stabbed knights, he stabbed infantrymen, commoners, and nobility. He stabbed anyone who needed stabbing in a battle and in all his stabbing he managed to never get stabbed himself. He was kicked and punched and knocked over and trodden on by horses but never stabbed. This had a beneficial side effect apart from not being killed. It meant he became a battle veteran, and as others fell to their deaths he found himself promoted and elevated through the ranks until eventually he was made a knight of the realm with his own horse and the promise of a little land if he ever got back to England, which by the time he was knighted, he hadn't seen for nearly twenty years.

That's because he was on a crusade. A crusade to take Jerusalem from the infidel Muslims. The Muslims, of course, considered the Christians, of which Joshua was one, the infidels, so they weren't too keen on giving it up. The fighting was bloody and sickening.

Carnage.

And, as usual, everyone had God on their side.

Joshua became an expert on desert survival and learned the routes from the Western Sahara to the Holy Land. He would guide and protect knights who had arrived by ship, and help them to the battlefields in the east. One day, as Joshua was leading a party of sixty knights on camels through southern Morocco, they were set upon by a hundred understandably irate Bedouins who were sick of the greedy Northern horses and soldiers drinking the oases dry and not burying their shit on the camel trails.

A fierce battle ensued and many were killed on both sides but after a while it became clear that the Bedouins were losing the day. A call went up among their ranks to order a retreat. The tribesmen fell back but one of their number, not hearing the call, ran to Joshua, who had been looking in the opposite direction, and knocked him from his horse. Joshua panicked; his heavy armor would be a handicap once he was off the horse. He stood up as quickly as he could but felt a knife tear through his chain mail and slice deep into the flesh on his arm. He shouted, more in surprise than pain, then brought his broadsword down heavily on his attacker's right shoulder. The Bedouin was almost cut in half from the blow and fell to the ground, dead.

Joshua strode angrily over to the corpse and pulled at its headdress in order to see the face of the first enemy who had managed to pierce his skin. He pulled back the black cloth that the Arab had worn and looked upon the face that changed his world forever.

It was a young girl, she couldn't have been more than thirteen, with clear coffee-colored skin and the darkest brown eyes, which were now as lifeless as polished gems. She reminded Joshua of a prostitute he had adored in Tangier.

He stumbled away and vomited on the corpse of a fallen comrade. It took him a moment or two to come to his senses, and then he knew. He was finished. He couldn't do this anymore, his time was up. With a heavy heart, he surmised that if a country is even sending its young women to fight you, it is because they are desperate for you to leave.

He threw down his sword, he took off his heavy armor, he took off his chain mail, he tied a tourniquet on his arm, he picked up a water canteen, looked at the position of the sun, found north, and started walking toward it.

The surviving knights called after him, asking where he was going. He told them he was going home.

He walked without stopping, without eating or sleeping. He never met a soul, friendly or no, until he reached the coastal town of Fez. He was in horrible condition when he arrived, his skin blistered and burned by the sun, his lips and eyelids cracked and chapped, the wound on his arm festering and infected. He fell at the city gates but was recognized by an English sentry who had served under him. He was taken to the town infirmary.

There he rested and was cared for but, as soon as he had recovered enough to move, which is to say not recovered much at all, he left his bed and walked down to the harbor, where he begged passage on a ship that was sailing to the Spanish port of Algeciras.

He hid belowdecks for the stormy five-day voyage, and when the ship arrived, the crew were happy to be rid of him, convinced by his brooding presence that he was accursed and that he was responsible for the savage crossing they had experienced.

As soon as he got off the ship, Joshua headed north. He walked out of town, through the hot, dry countryside, until it began to chill and grow greener, and still he walked. He walked through rain and sun and night and day until at last he fell into a muddy puddle at the side of a country road, his body racked with fever and completely unable to function, having taken so much punishment. His wound was now infested with little white maggots.

As he was about to die he looked up and saw the face of the ugliest old crone imaginable staring down at him. He saw the warts on her fat neck, her broken, spreading nose, and her piggy little eyes framed by her blond eyelashes. He saw the pockmarks and liver spots on her skin. He believed her to be an instrument of Satan, about to initiate his eternity of torment for all the killing he had done.

Especially the young girl.

His heart was broken and he was in hell.

He closed his eyes and tumbled into the darkness.

When he awoke he found himself lying on a bed of straw in a spotlessly clean, windowless room with a dirt floor. He had been stripped and washed and his wound had been cleaned and dressed. He felt like he had been away for a long time. He sat up, feeling a little dizzy, and saw that there was a black cat lying at the far side of the room in front of the embers of a dying fire. The cat, seeing he was awake, trotted over to him. It purred and arched its back as he rubbed the soft fur behind its ears, then, tiring of him, it trotted out the curtained door, leaving him alone.

He felt terribly thirsty, though the fog in his head began to clear a little and he no longer had a fever. He felt as weak as a kitten and, like a drunk who comes to after an elongated bender, he pored over his recent history. He wondered what had made him desert his comrades and start to walk home.

Of course, he regretted killing the girl but he had seen and taken part in many atrocities in war. That was what war was yet he somehow knew he was not going back. He knew he had not died and he knew he wanted, more than anything, to go home.

The old crone he had glimpsed walked into the room, hunched over a walking stick.

"You are awake?" she croaked in a voice that implied a rusted larynx.

"I am, madam," he said, surprised that she spoke his language. "I take it I have you to thank for saving me."

She nodded an assent as she poked her stick into the dying fire, stirring it a little. She poured him a cup of water from a wooden bucket and handed it to him. He drank gratefully.

"Thank you."

She nodded again.

He looked at the dressing on his arm. "Did you also attend to my wound? Did you bleed it?"

"I attended to it but I did not bleed it. You had already lost far too much blood. Let the leeches grow fat on the healthy," she cackled.

"It was infected. It must be bled," he protested.

She looked him in the eye, her left iris vibrating slightly, which he found unnerving. "If you want to die of superstition, go ahead, but I say to you: A wound must be cleaned and dressed. No more. Let the body do the work."

Somehow he knew she was right. Somehow he trusted her, and after all, she had undoubtedly saved his life as surely as that of the fire she poked with her stick.

He felt very tired and lay back down again, falling fast asleep once more.

When he awoke for the second time he felt much better. He was able to stand after a few moments. He saw that his clothing had been cleaned and mended and placed next to him, folded on the floor. He put on his breeches and shirt and walked outside.

He found he was in a clearing in a green forest. The room he had been in was all there was to the house.

A little shack in the woods.

There was no sign of the crone but the cat was watching him intently.

A chicken was roasting over an open fire. It smelled delicious and he realized it was the smell and his hunger that had awakened him. He almost ran to the fire, pulling the bird from the spit and devouring it, animal fat running through his cleaned fingers.

When he had eaten his fill, he sat back.

The cat was gone and the crone reappeared, riding through the forest on the back of a gaunt and depressed-looking mule.

"You have eaten?" she said.

He nodded, guiltily looking to the bones at his feet.

She was greatly amused, her laugh like the sound of coins rattling in a can. "Men! You are slaves to your appetites."

He smiled, agreeing, the grease from the chicken still shining on his chin.

And so began their happy interlude.

It turned out that the crone, whose name ironically was Bonita, was the midwife to a small town a few miles away through the forest. Like all the women of her profession at that time, she was treated with great suspicion by the ignorant populace, for often midwives were considered witches.

This was because their art and skills were misunderstood greatly by men.

Bonita's appearance and the fact that she very rarely lost a child or a mother didn't help much either. She was altogether far too good at what she did, so it was only a matter of time before the ignorant pitchfork mob came calling.

It happened after Joshua had been there for three months. He lived happily with Bonita, he read, for she had many interesting books, he swam in the river near the shack, and he ate her delicious cooking. She would occasionally venture into town to deliver a child but he never went with her, having grown tired of the world and its opinions.

He began to forget about England, thinking perhaps that this was his home. In the forest with the ugly old woman.

Then, one night, after a tasty supper of clay-baked stoat, as Bonita and Joshua sat quietly together as was their habit, a mob of villagers led by a priest came marching to the cottage. Joshua picked up a stick to fight them but Bonita made him put it down.

The priest, a handsome black-haired young man, his brown eyes glinting in the drama and torchlight, read from a parchment that Bonita was to be charged with the heinous crime of dabbling in black magic, specifically concerning a vicious unsolved murder in the nearby town. It seemed that a beautiful local teenage girl had been horribly mutilated and her little body dumped by the city wall. The conclusion was that only one in league with the devil could have committed an act so dastardly.

To the mob the answer seemed simple, as it always does.

Joshua approached the priest and protested, saying that Bonita was a good, kind woman and this could not possibly be true. The priest, knowing from local gossip that Joshua was a Holy Knight who had fought in the Crusades, was duty bound to hear the plea and offered a compromise. Rather than burn the old woman on the spot, they would take her to town and submit her to a proper trial and torture. If she confessed, all well and good; if not, what was left of her would be free to go.

Joshua protested still, so the priest asked Bonita what she would prefer, death now or maybe life but definitely torture first.

She chose life, as she always did.

Joshua had to be restrained as she was taken away.

He followed the mob to the village and watched as they threw Bonita into the local jail.

He then followed the priest to his apartments and cornered him.

He asked why Bonita had been chosen. The priest said that he had attended the body of the girl when she was found, that he had never seen such a horrific sight in his life.

The girl had been hacked apart, there was a wooden stake stuck in her vagina. There had been semen and mud sprayed on her innocent face.

Joshua asked why, if there was semen on the body, they had arrested a woman. Surely a man would be a suspect.

The priest replied that the semen had come from Satan or one of his demons who had committed the act along with Bonita. Then he summoned some officers and had Joshua thrown out onto the street.

Joshua went to the jailhouse where the old woman was being kept.

He could not see her but he sat underneath the barred window in full view of the guards.

He thought about his life in the Crusades, he thought about all the killing, killing in the name of God. He thought of the good men he had seen die, he thought of all the death he had seen, the death he had inflicted.

Then he thought of Hughes, the only man he had killed in anger.

Hughes was a knight he had served with almost ten years before. Not many men take pleasure from killing, although Joshua admitted to himself he had felt satisfaction in the act of surviving an enemy in combat, but every now and again he had encountered men who loved to kill. As an officer, Joshua had placed these men in the front of any battle, for they were fearless warriors who fought bravely but always ended up being killed themselves because they were reckless and bloodthirsty, therefore they made mistakes.

Once, though, he'd met a killer unlike any other; this was Hughes.

Hughes was a redheaded Welshman, a small, squat man with a strange intensity in his sharp green eyes.

For Hughes, killing was sexual.

Infantrymen hated to go into battle next to him, for they could see him masturbating as he sat on his horse, his chain-mail gloves drawing blood from his erect penis.

Joshua had heard rumors of Hughes's perversity but ignored them, for the man was a fearsome killer and he needed as many of those as he could get to fight for God against the heathens.

After a long battle just outside of Damascus, Joshua was heading to an oasis to wash the blood from his clothes when he came upon Hughes.

Hughes had grabbed a young Arab prisoner and taken him to a quiet spot. He had slit the boy's throat and, as the young man was dying, was anally violating him. The boy was crying and his blood sprayed and squirted over Hughes's filthy, grasping hands.

Hughes was whispering coarsely in the boy's ear, "You like it! You like it! You like it!"

Joshua was horrified. He took his sword from its scabbard as Hughes turned to look at him. Far from being afraid, Hughes thought his captain had come to join the fun. He offered the boy to Joshua. Disgusted and repelled beyond reason, Joshua severed Hughes's head from his body in a single forceful sweep of his weapon.

He had buried the Arab boy and left Hughes's body for the vultures.

He thought of Hughes again.

The one who had killed the young girl would have to be one of the thankfully rare creatures like Hughes.

As the sun rose over the small town, news reached the jailhouse that another murder, exactly like the one before, had occurred. Joshua, although saddened by the murder, was relieved for Bonita. Surely now the authorities would set the old woman free.

But he was wrong.

The mob formed again outside the jail, demanding the burning of Bonita, claiming she must have taken the form of some kind of animal, a *familiar,* and crept out of her cell during the night to commit the crime.

The priest arrived and quieted the mob by promising them a burning but saying that she had to be tortured first, lest they leave any of her accomplices undiscovered. With this he gave a pointed look to Joshua, who was relieved to have sat the entire night through in full view of the prison guards.

Joshua was immediately arrested and brought before the priest in his private chambers. The priest had the guards wait outside. As soon as they were alone Joshua protested.

"You cannot believe that Bonita is the killer here, not after last night. I was here all night. Nothing came or went from her cell."

The priest nodded. "God is perfect, but sometimes his sheep are too enthusiastic in his service," he said, gesturing to the mob outside the window. "I believe you are a good man and a God-fearing one, also I respect your position as a Crusader. Therefore I will be candid with you. If you continue to protest the innocence of the witch, the townspeople will see you as her accomplice and demand your hide too. I suggest you leave forthwith."

Joshua stood his ground. "She is no witch, she is a harmless and kind old woman."

"I do not think Bonita is the killer, but unless we have someone in her place that the mob believes is guilty, then I am afraid the church must do what any tired mother does to quiet her unruly children."

"What's that?" asked Joshua.

The priest sighed. "Give them what they want."

Joshua was about to protest again but the priest silenced him by raising his finger. "I will give you one day. Find the monster, or I will burn the old mother."

The priest was a clergyman but he was not an idiot. He knew that the devil was not abroad at night in the form of a cat or a wolf or any other animal. He lives eternally in the hearts of men.

So Joshua left the priest, and with not a thought to his personal safety, stayed in the small town and set out to find the killer although he did not know where to begin.

How do you catch such an animal?

He went to the sites of the murders. They had both been committed within a stone's throw from the town cess pit, a place that was understandably avoided by most of the populace. The girls had been killed by being sliced cleanly across the throat; their bodies had been cut in half at the waist.

Joshua thought of Hughes. How would he have tried to hide himself in civilian life, how could he?

He was a butcher.

A butcher?

The town butcher, as Joshua found out, was in his seventies and had six daughters of his own. He seemed an unlikely candidate. Joshua sat outside the butcher shop and looked around the street in the hope of an idea.

A butcher shop, a barbershop, two taverns, an apothecary, and a church. Not much of a town. You could get a drink and a haircut and some lotion for your boils before going to pray that you wouldn't get too drunk.

Actually it was better than it used to be. The barbershop was new, the barber arriving from the south only a few months earlier and setting up shop.

A barbershop?

In the Middle Ages barbers performed surgery and dentistry in their establishments.

They were knivesmen. Anything with a blade.

Joshua solved the crime. He exposed the local barber as the ruthless sex killer by luring him into a trap, watched by the priest and some townsfolk. Joshua paid a young homeless girl to enter the store and flirt with the barber, arranging to meet him later for a sexual encounter.

She was bait.

The barber, like most serial killers, was a moron and didn't realize he was being set up. He was caught en flagrante just as he was about to slaughter the girl.

Joshua watched the mob fall on the barber, watched them pull him apart with their bare hands. Even after his experiences in battle, after all that he had seen, he never ceased to be repulsed by how savage people could be.

He gently guided the killer's intended victim away, sparing her even the sight of vengeance. He would never allow any young girl to be harmed again if he could help it.

The grateful town allowed Bonita to leave jail and she returned to the forest with Joshua. The townsfolk were glad to not have to look at her too often. After all, she might not be a killer but there was no denying she was hideous. They had no idea how Joshua could stand to be in her company, how he could look at her day after day.

What they didn't know was that Joshua had seen real ugliness and that Bonita was no match for that.

What they also didn't know was that every night, after the excellent meal she cooked for him, she took the form of a sultry raven-haired young girl and made enthusiastic and perfect love to him, then held him tenderly until he fell asleep, exhausted and blissful.

Then she took the form of a cat and slept by the fire.

THE OTHER SIDE

"I DON'T GET IT," said Fraser. "If she was a witch, why didn't she just escape from the prison or even just escape when they came looking for her?"

"She wanted to see what Joshua would do for her."

"Bloody women," said Fraser. "They've always got an agenda."

"You liked it? The story?" asked V.

"Yeah, it was okay," said Fraser, not wanting to sound too enthusiastic, but the truth is he had been riveted, and had even cried a little at the end although he thought he'd managed to hide that from the poet. He hadn't.

"Is it a true story?" he asked.

"Partly."

"Which parts?"

"The true parts." V smiled.

"Oh, I'm tired of this rubbish!" snapped Fraser, but the truth was he had been so engrossed in the story that he hadn't noticed the landscape had changed a little as he had walked. Grass, it seemed, now grew here and there underfoot, some life appearing, and it seemed to Fraser that in the distance, a small hill rose up to obscure the horizon. He turned to mention this to V and noticed that the poet himself had changed. He looked to have gotten taller and thinner and younger.

"What?" asked Virgil when he noticed Fraser was staring at him. His voice was now deeper and more impressive.

"Things are changing," said Fraser. "You look different, the lay of the land looks different. What's going on?"

"Ah." Virgil smiled. "You just heard a story, you are being affected by it. Nothing has changed. I am the same, the lay of the land is the same."

"But it all looks different," protested Fraser.

"That's because the story, like all stories, has altered you slightly. Everything will look a little different."

And it did.

Fraser's perspective was indeed changing.

They walked on, the sinner and the poet, to the crest of the small hill. They reached the top and looked over.

It seemed they had been on a plateau, for down below, laid out like a painting, was the most beautiful valley Fraser had ever seen. A large clear blue lake sat on the valley floor, and on the shore, a tower.

From this distance Fraser couldn't be sure but it looked a little like a place he had seen in photographs. In a biography he had read. It looked like Bollingen.

Carl Jung's home.

THE ROAD TO GOD: FOUR

PALM SPRINGS IS A VULGAR LITTLE BURG, as a town that exists solely for its climate must be. There is some local tourist propaganda that claims there are restorative warm mineral springs in the area but none of the residents pay any attention to that rubbish. Anyway, very few rich seniors want to sit in smelly boiling water, they just like this town because it's hot.

It's hot, very hot, and it keeps the thin blood of the diseased and the elderly at a bearable temperature as they drive little electric buggies around manufactured lawns created by stolen lakes in search of little white golf balls and wait to die. Many think that the icy stillness of death cannot reach them in the desert, so they retire there to escape. But there is no escape, just as there is no party in Clouston Street.

Death will find them, it just takes a little longer, so they get to spend more time with their precious white balls.

Because the town attracts the weak and infirm, it also attracts the evil and avaricious—after all, if you have a fair-sized hamlet of elderly sheep, you can bet that word will get around the vulture community. So jailbirds perch outside the town in a dusty fence-post dump called Desert Hot Springs (where, strangely, there actually are restorative mineral springs although most are surrounded by trashy motels) and wait for opportunity.

However, the frail and weak are not stupid and poor, like those who would prey on them, so they hire security, and lots of it. Armed security, thugs who sweat uncomfortably in cheap nylon uniforms, give the stink-eye to anyone under seventy who is not another security guard or a cop.

And the old folks arm themselves too, with giant shiny revolvers, which look big and clean and young in their reptilian, liver-spotted hands.

And everybody waits for trouble. Waiting for death and robbery and crime and terror—*I like to be in America, La La La La America.* The atmosphere of the place is stifling, and the heat is the least of it.

A few psychics who have been there have guessed the awful truth of the place. It was never designed or meant to have humans live there, it is not an oasis or a strategic position. The land resents the presence of people.

It is not the worst case of this, of course. That distinction belongs to the town of Las Vegas, which is truly the capital city of the corrupted soul. In Las Vegas the land actually has a plan: It is waiting until the town reaches its maximum size, then the desert will swallow it and all the dirty, greedy cash-eating robots who live there and shit them into hell, where they belong.

Or perhaps that is Los Angeles.

Saul and Leon visited all three cities before they became holy and the first was Palm Springs.

They arrived in town in the cabin of the soft-furnishings truck that they had rode in from Florida. Leon loved the back of the truck, it reminded him of the old days back home with Mom. She had also wrapped the furniture in thick plastic to keep it from getting dirty. Saul hated it for the same reason but it did give him a chance to reflect on their recent adventures.

Saul knew that what he had seen in religion was going to be very important in his life. He had seen that some people were so desperate to believe in anything that the slightest piece of sorcery and/or show business would have them thrusting any cash they had on you, and they would be full of gratitude and love for you being gracious enough to accept it.

Once he knew this it was only a matter of time before he got into religion, especially armed with the singular talents of his brother.

And lo it was the Holy United Church of America was conceived in the back of a big rig on a freeway heading toward the Pacific.

Leon's thoughts were less profound. He was embarrassed about getting caught having sex with the minister's wife, but Saul, a born talent agent, put him at his ease.

"It's who you are, buddy. Women find you irresistible, it's not your fault. It's just something we're going to have to look out for in the future."

"I'm so sorry, bro," said Leon.

"C'mon, Leon. That gal was desperate for you from day one. I watched her the first time we were in church. If her husband hadn't a been actually preaching that day, her snatch would have leapt out of her panties and gobbled up your sausage like a hungry cougar, right there in front of the congregation."

Leon laughed, then so did Saul.

Always laugh second.

They had built a little den for themselves out of sofas and easy chairs, and snuck out to get snacks when the driver took his breaks. It was too uncomfortable to wait for the driver to stop when they needed to pee—he seemed to have a bladder the size of an oil tanker—so Saul took a couple of quart-sized empty oil containers from the Dumpster at a truck stop and the boys used them to piss in; they were perfect because the oil covered the smell of wee and the containers had air-tight sealing caps. Taking a dump was a rare luxury, never in the back of the truck, they had to wait until they had stopped somewhere and then they had to make sure the driver was sitting down eating.

Saul nearly got left behind. He was in the bathroom when the driver unexpectedly got up and left a diner just outside of Houston. Leon had been watching the driver from the parking lot but he hadn't seen him pay the bill. As the driver headed to the truck, Leon stopped him.

He couldn't think of anything to say, so in desperation he asked, "Excuse me, sir, do you believe in Jesus?"

The driver, a short blond middle-aged man with pale skin and alarmingly large dark brown freckles that made him look a little like a ghostly leopard, eyed Leon with the wary look of a seasoned traveler.

"Yeah," said the driver.

"That's great," said Leon, floundering, "'cause . . . er . . . he believes in you."

"What do you want, kid?" asked the driver in an accent Leon could not recognize.

Over the driver's shoulder, Leon saw Saul emerge from the bathroom. Saul saw Leon talking with the driver and he knew they were in trouble. He immediately ran to his brother's side.

"Hi . . . er . . . Bob," said Saul. "What's going on?"

"Oh, hi to you too . . . Bob," spluttered Leon with all the improvisational aplomb of a bucket of lard. "I was just telling our friend here that Jesus loves him."

"Oh, that he does, that he does." Saul smiled at the driver.

"You're both named Bob?" the driver asked suspiciously.

"We're brothers!" blurted Leon, panicking.

Saul winced. The driver looked confused.

"We're trainee monks," explained Saul.

"And you're both named Bob?"

"Yes, it's a coincidence. God's way of remaining anonymous, huh?"

"Oh, yeah, I suppose." The driver nodded. "Monks, well, that's . . . nice. I suppose you want money," he said, rummaging in his pockets for change.

Saul took a chance. He hated sitting in the back of the truck. "Actually, no, God bless you. We were going to ask you for a ride."

The driver thought for a moment. He did get very bored on the road and occasionally would pick up a hitchhiker. These kids looked harmless enough. The skinny one looked like he might blow over in a strong wind and the fat one could hardly move without getting out of breath. Plus they were Christians.

"Where you headed?" asked the driver.

"West," said Saul. "Under the Lord's guidance. We're traveling west as part of our missionary work."

"Well, I'm going to Phoenix to deliver my load and then on to Palm Springs to see my girlfriend. Deliver another load when I see her."

He laughed, his dark, broken teeth showing against his ashy skin, making him look like a photographic negative.

Both Leon and Saul were slightly surprised by the idea of this odd-looking creature having a romantic partner but they made no comment.

"Then I guess the Lord wants us in Palm Springs," said Saul.

"Yeah, well, if He does, you must have pissed Him off some. Still, it's your funeral."

And with that, they were in. They got to sit up front in the cab and talk to the driver and look out the window.

The driver was Mungo, named for a saint. He was French Canadian originally, from Montreal, but had come to the U.S. after falling in love with a girl from Birmingham, Alabama. The romance had fizzled out but Mungo had stayed on in America, it seemed too much trouble to go home.

Jeez, so this guy has been laid at least twice, thought Leon. Women will do anything.

Mungo had a huge collection of hardcore pornographic magazines in the cab of the truck and encouraged the boys to help themselves. He got a thrill out of seeing the young men enjoy the pictures, although it was Saul who loved the porn. Leon preferred live women but then again he wasn't afraid of them and didn't deify them. He didn't even romanticize women, like most men. He saw them for what they are. Human. Therefore objectification didn't come easy to him. He had never confided in anyone, not even his brother, that he thought the Virgin Mary had been lying her ass off about the whole Immaculate Conception thing. Saul would have been disgusted, he would have said the Virgin Mary was the only woman, including their mother, you could even halfway trust.

Saul loved the porn, he drooled over the murkiest stuff, and was particularly fascinated by a spread of a chubby young lady with dead eyes being mounted by a moth-eaten and oddly sardonic German Shepherd.

Mungo thought it was hysterical.

Leon thought they were both fucked up.

When the porn was put away the Bible came out.

Mungo was the proud owner of a magnificent black leather James VI version that he had bought from a yard sale after a Negro church had burned down in Louisiana. The congregation had sold everything they could to pay for rebuilding.

The church was set on fire by Dagwood Batters, an untreated schizophrenic who thought that black people were the lackeys of Old Nick.

The boys took turns reading passages from the Bible out loud to Mungo, who nodded and smiled or frowned in the appropriate places.

And so, like the pioneers of old, armed with the Good Book that they had grabbed at a bargain from the misery of others and split-beaver misogyny, they ate up the miles to the American West.

Mungo dropped them in front of a coffee shop on the main drag in Palm Springs and then headed off to his assignation with his girlfriend, Apples, a retired dental hygienist from Orange County, who had her own condo right on the third hole of the Heavenly Gates estate.

She had paid for it with the proceeds from her second divorce.

The boys looked up and down the street, at the nasty little souvenir stores, the crappy restaurants, and the curiously unattractive populace. They felt the oppressive one-hundred-degree desert heat beat down on them in sharp contrast to the chilly air-conditioned cab.

They thought what many do when they find themselves in Palm Springs for the first time: We have got to get out of here.

Only the elderly want to stay in Palm Springs and that's only because the alternative is even less appealing.

Saul and Leon got a sign from God.

It was written on the front of a Greyhound bus.

LAS VEGAS.

LA VIE NOUVELLE

AFTER THE DEATH OF HER LAST LOVER, Bruce, the Australian diplomat who had drunkenly stumbled in front of a Metro train, Claudette had felt she had to clean out her life and make it simple to the point of monastic.

She had lived in the large, rambling apartment she had inherited from Guillame, and over the years she had filled it with knickknacks and books and sofas and paintings and elastic bands and cotton buds and pieces of string and pamphlets and all the other rubbish that builds up in a home the longer one stays in it.

When Bruce died, she rented a room at the nearby Hôtel l'Abbaye and had contractors come and put all of her possessions, except for one framed photograph of each of her lovers, and all of her furniture into the back of a truck and take them away and sell them or burn them or dump them, she didn't care.

She just wanted everything gone.

Guillame had left her wealthy and she hadn't been foolish enough to give away the money. She loved the apartment and could not bear to part with it, so once it was cleaned out, she hired a decorator, Monsieur Garrido, a dark, squat man who was originally from Santiago de Compostela in northern Spain, to completely redecorate the place under very strict instructions.

The floors were sanded, the walls painted white, and she bought one large comfortable bed that she never slept in with any man. Her sheets were expensive white linen. She had one dining-room table with one chair, one bookcase, one reading lamp, one easy chair, one knife, one fork, one spoon. One cup.

She had one wall decoration. A wooden crucifix that she had bought in one of the many neighborhood stores that catered to the pilgrims who flocked to the nearby Saint-Sulpice. It hung above her bed.

Long, thick white curtains hung on each of the tall windows. The effect was meant to be stark and sad. Claudette wanted to enhance her solitude, she wanted the place to look as bleak as she felt, but in fact the result was completely the opposite. The old French apartment was so artfully constructed and had been lived in so much that Claudette's spartan style change had only improved it. It was breathtaking. Without clutter, the cornicing on the ceilings stood out, the marble of the fireplaces shone, and the sanded wooden parquets looked rich and warm.

Claudette's enforced period of minimalist solitude had only made everything more beautiful.

They kissed all the way to the fifth floor—the tiny elevator familiar to many old Parisian buildings seemed to insist on it—and when Claudette unlocked her door and let George enter, he felt a rush of adrenaline and approbation.

The Paris night filled the apartment with a dreamlike glow.

What they both failed to see was the ghost of Guillame, who had haunted his old home for the years since his death. He had been standing by the window in the living room, and when he saw Claudette enter with George, he smiled softly to himself, blew a kiss to the new lovers, and left, never to return. George and Claudette kissed in the hallway and the heat and joy of their passion began to turn to sex. Somehow, awkwardly and with some laughter and stumbling, they managed to make their way down the narrow hallway to the bedroom and remove their clothes at the same time. They both lost breath at the feel of each other's flesh for the first time, then they inhaled each other, and when Claudette put her small, cool hand around George's hot, hard cock, he had an overwhelming feeling of safety. Which surprised him a little but delighted him more.

Claudette parted from George and crossed the room. She drew the thick curtains closed and George gazed at her body, the most desirable and most female sight he had ever seen, backlit in the drape-muted halogen glow from the street. She turned and smiled at him and as she walked toward him he felt thrilled and nervous.

Claudette felt potent and fragile all at the same time. She could see the effect she was having on George and she could feel the effect he had on her. She had been wet since her hand touched his in Les Deux Magots.

Somehow this was to be her first time and somehow this was to be his first time.

They were hopelessly aroused and tumbling deeply into the physical manifestation of the biggest love either one of them would or could ever experience.

They were Holy Virgins.

All the ghosts of Paris gathered that night.

In the moonlit gardens of Luxembourg, the dead waited for the consummation of the Passion of Claudette and George. They stood by the statues or in the fountains, on the rides in the children's playground, or on the water of the large octagonal boating pond in front of the palace itself. The sweet suicide girls of the Resistance, the missing Jews, the Protestant heretics, the Catholic philosophers, the soldiers, the pox-ridden prostitutes, the betrayed revolutionaries, the murdered aristocrats, and the neglected children. The drunken drivers and the car-crash princesses. The divine Danton and the crones of the guillotine. The vomit-covered rock stars and the true Communists from the barricades.

All of Claudette's lovers.

Guillame Maupassant stood among them at last.

George's parents drifted shyly through the big green iron gates into the garden and took their place with the others.

And in the darkness and the silence as George and Claudette came together, the dead were set free.

* * *

Lovemaking took hold of George and Claudette and became like a third entity. They kept changing position and going through the moves that they had both learned in their respective sex lives but the lovemaking kept returning them to the missionary position, where they could look each other in the eyes as they climaxed.

They fucked and rested for a few moments, and fucked again, then rested, then fucked again. They made love three times before cock crow, when they both eventually lay exhausted, wrapped in each other.

Morpheus transported Claudette to the shadows and peace and dopamine-inducing, restorative slumber of God's favorites, whereas George began a tumble into dreamland.

As the lovers slept, millions of George's sperm died in Claudette's vagina and fallopian tubes.

Millions.

But not all.

THE TOWER

IN HIS LIFETIME, Carl Jung purchased a small tower on the shore of Lake Zurich, and as the years passed he added rooms and wings to it until eventually the place was much more elaborate and grand than it had been originally but it always remained his private place, his haven, his getaway from the world with all its questioning neurotics and judgmental academics. It was where he felt most at home.

Fraser read a biography of Jung after he started meeting him in dreams, and he identified very strongly with the doctor's desire to build a safe haven, a place of refuge from trouble. When Fraser was exposed as a kinky sex maniac in the tabloid press, he had wished he had his own little Bollingen to run off to, so he felt strangely at home as he walked along the shoreline of the lake with the poet Virgil as they headed to Jung's tower.

It seemed, as they got closer, that the tower was in the simple condition it had been when Jung purchased it, and Fraser saw that they were not in fact on the shore of Lake Zurich but actually on the edge of Hogganfield Loch, a small, shallow man-made boating pond in the downscale Riddrie area of Glasgow.

As they approached the door it was flung open by a delighted and slightly tipsy Jung, who had resumed his easily identifiable elder statesman guise. He strode purposely across the lawn and gave Fraser a bear hug.

"Fraser! How delightful! How delightful! I was wondering if Virgil would ever get you here." He winked at the poet, who laughed.

"He's a grumpy little spud, isn't he?" chuckled the poet, nodding at Fraser.

"He can be," agreed Jung, "but he doesn't mean it. He's just conflicted." Jung held out his hands as if trying to gauge the weight of two very similar-sized grapefruits.

"Sacred . . . profane . . . sacred . . . profane."

Jung and Virgil both had a good laugh at that and Fraser felt excluded. Jung noticed.

"Oh come, Fraser, don't pout! Come in, come in, both of you. I've made blackberry wine, and Toni and Emma are off hang-gliding, we have the place to ourselves. Just the boys."

"I can't," said Virgil. "I've got a doctor arriving. You know how arrogant they can be."

"Watch it, cheeky," laughed Jung, and the two great men hugged before Virgil took his leave.

Before he left, Virgil also hugged Fraser, who noticed the poet was now a full foot taller than him and at least ten years younger.

"See you." Virgil smiled through his now-perfect white teeth. "Don't be too tough on yourself, okay?"

Fraser nodded dumbly and the poet was gone.

Jung put an arm around Fraser's shoulder and ushered him into the tower.

Fraser and Carl sat in leather armchairs facing each other in front of the blazing log fire burning in the grate. The flames crackled theatrically but didn't give off much heat, and Fraser still felt cold in the circular, bare-brick-walled room.

"I'm cold," he said. "I suppose that's because I'm dead."

Jung smiled. "You're not dead. Not yet anyway."

"Well, I'm not dreaming and I'm talking to you and you're dead."

"Yes, I am," agreed the doctor as he sipped his wine. He relished the taste and lifted the glass to Fraser. "You sure you won't have some?"

Fraser shook his head sadly. "No, thanks. I've been hammering it too much recently. I think it's time I gave it a miss for a while."

Jung nodded, genuinely sympathetic.

"Look, if I'm not dead and I'm not dreaming, what exactly is happening?"

Jung sighed, put down his glass. "You're in crisis, Fraser. This is a fork in the road for you. We are in your subconscious. You're having a near-death experience but you're not dead yet."

"I'm in a coma?"

"No, you're dying but you're not all the way there. You are unconscious, certainly, but this is not a normal dream, if that is not too ludicrous a proposal. We are deeper and further in. We are not only in your unconscious, we are in the Great Unconscious. The Collective Unconscious, which, I may add, was my discovery and not something I stole from a student of mine."

"Oh, yeah, I think I read something about that."

"Enough!" snapped the doctor. "We are here to talk about you."

And that's what they did.

For the first time in his life Fraser totally opened himself up to the possibilities of himself. It wasn't that he hadn't been honest with Carl in the past, in fact he had, but he had omitted certain things and ignored others, dismissing them as unimportant. He freed himself from that quantitive judgment and just told the Great Psychotherapist everything, absolutely everything in his life he could remember, allowing the good doctor to interrupt him when he felt it was relevant, to point out something to Fraser, or to clarify a fact for himself.

They had all the time in the world. Not an engineer or a referee in sight.

Jung was particularly interested in a small point that Fraser had considered irrelevant.

It seemed that, when Fraser was three years old, his mother had fallen ill, developed some malignant growths in her uterus, and had to have a full hysterectomy. The operation was difficult and involved enough complications for her to spend six weeks in hospital. Fraser's father was embarrassed by the nature of the complaint and referred to the whole affair as his wife's "women's problems."

Everyone thought Fraser too young to understand why his mother was going away, so they just didn't tell him. One day she was there, the next day she wasn't and Fraser had been farmed out to his maternal grandmother, a giant wide-beamed frigate of a woman, who was well past the time in her life when she was up to dealing with and entertaining an energetic toddler.

Fraser pined for his mother, he cried and asked questions, and he was told she was away with women's problems. She would be back very soon.

The hospital had strict visiting rules. Scotland at this time was awash with ludicrous restrictions. It made people feel that order had been restored after the horrors of the bombing raids and mayhem of World War II. No children under five except in maternity, and even then only between four and five on a Sunday.

So when he was three years old, Fraser got an eye infection caused by standing at the letterbox of his grandmother's house, lifting the flap with his tubby little fingers and peering out, hoping to see his mother return. The resulting draft blew pollen into his tear ducts, causing them to swell his eyes almost shut. He had looked like a midget prizefighter who had just lost a title bout.

When his mother eventually returned, no one mentioned her absence but Fraser sensed she felt deeply guilty about having deserted him.

Jung felt this was extremely significant.

"Why?" asked Fraser. "It wasn't like she did it on purpose. She was ill, for God's sake."

"I'm not saying she was wrong to be ill but your family was wrong to not talk to you about it."

"I was only three."

"Exactly. Just as you are dealing with separation anxiety, your mother disappears. I am amazed you are not even worse."

Fraser was skeptical. "I'm not going to blame all my problems on my mother. It's a ridiculously simple cliché. I'm surprised at you."

"Your mother is not to blame for all of your problems but it is extremely important to find out where the trouble begins, and I am fairly sure, for you it began with this event. You learned not to trust. If you can't trust, you can't be trustworthy. Nothing is reliable to you, and you in turn are not reliable to yourself or anyone else. This causes you to feel shame, terror, self-loathing, depression, even suicidal."

"Come on, that's a bit of stretch, don't you think? You sure about that?" said Fraser. He felt that Carl was phoning it in sometimes.

Jung nodded, tapping his pipe on the fireplace to clean it. "Oh, yes, I'm sure—and I am not phoning anything in," he grumbled.

And on they talked. Well, Fraser talked mostly, Jung listening intently as he smoked his pipe, the blue-gray smoke spiraling up the tower and collecting in the rafters. At last Fraser felt he was finished. Everything was out, there was nothing he could remember that he hadn't mentioned or discussed with Carl.

The two men sat in silence for a while. At length Jung asked, "Do you believe in God?"

Fraser thought for a moment, then said that, in light of recent events, yes, he did believe in God. He had been hanging around with dead people for what seemed like days. That would imply there was an afterlife, which in turn suggested that there was a God.

"Why would an afterlife suggest a God any more than life itself?" asked Jung.

"I suppose they both suggest God," said Fraser.

Jung agreed but then said that just because Fraser had been with Virgil and H.P. Lovecraft and Brinsley Sheridan and himself, it didn't mean there was an afterlife. Perhaps he was imagining the whole thing. Perhaps everything was a dream and nothing was ever real or ever had been.

Fraser thought about that for a moment. "I think that's a dead end," he said.

"I'm inclined to agree," said Jung. "Perhaps it's more productive to say that all dreams are real."

Another long silence stretched between them.

"What now?" said Fraser at length.

"Now you try to go back," replied the old man.

"How? I don't know where to start."

"Get up. Open the door and start walking. There is no poet this time to guide you but you have a lot more information at your fingertips. It's a dangerous trip. Good luck."

"Will I die?"

"Everyone dies, Fraser."

Fraser nodded. He stood up, as did Carl, and the two men embraced. Before Fraser opened the door, he turned and looked back.

"Will I see you again?" he asked, sounding a little girly.

"I hope so," replied Carl.

Fraser nodded and stepped outside.

Of course, the landscape had changed again, he had expected that much, but he had not expected what he saw before him.

Belgium.

POPPY SEEDS

AS ANY REPUTABLE PRACTITIONER of medicine will allow, the human body is extremely complex and in many ways mysterious. Maladies and problems can spring up and/or disappear without any logical or scientific explanation. Strict scientists, those who study failure incessantly, say that this is for reasons that have yet to be discovered. Groovier, more shamanistic students of human biology will say that the body is intertwined with the soul and, even though science has as yet been unable to detect it, the soul is the single most important driving force in humans, controlling everything from the autoimmune system to the need to defecate.

In George's case, there was certainly a mystery occurring. It had nothing to do with his cancer but, as he lay in a deep sleep next to the incandescent Claudette in the most comfortable bed in the known Universe, his body began to shut down.

He was dying.

Quickly.

He ran down the length of the trench, mortar shells exploding behind him with hideously workmanlike thuds, not the kind of showbiz special effects he had expected. The big noise came from the guns on his own side and they seemed even more terrifying even though they were aimed at some poor sods miles away.

He stumbled just as he heard a bullet *swiss* neutrally by his head, missing by inches but murderously indifferent to him. He fell into a muddy hole on top of another soldier who was crouched in the fetal position with his eyes shut tight and his hands over his ears.

The fetal soldier opened his eyes for a moment and then a look of amazed and dazed recognition changed his expression from terror to bewilderment.

"George?" he whispered.

"Hello, Fraser," said George.

THE ROAD TO GOD: FIVE

CADENCE POWERS LOVED VEGAS HOOKERS. They would suck the pleasure and money from you with a speed and efficiency that left you breathless. Getting a blowjob from one of these avaricious sirens was the sexual equivalent of a roller-coaster ride. It was artificially created excitement and that's what Vegas is all about. Showbiz! Making something thrilling out of absolutely nothing. All smoke and mirrors, an entertainment resort in the middle of a deadly arid plain. It was fantastic. The devil's delight, a thumbing of the nose at God with all his trees and rocks and little wildlifey squirrels and bunny rabbits, all that Disney bullshit.

Cadence knelt at the glass-topped coffee table and genuflected before the cocaine, sucking the white powder into his nose with all the joyless violence of a blowjob from Tiffany. Tiffany, the hooker, was in the can rinsing her vagina and preparing it for the next customer. *Sanitized for your convenience.*

She had had so much reconstructive surgery that she could probably make do with wiping herself with a damp cloth. She was nonstick.

Men walked on the moon to create this technology.

After Tiffany left, Cadence called Room 1153.

"Hey, dawg, wassup?" he said, in the strange way that white talent agents from Los Angeles do in an attempt to sound like young black men from underprivileged backgrounds. A linguistic fashion as peculiar as the lisp that everybody in medieval Spain had to adopt after the king developed a speech impediment.

"Chillin. Whas wit choo," replied Rory, also a soft whiteboy.

"Jus watchin *Cosby.* Wanna get a drink?"

"See you in the bar in ten."

"S'all good," said Cadence and hung up.

Cadence and Rory were junior talent agents at CAM, Creative Artistic Management, an enormous Orwellian talent agency based in Los Angeles that represented movie stars and writers and directors and producers. They were in town for the Las Vegas Comedy Festival—a bullshit junket that none of the senior agents would even think of attending.

Cadence had left his fiancée back in L.A. and took advantage of flying solo to treat himself to a gram or two of the old Bolivian marching powder and engage the services of Tiffany, whom he had found in the classifieds of *L.A. Weekly,* a free left-wing newspaper and listings mag that subsidized itself with, among other things, ads from prostitutes. He had booked her himself. He could have had his assistant do it but he didn't trust the little shit. He didn't trust anyone at CAM and that was one of the reasons he was a rising star at the organization. At twenty-five he was on the way up. This would be his last trip to one of these gnarly loser conventions, going to see fifteen stand-up comedians every night for three nights, with all of them doing their same tired shtick about alienation and airplane peanuts. From now on he was going to be at film festivals or fucking nothing. He would have to take Lauren with him, though, she was getting a bit pissed at him for being out so much, but she was so dull. All she could talk about was fucking aerobics and wheatgrass. She was so L.A. it made him sick.

He didn't like Lauren much at all but he was marrying her because she was perfect for him. Looked great on his arm, knew the way he liked his dick sucked. What more could you ask?

He'd have to stop hanging with Rory, though. He creeped people out with all that phony ghetto-speak.

Cadence wanted to get ahead and get head and that was about it. He was a simple man, unpleasant but simple. A type that show business pulls to its ample prosthetic bosom and showers with glittering prizes.

He put on his jacket, checked his nostrils in the mirror, and stepped out into the night.

The comedians were worse than usual and he couldn't figure out why anyone was laughing. The place was packed with the usual polyester retards that flock to Vegas for a little piece of glamour. Vegas, as glitzy as a trailer park at Christmas, called to the stupid, and that was what Cadence wanted to see. He was looking for someone who appealed to the masses. He was looking for a comedian whom he could package, someone who was lovable and moronic and safe enough to develop a prime-time situation comedy for.

He needed a guy who could be the comic anchor while his life went crazy with hilarious results. He needed a comedy Nemo, an everyman to put with his nagging wife/boss, his goofy brother/neighbor, his dorky friends/in-laws, and his adorable kids/dog.

A hit sitcom was the way to make a star, and making a star is what made a star agent. Movies were too tough and political but TV was a machine, it devoured product, it needed more talent every year, performers to be shaved and dieted into acceptance by the mob.

Sanitized for your convenience.

There was nothing here tonight, though. The customers were just laughing because they were drunk. Cadence could tell the difference; real laughs sounded a bit like music, drunk laughter sounded like dogs barking.

He was bored.

"Rory, let's get the fuck out of here," he whispered to his tubby bespectacled colleague.

"Fuckin A, dawg," said Rory.

The two agents slipped out while the unfunny lanky doofus on the stage complained that bananas were too difficult to peel. They screwed up—the doofus went on to become the richest and highest-paid sitcom star America had ever seen.

When they got outside the club, the two whiteboys tried to grab one of the minivan cabs that shuttle the punters around Vegas but four big, clean, drunken girls from Minnesota jumped in beside them. The girls were college age and desperate to be wild and dangerous. To them this meant flashing their breasts at anyone who crossed their path. Cadence and Rory were delighted at this little sexy windfall.

"Where we goin, ladies?" asked Cadence as the girls gate-crashed the back of the cab.

The girls wanted to go to Mr. Bambaloni's, a karaoke bar just off the Strip. Cadence thought, Fuck it, why not. It was about as much fun as anything else in this shitty town. (He had already been in Vegas for two days, which is like being anywhere else for two years.)

They stumbled into the club just as Leon stepped up to the mike.

Within a few seconds Cadence was a believer.

Here was his destiny.

A great, big, fat fucking star.

WAR

"WHIT'S GOIN OAN HERE?" the Scottish soldier shouted down from the rim of the trench.

George had just landed on Fraser and they just had time to say hello before Corporal Adam McLachlan of the Argyll and Sutherland Highlanders, a movie-star-handsome twenty-eight-year-old battle-hardened veteran from Glasgow, found them in what looked like a cowardly little embrace.

"Getting cover, sir," yelled Fraser over the noise of the shelling.

"Awright, but try no tae look like a couple o' wee girls, will ye, ye'll have the bloody Bosch laughing if they catch ye."

"Yessir."

"I'm goin over tae C company, ther sergeant jist bought it, ther runnin aboot lik heidless chickens. When you boys ur finished wi' yer cuddle ye might do us aw a wee favor an shoot some fuckin Germans."

He was one of those warriors on the battlefield who made you think you might get out of this alive. Relentlessly courageous and a survivor himself. He had been in the army since 1914 and was still alive three years later. An unbelievable run of luck for an infantryman in this war.

"Keep yer heids doon, boys." He winked at them and then was gone, ducking under a hail of shrapnel and dirt that made his tin hat jingle like a faulty telephone.

George noticed that he and Fraser were both young again and were in damp and itchy army uniforms. He had never seen Fraser look so scared. He hadn't really seen him at all, except for when he caught the TV show, since the last time they had both been wandering Clouston Street on a snowy Saturday night in February looking for a party.

"What is going on here?"

Fraser looked at him, terror in his eyes. "We're in hell."

George nodded. He didn't believe Fraser. Somewhere in his psyche he knew he was dreaming, so the situation didn't touch him the way it might otherwise.

He had, though, a dreadful feeling of unease.

Fraser continued, "I'm dead. You're dead. We are the dead. I've been here for weeks, man. It's fucking mental here. I'm scared."

He was crying and George felt sorry for him. He hadn't been friendly with the guy for years but he was in a terrible mess.

George vaguely wondered why he was dreaming about Fraser.

Fraser told him of Brinsley and H.P. Lovecraft and his journey with Virgil and his discussions with Jung. He told him how he had left Jung's tower and must have taken a wrong turn, for within moments had found himself here in Ypres in 1917. He had given up the notion that he might escape.

George thought that the poor bastard was out of his mind.

"Relax. This is not real," said George, trying to calm him down. "Look." George climbed the little wooden ladder out of the trench to show Fraser that the bullets could not harm him.

Fraser screamed at him to get down but it was too late. A sniper bullet caught George in the right shoulder, bursting his collarbone to chips and spraying blood and bone over his face and neck.

George was conscious as he fell to the mud and dirt and shit and dead vermin on the trench floor. He was in agony, his face already paling from shock.

"What the fuck?" he whispered.

"Shut up," barked Fraser, who grabbed a dirty blanket from his pack and pressed it against George's wound, the filthy wool drinking up the blood like a greedy vampire.

George was crying now, the pain and the trauma turning him into an infant. "Jesus, I'm dying, I'm fucking dying, oh God I want my ma."

"Shhh," said Fraser. "I've seen this, you'll last longer if you don't speak. Save your strength. Just breathe, George, breathe as deeply as you can, keep breathing."

George did as he was told. Like a lot of young men in this war, he could not understand how he had gone from the bed of a beautiful woman in Paris to dying like a rat in a stinkhole in such a short period of time.

"I don't deserve this," he cried.

Fraser smoothed George's hair back with his shaking hand, trying not to be afraid for a moment in order to comfort the dying man.

"Nobody deserves this," he said.

"Nobody."

"Jesus, Ah telt ye tae keep yer heid doon." Corporal McLachlan was clambering back into the trench. A professional soldier, he was already pulling a med kit from his pack. Fraser got out of the way and let the senior man in to look at the wound. McLachlan lifted the swabbing and looked at the damage, his expression all business, not allowing the wounded man to see him wince.

"Ye'll be awright, son, ther noo, everythin's gonnae be awright."

George closed his eyes.

"Is he dead?" Fraser asked.

"Naw, Ah think he might make it if we kin get him tae the infirmary. They could stitch this mess or tar it or whatever the hell it is that they dae. He hus tae stoap bleedin tho."

"Where's the infirmary?"

"Ither side o' C company, aboot a hunner yerds away. Problem is, Ah've jist been tae C company, thur sarge was deid right enough, along wi' the rest o' them. Thur's nae C company noo, it's no-man's-land."

McLachlan ran across the trench and picked up a stretcher that was propped against the wooden-planked wall.

Fraser was aghast. "You're not serious? We can't carry him over no-man's-land. We'll all get killed."

McLachlan looked Fraser dead in the eye. "Listen, son. Ah've lastit three years in this war an d'ye know why? Cuz ither sodjers wur brave enough tae help me. Ah git shot an ah wid huv bled tae death if ma comrades hudnae goat me tae safety. Ah cannae thank any o' these boys cuz thir aw deid. Thur's nae rules in this place 'cept the wans ye make yersel. Here's ma rules. Help ither boys stay alive. Noo you help me get this lad oan this stretcher and grab an end or Ah swear tae God I will take oot ma gun and put a bullet in you masel. Yer nae guid here if ye wilnae help yer pals."

There was no doubt that the corporal was serious.

Fraser helped get George, who was still moaning, onto the stretcher, and when he was strapped in he and McLachlan manhandled the bundle up the trench wall.

Bullets and dirt and noise exploded around them and Fraser froze but McLachlan was a man possessed. He yelled at Fraser, "MOVE! GO! GO! GO! NOW!"

The two men ran with their load across the mud that had once been a cattle-grazing field as it blew up into their faces and eyes like hell had lost its lid.

Fraser could see a red cross painted on a white board up ahead and he ran toward it. Suddenly he felt the other end of the stretcher go limp.

McLachlan had been shot in the head. He lay on the ground. Dead.

When his body was recovered he was buried with thousands of other soldiers in a graveyard in Arras. After the war, in the regimental memorial book that sits in Edinburgh Castle, it would read "Cpl. Adam McLachlan—God's finger touched him and he slept," which the military brass felt sounded more poetic than "He was shot in the head and he died."

Fraser would have had a better chance of making it if he dropped the stretcher and ran the rest of the way alone but then George would die where he lay. So Fraser, the phony TV evangelist, the drunken, selfish media prick, the whoremaster, gossip, and sot, dragged George by himself for the last fifty yards to the hospital as the bullets whistled and hissed by his head and as the mortars pounded around him.

Sacred . . . profane . . . sacred . . . profane.

The surgeon was able to close up George's wound and luckily the bullet had passed through, he would live. For now.

Fraser was sitting by the side of his cot. He motioned to George to look at the next bed.

Lying there groaning incoherently in agony, a dark slowly growing bloodstain on the sheet covering his middle, was Willie Elmslie. The boy who had given Fraser cheap wine and who George had beaten with a fishing rod when they were thirteen.

George looked at him. "This is not hell," he said decisively and turned back to meet Fraser's eye. "In hell we couldn't die, there would be no release. Death cannot happen or threaten us if we are already dead. This is a dream."

"A nightmare," said Fraser.

"A nightmare, then," agreed George. "But we are alive. I am not staying here, Fraser, and I am not dying yet. I have some things to do and I need to get them done. Also, I love someone."

"What does that mean?" said Fraser.

"It means I will cling to life to be with them as long as God will allow."

Fraser did not remember his old schoolmate as someone who had such a prosaic line of chat. "What happened to you, George?" he asked.

"I got shot," said George.

"Not now, I mean before. What brought you here?"

"I got shot," said George.

And after a fashion, Fraser understood.

Fraser stood up. He walked over to the edge of the hospital trench and looked out over no-man's-land. He saw the body of Corporal McLachlan tangled in the mud and the barbed wire. He wept for the bravest man he had ever met.

Across the filthy divide was a young German private named Helmut Maunn, who much later would write the novel *Die Pampelmuse der Grausigkeit* about a poet who initially was attracted to the order and drama of the Nazis only to eventually become sickened with them and himself. The book would become a classic and eventually be made into a film starring the talented French actor Guillame Maupassant.

Helmut saw Fraser's head off in the distance. He raised his rifle, took careful aim, and held his breath as he squeezed the trigger.

The bullet caught Fraser directly in the face, smashing through teeth and bone.

God's finger touched him and he slept.

JERKS

IN AN ANCIENT LANGUAGE, *myo* is the word for muscle, and *clonus* means rapidly alternating contraction and relaxation. The sudden spasm of the major muscles as a person is falling asleep produces a little shock that wakes them up again; it is called a *myoclonic* jerk.

It is one of the thousands of little adventures that occur in the human body that are unsatisfactorily explained by contemporary medicine. Just about everyone experiences these tiny seizures at some point in their life and so they are considered normal, which of course doesn't tell you much.

The effect, common in everyone from newborn babies to octogenarians, is that of a feeling of stumbling or falling over. The best guess, or hypothesis, to use the word that academics like, that modern science has come up with to explain this phenomenon is that as the heart rate and breathing slow in preparation for sleep, the brain sometimes interprets this as the person dying and sends a jolt, or electrical impulse, through the body in order to wake it up. Bring it back to life, as it were.

In George's case, this was 100 percent accurate. His body was dying and his brain sent a thunderbolt through his system strong enough to jump-start a rusty truck.

Had Fraser and Corporal McLachlan not dragged him across no-man's-land, George would not have received the lightning bolt and would have died quietly in the bed next to Claudette. A postmortem would have revealed his cancer but nothing else, and his sudden expiration would have been a bit of a head-scratcher for a couple of French doctors for a while until they got too busy to think about it anymore.

Claudette would have finally snapped and ended her own life with the massive dose of sleeping pills she kept in the bathroom cabinet just in case.

But the fortunate George was carried by his comrades to safety and so he sat up with a start and found himself looking at the sleeping Claudette, her cheeks mushed into the pillow. It was still dark outside.

He did not remember anything. Some vague feeling of unease, something about Fraser Darby, but as he gazed at the sleeping beauty next to him, all the anxiety bled from his body and was replaced by wonder and awe.

He sighed and lay back on the pillow, his face close enough to hers that he could share her breath. In gratitude, he finally slept.

BEACHED

FRASER SWAM THROUGH WARM LIGHT-BLUE MILK. He was below the surface of something again but he could breathe. Breath filled him in a rush as if he'd had fifty extra-strong mints all at once, then went for a yodel on an Alp.

He couldn't see more than two or three inches in front of his face, or maybe it was two or three miles, it was hard to tell with the milk. It was a texture he didn't recognize, a sensation he only vaguely knew. Perhaps from the womb. He smiled a big, wide smile to himself. Carl would be very proud he was thinking like this.

Gradually he felt himself ascending until he broached the creamy surface and found he was about thirty feet from the shore of a tropical island. A small three-palm-tree job with a shiny white deserted sand beach. It was bright yellow daytime.

Up from the beach the three palm trees grew wildly, like Rastafarian bed-head. Fat bumblebees buzzed happily in the shade.

Fraser waded ashore and saw that he was naked. He looked around. No one about.

He suddenly felt a sadness that he had never experienced before, it hit him like a giant Georgia freight train. He fell to his knees and wept, his heart shattered, his soul broken in a billion pieces.

It was over.

He was dead.

After what could have been a few hours or a few days or a few years, Fraser looked up and saw an olive-skinned man with Brylcreamed hair walking down the beach toward him. He was barefoot and hatless but otherwise was in the uniform of a French policeman. He had his sleeves rolled up and was smoking an unfiltered cigarette.

Fraser cowered from him, terrified.

"Hey, relax," said the policeman in heavily accented English. "You are shaking like a Bethlehem shepherd. I have a message for you."

"Who from?" Fraser asked, trying to appear less afraid than he was.

The policeman laughed. "'Who from.' Very funny." He was really tickled.

Fraser smiled but had no idea what the policeman was laughing at.

The policeman handed Fraser an envelope. Fraser opened it. It was his final report card from when he had left school at sixteen. Under the teachers' additional-comments column was written in red ink:

Could do better.

Fraser looked up. He was about to ask what it meant when the policeman dealt him a vicious blow across the skull with his nightstick.

He blacked out.

He came to.

He heard himself moaning and at first everything was a bloody, smudgy mess but it seemed to burn off like a foggy marine layer. His vision finally focused with astonishing clarity on the anxious face of T-Bo, the teenager who had brutally beaten and mugged him only ten minutes before.

"Hey," said T-Bo. "You okay, man? I'm sorry. I'm really sorry. You okay?"

Fraser looked at him and smiled through bloodied and broken teeth.

"I am born again," he said.

RECOLLECTION

THIS FROM THE BEST-SELLING MEMOIRS of the flamboyant and charismatic, popular African-American television evangelist Bishop Thomas Leroy Bosley, published on the eve of his fiftieth birthday.

Although the bishop dictated the work himself, what many people do not know is that the book was in fact ghostwritten by a bitter old cynic named David Trundle, who as a young man received some acclaim for his screenplays for the Hollywood movies *Fingerplay* and *Big Friendly American Wedding Celebrity.* Bishop Bosley paid him $250,000 for the gig, a fraction of what he used to get for his scripts.

> The birth of my belief came almost immediately on the instance of my meeting with a man I shall call Rabbi. He never was in any way affiliated with the Jewish faith, but the term *Rabbi* was given to him by me. I felt that he truly was deserving of the term. His wisdom seemed as old as the Hebrew teachings and he was a great teacher to me. He certainly opened me up to the LORD, and even though we parted ways after a short time together and I have no idea what happened to him, I do believe it was God who sent him to me.

I believe the LORD chooses some unusual messengers to check that we are paying attention to his children when they bring us the Good News of the Gospels.

My child, you must never turn away a true messenger of the LORD because of his ethnicity, his profanities, his hygiene, or his apparent unworthiness. A man can have poop in his pants and Jesus in his heart.

"Then how will I know the messenger?" you ask.

I cannot answer for you. Feel in your heart. Pray for guidance. Ask the LORD.

The Rabbi was the last man I ever laid my hands on in anger or violence, Praise God. He was a man of God himself, although he said he was a hypocrite and that it was me who finally drove him to his true belief through the shock of the beating he received at my hands. My bloody hands. He said the experience "pushed him from the dry dock of sinfulness out into the ocean of God's love." Amen.

The details of my childhood have been documented in this book and in the press by my friends and enemies over the years, and much has been made of the disadvantages that I faced as a young man. While I do not negate or in any way minimize the situation that I faced then, I now believe that in no way did it excuse the life of crime that I had been infected with. I say the word *infected*. Amen.

I say the word *infected* advisedly, for many others faced the same torments as myself and did not succumb to sin. Were they morally superior to me? Were they closer to our LORD? I say, "Nay, they were not." The plain truth is that I was shackled by the devil and he had taken control of my person, my soul. It was Satan, Ole Blackbritches himself, who drove me into the arms of Jesus. His wickedness backfired on him. The night that my friends and I pounced on the Rabbi, to beat him up and rob him, I was in a place where I could only be saved by a divine act of grace, which struck me as a bolt from the blue much like our beloved St. Paul on his journey to Damascus. And the LORD saw fit to bless me with his sacred lightning bolt. Amen.

We attacked the poor Rabbi, who had wandered drunkenly from a nightclub, the den of his own iniquity. Yea, though he was a Rabbi, he was also a sinner. He fought us back fiercely but he was outnumbered by younger, fitter, angrier men, and he was incapacitated by his intake of alcohol and drugs. We took his wallet and his passport (for he was a foreigner). I believe we stole his watch also, and I seem to remember we also stole his pants, although I could not imagine why we did that. We ran off leaving him bleeding and unconscious in the filthy back alley.

My friends and I had by this time purchased a car with the profits of our sinful missions, a Chevrolet Caprice convertible, 1975, pimped out with a chrome roll bar and spin-back chunky rims. Amen.

We returned to it to count our takings and escape back to the projects, where we would be safe. During the fight with the Rabbi, I had made eye contact with him and felt that he was special, that he was filled with the love of the LORD.

The look had troubled me as we made our escape and as I sat in the car among my fellow thieves and watched them laugh and delight in our grisly exploits and count our ill-gotten gains. When we went through the Rabbi's effects, we found an invitation for him to attend a meeting of evangelists in Birmingham, Alabama. A convention of the Holy United Church of America. Praise God! It was at that point I had the terrible realization that we were guilty of attacking a man of the cloth. We had robbed and beaten one of the LORD's righteous servants. Shame consumed my soul. Suddenly it was as if the car was filled with a white light and a voice seemed to say:

"Turn back, Thomas Leroy. Repent thy sins, while thou have time."

I was afraid and exhilarated at the same time. I was suddenly filled with a terrific rage.

I grabbed the money from my colleagues, who were mystified by my behavior. I threw them from the car and drove back to the scene of the crime, to the Rabbi, who lay bleeding and unconscious in the alley.

I lifted him up and placed him in the passenger seat, so that I could take him and attend to his wounds. I begged his forgiveness. I tearfully admitted I had committed this horrible act of violence against him. He mystified me with the spirituality of his reply. Far from admonishing or condemning me, he whispered, "I am born again. Thank you, thank you, thank you," over and over again. I also wept, for with him and through him, I felt the beautiful, benign, forgiving presence of the LORD.

Amen. Praise Jesus. Amen.

THE ROAD TO GOD: SIX

FROM THE MOMENT THEY HAD BEEN BORN, their DNA contained a combination of madness and showmanship, so it was inevitable that Saul and Leon would have ended up in Los Angeles, the home of the attention-seeking spiritually disenfranchised. In the years that they were there they plowed the depths of greed, insanity, and nihilism, which is to say that they participated fully in the civic activity of Beverly Hills, their chosen parish. In their time in Bleaktown they saw their world change, they saw riches beyond imagining, and participated in the most discouraging acts of depravity, both together and separately. They saw fortunes, including their own, rise and fall and rise again, and they saw the thing that disappointed them both the most.

It was this: "A man profits nothing if he gains the whole world and loses his immortal soul."

What they did not see was the beauty, art, and holiness, which was a shame because that was also there.

Hope springs eternal—the Renaissance flowered under the Borgia popes. The Universe seeks balance and abhors a vacuum, and so Los Angeles also offers curative mysticism and mental health, but unfortunately the line between good and evil is blurred by the smog of money and cosmetic dentistry. It takes an expert to pick a safe route.

The devil smiles brilliantly through the brown fog, offering a three-picture deal and a two-week psychic retreat in Santa Fe complete with deep-tissue massage and recreational heroin.

In other words: In L.A. it is very difficult to tell who your friends are.

And, of course, even when you think you have the place and its people finally figured out: The ground keeps shifting.

Saul and Leon were lucky to escape with their lives and at least a shot at redemption.

Cadence Powers had led them to the pit, and after a short, brilliant burst of success, he was consumed by his own creation.

Saul and Leon, having found themselves stranded in Palm Springs with no method of escape, that is to say they had no money, took heed of the old maxim that the Lord helps those who help themselves.

They helped themselves to a purse that an old lady had left draped over the back of a chair in a coffee shop.

The coffee shop was called Stubb and Flask, named after the second and third mates on the *Pequod,* the doomed whaler of *Moby Dick.* It was one in a chain of stores that sold good, regular coffees with fancy-sounding names at a preposterous markup. This made the gullible customers feel they were getting a quality product, a little like Neiman Marcus or the Mormons. The literary connection of the name also made some customers feel well read, which indeed some of them were, but what's the point of being well read unless you can feel it—i.e., show off about it. Stubb and Flask coffee shops became immensely popular the world over until they were sabotaged by eco-warriors, who claimed the company was ruining the planet with plastic heat-retaining lids for their to-go cups: The lids had a half-life of fifty thousand years. The eco-warriors firebombed a few stores in Paris and New York and customers panicked, deciding to return to reasonably priced diner coffee and safety. No one wants to be hideously burned for a nonalcoholic beverage, no matter how delicious and intelligent.

In the purse that Leon and Saul stole there was three hundred dollars cash, twenty-six Vicodin pills (a powerful painkiller with a very pleasant narcotic buzz), a brochure for a pet funeral home in San Bernardino that provided open-casket ceremonies for cats and dogs, and a partially used tube of Preparation H, a salve for the treatment of hemorrhoids. It was an Aladdin's cave for the boys; the only thing they couldn't use was the pet undertaker literature but they kept it anyway as a souvenir. Saul later had the brochure framed and hung it in his office.

The boys used the money to buy two one-way tickets on a Greyhound bus from Palm Springs to Las Vegas, and after enjoying a latté each from Stubb and Flask, they took a couple of Vicodin and grooved all the way to Sin City.

Saul had developed juicy grapelike hemorrhoids from being so fat and damp and sitting on the plastic in the back of the truck from Florida, so before they left, he slid into the bathroom at the bus station and with his index finger liberally applied the healing balm to his angry anus.

The combination of theft, drugs, cash, and anal relief made Saul feel as good as he ever had and set a pattern for his life for years and years to come.

The boys slept on the bus, slumped in the uncomfortable seats, their heads touching.

In Vegas they got a room in the Bier Keller, a cheap and strangely Bavarian-themed motel about a mile east of the Strip, the main street in town. A twin room in the Bier Keller cost twenty dollars a night and, huddled in a dark bedroom named the Putsch Suite on a bed that would vibrate if you fed it twenty-five cents, the boys plotted their march to world domination.

Saul was of the opinion that Leon's talent was so great that they only had to let people know what he could do and cash and prizes would follow.

Leon was of the opinion that Saul could take care of everything.

They shook hands on their business arrangement in their dark room, the only contract they ever had.

Leon sings and performs and he gets 50 percent.

Saul takes care of everything else and he gets 50 percent. (Ironically, in later years Leon and his ghastly retinue of hangers-on would always talk about "taking care of business" but the only person who ever took care of Leon's business was Saul.)

Rather than plod aimlessly from audition to audition trying to find a spot in a chorus line, Saul had Leon sing every night at Mr. Bambaloni's. Soon people were turning up at the bar to hear Leon, not themselves, sing. Saul, in interviews he later gave, equated this time to fishing. He was just waiting for showbiz to bite, which it did the night Cadence Powers stumbled in.

After hearing Leon sing, Cadence approached him at the bar and gave him the old spiel about Los Angeles and Hollywood and opportunity, and perhaps he might like to talk etc. etc. Cadence knew he should play it cool. Passive/aggressive is key in talent negotiation but he also knew that this guy would get snapped up fast if he didn't get to him immediately. Leon listened to Cadence's pitch patiently for a few minutes, then pointed across the bar to Saul, who was sitting in a booth in the corner sipping a Shirley Temple.

"That's my manager. He takes care of everything."

Cadence looked over at the sweaty, acne-covered (Tootsiepop Ted had just killed LeShay Jackson and dumped her eyeless body on a hiking trail on Kennesaw Mountain) fat kid and thought that he would be able to snow the youngster with some big name-dropping and money talk.

He was wrong, of course. Saul was already much tougher than him. Saul burned Cadence for a cash advance and he and Leon moved to Los Angeles. Cadence paid for this move out of his own pocket and signed the boys into a partnership with him personally. He did not want to be marginalized by the more senior agents at CAM who would have stolen Leon from him at the earliest opportunity had he not protected himself in this way.

He got the boys a two-bedroom apartment on Sweetzer Boulevard in West Hollywood, not far from his own place, and set about getting Leon a series of "generals"—meetings with casting directors who could put Leon's name forward for him to be considered for upcoming projects.

Casting directors in Hollywood are usually gay men or middle-aged women, so Leon shone in these getting-to-know-you meetings.

He flirted and smiled and joked and charmed, but there are lots of extremely good-looking young men who can flirt and charm in Hollywood, it's one of the things that makes the town so obnoxious, so although he did well, that is to say he was liked, nothing came of any of these meetings.

Saul complained to Cadence that he had Leon go up for acting jobs when he was a singer. Cadence said, bullshit, everyone was an actor and he knew what he was doing. He just wanted enough people to know who Leon was before he had a showcase. He was raising Leon's profile.

"What's a showcase?" asked Leon.

"It's where you get to score your first goal," said Cadence.

The only other client of any importance that Cadence had was an English screenwriter named David Trundle. Trundle, although a mediocre talent, had managed to wrangle a scholarship for the prestigious UCLA screenwriting course that had been paid for by BAFTA, the British Academy for Film and Television Arts. He got this through his social and family connections in the U.K.

Trundle, a triumph of the English public-school system (which is what the English call their private-school system), was a well-mannered weasel who would succeed far beyond his potential. In another time he would have joined the British Foreign Office.

The screenwriting course itself is prestigious because it has produced a number of students who have written highly lucrative formulaic blockbuster movies for the big studios, movies about evil tornados or evil aliens or evil scientists or evil dinosaurs or serial killers or tough-but-likable maverick cops who don't play by the rules.

Cadence's biggest triumph at CAM was when he managed to get a million dollars for a spec script Trundle had written, a ludicrous thriller called *Fingerplay,* the story of identical twins Esau and Luke, who are separated in childhood. Esau becomes a scientist/serial killer and Luke becomes a tough but likable maverick cop who doesn't play by the rules.

Esau finds a way to forge fingerprints by genetically restructuring his own hands. He steals his brother's identity and frames him for a string of murders, and Luke, the good twin/cop, has to clear his name or he will go to the gas chamber and lose his girlfriend.

There is a poignant moment toward the end of the movie when Luke has to kill his bad self.

"Very Jungian," wrote the fawning and corrupt semiliterate chimp who reviewed films for a Chicago newspaper. The film starred the pompous, pseudo-intellectual, alcoholic movie actor Nicholas Kilmer in the roles of both cop and killer. It made two hundred million dollars at the box office and Kilmer won an Oscar for his work. The critics lauded his performance as breathtaking.

With the success of *Fingerplay,* Trundle became insufferable, he became a genius in his own mind, and he kept on and on at Cadence that he wasn't getting paid enough for his scripts (he burned through the million for *Fingerplay* very quickly) and demanded that Cadence find him a deal. Cadence was having trouble getting work for the Englishman because of his reputation for being extremely argumentative and difficult, characteristics that would be tolerated, even encouraged, in an actor or director but were unwise in writers, given that they were so easily replaced. Jesus, anyone can write if they have the time. How hard can it be?

Cadence told Trundle he had a plan for him to make huge dollars by creating a sitcom for television.

Trundle said that no way was he going to make television, he was an artist, but he listened more closely when Cadence told him the amounts involved should they be successful.

Trundle made sure that he was at the showcase early in order to properly suck up to Leon, just in case.

It is difficult for those who have never been actively involved to appreciate the depth of the pathological self-centeredness that infects entertainment executives and artists' representatives in Los Angeles. These are people who, with one or two exceptions, earn their living and base their self-worth completely on money, gossip, and how much they weigh. This is both a good and bad thing. It is bad for the executives and agents themselves because most of them, as they age, no matter how successful they have been in financial, career, and dietary terms, begin to realize the awful emptiness of their lives, and this makes them very sad and bitter.

The good thing is it makes them very easy to manipulate. These people are frantic, so the fashion among them is to suck in their guts and effect an attitude that they are slightly bored by everything.

Beneath the surface, little desperate ducks paddling furiously.

Cadence, being one of them, but a smarter-than-average example, understood this, so his plan for Leon's debut in Hollywood and what would come after was very well thought out, with maximum advantage for him.

He hadn't figured on Saul but he would only regret that later. Truth is, Cadence did a great job.

When Leon had been to see enough people around town and made a good enough impression, Cadence let slip to one or two other agents, and to his assistant, who was really a spy from another agency (Cadence had long ago guessed this and played the little Mata Hari for all he was worth), that Leon had a development offer on the table from one of the big television networks. A deal that meant the network was developing a sitcom for the charming young Southerner to star in.

When the rumor was established enough, he sent out invitations to hear Leon sing at a dingy little comedy club called the Maestro on Melrose Boulevard in West Hollywood.

Normally, of course, no one would attend an event like this, but Cadence picked a Monday night, when he knew there were no movie premieres or basketball games on, and he picked a club small enough to mean that he could only fit about fifty people into the room.

This meant tickets became scarce and this meant people wanted them. Consequently, there was a decent turnout of middle-range power players in the Maestro when Leon walked to the mike and Rufus, a bucktoothed, red-haired pianist hired for the occasion, hit the opening chords of "I Get Along Without You Very Well."

The effect of that night on Leon's standing within the entertainment community in L.A. was dramatic, and before long there actually was a development offer on the table for him.

Cadence packaged Leon with David Trundle as the creators of the sitcom *Oh Leon!* with himself and Saul as executive producers.

The show was about a young lounge singer in Las Vegas, Leon Johnson, played, of course, by Leon (the network thought that Leon's real surname of Martini sounded too ethnic and alcoholic), who has to raise his cute little brother, Petey, and deal with his wacky fat neighbor, Stan, who is a croupier at one of the big casinos.

After a difficult pilot in which they went through three different kids until they got the right child actor to play little Petey, the network ordered thirteen more episodes.

Leon sang a different song every episode.

The show premiered in the fall.

LE JARDIN

CLAUDETTE AWOKE JUST AFTER DAWN, the clean sunlight coloring the city lightly to perfection. She looked at George sleeping peacefully and kissed him on the lips. He smiled but did not awaken. She quietly got out of bed and walked to the bathroom. She looked at herself in the mirror, enjoying the little lines of age that were beginning to form around her eyes. French women do not fear aging in the way that their American sisters do. She washed and dressed quietly and wrote a little note for George. She left it on the pillow.

> Cher Georges,
> If you awake before I return do not think
> me callous or rude but I have gone to
> the patisserie to fetch breakfast for us.
> Thank you for sleeping with me.
> Claudette.
> X

George kept the note until the day he died. In fact, it was burned with him, in his inside jacket pocket.

She quietly closed the apartment door and headed down the stairs. She didn't want to be alone in the elevator. She clicked open the little door within the giant green doors of the entrance to the building and stepped out onto the street.

The patisserie at the corner of Rue de Vaugirard and Rue Madam consistently wins awards for its croissants and brioche. In a city of exceptional bakers, it is an exceptional bakery. The counter staff have the usual bleary-eyed grumpiness of all bakers from having to rise in the middle of the night. Like yeast.

Claudette was not too surprised to see a line of construction workers waiting for their take-out breakfasts; there was a lot of renovation being done at the nearby Catholic Institute of Paris.

Rather than wait in a line of amorous laborers, she decided to take a little walk around the park. The Jardin du Luxembourg is closed at night. Municipal workers open the gates at around seven A.M. and early-morning joggers plod around unimpeded by mothers with strollers or tourists who will show up later in the day.

It had been a long time since Claudette had been in the gardens this early and she wondered why. It was at its most beautiful at the beginning or the end of the day.

She strolled toward the boating pond at the park's center and sat down on one of the green metal chairs thoughtfully laid out by the local council.

She thought of the sex with George. She thought of their meeting and marveled at the intensity of emotion, the depth of feeling that she already had for him. She was a little frightened that he would not feel the same way this morning but she instinctively knew that would not be the case.

She was lost in reverie when she felt the bony old hand tap on her shoulder. She turned around to see a pitifully unpleasant-looking old man. His bloodshot, watery eyes seemed to have the look of a bludgeoned dead squid. White sprigs of hair peeped from under his black beret, sprouted from his ears, and crept from the nostrils of his giant sponge nose like little pallid hedges decorated with a nicotine tint. He had no bottom teeth and suspiciously perfect top ones that looked a little slack. In fact, they dropped down as he spoke, almost falling from his mouth.

"Do you have a cigarette for an old man, daughter?" he croaked in a voice from a bad character actor's repertoire.

Claudette smiled and dug a Lucky Strike from the pack in her purse. She lit it for the old man, who shut his eyes and inhaled deeply, drawing the blue smoke down as far as his breath would allow. He held the smoke, then released it in an almost euphoric exhale.

He looked at the label on the cigarette filter. "American?" he said.

She nodded. "They make good cigarettes, then don't smoke them."

The old man laughed, phlegm rattling around in his loose, jangly frame.

"I like Americans," he said. "They are lovers of liberty and civil disobedience and science. They are a great people. Have you been there?"

"Once," she replied. "I didn't like it very much."

He nodded. "I have never been. Perhaps that is why I like it so much."

She smiled at him. She felt sympathetic toward him, partially because he seemed so pitiful and partly because she had been so well fucked a few hours before. She was still glowing a little.

The old man sat beside her. "I don't talk to many people. They lose interest in you when you are old. Never grow old."

"I don't think I have a say in that," she said.

"I've been here in the park all night, you know. They close the gates but I have my ways. Policemen, hah! They are always locking gates and pushing people around, but not me. Laws were made to be broken, I say."

"You slept in the park?" she asked, concerned.

"I don't sleep anymore," he sighed. "I stay awake all night and listen to stories, or tell stories with the others. Do you want to hear a story?"

She looked at her watch but she wouldn't have felt right saying no.

"It won't take long." The old man grinned. "It's about a man who made these." He tapped his filthy mahogany fingernail against the glass of Claudette's watch face.

A strangely invasive gesture.

L'HORLOGER

ONCE UPON A TIME there was a clockmaker who believed in the divine right of kings.

His name was Jean Mancona and he came from the country town of Arras in northern France. His father was a clockmaker of no little skill, and nobility from all over the region came to visit his store and please themselves by wasting money on exquisitely crafted timepieces. It was not as if they had any need of them—who would ever give them trouble for being late?—but they were in fashion.

The king liked them.

Little Jean was a sickly, sensitive child, a pale boy who timidly avoided the roughhousing of the other children in the schoolyard. He was forever the victim of bullies who pressured him to give over any food or toys he may have been carrying with him. He soon learned to carry nothing he valued, but always had a little something to placate his tormentors.

One day in the schoolyard, two of the older boys were picking on him. They had him pinned to the ground and were tweaking his nose and ears, making him squeal like a little runty piglet. Their fun was abruptly ended when Maximilien, a boy his own age, demanded that the bullies leave poor little Jean alone.

Maximilien was a quiet boy, very clever in his studies but aloof from his classmates. The other children said he was sad because his mother and father were dead and he was being raised by his aged grandparents, who were so old and cold they were almost dead too.

The bullies turned on Maximilien and demanded to know who he thought he was. Max stood his ground and when the first and bigger of the two bullies approached him he hit him so hard in the face with a rock he had concealed in his hand that the bully's nose instantly gushed blood, terrifying him and his cohort.

The two aggressors ran off promising dire reprisals.

Jean got up and went over to his Samaritan. "Thank you," he said.

Max said nothing, just gave a little joyless smile. Embarrassed and shy.

"I hate those two, they're the worst. They hit me even after I give them things."

"Perhaps they learned a lesson today," said Max.

Little Jean nodded, in awe of his new best friend.

From that day on Jean stuck to his protector like glue. As promised, the two bullies, who were called Stefan and Charles, attempted a higher authority for justice. They told their teacher that Max had hit Stefan with a rock for no reason whatsoever. The teacher, who had been around naughty children all his adult life, as well as all of his childhood of course, saw through the tales.

He gave Max a verbal reprimand for being a little too rough, saying that the one who resorts to violence first is the moral loser. Max agreed, saying the bullies had been using violence way before he had arrived on the scene. The teacher said not to talk back but he almost winked at the boy, impressed as he was with the intense youngster's gumption.

The teacher had another reason for going lightly on Max. Max was the star pupil in school and the teacher had him in mind for a big job.

A new king had recently been crowned, Louis XVI, and he was set to visit the town. As the brightest and best in the school, little

Maximilien was chosen to read an address in Latin to the monarch, some fawning piece of rubbish about kings being God's ambassadors on Earth. Something that underlined the ancien régime—basically the birthright of the nobility to use others in any way they saw fit.

The king listened intently as the beautiful, serious little boy read with passion and he thought to himself how magnificent that one so young could have such a grasp of loyalty to the throne. He was moved.

"The little lad had quite an effect on me," he would say later to his favorite prostitute.

Max was proud and honored to be in the presence of the divine Louis, and his friend Jean almost burst with pride.

Bliss was it that dawn to be alive, and very heaven to be young—that beautiful day when Louis was still a tin-pot god and Maximilien Robespierre was still a hoodwinked child.

Years passed and the boys grew into themselves, Jean going into his father's profession, much to the old boy's delight. Jean was well suited for long periods of time sitting at a desk studying and creating intricate and delicate machinery.

Maximilien, the joyless protector of the less fortunate, studied the law and became a famous barrister, winning a celebrated case of the time allowing some local people in St. Omer to install newfangled lightning rods as developed by the wonderful American Benjamin Franklin. Maximilien was so successful he was made a judge at an early age.

Now there would be justice.

Maximilien admired Ben Franklin, he was very interested in Franklin's scientific work, which seemed to suggest that there was no such thing as divine rule. That the ancien régime was perhaps erroneous. Perhaps there was more to the Universe than the order dictated by the clergy and the nobility.

The people in power, the nobility, using the theatricality and superstition of the Church to spoon-feed the masses any old cabbage they required them to swallow.

Maximilien also read and reread the works of Jean-Jacques Rousseau.

The man who had written: "Man is born free but everywhere is in chains."

And, "You are lost if you forget that the fruits of the Earth belong to no one, and the Earth itself belongs to everyone."

Which actually native American people had been saying to each other for thousands of years, but they didn't write it down, so it didn't count. Also, at this time most of them were still tucked away quietly in their own private paradise awaiting the arrival of enlightenment, Christianity, and genocide. Maximilien's radical views alarmed his old friend Jean when the two met for dinner, as they did every month. Jean agreed that there certainly seemed to be change in the air but that it must be steered by King Louis himself, who had a divine mission from the Lord to shepherd His flock.

Jean would not ever make a stance against the king. It would be wrong, it would be treason, it would be heresy, it would be satanic.

Surrounded as he was by clocks, Jean could not see what time it was.

The clocks understood, they kept moving, motion, following the truth that change is the nature of God's mind, and resistance to it is the source of great pain.

Maximilien and Jean finally faced each other on opposite sides of a bloody revolution. By this time Max was known as "the Incorruptible"—he wouldn't let anything get in the way of his principles.

He found himself sitting in judgment of his old friend, whom he had saved so long ago.

Jean was brought before the Revolution for helping to smuggle aristocrats to safety. They had been his best customers, he knew many of them personally. He could not just let them die. They had families.

Jean said it was the will of God that the king rule.

Maximilien said that God had changed His mind. He was correct in this respect.

Maximilien sent his friend to the guillotine because principle came first. A scientific fact that surely Jean, as an artisan, understood.

Certain laws cannot be broken.

But Maximilien was incorrect in this respect.

Allowances can always be made for your friends to disagree with you. Disagreement, vehement disagreement, is healthy. Debate is impossible without it. Evil does not question itself, only hope questions itself. Even the incorruptible are corruptible if they cannot accept the possibility of being mistaken.

Infallibility is a sin in any man.

All laws can be broken and are.

Often.

Like when a bumblebee flies or an ancient regime is toppled.

MARAT

"IT'S A TERRIBLY SAD STORY," said Claudette.

"Yes."

"Is it true?"

"Oh yes, all of it. Well, I put in the part about the bumblebee. I thought it was a nice touch," said the old man.

Claudette smiled at him.

"I knew Robespierre, you know," he said. "I didn't like him much. Always fussing with his hair. He was a cold fish. He told me that story himself."

Claudette looked again at the old man. She had at first thought him a charming old eccentric but now suspected that he was deranged.

She wanted to get away but felt guilty.

"I really must go now, I have someone waiting," she said.

"A lover?"

Claudette blushed slightly.

The old man grinned. "I know about lovers, I know about love. I wasn't always like this, I was young and pretty and I had my Simone. History turned me to this. Fearful slander about me written by frightened sheep—that's what did this to me. I wasn't old, I was young, I still had work to do. A woman—a Girondin woman!—killed me and still

I got old. My comrades and I, we changed the entire world and were never forgiven for that. The liars made me old and they made me ugly and they made me mad but I was never those things."

He was getting animated now and Claudette felt a little alarmed. She looked around for a jogger but there didn't seem to be any.

"You know why they do that to me, daughter? You know why they attack me?"

Claudette shook her head.

"Because I dared to dream that things could be different. That there was a point in trying to make a change. Nothing is written, daughter, the world is magical and mystical but not in the way they told us. The magic and glory and wonder of the world is for everyone, not just for kings and princes and all those unworthy braggarts. For you and me, Les Sans Culottes. Never accept the status quo! Ask yourself this: If the Duke of Brunswick ever gets here, what have you done that will get you hung? Eh? Eh?"

He cackled, spittle forming at the side of his mouth.

Claudette edged away.

She found his ranting disturbing but didn't feel particularly threatened, the old man was too frail for that, but she didn't want a scene or any unpleasantness.

She had felt so good only a few moments before. She wanted to be back in the warm bed with her Georges.

The old man rattled on. "I'm not French—by birth, I mean. I'm Swiss. But I was never neutral. A pox on neutrality—cowardice and opportunism. I am French"—he pointed to his sunken chest as if it contained great treasure—"here."

She got up to leave.

The old man put his hand on her arm. His look softened.

"You have no children?" he asked.

She shook her head.

"You are too full and fresh not to have children. You must have them."

She nodded, pulling away.

"Name one for me," he croaked.

“What’s your name?” she asked softly.

“Jean-Paul,” he said, then closed his eyes.

Claudette trod briskly to the park entrance. The old revolutionary watched her leave, then walked over the water on the boating pond and back into the lies of imperialist history.

A NEW TESTAMENT

IT WAS STILL DARK BUT THE TOP WAS DOWN. He felt the warm wind blowing his hair, his tongue found the dried blood on the side of his mouth. His ribs and legs ached and his head felt like there was a tight band wrapped around it. He felt his heart palpitating as his body shook off the alcohol and he felt the cold stickiness of his urine-soaked trousers. He turned his head and looked at T-Bo, who was driving.

"Where are we?" he said.

"A1A. I didn't wanna take I-95, 'cause you never know who you gonna meet there. Also you look pretty beat up. Cops see me driving down the freeway at night in this ride with a white guy in your condition, they gonna wanna talk to me, ask me some questions."

Fraser nodded, felt a stab of pain in his neck, and decided to stay still for a while.

"Where are we going?"

"I got a buddy in rehab in one of them treatment centers in Delray Beach, 'bout ten miles up the road here. We gonna see him. I called him on his cell but no joy."

"Why are we going there?"

"I said I would bring him something and, well, I had to split town, some guys are lookin for me. This is kind of their car too."

"This is a stolen car?" asked Fraser.

"Not exactly, I share it with my homies, Silky and Wilson, but they a little mad at me right now. I took the money we got from you and the car and took off. When they get some metal they gonna come after me. I dissed them bad."

"I see. I can imagine they are a little irate at being 'dissed.' "

T-Bo glanced at Fraser. "You fuckin with me?"

Fraser smiled without opening his eyes. T-Bo laughed.

"I can't believe you, man. You get beat up bad and go through what you went through and you fuckin with me. You got balls, Homes."

"Thank you," said Fraser.

"I can give you your money back," said T-Bo.

"Keep it," said Fraser. "I don't need it anymore."

"What you talking about? Everybody needs a little money."

"Not me. Not anymore. I'm done with it."

"You prob'ly still a little groggy. I'll get back to you on that."

Fraser drifted off again for a few moments. When he opened his eyes again he looked at the condo buildings and the palm trees and caught glimpses of the sacred Atlantic through the gaps between the brassy neon of the motels and hotels.

"It's beautiful here."

T-Bo nodded. "Better in the daytime. You a preacher?" he said.

Fraser thought for a moment, went over his recent history in his head.

"Yes," he replied. "I am a flawed and beautiful child of God. I walk in His image and His Amazing Grace. I was lost but now I'm found."

T-Bo looked at the bloody, beaten drunk next to him. "What was you doin in that gay club? If you a preacher."

"I walk among the children of the Universe. I am no longer impeded by the constraints of fear, cowardice, and opportunism. I go where I please."

"Yeah, but bein a faggot is wrong. It's against the Bible."

"I don't read the Bible, I am only interested in the word of God."

"Well, the word of God is in the Bible."

"Yes, it is but it's a lot of other places too. The Bible has been through at least half a dozen translations by the time you read it. Plus, when the word of God is infected by the hand of man, that is, written down, it is tainted."

"You saying the Bible is infected?"

"Yes, Praise Jesus. Amen."

T-Bo shook his head and drove on in silence for a while. Then he asked, "You a faggot?"

Fraser painfully turned and looked at him. "If I say yes will you beat me up again?"

T-Bo looked away, embarrassed. "I'm sorry, man. I did wrong. I'm changing my ways. You're a Christian. Forgive me."

Fraser smiled and closed his eyes. "I forgive you," he said.

They drove on in silence for a few moments.

"What is the true word of God, then?" asked T-Bo softly.

Fraser didn't move. T-Bo thought perhaps he had passed out again but after a moment he spoke. "Help ither sodjirs," he said.

"Say what?"

"Help others," Fraser repeated.

"That's it?" said T-Bo.

"That's it," said Fraser.

Delray Beach is like a little time capsule on the east coast of Florida, wedged between the retirement communities of Boca Raton and beige celebrity hideaways of Palm Beach.

The beach itself is long and sandy and unspoiled. The coast road is peppered with beautiful homes and surprisingly cheap hotels. The main drag, Atlantic Avenue, is a throwback to the 1950s. Little mom-and-pop stores and burger joints that don't have twenty-five hundred branches elsewhere. A railway track runs through the center of town and every half hour or so the crossing bells ring, the barricades come down, and a giant freighter will rumble through.

Further up the street, toward the ocean, there is a drawbridge over the inland waterway, a pleasure boat canal that runs from Maine all the way down to Miami. When the drawbridge is up and a train is coming through it can take half an hour to travel three hundred yards down this street no matter how pimped out your Chevy Caprice is.

The town is popular with middle-aged bikers, optometrists on Harley-Davidsons, who roar up and down the road taking full advantage of Florida's no-helmet law to show off their rebelliousness, their danger, and their male pattern baldness.

At this time of night, though, the wild motorcycle gangs of Delray were tucked up in their stripy pajamas and the street was deserted. The restaurants and stores were closed. T-Bo made his way along Atlantic Avenue to the ocean. He parked the Caprice at a broken parking meter on the coast road and woke Fraser.

Fraser rubbed his eyes and looked out at the moonlight throwing white and silver flashes on the blue-black sparkling sea. He remembered Saknussem and shuddered.

"We gotta get you cleaned up, man, you a little stinky right now. Messing up my ride."

Fraser nodded.

T-Bo helped him out of the car and Fraser limped toward the ocean.

"Where you going?" asked T-Bo.

"I have been born again. I must be baptized."

"No, there's a shower here, people use it to clean the sand off themselves when they sunbathing. It's fresh water. Use that."

"No, I have to go to the ocean."

"Crap," said T-Bo. But he followed Fraser over the dark, deserted beach to the shore.

Fraser started taking off his clothes.

"You can't get nekkid here, man, you'll get arrested."

"What will they do? Charge me for having a body?"

T-Bo looked at Fraser's white skin, alien in the moonlight. "They'll charge you for showin it. No offense, but Victoria's Secret you ain't."

Fraser ignored him and stripped off. He walked into the cold water. The shock of the water had a sobering effect on him but he was changed. Changed forever. He wanted no part of his old self or the

Press Bar or his old life in television. He had been through the fire and had been tempered.

He worked for God now and no one else.

He opened his eyes underwater and there in his blurred, dark, salty vision was Virgil the poet.

He smiled at Fraser and said, "Congratulations, Rabbi."

Fraser smiled back and then blinked.

The poet was gone and only the sea remained.

He returned to the surface.

A doctor would probably have diagnosed Fraser with having some kind of brain damage, some kind of internal trauma that occurred during the beating, but as far as Fraser was concerned his brain had not been damaged.

It had been improved.

He ducked down under the surface and felt the surf cleansing him and massaging his bruised limbs.

T-Bo looked up and down the shoreline but there was no one around.

"Fuck it," he said out loud. Then he stripped naked and dived into the water.

T-Bo swam across to Fraser, who was floating on his back looking at the moonlight. He touched the beaten man's face tenderly. Fraser turned and looked at him directly in the eye. T-Bo's heart pounded and he felt himself get hard.

He kissed Fraser softly on the lips.

Fraser smiled at him.

"I'm not having sex at the moment," said Fraser gently, "and I have to tell you that if and when I do, it will probably be with someone who has ladies' equipment."

T-Bo was at a loss. Deeply embarrassed and angry, he wanted to hit Fraser again.

Fraser saw his rage building and spoke to him again. He had a calmness and an authority in his voice. No aggression. He was mildly surprised by the clarity of his tone—he was not yet fully aware of what had happened to him.

"There is no point in being angry, my friend. I did not make you what you are any more than you did yourself. You are a beautiful child of God and nothing you desire is shameful. You could drown me right here and compound your misery, you could run away and your pain will follow you, or you can let me help you."

T-Bo had never broached this subject in his life. This was the source of his shame. All his life he felt he was wrong, a freak, despising himself for what he felt. His moment of grace had arrived. The miracle was that he honored it by asking a question.

"How can you help me?" he said.

Fraser grinned. "I'll find you a nice boyfriend."

There was a quiet moment between the two men as they stood in the dark water. The danger of the situation was palpable and Fraser knew that T-Bo *was* thinking about killing him. T-Bo was thinking about killing Fraser but he couldn't do it. The crazy Scottish preacher was right.

T-Bo was, like Saint Paul, that which he always professed to despise. He felt an enormous weight leave him. He felt himself laughing, real, beautiful, hysterical, transcendent laughter.

Fraser laughed along with him.

The two men laughing—naughty children on a midnight swim.

After they had bathed, T-Bo got dressed and ran off to find Fraser something clean to wear. The only thing he could get was a bright orange floral sundress that an overweight lady had left to dry on a low hotel balcony.

He brought it back to Fraser, who was delighted with it.

"It's beautiful. When I was a wee boy, I remember my mother telling me a story about a man who grew nasturtiums on his roof. This is the color of nasturtiums."

"What are nasturtiums?" asked T-Bo.

"They're flowers. They are bright orange. Like this."

T-Bo nodded. He laughed at the sight of the big Scotsman in the sundress but then stopped when he saw that Fraser's feelings were hurt.

"Sorry, man," he said. "It's just—maybe you would have done better in that nightclub you was in if you had been wearing that."

Fraser smiled.

They sat down on the beach and watched the sun rise over the horizon. Fraser wiggled a broken front tooth loose and spat it from his mouth.

"Ah, that's the ticket," he said.

"You okay?" asked T-Bo.

"Never better," said Fraser, tasting his own blood in his mouth.

"You need to get back to Miami?" T-Bo said.

"No," said Fraser. "I need to go to Alabama. I have been asked to go there to preach the word of God. That's what I must do else I will end in the belly of the whale again."

T-Bo nodded. "Can I take you there?" he said.

"Yes," said Fraser.

Fraser was sleeping on the sand when T-Bo's cell phone rang. T-Bo answered and had a short conversation with the caller. Then he woke Fraser.

"Come on," he said. "You gotta meet Vermont."

And so Fraser began to rise.

THE ROAD TO GOD: SEVEN

OH LEON! HAD A TOUGH SLOT. It premiered against an established sitcom, *Roomies,* on one rival network and a new cop show, *Ballerina Detective,* on another. *Roomies* was the most popular show on television. It was a youthful, upbeat comedy about a group of six rich white twenty-somethings in Boston who had plenty of cash for disposable goods and air travel but not enough money to find their own apartments, so they had to share. None of them had any friends who weren't white. The cast were attractive and likable and the scripts were good.

It was a very unusual show indeed.

On the other hand, *Ballerina Detective* was standard TV fare. It was about a woman named Jenny Dakota who was a dancer with the New York City Ballet Company and for some reason also worked undercover for the FBI investigating serial killers. In the first episode she caught a crazed psychotic, danced the lead in *Swan Lake,* and still had time for a cheeky little joke with her partner, Jack Hardiman, a tough FBI Special Agent who had to pretend to be a ballet dancer in order to maintain their cover—with hilarious results!

There was an obvious sexual chemistry between the two leads, and although the show tested well in market research, it appealed directly to the same demographic as *Roomies,* and that audience—

women and gay men who love too much—was far too loyal to leave its favorite show.

This was before the rise of cable TV, so there were only three real players in the TV ratings game. The three big networks.

The network that *Oh Leon!* aired on, ABN—the American Broadcasting Network—was pleased with the initial figures for Leon's show. Although the total numbers were still well in favor of *Roomies,* there was a significant audience of males ages eighteen to thirty-five for Leon.

Then, after only three weeks, *Ballerina Detective* was axed and replaced with *America's Funniest Accidents,* a cheap clip show that consisted mostly of disastrous wedding mishaps caught on home video cameras. ABN moved *Oh Leon!* to Wednesday nights, where the only competition was a tired old family drama called *The Richardsons* and a lame high-concept sitcom called *Alien Monkey, M.D.,* starring a cute puppet as a friendly extraterrestrial chimpanzeeish doctor who shared a practice with a grumpy old doctor and a sexy girl doctor.

Oh Leon! became a hit, first with the target audience of men ages eighteen to thirty-five, who liked Leon's comedy neighbor Stan, played by roly-poly Midwest comedian Bo Ness. Bo joked about farting and beer, and regular American guys could relate. In time, though, women started watching the show too, because of Leon's looks and his great voice. Everyone loved the song at the end of each episode; eventually it became a national obsession to catch the closing number on *Oh Leon!* every week.

The character of little Petey, Leon's fictional younger brother, was not well liked and was dropped after twelve episodes. The child actor who played him, Jonathon Daimler-Thomason, went on to star as Pucky the clairvoyant midget in the blockbuster movie *Chariots of Magic.*

Over its first season of twenty-four episodes, *Oh Leon!* evolved into a show about two guys, Leon and Stan, who live next door to each other and are trying to make their way in the tough town of Las Vegas, Nevada, although, of course, the show was shot on a soundstage in Los Angeles, California. Leon's character was that of a caring man looking (unsuccessfully) for the right girl so that he could settle down and marry.

Bo Ness's character was the fat guy in his mid-thirties who liked to drink beer, watch football, and date strippers.

Do these guys get along?

No, sir! With hilarious results!

Off camera, Leon and Bo, his costar, got along famously. They both shared a love of obvious, pneumatic women and partying. They did the talk-show circuit together, joking on couches, and then Leon would get up to sing while Bo looked impressed.

They attended movie premieres and industry parties and became fixtures on the Hollywood circuit, always surrounded by blond, shiny women. Saul was everywhere that Leon went too, keeping an eye on him, making sure things didn't get out of hand, but he stayed in the background as much as a three-hundred-pound sweaty man can. He was noticed by the press, however, and the physiques of Saul and Bo got the little gang their nickname—the Fat Pack. Although Leon was as lean as a rail, he was seen as the leader, but anyone who spent any time around the brothers soon guessed who was really in charge.

The money was not terrific at first—season one salaries never are, and season two is not much better—but Leon and Saul were also producers of the show, so they'd get a piece of the real action when and if the show was sold into syndication (repeat showings on America's hundreds of small syndicated TV stations, not to mention foreign sales).

For that to kick in the show had to stay on the air for about five years or 105 episodes—the recognized number that was the industry standard to make a syndication sale. Given the viewing figures at the end of season one, that looked highly likely.

Season two went even better, and at the end of that year Saul began to exercise the power that being an executive producer, brother, and manager to Leon had given him.

The first two years the show was on the air and his brother was becoming a star, Saul had trodden carefully. He was a little unsure of how to deal with the network executives and his fellow producers but they started kissing his ass anyway because even if he wasn't really aware of how much power he was attaining, they were. He found his jokes got funnier, doughnuts would be carried to him even if he didn't ask, and strangest of all, women started to come on to him.

He couldn't believe it. All his life women had looked at him with a mixture of pity and disgust and he had grown to hate them, all of them, and now they had changed the rules. He was attractive now to some women because he had money and power. That made him hate them even more but at least now he could have revenge.

The first time a woman approached him without first getting paid was in a nightclub called the Foxy on the Sunset Strip. He had gone there with Leon and Bo and their coterie the night after the first big article about the Fat Pack had appeared in *Peephole* magazine, the weekly celebrity Bible.

A tall, stunning brunette in a silver dress came over to him as he stood in the VIP enclosure. She took him by the hand and led him to the ladies' restroom, to the cheers of Leon and Bo and the laughter of the ladies in the Plastic Pussy Posse, who later became known as the Snatch Batch.

She squeezed him into a stall and took his pants down, lifted his massive gut with the top of her head, and sucked his tiny penis while she gently scratched his enormous, swollen scrotum with her taloned fingernails for the thirty seconds it took for him to come in her mouth.

She swallowed his juice, licked her lips, and pulled up his pants for him, then she left without saying a word, although she put her card in his jacket pocket on the way out.

It read, "I'm Candy. Call me, sweetie," and had her number.

He sat down in the stall after she left. This didn't happen to him, this is the kind of thing that happened to Leon. Leon must have paid her, put her up to it.

He started crying, his heart breaking on every exhale.

After he'd pulled himself together, he headed back out to the club.

"Thanks, bro," he said as he returned to Leon, who was drinking a tequila and looking out at the dance floor trying to make his mind up who to fuck.

"For what?" asked Leon.

"The hooker in the john. That was very cool."

"I didn't do that, Saul. She was flying solo."

Saul had never felt better.

He later called the number and it turned out the woman, whose name was Candy Chambers, was in fact a hooker but she said she'd wanted to give Saul a freebie because she "liked his style."

She was a very astute businesswoman, and over the years he was in Hollywood, Saul spent hundreds of thousands of dollars for her services and she would eventually help topple his empire.

Cadence Powers became a pain in the ass to Saul, as did David Trundle. They both thought they knew the best way the show should go, from story lines to guest stars, even trying to pick the song that Leon would sing at the end of the episode. Saul began to feel that they were hindering him, trying to get between him and Leon, so he went to work on his brother, telling him that Cadence was trying to cheat them on their points on the syndication deal and that Trundle was saying that he was a bad actor and the show was only a hit because of the scripts that he and the other writers came up with.

Leon told Saul that he had to protect them from these guys.

Saul said he'd try.

During contract negotiations for seasons three and four, Cadence and Trundle found themselves being edged out. They fought like hell but the network knew that the power lay with Saul, that Leon and Saul were an unbreakable unit.

Saul wanted Cadence and Trundle gone, they were gone.

They sued, of course, standard business practice under the circumstances, and received, out of court, a sweet kiss-off financially but nothing like the amount they would have made if they had managed to stay in the game.

Saul was now in sole charge of Leon, his career and the show. Bo Ness's representatives tried to stop that but they also knew that, bottom line, Leon would be fine without the show but this was Bo's moment in the sun and they had to stay in there no matter what. *Oh Leon!* could not go on without Leon but it might without Bo.

They swallowed their pride and watched as Saul took the reins. Leon had become one of the biggest TV stars in America and all the old orphans, The Bastards, came out of the woodwork selling their stories and trying to cash in or get near their former school chum but Saul kept them all at bay.

He built a fortress of lackeys around his brother.

One of the supermarket tabloids found the old court records about their mother and that became a story for a few weeks until Saul booked Leon on one of the phony serious news shows on television and had him cry in an interview along with the journalist/ridiculous old matron who was asking the prearranged questions.

It actually helped Leon's career. Poor little orphan boy who single-handedly raised his obese brother.

America wept.

No one found out the truth about their fathers. That secret had died with Sophie.

They became richer and richer and more and more famous.

Of course, they moved from their apartment on Sweetzer but they wanted to stay together, so they bought an eleven-thousand-square-foot home in the Hollywood Hills that had been built in the French Baronial style in 1933. The same year Hitler had risen to power in Germany.

The boys lived in opposite wings of the house. Leon's wing was reserved for himself and whatever famous actress, singer, or model he was dating at that moment. He had fun but if ever he got too close to a woman, as he genuinely wanted to, Saul would have her removed in some way. He couldn't have Leon being used by some bitch.

In Saul's wing, he began to indulge in a gluttony that was breathtaking. He gave in to his every whim for food or sex or prescription medication. He loved prostitutes, peanut butter, and Vicodin, sometimes, many times, all three at once.

He hired hookers. Candy Chambers became his pimp and his regular accomplice in his private kinky sex games. He got heavily into sadomasochism in a dominant role. He liked nothing better than "turning out" a young girl. This meant introducing a girl to S&M by beating her ass black and blue with a paddle and then taking a shit on her face as he jerked himself off and Candy whispered obscenities in his ear. That really turned him on.

He got a rep as being a "tough trick" among L.A. prostitutes but work's work and he wasn't as bad as some action-movie producers.

As long as Saul made money, no one felt in a position to judge him, the only morality in Hollywood being success, and the girls saw themselves as hapless victims of a ruthless, male-dominated town. Every now and again, a hooker would refuse to indulge Saul, and once a girl named Dawn Hawthorn, who was just in from Nebraska and new to prostitution, was so repulsed by him she actually left the game, took a pay cut, and got a real job as a waitress.

Leon had been dating Roseanne Hannah for about two months when he came to see Saul. Roseanne was a serious actress and had been nominated for a Golden Globe for her portrayal of Barbara, the female cop who has to choose between her career and the man she loves, in the movie *Fingerplay*. Roseanne had stayed in touch with David Trundle and had a copy of his latest script. He had returned to his first love, writing screenplays, and had produced a brilliant, intense, dramatic work based on the true story of *Tootsiepop Ted,* the Atlanta serial killer. It was called *Killing by Starlight*.

Roseanne had read it and given it to Leon because she thought he would be perfect for the leading role of Detective Kenny Irwin, the slow-talking Southern policeman who finally catches the maniac. A tough but likable maverick cop who doesn't play by the rules.

Leon read the script before taking it to Saul. He had never done that before but he really liked Roseanne and he knew how smart she was. (If she was really smart, she would have given the script to Saul first.)

He told Saul he desperately wanted to do the movie. He wanted to do a serious role. He was tired of being some lightweight TV guy, he wanted a serious role in a proper big, dramatic movie. He wanted to win an award. Plus, think of the publicity angle—they used to ride on the bus that Tootsiepop Ted drove! Saul listened, took a deep breath, and said he would read the script and see what he could do.

Saul did read the script and was surprised to find that he agreed with Roseanne and his brother. It might be a smart move for Leon to do a dramatic role, the sitcom wouldn't last forever, and look at Frank Sinatra in *From Here to Eternity.* And the publicity angle really was good.

He called Trundle, and although the two men had been involved in a bitter lawsuit only eighteen months previously, they had both been in town long enough to know that business comes first.

Saul said he had read *Killing by Starlight* and wanted to know what studio it was at. Trundle said it wasn't anywhere, he hadn't sold it yet.

Saul offered him a million dollars for it and Trundle agreed. Done deal.

Saul owned the project and could now set it up wherever he pleased with his brother as the star. He made a mental note to get rid of Roseanne.

Roseanne didn't mind being dumped.

Trundle had promised her 10 percent if Leon took the bait. He gave her fifty thousand dollars.

Trundle had actually written the role for Leon. The first night he talked to him, at his showcase on Melrose, Leon had mentioned that Tootsiepop Ted, who was in the news, having just lost yet another appeal that week, used to drive his school bus. Trundle had stored that away as a useful piece of information.

It was a little more difficult to set up the movie than Saul thought. Although Leon was a big comedy star on TV, the studios were wary of him in a dramatic role. Eventually he got a deal at Uniwarn Pictures, though with the stipulation that he get a big female star to play the part of Blanche, the detective's loyal and beautiful wife. That was easy enough. Leon had moved on from Roseanne to Meg Roberts, America's flame-haired, green-eyed, twenty-million-dollar-a-movie sweetheart. She had met him at a charity event for underprivileged dogs and left her husband of three years for him that very night.

She jumped at the chance of working with him.

Saul was slightly worried because she was as nuts as his late mother and was well known for being an ardent follower of Brainyism.

* * *

Brainyism was the latest funky religion that was catching on with the privileged and bored in the entertainment business in Los Angeles. A bit like the way Christianity had caught on with upper-class Romans.

Brainastics, or Boondtists, as they called themselves, were members of a cult that had built up in Hollywood around the teachings of a bankrupt ex–carnival roustabout who had died in the 1970s, Darren Boondt.

Boondt had given up the carnival and had come west in 1956 to seek his fortune. He failed in the profession he thought he would excel in—writing commercial jingles—achieving only one minor success, a radio ad he wrote and sang for Kliphorn canned peas. It went, to the tune of "Frere Jacques":

Kliphorn canned peas please
Kliphorn canned peas please
For me and you
And Grandma too
They go well with chicken
They go well with chicken
And taters too
Taters too.

Not much, but it kept him going for a few months while the ads ran on the local stations. He got no follow-up work, so he had to improvise some way of making cash. Boondt had grown up in the thirties when people believed in the supernatural power of computers. In the fifties, science was still all the rage, so he claimed to have invented a machine that he said could cleanse the soul, unleashing its true energy. It had a lot of wires and dials and the machine certainly looked the part but really it was just a blood pressure pump, some bits of a telephone and part of a prop a friend of his had managed to steal from the set of *This Island Earth* while working as an extra.

The customer or patient or devotee or whatever was hooked up to the machine by little suction cups cannibalized from a children's bow-and-arrow set, and then the operator or priest or technician or whatever would chant some gibberish about Jehovah, Ancient Egypt, and Cherokees. He thought he might be able to charge a few suckers a few bucks for it but was amazed at how popular it became. He invented a whole spiel and legend to go around the machine, which he called the Boondtdock.

"Plug In to the Power of God."

Predictably, once a few gullible movie stars fell for it, then the rest of the town followed in the hope that somehow moviestardomness would rub off on them if they did the things that movie stars did. Like have themselves connected to the Boondtdock and joining the Church of Brainyism, which is what you had to do in order for the Boondtdock to function properly.

Boondt came up with this after reading about tithing in the ancient church and finding out what it was.

The original Boondtdock was placed under glass and treasured as a sacred relic by the faithful. New, flashier Boondtdocks were built and some of the richer Brainastics had their own personal machines at home.

Boondt died young but rich and Brainyism became popular with people who were very ambitious and a bit stupid. It was the fastest-growing religion in America at the time and Meg Roberts was very involved.

Saul hated the thought of Leon being around these nutters but he needed Meg to get the movie made, so he took the risk. Brainastics were famous for their lack of humor and for being very sensitive about their faith. They would viciously counterattack anyone they even suspected of making fun of them or casting aspersions on their beliefs. In this respect they were like any other emerging religion.

The award-winning Scandinavian director Janus Borg was set to helm *Killing by Starlight,* and in the role of Tootsiepop Ted they got Guillame Maupassant, the classy French actor who had just won the Palm d'Or in Cannes for his role in *Le Pamplemousse du L'Horreur.*

They hired Stevie Zabadan, an expensive hack, to rewrite the role of Ted as a French immigrant. Two weeks before shooting was set to begin, Saul had a small party for the cast, some crew, the director, studio executives, and producers. Everyone was outside by the pool enjoying the beautiful California evening when Guillame and his companion arrived late, having just gotten off the plane from Paris.

Leon took one look at Claudette and he knew that this was it.

He was in love.

COMBAT

CLAUDETTE WAS IN LOVE.

It scared her that she should feel this way for a man she'd only just met and, over breakfast, she told him so. She said that if he felt threatened or weird, he should go and break her heart now before it got any worse.

George told her that he had the same problem, that he was in love with her and he wondered if he just felt that way because he was losing his marbles on account of his impending death. Thus they remained honest in the face of convention, and after finishing the pastries and coffee they went back to bed and made love again.

Their entire morning was spent enjoying each other until they were both spent, hungry, and a little bit stir crazy. They went out for lunch.

They had to go out because if they were indoors for more than half an hour together, they were pawing and mauling at each other, trying to climb inside each other. They needed the civilizing effect of polite society or they'd never get anything done.

They returned to Les Deux Magots, the café where they had met, because they were too stoned on their carnally released endorphins to think of anywhere else. They sat at the same table where Claudette had lit George's cigarette the night before and they caught up on the blanks that they had in each other's stories.

Claudette grew thoughtful when listening to George, and when he asked her what was on her mind she hesitated, but he persisted.

"We have to do battle," she said.

"No," said George. "It is a foregone conclusion. It's lung cancer. I'm not going through what my folks went through. It's painful, undignified, and shitty. I'm screwed. I'm not going to spend the time I have left with my arse hanging out of a hospital gown with everybody telling me I look younger with no hair. When the pain becomes too great, I'll jump."

But Claudette would not back down. She was stronger and fiercer than any hostile lawyer he had faced in a Scottish courtroom; also she said the battle was not only for him, it was for her.

"Death has always snuck up on me and taken what I love in a surprise attack. This time I can see him coming and I will do battle with him. I will not ever back down from the son of a bitch!"

George fell in love with her again.

"I can't," he said.

"You don't have to. I can," she said. And she took out her cell phone.

Alain Pantelic was the preeminent cancer specialist in Europe. He had finally stopped treating individual patients about seven years ago and devoted his time to research against his hated enemy.

In quiet moments, away from work or colleagues, he gave cancer a personality. He saw it as a soulless civil servant who wouldn't bend the rules for a child or someone who had extenuating circumstances, and he loathed it for that.

He never talked to anyone about this; his colleagues and his wife, also a doctor, would have considered it fanciful and frivolous, so he attacked his foe in his quiet, detached, methodical way. He was as fearsome a warrior as anyone had ever faced, and every now and again, he felt he had the bastard on the ropes.

But today was not one of those days.

He had agreed to talk to George as a favor to Claudette, whom he had known for years—Guillame had been one of his best friends, the two men had grown up together. He had been almost as crushed as she was when he died.

She called him from the restaurant and he was in his office, only a few blocks away, so they went straight over. He had a conversation with George, discussing the diagnosis that had been made at the Western Infirmary in Glasgow. Alain said they had excellent doctors there—very up on the latest techniques and innovations. They had to be—Scotland has the highest rate of cancer per capita in Western Europe.

Alain said some of the most exciting work in the research field was being done at Glasgow University. He got the name of George's physician and agreed to get in touch with him. He referred George to a doctor in Paris who would perform a duplicate and slightly more extensive set of tests but Alain's prognosis was the same as George's. He asked Claudette in French if she would ask George to leave the room.

In English, Claudette said, "Georges, he wants to talk to me alone. Is that okay with you?"

George said it was. He had actually understood the doctor anyway but didn't want to embarrass him. He seemed very nice. George shook the doctor's hand and said he would wait for Claudette outside.

Alain told Claudette that if the tests came back the way they had in Glasgow—and he suspected they would—then George was indeed doomed. They just weren't at the point where they could beat this.

"If I were practicing and he were a patient, I would encourage him to enter treatment immediately, in the attempt to prolong his life. You never know, but if he were my friend, as he is yours, I would tell him to get his affairs in order."

Claudette nodded grimly. The mad old man in the park flashed through her mind.

"Thank you for doing this," she said.

"Of course," said Alain, and they kissed on each cheek before she left.

Claudette got back on her cell and made an appointment for George's further tests and then booked them two seats on a plane flying to Scotland the following day.

"Why?" said George.

"We have to put your affairs in order," she said.

He felt a dull pain in the center of his back.

MIRACLES

THEY MET VERMONT at the children's playground next to the swing bridge. It was deserted this early in the morning but soon the tired mothers would arrive with their tiny insomniacs. Vermont burned a rock and inhaled deeply on the little glass pipe, sucking down the smoke to the core of his being. The effect was wonderful, uplifting and soothing all at the same time. It was as if he had been tightly stretched on the rack and then rescued, the bindings pulling at him had been released and he could relax again.

Heaven.

T-Bo and Fraser watched him.

T-Bo felt slightly guilty. Vermont had been in a treatment center in Delray as part of a court-ordered rehab funded by the Friends of African-American Youth, a humanitarian group supported by local businesses that contributed to the treatment costs of selected young addicts and alcoholics from the projects. They couldn't help them all; only the U.S. government had that kind of money and they certainly were not going to be spending it on young black junkies. Unless, of course, it was to lock them up.

Vermont had been caught burglarizing a pharmacy and his attorney had pled the junkie defense, although Vermont had been trying to get cash as much as anything else he could get his hands on. The judge bought it and sent him to the sobriety holiday camp in Delray: If he completed treatment and got a certificate from the center, he would get off with probation, but as it turned out, twenty-eight days without a smoke was just too much for the young man and he had called T-Bo the previous day begging him to bring up some rock. He had lasted fifteen days and it's not as if he was addicted like those other crazy bastards in the rehab. Just a little rock now and again, Jesus Christ, it wasn't like he did it every day.

Goddammit, he hadn't even had any in two weeks. Two weeks!

Shit, it was even legal somewhere in Europe—Holland or something.

Like many people, mostly politicians, Vermont confused the legality of a substance with its addictive properties, forgetting always the biggest killer of all, alcohol, was legal, white, and sanitized for your convenience.

He was a handsome young man—striking light brown eyes with whites that contrasted against his shiny black skin, but as he smoked, the whites of his eyes got redder and he seemed to disappear a little bit.

He offered the little burnt pipe to Fraser, who refused, then T-Bo, who did likewise. He got T-Bo to run through the story again.

"So you stole the ride and the money and took off with the guy you robbed?"

"Pretty much," said T-Bo.

"Them fuckas gonna shoot you, Dawg."

"Yeah, that'd be my guess too," said T-Bo.

Vermont nodded. He was twenty years old but had already seen too many of his friends die.

"What you gonna do?" he said.

"Stay away," said T-Bo. "I'm gonna drive the Rabbi here to his conference of preachers in Alabama."

Vermont nodded. "Negro, you're fuckin crazy."

T-Bo smiled. So did Vermont. "I'll come with you," he said. "They gonna kick me out of this place now anyhow, they test my piss an' my ass is goin to jail."

T-Bo looked at Fraser. "That okay with you, Rabbi?"

Fraser smiled and nodded.

"You're in," said T-Bo.

Vermont looked at Fraser. "The crazy old Jew in the pattern dress is running things here?"

T-Bo nodded. "He's a holyman, Vermont. He's not a Jew. The word *rabbi* means teacher. He taught me that."

Fraser smiled the bloody gap-tooth grin that made him look even more unhinged.

"I wouldn't mind being a Jew," he said. "They make great soup."

"Whatever," said Vermont. "You gotta drive me to the rehab, I gotta pick up my shit from my room."

Fraser put his hand on Vermont's shoulder, looked him in the eyes, and told him, "I think you would feel better if you didn't smoke anymore."

Vermont held Fraser's stare and suddenly knew the fool was right.

What the fuck was he doing with this crap? He took the pipe and the tiny grip-lock baggy of rocks and put them in the trash can next to the swings.

"Push it right down," said Fraser. "You don't want any children picking it up."

"Yeah, right," said Vermont, doing as Fraser asked. "Fuckin drag queen has me cleaning the damn park now."

T-Bo laughed.

Then there were three and they headed to the car.

The redness began to clear from Vermont's eyes.

Getting out of Delray proved to be slightly more difficult than T-Bo thought it was going to be.

Miracles Treatment Center made its money from insurance companies. They accepted coke addicts, heroin addicts, alcoholics, anorexics, overeaters, degenerate gamblers, sexual deviants, and anyone else who could get their policy to cover the cost of the recovery from whatever flavor of lunacy they were suffering from. Miracles sold the idea that all addictions were the same and that therefore they all required the same treatment. The center made no distinction between anorexics or alcoholics or addicts. This is extremely dubious medically (anorexia being an "addiction to not eating" is definitely a stretch) but makes wonderful financial sense.

One size fits all, very cost effective, and Miracles was not a charity, it was a business.

As Vermont snuck out from his room with his little backpack of belongings to meet Fraser and T-Bo, who were parked a block away, he was confronted by another patient, Cherry, a skeletal anorexic who had lost all her stripping work because she grossed out the customers.

Cherry had not slept in two days, she was high on not eating. She was starving. Her body was in an almost constant state of panic. It would not let her sleep; instead, it sent her out to look for food even though she would refuse to eat it. She demanded to know where Vermont was going. He said he was leaving and she said she wanted to go too. She hated it here, they were always talking to her about food, she wasn't even interested in fucking food.

Vermont said no but she threatened to call the staff, who would in turn call the cops on Vermont because he was under a court order.

They would do that later anyway but if the cops knew he'd been gone for a few hours, they wouldn't even bother looking for him. It would make everyone's life a lot easier if he could slip out unnoticed.

He agreed to take Cherry to the car and let the others decide.

"No," said T-Bo.

"Yes," said Fraser.

She got in the back next to Vermont. She didn't take up much room.

Before they could get out of town, they had to get past the roadworks that are a constant fixture on I-95 in Florida. By this time, the morning rush hour had started and they got stuck sitting in traffic.

Fraser noticed a Hooters restaurant at the side of the road. "I'm hungry," he said. "Let's eat."

"We should get on the road first," said T-Bo. "We got a long way to go."

But Fraser would have none of it. "You can buy us breakfast, T-Bo. You can use some of the money you stole from me," he said happily.

T-Bo sheepishly turned into the parking lot.

The three men got out but Cherry sat in the car.

"I'll wait here," she said, hugging herself.

Fraser put his hand on her cheek. She had a soft light beard beginning to grow. Her body, in an attempt to compensate for the lack of fat, was frantically growing hair to keep her temperature stable.

"You look thin, Cherry, you must be hungry," he said.

She looked at him for a second. Vermont waited for Fraser to receive the torrent of abuse but to his surprise Cherry suddenly said, "You know, when I think about it, I am fucking starving."

And she got out of the car too.

Hooters girls, the waiting staff in Hooters restaurants, wear bright-orange hot pants and tight white T-shirts. It's a great marketing tool to entice men, to suggest their food will be served to them by a sexy, scantily clad girl, but most times when a man walked into a Hooters he wished the girls were wearing more. The aesthetic requirements to be a Hooters girl who actually waited on tables as opposed to a Hooters girl who appeared in Hooters advertising were very different.

Hooters had a bit of a problem living up to its promise but many folks do and they shouldn't be judged harshly for that. What they should be judged harshly for is their terrible food; it is both tasteless and fried, which is almost impossible. The Hooters girls are the stars and the draw of the restaurants, and the management prefer it if everyone else stay in the background.

Fraser and his disciples had been placed in an out-of-the-way corner booth by the manager, who was not a girl at all but a young Texan Reserve Marine named Chad Butterworth.

Chad was a wiry martinet who was very tough on the girls. He treated them as if they were a battalion in a combat zone, and on some nights the girls would have been inclined to agree with that perspective.

After he finished his pancake breakfast, Fraser sipped his coffee and stared out the window at a pigeon that was trying to retrieve a piece of gum that had been stuck to the sidewalk. Every time the bird thought it had a morsel, the gum snapped back cruelly and the pigeon looked around as if it didn't want anyone to see it make a fool of itself.

Whenever the pigeon looked in Fraser's direction he pretended to be looking at something else so as not to embarrass it.

T-Bo and Vermont watched Cherry finish her second breakfast. She wiped her toast on the plate to scoop up the remains of her fried eggs. When she was done she sat back in her chair and burped.

"I think she's cured," said T-Bo.

"That's the most I've seen her eat. If I added up all the food I ever seen her eat—and I sit next to her in the dining hall—I still never get half of what she just ate."

"I was hungry," said Cherry.

"You go to the bathroom now and barf it up, that your deal?" asked T-Bo.

"Don't be gross," said Cherry. She let out a sigh and unbuckled her belt. It didn't look as if she had any plans to go anywhere unless she was carried.

"It's a miracle," said Vermont.

"It's the Rabbi," said T-Bo. "That makes three."

"How come?" Vermont asked. "What else he do?"

"He got her to eat, he got you to put down the crack pipe, and . . ." T-Bo turned and looked at Fraser.

Fraser smiled at him and nodded encouragingly.

"He got me to admit I'm gay."

Vermont raised his eyebrows. "How'd he do that?"

"You knew?" said T-Bo.

"Nigger, everybody knew but you. I even think you knew, you just wasn't listenin."

When they got in the car to leave, Cherry sat in the back next to Fraser and fell asleep almost instantly. Vermont sat up front next to T-Bo to prove he wasn't homophobic, although he was at pains to point out he was not gay himself.

So the brain-damaged, dentally challenged Scottish holyman in the orange dress; the street-fighting, gay Watusi; the crackhead on the lam; and the ninety-pound stripper peeled out of Delray in the purple, pimped-out Chevy Caprice and headed for the Florida Turnpike.

An accident waiting to happen.

THE ROAD TO GOD: EIGHT

THE SHOOT FOR *KILLING BY STARLIGHT* WAS A NIGHTMARE, even by Hollywood standards. The production was six months late in starting because when Borg, the director, turned up to look at the sets that had been built on the soundstages in Burbank, he went apeshit. He screamed and threw his Stubb and Flask double Americano with an extra shot at the plywood backdrop that was meant to be Tootsiepop Ted's cell the night before his execution.

"It's like a fecking TV show! Is he presenting *American Funny Veedyos* or is he fecking waiting for hexocution? This is fecking sheet! I cain't work with this sheet!"

And he stormed off the movie, going straight to Van Nuys Airport, where he boarded a chartered Gulfstream V and flew back to Scandinavia.

As he boarded the plane his coffee was running down the fake prison walls, and the design team that had worked through the night to get the work done in time stared blankly at one another. There was nothing wrong with the set, of course, but Borg had to establish that he was an artist and was in charge of this production and that he would not be pushed around by the suits, even if they were paying his wages. This is standard industry practice for big-time moviemakers.

Line producers, the people who actually physically produce (orchestrate the production of) the films, call this "throwing the toys from the stroller." It allows the directors to feel powerful and everyone else to feel they are in the presence of a genius, so no one really minds except the people who are paying for it.

In this particular case, though, Borg had an ulterior motive. He had been offered a large sum of money to direct a commercial for Svendesson Herring Fisheries in his native Norway. It would only take him two weeks to prep and shoot the commercial but the dates clashed with the movie, so he used the delay, when he was supposedly frustrated about the production values in Hollywood, to film a trawler full of supermodels in wet-weather gear having netloads of live fish dumped on them to a Lenny Kravitz backing track.

The TV ad was shown in more than fifty countries and Svendesson's share of the herring market went up by 8 percent.

This hiccup should only have delayed the film by two weeks but then the revised schedule clashed with Meg Roberts's publicity schedule on another movie she had made the year previously, *Calendar of Love,* the tender story of a Louisiana woman who learns to love again after her husband is killed by an escaped bear. It was a terrible movie, written by the Same Idiot who penned the self-help book *Men Are Asteroids, Women Are Meteorites* that Meg was addicted to.

She could not back out of her duties to *Calendar* since she was also the executive producer and had her own money in the project. This delay in turn ran into Leon's shooting schedule for *Oh Leon!,* which was going into its fifth season and which he was contractually obligated to.

Guillame and Claudette used the delays to have an extended holiday touring South America. In Colombia they were received with great pomp and ceremony by the government. The president, Juan Carlos Menendez, who would later be assassinated by his own son, had loved *Pamplemousse* and was desperate to meet Guillame. Meg and Leon's relationship had taken a downturn the night of the cast party when he drooled over Claudette, embarrassing her in front of everyone with his obvious infatuation, so by the time everyone was ready to begin shooting, the male and female leads were now ex-boyfriend and ex-girlfriend, which led to a frosty environment on the set, to say the least.

Meg was now dating a man she had met through the Church of Brainyism, Crag Harding, the former pro wrestler who was trying to break into action movies. He came to work every day with her. Every time he saw Leon he glared at him with his trademark "scary stare" that he had used to great effect in the World Wrestling Foundation and that he would later employ as the angry robot hell-bent on revenge in the highly successful *Killdroid* and *Killdroid 2: Return of the Killdroid.*

Leon complained to Saul that Crag Harding made him uncomfortable: "I can't work with that psycho gorilla around, he's freaking me out."

Saul talked to Meg: "Please don't bring Crag to the set. He's freaking Leon out."

Meg talked to Saul: "Get out of my trailer, you fat pervert."

And things went downhill from there.

By the time the shooting actually started, the head of Uniwarn, who had green-lit the project, Mike Thorne, had been fired and replaced by a new man, the legendary Jeffrey Wiesner, Hollywood's Mr. Fixit (even if it's not broken or even in need of maintenance). Wiesner, an ex–car salesman from Baltimore, had been a high-ranking executive at the Disney Corporation and had had great success with a series of feel-good family comedies he'd commissioned. He had a reputation as a "very strong personality," which meant he was a megalomaniac and a bully.

Wiesner was delighted to inherit a project that had Janus Borg and Meg Roberts and Leon Martini attached, even if it meant dealing with Saul Martini, who was renowned as a deviant monster. What he was less thrilled about was the script itself.

Trundle's script was excellent and covered the guilt and conflict of Tootsiepop Ted and the anguish of his victims along with the frustration of the law-enforcement agent who doggedly pursued him, but Wiesner felt it was too dark and much too grisly.

He wanted changes.

He called Saul to his office and told him that he wanted less killing and that more should be made of the relationship between the policeman and his wife, which should be less tense and more lighthearted. He also felt they should have a kid, in fact a couple of kids, and a dog.

Also he wanted Leon to sing in the movie.

Saul tried to get around him but Wiesner would not budge. He wanted changes or he would cancel the whole thing, big-time stars and director or not.

This was the reason Wiesner had been hired by the board of Uniwarn: He would not cater to the artistic types whom they saw as ruining the industry.

Saul hired Zabadan again to make some more changes and find places to put in songs. As production continued, Wiesner's demands on the script got more and more ludicrous, and he forced them to reshoot a vast array of scenes. This in turn forced the budget up, which Saul, as producer, would be blamed for.

Killing by Starlight became almost unrecognizable from the original script. The homicide detective played by Leon now sang at every opportunity—in the bar with his cop buddies, in the house to get his kids to sleep, in a flashback when he sang to his new bride at their wedding, and in one memorable scene he crooned a sensitive ballad to a corpse hidden tastefully under a blanket in the city morgue. The murders were reshot to ensure there was no blood and the victims were seen as to somehow deserve their fate for their life of prostitution. Meg's character, the policeman's wife, was given a few monologues where she peeled an orange and talked to her gay friend about her feelings.

Of course, the changes did not go unnoticed by the actors or director. Leon whined a little but was secretly relieved to have singing added, since this was one area where he knew he was a star. Guillame complained loudly that his character was ridiculous and point-blank refused to wear the "evil eyebrows" that Wiesner wanted. He actually barged into Wiesner's office and demanded to be released from the movie. Wiesner told him no and managed to placate him with a million-dollar bonus. Guillame was French and an artist but he wasn't an idiot, and anyway, Wiesner backed down on the eyebrows. Meg actually liked the changes and called Wiesner to thank him. Janus Borg didn't give a damn and nobody cared what Trundle thought.

Saul was crushed, though. All this time he had been in charge, he had steered Leon's career and been the one who took care of business, but he sensed, as the might of Wiesner and Uniwarn took over, that his grip on his brother was slipping. They hardly talked and he knew that in his brother's eyes Wiesner had diminished him. He was no longer in control of *Killing by Starlight* or, it seemed, anything else. Toward the end of the shoot, Wiesner, who was a lot happier with the way things were going, called Leon into his office. He told him how happy he was that the changes had been made, and that he felt this was going to be a great big hit movie for both of them. Saul thanked him and agreed, wary of Wiesner's good humor. Wiesner said that he'd had some market research done and found that the title, *Killing by Starlight,* which personally he loved, didn't test well. People thought it was a horror movie.

Saul said that in a way it was but Wiesner plowed on, ignoring him. He told Saul he had at great expense hired a firm to find the top dozen words that made modern-day Americans feel good. He wanted to have a title that contained at least some of these words.

The words were, in no particular order: *wedding, mega, celebrity, America* or *American, friend* or *friendly, shrimp, dollars, holy* (although this word had actually tied with *bikini*), *vacation, big, united,* and *buffet.*

Wiesner said he had considered a bunch of new titles for the movie, including *One United American, The Shrimp Vacation, Holy Bikini!,* and *Megadollar Buffet,* but had settled on *Big Friendly American Wedding Celebrity* because it contained the most words and it was truest to the plot.

"How can you call a movie about a serial killer who ate the eyes of his victims *Big Friendly American Wedding Celebrity*?" yelled Saul, finally at the end of his tether.

Wiesner explained, "Because in the movie, the crimes are *big*, the cop played by your brother is *friendly* and *American*, there is a flashback to his *wedding*—with Meg Roberts, for Christ's sake—and she is a *celebrity*."

Saul slumped in his chair.

"Plus," Wiesner continued reasonably, "I am the head of the studio and I can do what I fucking want. Now get out."

And out Saul went. Every night.

In frustration he ate more, drank more, fucked harder, and took more Vicodin, his rage and despair taken out on his unfortunate body or the unfortunate bodies of the call girls who turned up at his home in the Hills.

The reshoots and script changes meant the movie ran over-schedule by an extra three months and by the time shooting finished Saul was a wreck.

Leon returned to the sitcom, happy to be back. He didn't tell Saul but he started attending Brainyism meetings and got hooked up to the Boondtdock.

Meg broke up with Crag because he was afraid of intimacy. She got bored with Brainyism and moved on to hypnoyoga.

Guillame and Claudette returned to Paris, relieved to be home. Claudette made Guillame swear he would never work in America again, Guillame agreed, and he bought her a stupidly expensive necklace with some of his million-dollar bonus.

When he died she gave it to UNICEF to raise money for children who needed it.

Claudette was supportive of Guillame during the nightmare shoot in Hollywood, so she never mentioned what happened with Leon when they were there. It would only have made him angry and he already had enough on his plate.

She often thought about telling him afterward but he died before she could, and it wasn't that important anyway.

CLAUDETTE AND LEON

THE NIGHT THAT GUILLAME AND CLAUDETTE arrived in Los Angeles they had been having one of their rare arguments. Their plane had been delayed coming out of Charles de Gaulle due to a baggage handlers' dispute about tea breaks, then the flight itself had been bumpy and busy, so neither of them had slept, and so when they finally arrived at their hotel in L.A., Claudette had wanted to go to bed. Guillame said no, they had to go to the party, he would not go alone, and it was disrespectful of her not to come with him.

She was too tired and grumpy to realize he was afraid not to go and afraid to go alone, so they had snapped at each other but she relented, and in the back of the car that Saul had sent for them, as they made their way over to the party, she leaned over and kissed his ear and tickled him until he was himself again.

Everybody fussed over them at the party. Meg Roberts, who seemed a little vivid in person until she explained to them that she'd just had an intensive face peel, had presents for both of them. She gave them signed copies of *Men Are Asteroids, Women Are Meteorites* and a candle each. One had the word *serenity* written on it, the other had the word *achieve.*

It was all very polite and friendly. Everyone congratulated Guillame on his award and said his performance in *Pamplemousse* was remarkable and how much they had loved him and the film, although they didn't mention that they hadn't actually seen it.

Leon was very obviously taken with Claudette and he followed her around like a puppy. She was charmed by his enthusiasm and Guillame didn't mind; he had seen men have this reaction to her before and trusted her, and also he had been drawn into a conversation about his character with the director.

Borg thought that it would be great for the movie the more normal and suburban Ted appeared so that when he carried out his crimes, the murders—which he was determined to shoot in graphic detail and fuck the studio if they had a problem with that—the contrast would be spectacular.

Guillame concurred, saying that he took the role because of the interesting juxtaposition between bourgeois family man and serial killer.

Although it was obvious how to portray a killer in the act of killing, Guillame wondered aloud how to portray normality.

"He should play golf!" declared Borg.

"Did he play golf in life?" asked Guillame.

"I have no idea but it is unimportant. He was also not French. What we are driving at here is the essence of Tootsiepop Ted."

Guillame was delighted. He loved to play golf, as did Borg.

"We should have a round tomorrow, for rehearsal," said Guillame.

"Excellent," Borg agreed.

Leon steered Claudette to the piano.

"Do you play golf?" he asked her.

She laughed. "*Non, monsieur,* I do not play golf."

"What's funny? Women play golf."

"Not this one," said Claudette.

Leon sat at the piano. He had learned that the impact of his singing could be enhanced if he accompanied himself, so had learned how to tinkle a few chords. He played and Claudette listened as he sang. A few of the guests drifted from the party but there were quite a few powerful people in attendance, so no one wanted to appear too enthusiastic, just polite admiration would be appropriate.

Leon ran through his repertoire, giving it all to Claudette with both barrels, and as he did so he admired her composure, which made him want her even more. He had seen that under this kind of seductive pressure most women buckled, became embarrassed, or even came on to him, but she enjoyed his singing and clapped politely with the others when he was done.

"You sing beautifully, thank you," she told him.

Then excused herself and went to find Guillame.

She had just come out of the bath and was sitting in her robe happily devouring one of the delicious complimentary chocolates the hotel had put out for them when he knocked at the door.

She was surprised to see him. She said that unfortunately Guillame was not there, he had gone off to play golf with Borg. Leon said that he wasn't here to see Guillame and walked into the room, closing the door behind him.

He looked at her, fresh from the bath, hugging the big white terry-cloth robe around herself like a security blanket. She was the most enchanting thing he had ever seen.

"Claudette, I have a blowjob in mind," he said softly.

Claudette couldn't quite believe her ears. "Pardon?"

"I need your mouth on me," he said, using that tone that always worked for him.

Claudette went to the door and opened it.

"Please leave," she said flatly.

Leon was genuinely mystified. He had never really encountered this kind of thing before. He had mistakenly believed the press and gossip about himself. He had read in *Peephole* magazine that he was the most eligible single man in the world. "This sexy bachelor can have any woman he wants," they had written, and they were known for their accuracy.

In his confusion he thought this was a game. He went to her and tried to embrace her, putting his hands on her robe and forcing it open so that he could see her magnificent body.

He gasped. Not at the sight of the naked Claudette, although she was indeed breathtaking, but at the sharp pain he felt in his testicles as she kneed him in the nuts. He still couldn't get a breath after she had thrown him into the hotel corridor and slammed the door of the suite.

He had to hide his face as a chambermaid looked out a room she was servicing to see what was going on.

He was deeply ashamed.

He didn't want anyone to see he'd been rejected.

TURNPIKE

THAT A CAREER CRIMINAL LIKE T-BO would have chosen to ride around in as distinctive a car as the one he had needs a little explanation. The car itself was not owned by T-Bo alone. He had paid cash for it from stolen money he had acquired from his mugging escapades with Silky, Wilson, and occasionally Vermont, although Vermont was usually too high to do much but smoke more crack, so they didn't really consider him as having a share.

The last time they took him on a job he had almost gotten them arrested by pulling an attitude with a cop who wanted to know why they were running down the street. The three other boys were together enough to know that the way to fool cops was to be polite and act respectful but unafraid. Vermont had been neither, yelling at the cop, who was black, that he was an Uncle Tom doing whitey's dirty work for him. The boys managed to get away by saying their friend was a little drunk after having been to the school prom where his girlfriend had ditched him for a white boy. The cop, Buford Manning, didn't buy it for a minute but he was on his own, it was the end of his shift, his wife was nine months pregnant, and he wanted to go home. He was quite happy to drop the whole thing if he didn't lose face. T-Bo, Silky, and Wilson played the forelock tugging just right and managed to get away but they never took Vermont out again. He was fun to party with but he was a liability in the field.

They bought the car together for status and protection. If they had kept the cash and that became known, even if they had it secreted somewhere, they would have become targets for other guys in the neighborhood. One or maybe all of them could be kidnapped or tortured until they had given up the goods. Also, if they kept the money in cash, then they had to believe that one of them would not at some point abscond with all the money. The boys were uneducated but they were not stupid, so they plowed a chunk of money into the car. They could ride in it together, they could chase girls, look good, and feel cool. Just what every teenager wants.

Buying a car also involved less paperwork than most other big purchases, so it was easier to have the legality forged should you be stopped by a cop, and if you are young and black and in a pimped ride, you will definitely be stopped by a cop.

That's one of the things that gives the car status with other kids.

So the car was owned three ways and they had put more money into it, getting it just the way they wanted it, and now T-Bo had stolen it. There was no chance the other boys would report the car as stolen, and they had no idea in which direction T-Bo was headed, but if they ever saw him again they would have to shoot him. They knew it and T-Bo knew it. So he was never going back to Miami.

He thought about this as he drove north on the Florida Turnpike with his new gang. He felt bad about taking the car and promised himself that one day he would make it up to his friends.

He also began to countenance the thought that he would have to make amends to the people he had mugged. He shook that off. Too much too soon.

Fraser was looking at the flat, wet countryside and thinking about the French policeman who had banjaxed him with the truncheon. He said he shook like a Bethlehem shepherd. What did he mean by that? He wondered who had written *Could do better* on his report card.

Jesus?

Probably.

He wondered what Carl would make of all this.

Vermont was thinking about crack cocaine. He had always promised himself he would never turn out to be a drunk like his old man. He had hated the way the fool had drooled on himself and been a laughingstock among the family and in the neighborhood and yet he felt he had done the exact same thing to himself with the pipe. He was done with that shit. He felt free; the open-top car added to the sensation. He felt as good as he had ever felt in his life. He held his hands up in the air and with sheer delight he screamed, "Yee fucking haw!" in his best cowboy.

The others smiled.

Cherry had not eaten as much as she had in Hooters in one sitting since before she started having her period. She felt good too but a bit sick. She felt her rib cage with her fingers, she touched her nipples through her shirt, trying to find where her breasts used to be. At twenty-three she thought she should be at the absolute peak of her physical beauty as a woman and yet here she was like a fucking scarecrow. She decided she really needed to put on some weight. Her body, unaccustomed to the calorie intake and fried food, was in a mild state of toxic shock and her digestive tract was in some kind of emergency mode.

"I need to go to the bathroom," she said.

"Me too," said Fraser.

T-Bo said he would pull in at the next stop.

Mickey Day was an angry man.

He had been angry when he worked as a high-school math teacher in Boston. He thought it might be because the students were such a pain in the ass but when he retired the anger didn't go away. He thought maybe it was because of his wife, Agnes, who was such a fucking chowderhead, but he could get plenty angry these days and Agnes had been in her grave for two years. Maybe it was because he didn't have kids or because of the government or the media or all of the above. He guessed it came down to one absolute truth: Other people were just fucking assholes. They consistently proved his point by the way they drove or acted around him. You had to carry a gun for protection. It made him feel better knowing it was there, sitting in the glove compartment like buried treasure.

He had tried to get away from being angry. After he retired, he and Agnes had sold everything and bought an RV, a big camper wagon that they were going to go out on the open road with. They were going to tour America, get out and away from all the assholes, but Agnes fucked up; she died of a heart attack three weeks out of Boston. He went back, cremated her, and went out on the road again and here he was, sixty-three years old, bald, varicose veins, high blood pressure, and blowing around the country like a fucking tumbleweed.

No wonder he was fucking angry.

He needed gas, so he pulled into the next stop.

It wasn't much of a crash and it would have been difficult to say who was at fault but the fact that the Chevy had the roof down didn't help. T-Bo was pulling out of the rest area and Mickey Day was pulling in. The big RV crashed into the passenger side of the Caprice, hitting Vermont and Fraser, who were on that side of the car. Vermont had a few bumps and bruises and Fraser had a few more than he'd had before but otherwise everyone was okay.

Mickey was furious and adrenalized. He stuck his gun in his waistband under his shirt, got down from the RV, and yelled at T-Bo, "You slammed into me!"

T-Bo did not want trouble, they didn't need cops around. "It's cool, man, it's all good. Everybody's okay."

"I am not fucking okay!" shouted Mickey. "Look what you did to my vehicle." He pointed to a smashed headlight on the camper, which had survived the impact in far better shape than the Chevy, which had a buckled front wheel and a mashed front wing.

It was no longer drivable.

"Be cool. It's all good," cooed Vermont, stepping wide and away from Mickey so that he couldn't look at both him and T-Bo at the same time. The ghetto kids were going into autopilot. They had to get out of this, and soon.

Cherry started crying and Fraser put his arm around her.

“Now look what you’ve done,” he said to no one in particular.

Mickey took stock of the situation. Two niggers, probably on crack, a mangy-looking fag in a dress, and some skinny junkie girl. He knew this was dangerous. He panicked and pulled out the gun.

“Stay where you are,” he said, not knowing who he meant.

Everyone stood still.

Except Fraser.

Fraser had never seen a handgun before except in the movies, so he had no real concept of what danger he was in, and even if he had known he wouldn’t have cared. He worked for God now.

He left Cherry and started walking toward the shaking Mickey.

“Get back, faggot!” Mickey yelled at him.

Fraser smiled the big gap-tooth grin and told Mickey it was all right.

Mickey was actually about to pull the trigger when he felt a shooting, searing pain tear across his body. His legs buckled and he fell like a stone. He was out.

“What the fuck?” said Vermont. No one had been anywhere near him.

Other drivers and customers at the rest stop were looking over.

“Quick, get in the bus,” said T-Bo.

“It’s an RV,” said Cherry.

“Just fucking get in it,” said T-Bo.

Cherry and Vermont bundled into the camper. Fraser was leaning over Mickey, who was convulsing and foaming at the mouth. T-Bo ran over to them.

“We gotta get out of here, Rabbi.”

“Okay.” Fraser smiled. “Help me carry him.”

T-Bo didn’t want to take Mickey but he was between the devil and the deep blue sea. Taking the camper without Mickey in it was grand theft auto and probably an assault charge or worse if the old fuck died. Taking him and the vehicle was carjacking and assault or worse if the old fuck died.

Staying was not an option. No cops or judges were going to believe a crackhead, a homeboy, a stripper, and a foreigner in a dress that the whole thing was just a huge misunderstanding, especially when they saw the gun.

The fastest way out of there was not to argue with the Rabbi, so he helped Fraser drag the convulsing senior, who was beginning to turn blue, into the camper.

He started it up and got back onto the turnpike.

The handgun was left lying in the road next to the damaged car.

T-Bo was smart enough to realize that someone at the gas station might have taken the camper's number (although if they tried tracing the Chevy, all they would get was a fictional bartender in Miami named Desmond Cosby), and that traveling on the turnpike would probably be a mistake, so he got off at the next exit.

They would take the back roads north.

Fraser was sitting with Mickey, who had stopped convulsing but still not regained consciousness, as T-Bo drove into a hick town in northern Florida looking for a place for them to hunker down for the night.

Fraser kept whispering in the old man's ear, "Come back, come back, come back."

T-Bo was exhausted, this place would do. It looked like nothing had happened here for years. He read the town's name on the roadside sign.

CRAWFORD'S CREEK.

PLEASE DRIVE CAREFULLY.

SCOTLAND

EDINBURGH AND GLASGOW are only about forty-five miles apart and there is no direct scheduled flight from Paris to Glasgow, so George and Claudette flew into Edinburgh Airport instead. It was a little plane, the demand not being high, and George could not get comfortable in his seat.

The pain in his back had not gone away, in fact it was getting worse. Much worse. Before they boarded, George had snuck into the pharmacy at the airport and bought some aspirin. He had taken twice the recommended dose and they had absolutely no effect. An hour into the flight as they crossed over the border into Scotland, he was in agony and as they began their descent he finally confessed to Claudette.

"The pain is here," he said.

She nodded as if she had been expecting it. She went into her handbag and brought out a heavy amber glass bottle and a dropper. She opened the bottle and sucked up a little of the clear liquid.

"Open wide."

"What is this?"

"Morphine," she said.

"Where did you get it?"

"Never mind," she said, thinking how reluctant Alain had been to prescribe the drug for her.

He opened his mouth and she dropped the sacred liquid onto his tongue.

It felt like Communion.

George felt profound relief almost instantly, then he started to feel good.

Very good indeed.

Claudette had booked a rental car, and as she drove from the airport to the first stop on their itinerary she almost killed them both half a dozen times by driving on the wrong side of the road but George didn't mind. He thought her driving was charming and was trying to concentrate on giving her the correct directions, which he found a little more difficult than he might ordinarily.

It took them less than an hour. Huge gray clouds hung low over the city like giant sheets of battered iron. They filtered out any warmth from the sun, allowing only cold, clear blue light and the threat of rain.

George's parents were buried next to his grandparents on his father's side in a family plot in the giant graveyard on a hill in the east end of Glasgow called the Necropolis—the city of the dead. They parked the car and walked up the hill past the ostentatious and Baroque soot-blackened tombs of the Tobacco Lords and the Victorian wealthy to the newer, smaller graves on the far side of the hill overlooking the nearby motorway. They stood in the shadow of a giant monument to John Knox, the founder of the Church of Scotland.

Claudette looked up at the statue of the austere bearded misogynist as they passed. "Who was this? He must have been very important."

George told her, told her that he was no lover of Catholics or women and would be very upset that his fienian mother was resting among good Scottish Protestants.

"Perhaps he's changed his mind. Perhaps he realizes it doesn't matter."

"Perhaps," agreed George, but doubted it.

They reached the marker. A flat granite slab. It read:

INGRAM
Robert James Ingram, 1890–1963
Margaret Jane Ingram nee Brodie, 1894–1974
Elizabeth Margaret Ingram, 1923–1979
James George Ingram, 1928–1986
Susan Andrea Julia Ingram nee O'Reilly, 1932–1987

They stood in silence for a moment looking at the grave. A bitter-cold wind blew from the east and Claudette wrapped her coat tightly around her. George did not seem to feel the cold.

"Robert was my grandfather, I don't remember him. Margaret was my gran—I called her Nana Peggy. She had a giant arse and always wore an apron, I seem to remember. She made chips—pommes frites—that had wee black dots on them, I think because she didn't clean the pan often enough. She sang a lot. Elizabeth—Betty—my dad's sister, sad wee woman, never married, died of some kind of kidney disease, and then my mum and dad."

Claudette put her hand on George's cheek. He turned and smiled at her sadly.

"There's room for one more in the plot. Quite an honor to be buried up here. Doesn't happen much anymore."

"Is that what you want?"

"No," said George. "I don't want to be lying around this place with all these dead people. It's depressing."

She nodded.

"My mother used to drag me up here every now and again when I was a kid," he said. "She thought it was comforting to know where you were going to end up. I just thought it was creepy."

"What do you think now?"

George looked out at the thousands of graves, most of them broken down and forgotten, covered in weeds.

"I think they should get a bulldozer in here and knock all these fucking tombstones down. Build a swing park for kids."

She smiled. "I love you, Georges."

"Merci, chérie. Je t'aime aussi," said George, feeling gloriously European and windswept.

The pain in his back was becoming fierce again.

"Any more of that happy juice?"

Claudette drove the car to a nearby bus stop they had picked out on the way in to the housing estate. She sat in the car alone and lit a cigarette. She kept the engine running and turned on the radio to a local station. Radio Clyde. There was a phone-in competition; two listeners were competing for the prize of a night out at the Glasgow Pavilion to see a singer named Christian. Claudette wondered if he was Catholic or Protestant—that seemed to still be important in this country.

The door was open and George didn't need his key, which was lucky because he'd thrown it away at a service station in the Lake District a few days ago.

Jesus, was that all? A few days?

He walked inside the house and heard Sheila pottering about in the kitchen. She was listening to the phone-in competition on the radio. She looked up as he walked in. She seemed angry. She walked over and turned off the radio and then folded her arms and looked at him.

"Hi," he said.

He thought how far away she looked; he felt like she was someone he had known a long time ago and who he had lost touch with, which he supposed she was. She looked pissed off but she had always looked that way around him. He knew now, of course, that it was because she didn't like him, and he guessed she had a point. He had never really showered her with affection or attention, he hadn't made a fuss over her the way he would have if he'd been in love with her. When he was nice to her it was to calm her down or to stop her getting upset. Not very good reasons, he thought. He realized he'd been patronizing her for years.

"I'm sorry," he said.

"Uh-huh," said Sheila. Her hair had gotten thinner since she was a teenager; George vaguely wondered if women went bald. She was still good-looking, though, dark brown eyes like a cow, and she was sturdy. She'd make a good wife for a farmer maybe.

He decided he was being cruel. "I'm sorry. I've been cruel," he said.

"Not a note, not a phone call, nothing. We called the police and had them looking for you. Where have you been?"

"Paris."

"Paris! What the hell were you doing in Paris?"

"Well—" said George.

Sheila butted in, "Let me guess, another woman?"

"Yes," he said.

"You bastard. You never think of anyone but yourself, do you?"

"I'm sorry you're upset."

"I want you out. I won't take you back no matter how much you beg. Who is it? Is it that slag Glenda from your office?"

"No. You don't know her."

"It's over, George. This is the last straw. I can take your distance and your moodiness but I will not accept infidelity."

"Yes, all right."

"I have men approach me, George. Barry Symington at the leisure center has asked me out more than once."

"The swimming instructor?" asked George, surprised. "I thought he was gay."

"No, he's not gay, and he's got a fucking good body. I've seen him in his trunks."

George nodded.

"I want you out. You can go back to Paris with your fancy woman for all I care."

He nodded again. "I want to say something to you before I go. I want to tell you that I think you are a very good person and I want to thank you for our daughter. Thanks for putting up with me all these years, you deserved better."

"You're damn right I did," she said. She had tears in her eyes.

"Good luck," he said.

Then he walked over to her and kissed her gently on the forehead. She looked at him, sensing something was different.

"Everything is going to be okay. All is well. This is the right thing for us to do," he said.

And somewhere deep down inside her, past the hurt and the pain and the humiliation and the anger and the pride and the resentment and the fear, she knew that he was right.

She couldn't speak, so she just nodded.

He smiled.

"Thank you for everything, Sheila," he said, then turned and walked out the door.

"How did it go?" asked Claudette.

"Pretty well, given the circumstances," said George.

"This next will take longer," she said. "My cell phone works in the U.K. Call me when it's over."

He said he would and she dropped him off at the school gates.

Our Lady's High School had been rebuilt in the early eighties and looked even more like a factory now than it did the first time around. George marveled at the absolute insensitivity of modern municipal architecture. Everything was utilitarian, no art, no joy, why the fuck would anyone be in this building without getting a paycheck. This was, of course, exactly the view held by the vast majority of the student body.

Using Claudette's cell, he had called Nancy on her cell phone and asked her to meet him outside the school gates. She had been in a double history with Mr. Johnson (a.k.a. The Bladder, Leaky McSqueaky, and Trouserman), a shambolic old duffer who seemed to always have a little urine stain on the front of his pants, nine times out of ten shaped like a map of Africa. The dark incontinent.

Leaky McSqueaky had been as happy as she was for her to go—she told him it was a family emergency—as he knew she had absolutely no interest in the Covenanters. Christ, he could hardly keep awake himself.

Nancy worked hard at doing the gum-chewing teenage apathy thing as they walked along the side of the iron perimeter fence that surrounded the school. George was struck by how much she looked like his mother in old photographs. A dark-haired, green-eyed Celtic goddess in the making; soon the puppy fat would fall from her and she'd be grown. Boadicea in Banana Republic.

"You and Mum are getting divorced, right?" she said, feigning disinterest.

"Well, we're certainly splitting up," said George.

"It's okay with me. You don't get along very well anyway. Sandra Patterson's mum and dad are split up and she says it's better."

"Yeah, I'm sure it is."

"Is that all you wanted to tell me, 'cause we're doing the Covenanters."

"No," said George. "Listen. I'm going away. Oh fuck, there is no easy way to say this, Nancy, I'm not lying to you."

She was shocked. She had never heard her father swear in her life. She looked at him, her eyes wide.

As most parents have thought at some point while looking at their child, he could hardly believe that he was related to, never mind a parent of, a creature so beautiful.

"Nancy. I've got cancer. I'm dying. I got the same as your Nana and Papa died of."

She looked horrified, all the color and cool drained from her in an instant.

She was a little girl again.

"No," she said in a tiny voice against the inevitable.

"Yes. I'm sorry," he said, instantly regretting telling her the truth.

She clung on to him, wrapped her hand around his neck the way she used to when she was four years old.

"Daddy, Daddy, Daddy, no, no." Her heart breaking a thousand times on every exhale.

George was shocked for a moment by the sudden intensity and grief that poured out of her. Save for a dream of a closed cathedral, he had not cried himself until this moment, and now he wept. They clung to each other to stop from drowning in a sea of tears.

Claudette knew she would have time to kill. She looked in the glove compartment of the rental car and found a tourist leaflet for Stirling Castle. It had been the site of sieges and battles and murders and atrocities down through the years, all the things tourists enjoy in a historical monument. She drove there, only ten miles, and walked its battlements and looked out over the surrounding green plains.

Rain began to fall and she went inside to look at the museum to the castle regiment. The Argyll and Sutherland Highlanders. She wandered past battle standards and wall-mounted costumes and armor, past swords and muskets, all the equipment used in the forging of an empire.

She lingered by the exhibit on the First World War. There was an old sepia photograph of a young soldier with his wife and children before he marched off to battle. The shot was posed in the serious formality of the day but the family looked so real, so normal. Mum, Dad, and three kids, dressed for a Sunday. She looked at the soldier and was struck by how handsome he must have been, Lance Corporal Adam McLachlan.

At that moment, the one sperm of George's that had survived its long and perilous journey stormed Claudette's egg. It dug in like the battle-hardened trouper it had become, and together the new allies advanced on the uterine wall.

Hallelujah.

George and Nancy went to the City Bakeries tea shop in the town center. They had hot, sweet Earl Gray and cream cookies. They hadn't done that in years. They talked for two hours. George told her what the doctors had said, what decision he had made about his life and how it would end, and then for some reason they started talking about family holidays years ago, when she was a kid. They got calm for a while, then it was time for him to go. She begged him to stay but he said that he had to go, that apart from anything else he was not going to die slowly in front of her until finally he expired and was released from his agony and everyone would be relieved.

"Don't be selfish, Dad," she said.

"Don't you be selfish," he said.

The pain was returning, stronger and more urgent, and he wanted to get to Claudette and the magic bottle. He needed the genie.

They stood outside the little tea shop. She wanted to leave first.

"Good-bye," she said.

"Good-bye," he said.

She turned and walked a few yards, then she looked back at him.

He smiled at her. "Help others," he said.

She nodded, and ran off.

On the evening plane back to Paris, George slept, the morphine soothing his furrowed brow along with the cool hand of his love.

THE ROAD TO GOD: NINE

THE PUNISHMENT THAT SAUL'S BODY HAD TAKEN over the years in Hollywood showed in the broken veins on his nose and cheeks, his high-blood-pressure readings, and his ever-increasing obesity. His face had gotten so fat his eyes were little bloodshot dots of mistrust. The punishment that his soul had taken was visible in his acts of depravity and greed. He truly had become a monster inside and out yet his mind still functioned as sharply as it did when he was scoring homemade acid from Benny Alderton. This was fortunate because when *Big Friendly American Wedding Celebrity* came out to horrific reviews, he had to spin as much as he could to try to keep from looking like he was to blame, which this time he actually wasn't.

That doesn't matter, though, his reputation was distasteful enough for the town to turn against him. The hyenas of Hollywood sensed his weakness and gathered for a wilding, the bloody orgy when they bring down one of their own.

Saul might have survived but he was ugly and fat, so he was really despised. Advance word on the movie was dreadful. It performed badly in front of test audiences, who had expected a feel-good comedy about a big, friendly American who went to a wedding and became a celebrity or something. They had not expected a ridiculous, confused musical about a serial killer. It got a big thumbs-down.

The studio gambled, trying to snow the public with a massive advertising campaign and putting the movie on a huge number of screens its opening weekend. This is standard industry practice; they figure that if they sell the movie hard and all the suckers go the first few days, by the time the chumps have figured out the film is a piece of shit, their money is safely on its way to the bank.

This is done time and time again and people still fall for it, but every so often the audiences get a whiff of something, some kind of warning flare goes up in the collective unconscious, and they stay away.

So it was with *Big Friendly American Wedding Celebrity.* The movie stiffed, it did not even recoup the cost of paying its stars' salaries, never mind production or advertising costs.

Saul began to teeter.

Sensing that the time was right, the publishing house Havering announced they had purchased the rights to a tell-all book about prostitution in Hollywood as written by a genuine madam to the stars, Candy Chambers.

The book, *Hot Lunch/Cold Hearts,* graphically described the sexual predilections of, among others, Bo Ness and Saul. (Leon was actually a little too vanilla to be interesting; he only ever had sex with one woman at a time and didn't use prostitutes.) The publishers released some advance material from the book to *Peephole* magazine.

Saul became a laughingstock. His power disappeared almost overnight. He still had money but CAM took over the day-to-day running of Leon's life and left Saul with looking after "development," which meant he would be given a salary by Leon if he just kept out of the way.

Uniwarn canceled Saul's production deal under a morality clause. It had stated that the studio could terminate any agreement if a producer brought them into disrepute, which technically meant they could fire anyone who made a movie that got a bad review, which technically meant they could fire anyone they pleased. Which they did, often.

Hollywood turned its back on Saul. He couldn't get his calls returned. The only person who would talk to him, through the miracle of electricity, was the spotty teenage screenwriting hopeful who manned the night shift at the Fatburger drive-thru.

Saul and Leon still lived together in the big house in the Hills but they rarely saw each other. Leon was out at work all day and Saul became practically nocturnal. He would get up around five P.M., get on the phone to do some business, that is, phone some people who didn't want to talk to him, then he got moving and shaking with his slimy retinue of party friends—the hookers and dealers and hangers-on who didn't have a better gig or contact—at around nine.

Saul had gone the whole hog, he had tinfoil put on the windows of the rooms in his area of the house so that sunlight could not find him, and he lived for drugs, food, and the next orgasm.

Then it ended.

It was fast.

He got up one afternoon and went to the bathroom. Leon wasn't home yet. He sat his massive bulk down on the bowl and suddenly felt tingling, intense tingling, all down the left side of his body. He picked up the telephone next to the toilet but he couldn't remember what to do with it. He dialed 911, the only number he could think of, and when the emergency services operator came on he said, "Mommy, I want bananas—" then collapsed on the floor.

Emergency services traced the call—the line was still open and the operator could hear Saul convulsing.

Fifteen minutes later the paramedics burst down the front door and found Saul on the bathroom floor.

He was breathing but the stroke had done a massive amount of damage to his brain. They rushed him to Cedars-Sinai Medical Center, where he was immediately taken into the ICU. Tim Flannigan, the paramedic who drove the ambulance, called the news channel he had a deal with, then called the studio to alert Leon.

At first Leon came to see him every day before he went to work. Saul regained consciousness and he could see and hear but he couldn't speak and was paralyzed from the neck down. He had no sense of up or down or time, he never really knew when he was sleeping or when he was awake.

He was half dead.

One day, Leon came in and sat next to the bed and told him that he had talked to the doctors and they said that sometimes people recovered a little bit, one day he might even walk again. Saul just sat and glared out from his fleshy prison, vaguely aware that every now and again a nurse would come and change the TV channel, his drip, or his diaper.

Over time, Leon's visits got a bit more spread out. He got very busy, the ratings for *Oh Leon!* were beginning to dip, and he had to do a lot of extra publicity. Also, he was getting more into Brainyism and attended meetings as often as he could. He made sure Saul had fresh flowers in his room every day and a little bowl of fruit. Saul couldn't eat the fruit, of course, he could only look at it. Saul got his food through a plastic straw, a sickly sweet mush prepared for him in the hospital kitchen.

Sometimes one of the orderlies would take the fruit and give it to one of the children in the pediatric ward or even just put it in the staff room.

They figured Saul wouldn't mind.

When he noticed, Saul was furious. He tried to convey his rage at the fruit theft by blinking his eyes furiously but everyone thought he was just asking for his bedsores to be treated or he had sweat in his eyes, and indeed sometimes that was all it was.

Sometimes Saul got a hospital visitor. Well-meaning volunteers who would sit by his bed and read him books or entertainment magazines. He hated this more than anything, he hated the sound of their chipper, upbeat voices, he hated hearing how the world was moving along just fine without him. He screamed for death but no sound came and neither did the Reaper.

But someone did.

It was a smoggy California afternoon and the air-conditioning in Saul's room was on the fritz. The hospital was chockablock and there was nowhere to move him to. He lay in bed, a light sheet covering his useless bulk while a fan blew warm air over him. The saline drip in his arm kept him from dehydrating and every so often a nurse would come in and pour a little water into his mouth and swab his face and neck with a cold towel.

When the fat, shiny-faced man came into the room, Saul presumed he was a volunteer visitor, but this one was different. Usually they were timid and tried not to look at him too much. He guessed he must be hideous. He certainly was no oil painting when he could move around but lying here naked and helpless like the carrion of a beached whale that had begun to rot even before it died probably hadn't enhanced his beauty. He supposed he smelled pretty bad too.

The fat visitor didn't seem embarrassed by Saul's ugliness or helplessness. He seemed a little hostile, angry even. Saul wondered how his visitor could stand the heat; he was wearing a Harris tweed jacket and plus fours and a cap. Not a baseball cap but a cloth cap, like a turn-of-the-century longshoreman.

The visitor was almost as fat as Saul but he also had an athleticism, a grace that Saul had never had. Saul watched him as he wandered around the room, inspecting it, tapping monitors, and looking in cupboards.

Jeez, don't you have any booze in here? I guess not, huh—hospital, he said to himself.

He helped himself to a piece of fruit. He bit into a soft plum and ignored the juice as it rolled down his chin and onto his dirty white shirt.

For some reason Saul was afraid of the visitor, who had been in the room for five minutes but hadn't spoken to him or tried to communicate. Just eyed him with a kind of contempt. This was very unusual.

The fat visitor stood at the end of the bed. He grabbed the sheet and whisked it off, revealing Saul's hideous naked body. The visitor stared at him for a long moment. Saul was terrified. He blinked for help but none came.

"You're a fat one," said the visitor. "Of course, I'm fat myself, but not like you."

He walked around and sat on the chair next to the bed. He put his face close to Saul's. Saul thought it looked as if his visitor was wearing makeup—lipstick maybe? He smelled of whisky and he seemed somehow familiar.

He thought the fat man was here to kill him.

"I'm not here to kill you," said the fat man, as if reading the stroke victim's mind. "But I bet you'd like that, wouldn't you?"

Saul blinked.

"Was that a yes or a no? Oh, it doesn't matter, it doesn't make any difference now what you want or think, does it?"

Saul didn't blink.

"I'm not a killer and I was never like you. Gossip and lies and ignorance would tell you different but that's Hollywood, huh? Even when you're not guilty, just being accused is enough in the eyes of this fucking place. A world to itself. I was never like you."

The fat visitor got up and walked to the window. He looked out at the Hollywood sign, just visible up on the hill through the brown haze. "It used to read Hollywoodland, you know. Like it really was another country—England—Ireland—Hollywoodland."

He turned and looked at Saul again. "I was framed, buddy. Railroaded."

He walked back, took off his cap, and sat next to Saul again.

"My name is Roscoe. I'm a volunteer. Do you want to hear a story?"

Of course, Saul had no option.

THE SAINT

ONCE UPON A TIME there was a holyman who believed in the value of martyrdom. Francis was Italian, born into a family of wealth and privilege. His father was a successful cloth merchant and his mother was the daughter of an ancient and revered family. He was loved and adored by his parents, who indulged his every whim. He grew up spoiled and selfish and ran with a pack of other young men from similar backgrounds. They drank and caroused and had the time of their lives, giving no thought to those less fortunate than themselves. Every so often, though, as he paraded through town in smart livery, Francis would catch sight of a beggar or a cripple or a hungry child and he felt a snag, a tug at his heart. As he grew older, the enthusiasm with which he pursued his revels began to pale and he began to look for purpose, for a meaning in his life.

He resolved that he should enter the military. The austere life of a soldier would be a counterweight to his epoch of comfortable but empty luxury. He signed up with a local warlord, a noble who was intent on acquiring the land of a distant relative who lived on the other side of the hill.

Francis learned the arts of war but he was no soldier, and in his first battle he was captured and taken prisoner by the opposing forces, who also won the day.

The lord whom Francis had hitched his banner to was killed in the fray.

Francis was thrown in a deep dungeon and had to sleep with other prisoners on a dark, damp floor that crawled with vermin and disease. His constitution was weak and he became deathly ill. A fever gripped him and he began to hallucinate; wild dreams and visions came upon him in his cell.

He dreamed he was called to arms with another noble, one who flew the banner of a red cross on a white background. He dreamed of a beautiful woman in tattered clothes who wept for him, he dreamed of the Messiah in his moment of doubt.

In negotiation with his hometown, his captors agreed to his release and he was returned to the bosom of his family, where he made a full recovery from his illness. Although he remembered little of his feverish nightmares, he felt haunted by his experience in the mire of the enemy prison.

His father told him that it was time for him to take the reins of the family business and fortune, and Francis tried to please the old man but he could find no enthusiasm or fire for the task. Money and business and figures bored him. He felt that they were somehow beneath him, that he had a higher calling.

It is to be remembered that he was a child of wealth and privilege and he wanted to better himself from that background. His mother paraded a string of marriage candidates before him, beautiful local girls, girls from noble families in other towns. His mother was desperate for him to marry but still the old ennui would not desert him and he felt that he could not.

In a desperate search to shake off the black cloud of despair that he felt followed him everywhere, he began visiting holy sites. He was a Christian by faith and sought the graves of great Christians who came before him.

He went to the site of a dead saint's grave and was appalled by its unkempt and neglected appearance. Surely one of the fathers of the Church deserved to be remembered with greater glory than this dirty boulder of a headstone. There should be a shrine. In protest, he took out his purse and emptied all his money on the grave so that the other pilgrims could see; he for one intended to help build a decent monument to a great one.

As his money fell from his hands to the grave, he felt lighter and lighter. It seemed like the coins fell through the air slowly, and for a moment he felt he was back in the prison cell and was in the throes of a vision.

The money clanged against the cold stone and shook him into awakening. He felt his heart pump and a joy surged through his body.

It was the money.

The money and the privilege.

This was the source of his discomfort.

He turned to a ragged beggar who stood next to him at the shrine. The beggar, who had already noted with a thrill the fall of the money, was delighted when Francis suggested that they swap clothes.

Francis wanted to be dressed in rags. It made him feel holy. The beggar stole the money and ran off in his new suit before the mad aristocrat changed his mind.

Francis stood by the grave all day so that everyone could see how pious he had become. He was recognized by some natives of his hometown, who informed his family what he was up to. His father, exasperated by his son's foolishness, had some of the men in his employ go to the tomb and grab the boy. He told them to try to beat some sense into the fool.

They did their best but Francis rejoiced at his suffering and in the end his father locked him up in an attic in the house. It was seen as shameful to have insanity in the family and it was the custom at the time to lock the mad away from sight lest the family fall into disrepute.

When his father was away on business, his mother allowed him to escape and he ran to the church for sanctuary.

When his father returned, he demanded his son come home but Francis told him he no longer was his son. He had a different father, one "who art in heaven," and he would answer only to Him.

Francis worked among the poor, dressing wounds, tending the sick, distributing alms from the charitable, and offering solace to the miserable and the dying by preaching the good news of the life that awaited them in heaven.

He was seen as a madman by his former friends, and when they encountered him in his rags in the street, they beat him and insulted him as they would have any other traitor to their kind. Francis wanted to help others, it was the only thing that made him feel good, but in his enthusiasm for doing good he sometimes got carried away, and in his desire to emulate the good carpenter of Nazareth, he occasionally fell into a mistaken zeal, which resulted in the sin of infallibility.

He was still tainted with the desire for victory.

As time passed and he did not falter from his marriage to Lady Poverty, he began to be seen by those who are looking for such things as a holyman. After all, he had given up everything to do the work of God, and surely that was better than someone who just did the work of God without having to give up a nice house and flashy velvet pantaloons.

People were no smarter in those days than they are today.

Francis became a celebrity.

He founded his own gang of holymen who had to dress in rags like him and help the poor; there was a separate order of women who did the same.

Things were fine for a while, then the old misery came back to him. Francis needed more pain. He whipped and starved his body but that didn't do much good, so he gave it some thought and eventually he hit upon a scheme.

He elected to take only twelve of his followers, choosing the number to be just like Jesus (just because he had embraced poverty did not mean he had lost all ambition), and go to North Africa to convert the people of Islam to Christianity. This was at a time when the Muslims and Christians were locked in bloody and brutal war.

To embark on this mission was almost certain suicide.

Francis and his disciples boarded a ship and headed into the heart of the fray. They crossed stormy seas and were tossed onto a faraway shore. They walked south. In time, they reached a castle in the desert where Christian forces were being held siege by a vast Muslim army.

Francis fearlessly walked into the enemy camp carrying a wooden cross before him, his fanatic followers trudging behind, heads bowed, awaiting decapitation.

The Saracen soldiers could not believe what they were seeing; most thought it some kind of a joke, until a superior officer ordered his men to throw the monks in irons.

Word of the incursion by Christian fanatics reached the commander of the Islamic forces, the great Saladin. He ordered that Francis be brought before him.

Francis stood before the throne of the sultan.

"What do you want here, Holyman?" asked Saladin.

"I want you and your people to convert to the one true God," said Francis.

Saladin laughed, his eyes crinkling at the corners, his teeth bright though his dark beard.

"We are converts to the one true God. There is but one God, Allah, and Mohammed is his prophet."

"No," said Francis. "God is God. The Father, the Son, and the Holy Spirit. Amen."

Saladin smiled. "Well, we can't both be right."

Francis was strident. "I know. I am right and you are an infidel. Turn to Christ or spend an eternity in hell."

"Oh, come, come, priest. Enough fire and brimstone." The sultan gestured to the silver pot and glasses in front of him. "Have some mint tea."

Saladin's guards glanced at one another, confused as to their leader's hospitality to the prisoner.

Francis refused to sit and have tea. He began to mutter the Lord's Prayer over and over again quietly to himself, in preparation for his execution.

Saladin walked up to him and clasped him on the shoulder.

"Priest," he said, "you are brave and you are committed to your faith and both of these are admirable traits but you do me a disservice if you presume me stupid. You think I cannot see through your plan?"

Francis opened his eyes and faced the sultan.

The sultan stared at him intently. "You seek martyrdom, I understand. Sure passage to paradise and the praise of those who will follow."

Francis said nothing.

Saladin continued, "But those who make martyrs are tyrants or fools or both, and I am neither. I am a soldier defending my homeland."

"You are a heathen. An unbeliever," stated Francis defiantly and without humor.

The sultan sighed deeply. "Yes, well, we'll have to agree to disagree on that but here is what I am going to do with you, brave Christian. I am sending you home, under guard to protect your safety. My best soldiers will ensure that you reach your own armies unharmed, even if it puts their own lives in danger. It would be well if they were not martyred protecting you, history may frown on that no matter who wins."

Francis was confused.

"I have enjoyed this, priest," said Saladin, "but if you will excuse me I am very busy. May you die an old man in the company of your great-grandchildren. *Inshallah*."

He snapped his fingers and Francis was led away.

Francis did not live to be an old man. He died at forty-five. It is said he suffered the stigmata, the wounds on his body imitating those inflicted on Christ.

This may be true, the wounds on Francis may have appeared due to the influence of a supernatural power.

Perhaps God's finger touched him and he slept.

But there is one thing that all agree on.

He was not killed by a Muslim.

THE ROAD TO GOD: TEN

"IN A PERFECT WORLD," said Roscoe, "you would have Chaplin as Francis and Valentino as Saladin, but who could ever afford that sort of casting, huh?"

Saul had been transported by Roscoe's story. He had seen it as though it were a movie, a huge, magnificent epic where he could hear the thoughts of the actors and where the music on the sound track filled him with wonder. Another strange thing was that, in Saul's head, the part of Francis was played by Chaplin and Saladin was played by Valentino.

He cast himself as the beggar at the tomb who stole the money and made off with the fine clothes, which of course was ridiculous because nothing that Chaplin wore would have fit him. Except perhaps the pants.

When he arrived at Sennett Studios in 1910, Chaplin had borrowed Fatty Arbuckle's pants from wardrobe. He felt that the Little Tramp would look more comical in a pair of giant trousers that were obviously too big for him.

"Okay," said Roscoe. "I gotta go, people to do, things to see, ha-ha." He seemed to have cheered up considerably at the telling of a story.

"You look after yourself," he said, putting his cap back on. "And here's a tip. If you ever get out of that bed"—he leaned very close and whispered in Saul's ear—"get the fuck out of Hollywoodland."

And off he fucked.

Saul lay there for a while, trying to conjure up the story again, but it had left him. He became aware of an itch on his nose. He tried ignoring it but it got worse. He wished the nurse would come in and wipe his face, that would do it. The itch grew, it was torture, he couldn't bear it, tears of despair rolled down his cheeks and from deep within his body a cry welled up and to his amazement he yelled, "Help!"

Then fainted at the sound of his own voice.

THE BEGINNING OF THE END

CRAWFORD'S CREEK HAD CHANGED OVER THE YEARS. Where once there had been three churches, now there was only one.

The one true Church.

The Christian Reformed Fellowship of Born Again Snake Handling Pentecostal Baptists (Reformed).

The other churches had been boarded up, and slowly the vegetation of the forest began to creep over them, returning them to the dark mire from which they came.

The town itself had, in essence, died. When the interstate was built six miles to the west and the anthrax was found in the swamp, it seemed that no one wanted to live there anymore. When the young grew to maturity they moved away as quickly as they could, if they were lucky to a college, or if less fortunate they headed north to the plastics factories in St. Augustine. In time, the ones who didn't run died off and were interred in the little churchyard in the woods.

All that remained were a few houses and the gas station that used to be the old truck stop where Saul and Leon had hitched their star to a wagon. Like many struggling businesses, the gas station had to diversify in order to survive. It got practically no passing trade because practically nobody passed, so they branched out to selling fireworks, liquor, guns, hunting knives and clothing, ammunition, greeting cards, and baby clothes—and they stayed open twenty-four hours.

People came from miles around.

Not so for the one true Church. It did not have the savvy to diversify. It was tucked away in the clearing of the old battle site about a half-mile away from Main Street and it got no business from the town. The only people who lived there were the new owners of the gas station, the Gupta family, who had moved from Bangladesh to Florida in the mid-nineties, and they were Hindus. Snake handling was a bit too "out there" for them.

The lights were on in the Gupta gas station as the big RV rolled into town. Rasheed Gupta, the fifty-five-year-old patriarch of the Gupta clan, who always took the deadly quiet night shift, watched as the big camper rattled to a stop at the gas pump.

He watched the young black man get out, then felt under the counter and undid the safety clip that held his shotgun in place. He had never seen a young black man in a vehicle like this. It didn't gel, it sent little warning pulses of fear through his system. He watched as another young black man got out and stretched, then a strange-looking white man in an orange dress, and a skeleton in a miniskirt.

He pulled the gun from its mooring and sat it on his lap.

T-Bo walked up to the bulletproof window and passed a twenty-dollar bill under the slot.

"Evening. Pump four."

Rasheed nodded and took the money, glancing over at the freaks on the forecourt.

T-Bo turned and saw the others. "I told you guys to stay inside," he growled in a stage whisper.

The others ignored him except Fraser, who called happily, "Remember to get chocolate biscuits."

T-Bo turned back to Mr. Gupta and smiled. "We're a band. Comedy troupe—musical comedy."

Rasheed nodded slowly. "Okay," he said.

"We're looking to get to Birmingham, Alabama. We on the right road?" asked T-Bo.

"Oh no, sir," said Rasheed, relieved the young man had asked him a question. It somehow made him seem less menacing. "You should be on the interstate, about six miles west. There is no traffic comes through this way."

T-Bo nodded.

"This is Crawford's Creek," said Rasheed, like that should mean something.

T-Bo thanked him and bought the chocolate cookies that Fraser had insisted on. He gassed up the truck and rounded the others back inside. He admonished them for showing themselves. If there had been a cop around, he would have been bound to ask a weird-looking group like this some tough questions.

"They can't put you in jail for the way you look," said Fraser, munching his first Oreo.

"You haven't been in the States long, have you, Padre?" said Cherry.

T-Bo had got the information he needed. There was nothing here to worry about and he could rest. He was exhausted and not one of the others was capable of driving. He pulled out of the gas station and headed down the road a few hundred yards past the boarded-up and ruined town. He turned down a lane and parked the camper in a little clearing in the forest. He turned out the lights and told everyone to get some sleep.

Potter Templeton woke them up.

He tapped the barrel of the big shotgun against the glass of the windshield. T-Bo opened his eyes, saw the gun, saw the face of the toothless hillbilly behind it, and knew they were in deep, deep shit. Potter marched them at gunpoint through the clearing. The croaking bullfrogs sounded like an angry and hostile crowd hidden just out of sight. He made T-Bo and Vermont carry the still-comatose Mickey Day, and he had Cherry and Fraser put their hands behind their heads like he had seen in a TV show years ago.

T-Bo, Cherry, and Vermont were terrified but Fraser seemed delighted with this turn of events, saying that Potter looked like his uncle Jack on his mother's side. Potter told him to shut the hell up and Fraser pouted at the brusque tone.

Potter had them climb the creaking and broken stairs into the dilapidated church. The windows were smashed and the light, swampy rain drifted through the holes in the roof. The pews were smashed and broken into one another, and a battered and rusty drum kit lay in ruins near the door.

Standing at the far end of the church in the pulpit, aged and badly damaged but still upright, was the Reverend Alexander Pinkerton. He was a dark and sinister shadow framed by the ridiculously theatrical rays of moonlight that shone into the church through the broken stained glass behind him.

T-Bo thought the whole thing was like a bad dream. A very fucking bad dream.

"Who are you?" demanded Pinkerton.

There was a moment of uncomfortable silence. T-Bo grasped for a story but Fraser spoke.

"We are beautiful and flawed children of God, as you are. We are headed to the meeting of souls in Birmingham, Alabama, where we will spread the good news among those gathered there. You may join us if you like. We have chocolate biscuits."

Pinkerton seemed confused; he peered into the darkness at Fraser.

Then he climbed down from the pulpit and walked up to him, stopping only when their faces were inches apart.

"You have seen the Holy Postman?" said Pinkerton.

"The French guy?" said Fraser.

"Yes! Yes! The Frenchman, the Frenchman!" Pinkerton started jumping up and down happily, and the others looked at one another with discomfort. T-Bo snuck a glance at Potter, who seemed as baffled as he was.

"He's not a postman, he's a policeman. They have blue uniforms," Fraser said.

But Pinkerton wasn't listening. He ran to the back of the church and dug under some old blankets and brought out two gallon jugs of moonshine and held them aloft.

"Praise Jesus! Praise Almighty God! Free at last! Free at last! This calls for a celebration," he cried.

Everyone sat in a circle, except, of course, the unfortunate Mr. Day, who was laid down on a pew, and the jugs were passed around. Everyone was expected to drink in this ramshackle communion, and Potter followed the whisky around the circle with his rifle to make sure there were no heretics. As the Oreos were broken and taken and the whisky jugs were passed and the powerful brew took everyone in its grip, the Reverend Pinkerton told his tale.

He said that many years ago he had mistakenly invited two demons into the Church. They had taken the form of young boys and one of them could sing like he was a member of God's angelic choir. The demons were clever and tricked the Reverend into trusting them, then they raped his wife when he was out doing God's work.

One of the demons had hit his wife with a household appliance and knocked her out. When she awoke her soul had been snatched away and she was rendered a heathen, she spoke in garbled tongues for three days about needing to have her physical needs met, then she fled to the north.

The last the Reverend had heard of her, she was working as a cocktail waitress in Atlantic City and was an active member of a devil-worshipping group.

The Reverend told that he himself had been struck with the same household appliance that had been turned against his wife, and he had fallen into a deep coma as if he were dead. In his coma he had a vision of a man he called the Holy Postman, who told him—in a French accent, no less—that he should stop annoying innocent snakes and look for something else to handle, maybe something in a dress.

When he awoke the Reverend was confused as to the meaning of the vision, and all these years, as his parishioners had died off or left, he had pondered over it. Everyone said he had lost his mind and all had deserted him except the ever-faithful Potter, who never would leave the graves of his wife and child. The two men had lived in the forest in the church and worshipped together every day.

Every day the Reverend would preach even though there was only Potter to listen. Every day Potter would pray over the graves of his loved ones. They made holy moonshine to ease their pain and to barter with locals for food and toilet paper. He no longer felt the lure of the deadly things and had changed the name of his church from the Christian Reformed Fellowship of Born Again Snake Handling Pentecostal Baptists to the Christian Reformed Fellowship of Born Again Snake Handling Pentecostal Baptists (Reformed)—as in they didn't handle snakes anymore.

The Reverend told the gathered drunken congregation, whom he preached to at gunpoint, that tonight he understood his vision. Fraser was the "something in a dress" and he had come to lead all of them out of the darkness.

Potter asked Fraser if this was true, and Fraser smiled his big bloody grin at him and said, with a little difficulty because of the illegal-booze intake, that yes, it was.

Potter, tanked to the gills, put the gun down, fell to his knees, and cried, "Thank you, Jesus."

T-Bo, Vermont, and Cherry, who were also shitfaced by that time, cheered and cried. Then everyone, excepting Mickey Day of course, stood and held hands and said the Lord's Prayer, led by the Reverend himself.

Soon after, the cheap booze forced them all into unconsciousness.

Fraser was caught up in a hurricane—he dreamed of disillusioned crusaders and ugly witches, he dreamed of revolutions and murders and clockmakers and lies, he dreamed of dead movie stars and religious fanatics and Moorish generals, he dreamed of the death of his old friend George and he wept and shook and sweated. Then he got up. He left the others asleep on the floor and broken pews and he walked outside the ruined church and into the Florida night.

He walked by the bank of a still pond in the moonlight. He could still hear the bullfrogs croaking. He looked like his old self. His bruises were gone, his mouth uninjured, and he noticed he was wearing the suit he wore to funerals or business meetings. His shoes were shined and his hair was combed and he smelled of deodorant and toothpaste.

He looked at the dark water, where he could just make out the shapes of creatures that stirred, surfaced, and submerged, sending ripples out toward him. To his right he saw a broken antler lying by the path. It seemed to be a signpost and pointed him in a direction away from the dark mire. He headed in the direction indicated and after a few hundred feet he happened on his old friend.

"Carl!" he cried delightedly.

"Hello, Fraser." Jung smiled, and the two men embraced warmly.

Jung led Fraser to a couple of striped deck chairs he had set up in the woods.

They sat looking out into the dark forest and Jung lit his pipe.

"I've come to say good-bye," said Jung.

"Why?" said Fraser.

The old man puffed a big blue smoke ring out into the night. "I can't treat you anymore," he said. "It's not you. It's me."

"What are you talking about?" squeaked Fraser. "Are you breaking up with me?"

"Look, Fraser, we both know this can't go on. It doesn't make sense. I'm dead. I've been dead for years."

"I've gone completely insane, haven't I?" groaned Fraser. "It's brain damage from the beating I took or the moonshine whisky or both."

Jung thought for a moment. "No," he said at last. "You are certainly not the man you were but you were never particularly enamored of him anyway."

"True," said Fraser.

"You have deserted the realm of cynical reason, and there will always be a part of you that is suspicious of that. Debate is healthy, only evil does not question itself."

"I had such dreams, such vivid, nonsensical dreams, they felt real. I thought I was dead, I thought my old school friend George had needed my help. It's all crazy shite, isn't it?"

"*Crazy shite* is not a clinical term that I am familiar with," said the doctor, smiling, "but I will tell you something. I admire you."

Fraser was thunderstruck.

"Me?" he said. "I'm a disgraced, runaway, alcoholic minor television celebrity with brain damage. You are one of the most revered and respected healers and teachers in history. What could you possibly admire in me?"

"Your tenacity," said Jung. "It took me until I was an old man and could smell death before I finally shook off the mental and spiritual chains of the frightened engineers and referees who attempt to control the thoughts of us and our fellow pilgrims. You have been thrown to the ravages of the collective unconscious and you survive with questions and innocence and self-doubt. You have been mauled by fear and poisonous self-judgment but have not succumbed to it. You live your life as it arrives."

Suddenly Jung and Fraser both were dressed as dashing Cossacks and had glasses of chilled vodka in their hands. Jung raised his in a toast.

"To my friend Fraser Darby," he said. "You, sir, are interesting!"

Fraser laughed and they clinked glasses, but before Fraser could drink he was back in the church sitting on the floor screaming.

He was awake and he was blind.

THE ROAD TO GOD: ELEVEN

SAUL WAS AWAKE and could see the concern on his brother's face. He could also see the doctor, the one with the wart on his cheek who smelled of mouthwash and nicotine. He saw the cute nurse and the ugly nurse and he saw that the window in his room was open. He looked at them blankly for a moment, then said, "Where's Roscoe?"

They reacted with surprise and the cute nurse said, "I told you."

Leon came forward and leaned in. "Can you hear me, buddy?"

"Of course I can hear you," said Saul, his voice quiet and raspy from lack of use. "You've got your big ugly mug right in my face."

Leon smiled, tears rolling down his cheeks. He hugged Saul. "Oh fuck, Solly. I thought you were gone, buddy. I thought I'd lost you."

"Cut it out," growled Saul. But he was delighted. His brother had not hugged him like this in years. He tried to hug him back but only his left arm would move, and even then just an inch or two from the bed.

But it did move.

The doctor asked Leon to stand back so that he could examine Saul. He peered and he prodded and he took out his little stick and pressed it on Saul's tongue; he didn't really know what he was looking for but he wanted to impress the cute nurse. When he was finished he leaned back and said, "Hmmmm, inconclusive," in the way he had seen on TV and in the movies. "We'll need to perform more tests."

The cute nurse got a little damp. This was a real man.

"How do you feel, Solly?" Leon asked.

"I'm changed, Leon," said Saul. "I feel like I'm born again."

Saul had thought he had been in his state of stasis for a month or two; he was horrified and shocked to find he had been down for almost a year. A year of his fucking life spent in a bed with nothing to do but blink and poop. He felt cheated. Why him?

In the time that Saul had been incapacitated a lot had happened in his life and the life of his brother. *Oh Leon!* had been canceled and Candy Chambers had sued Saul for fifteen million dollars for emotional and physical abuse.

Saul was horrified at this. Candy Chambers was a hooker whom he had paid. Leon agreed but said that their lawyers had told him that she had a good case and the action would certainly generate a lot of hostile publicity. Plus a long, drawn-out legal battle could cost that much anyway, so they advised Leon to settle out of court, which he had done for ten million.

Saul nearly had another stroke but that was not the worst of it.

Leon admitted to Saul his involvement with the Church of Brainyism and said that he had invested in the Church's new headquarters on Hollywood Boulevard. It should have been a safe investment, the property alone was worth so much, and then when the renovations were finished they were going to rent out rooms to Boondtist pilgrims who were visiting town. It should have been a gold mine but the developer, Harry Crenshaw, a longtime elder of the Church, had absconded with the money. The Church itself was blameless, said Leon, a lot of people had been burned, including the Grand High Boondtrah himself.

Saul asked him how much.

Twelve million.

In the time that Saul had been out of commission Leon had lost twenty-two million dollars; Saul's medical expenses and the bills for fresh fruit and flowers every day drove the number up to twenty-four million.

Leon sat on the edge of Saul's bed and wept with shame.

If Saul could have gotten out of the bed and killed Leon, he would have done it, but instead, realizing the limitations of his condition, he said, "It's okay, I'm back now. I'll take care of everything."

Leon nodded.

"No more Brainyism, okay?"

Leon nodded again.

Saul thought that to be involved in something called Brainyism, it might help if you had a fucking brain instead of being a fucking singing cock. But he didn't want to hurt his brother's feelings and he knew he still needed the skinny prick, probably now more than ever, so he didn't say anything. Instead, he yelled at the nurse to bring him a phone.

Saul had all the accountants and managers and lawyers who took care of and mishandled his and Leon's fortune when he was incapacitated fired. He toyed with the idea of suing the bastards who had allowed Leon to make such a fucking mess of things but he kept thinking about Roscoe.

There was something urgent and dire about the fat man's warning to leave Hollywoodland.

Saul was haunted by the thought that if he stayed in this town, things would not only get as bad as they were before but somehow worse, although he had a little difficulty imagining what that would look like.

Leon hung around the hospital all the time, sheepishly trying to take care of his brother even though he couldn't think of what to do, so he just sat in Saul's room next to the bed and flipped through the channels on the TV while Saul mulled over his next move. Saul's speech had returned and he had partial use of his left arm and that was about it. Occasionally, he thought he felt some tingling in his penis but he surmised this was just wishful thinking, like the phantom itches an amputee feels in the missing limb. The doctors said he might or might not improve, that the test results had proved inconclusive. Saul took from this that they didn't have a fucking clue.

We don't have a fucking clue is the lay term for the medical expression *inconclusive.*

Saul and Leon weren't broke but Saul was aware that if he wanted to continue to have the best medical attention and live in luxury and as much comfort as his condition would allow, then they had to earn some money. The only way he knew how to do it was to pimp out his brother, but Leon's stock had fallen considerably in Hollywoodland, and he himself was afraid to stay there anyway.

Roscoe had told him to get out.

He asked about Roscoe a few times but no one seemed to know who he was talking about, so he let it slide.

One long, hot afternoon, Saul was deeply depressed and was just about to ask Leon to turn off the television when he noticed a channel his brother had skipped past.

"Go back!" he said.

Leon flipped the channel back to what Saul wanted.

A religious channel.

A man with a preposterous hairdo in a garish yellow suit and bootlace tie was preaching fire and brimstone to a massive audience in a huge auditorium in Texas. A number was flashing across the bottom of the screen telling callers where to call to pledge their donations. Saul knew his prayers had been answered.

This was the way out of this sick and twisted fucking town.

Saul had Leon bring in some high-ranking Boondtists to his bedside on the premise that he was interested in joining the Church. Saul had no intention of doing this, of course, but he pumped the Brainyists about the birth of their faith, about Boondt himself, and about their tax-exempt status as a religion. He asked about their recruitment techniques and their structure of management.

During this time Saul also asked for, and got, visits from Catholic priests, Protestant ministers, Mormons, Muslims, Jehovah's Witnesses, rabbis, gurus, shamans, and snake oil salesmen of every description who peddle their services to the sick, the scared, and the dying in the hospitals of Southern California.

Saul thought back to the sermons he had witnessed in the snake-handling church of Crawford's Creek, how these dirt-poor farmers had been only too happy to hand over what little cash they had if they were convinced that they had been in the presence of a little miracle or two.

Saul devoured historical and religious texts. Leon hired an out-of-work actor to sit by Saul's bed and turn pages for him. He had to fire three before they finally got one who would shut up. He studied the rise and fall of ancient religions, he studied the spread of empires and the careers of dictators. He read and reread, from the indecipherable Kierkegaard to the sound-bite-friendly Nietzsche. He read Kahlil Gibran and Tolkien and C. S. Lewis and Joseph Campbell and Jung. He read Saint Thomas Aquinas.

He read *Men Are Asteroids, Women Are Meteorites,* he read *Peephole* magazine, he watched daytime talk shows and hours and hours of religious television. He was in awe of the thirst that people had for someone to tell them that everything was going to be all right. He marveled at the gullibility and vulnerability of his fellow humans. No wonder the churches called them sheep. They were woolly-headed pack animals being herded around for the benefit of whoever knew how to control the dogs.

He read about branding and tipping points and all other aspects of advertising.

He thought about what Wiesner had done to *Killing by Starlight.* He remembered that the executive had renamed the movie using words that appealed to Americans regardless of their relevance to the plot. Saul tried to remember the words—*wedding, celebrity, united, America* or *American.*

Finally, when he had gathered enough information and his plan was completely formed, he was ready to make his announcement to his brother. It was the middle of the night. Saul screamed for the nurse. He demanded that she phone Leon and tell him to get here right away.

Something big had happened.

Leon rushed right over. Saul was sitting up in bed, a beatific smile on his fat mug, not unlike the look that Fraser had used to such great effect when working on Scottish television.

"Leon, oh Praise the Lord, Leon. Thank God you are all right."

"What is it, Solly? What's going on?"

"Leon, it's going to sound weird but something has happened. I was lying here in the dark and I felt myself dying, I felt my body give up the ghost, and I cried out, 'Oh Lord God, take me if You must but please look after my brother.' "

Leon was hooked. Saul knew the way to get Leon really interested was to give him a starring role.

He continued, "Then the room lit up and a great wind blew through and I felt I was on a mountaintop and a tall handsome man in a long white robe and a beard appeared to me."

"Jesus?" whispered Leon.

"He didn't say. He only said this: 'Saul, you have been a wicked and evil sinner. Leon thy brother has also followed the path unto darkness. The time is at hand to repent. I healed you for a reason. You two brothers are to turn from your wickedness and do my work. If you do not, then you will be cast into the fiery pit.' "

Leon was transfixed. "What do we do?" he asked.

Saul raised his left hand and placed it in the hand of his brother. He looked up at him and smiled sadly, tears in his eyes. "We must do Our Lord's bidding," he said.

Leon fell to his knees.

Saul placed his hand on his brother's head. "It's going to be all right, Leon," he said.

Leon wept.

CHEZ NOUS

GEORGE WAS AWAKE BEFORE CLAUDETTE. The pain in his back drilled away at him but it was lower grade than before. He thought he must have a bit of the old morphine coursing around, thank God. He watched her for a little, then got up and padded through to the little kitchen.

He had a raging thirst like he'd been drunk for a week. He pulled a little bottle of Orangina from the fridge, twisted off the top, and drank it down.

"Holy crap," he gasped aloud with delight.

He threw the Orangina bottle in the trash and went through to the sitting room. His other bottle, the little morphine bottle, was sitting on the table but he didn't want to take it just yet, it made him feel dopey and strange, plus he wanted to feel the pain intensify because it would help him go through with his plan for the day.

It was still early morning and the street outside was quiet. He heard the occasional *putt-putt* of a moped, that shameful combination of hair dryer and bicycle that the French seem unembarrassed about being seen on.

He thought over the last few days of his good-byes in Scotland and he was happy about that. He had been deeply touched by the reaction of his daughter. He thought about how much he'd miss her. He thought about his wife; that made him sad. She was such an unhappy, angry woman, and he suspected he had helped her get that way by staying with her and not loving her. He hoped she'd get a little more fun out of life, maybe with Barry Symington, the swimming instructor from the leisure center, although George really had a hard time believing that Barry wasn't gay.

Then he thought about Claudette and wondered about all of that.

Everything had happened so fast yet he felt that he had known her for his entire life. He thought about what had happened to him by knowing her. He had become wild and sexy and interesting in the space of a few days.

A phrase he had heard somewhere popped into his head: "Nothing became him in his life like the leaving of it."

He thought about the sex he had had with Claudette, not only on their first night but on the return from Scotland. They had gotten a little drunk on the best wine he had ever tasted, a fruity bouquet that seemed to go very well with morphine. They had eaten bread and cheese and fruit and chocolate and then made love on the wooden floor he was now looking at.

He thought about the phrase *made love*. He speculated that if you "made love" without having the correct ingredients, then it probably wouldn't taste as good.

He thought about the sex again, he thought about how she looked at him as she took him in her mouth, and that it had excited him beyond belief. She had touched the tip of his penis with her tongue and gently stroked his bottom. She had left little lipstick marks on the top of his thighs.

He felt himself get hard again and thought that he'd better go through to the bedroom and wake her up but the pain was really beginning to bite now and anyway, he knew he couldn't. He wouldn't be going there to make love, he'd be going there to take it, and although Claudette would be happy to give it, he knew it was time.

It was time.

He put on his clothes as quietly as he could, then he kissed the sleeping beauty on the head and left her a little note that read:

Chere Claudette,
Quand tu reveille s.t.p. ne me pensez pas
grossier ou irrespectueux mais j'ai du le laisser.
C'est temps.
Si je ne t'ai pas convaincu pourtant je le dirai
encore.
Tu a l'amour de ma vie.
Merci de tout.
Ton Amour
Georges.
X

He felt a little of ripple of gratitude for his high-school French teacher, Miss Major (a.k.a. Beanpole and Le Stick). Claudette kept the note until the day she died. It was far from perfect but it was the most beautiful and poetic French she had ever read. It was folded and tucked away in her jacket pocket when she was burned.

George took a last look at her. His face was calm, giving no indication of the pain that was roaring and bucking wildly inside of him.

He walked out of the apartment to his suicide.

LAMB OF GOD

ONCE FRASER REALIZED that he was only blind and that it wasn't anything serious, he calmed down considerably. He had been terrified for a moment or two that he was about to be thrown back to the trenches or into the hands of the grumpy boatman. His screaming had woken everyone else up, including the confused Mickey Day.

The Reverend explained to Fraser that occasionally when people drank the holy moonshine they would be rendered sightless for a time, but as far as he knew, their vision had almost always returned. Fraser said that was just fine with him, that his eyes could use a rest anyway, and as long as someone handed him a chocolate biscuit, he was good.

The rest of the troop were unharmed except for the vicious hangovers they had been stricken with, but they were soon helped by Potter, who went outside and picked eight watermelons from the patch near the swamp. They were still cold and dewey from the night and when they were cracked open they spilled their life-restoring red juice as freely as enthusiastic martyrs.

They were manna.

Pinkerton held a piece of dripping watermelon over Mickey's mouth to give the groggy, dehydrated old man some moisture. The red juice dipped over Mickey's cracked lips in a fruity communion, and as the liquid dribbled down his throat, he coughed and spluttered.

He looked warily at the strange crew around him. They looked warily back. "What's happening here?" he croaked in a tired frog voice.

T-Bo gave him the whole story, about him taking out the gun and having a fit and how they had panicked and that his camper was unharmed and sitting outside of the church.

Mickey told them that while he was out he'd suffered strange dreams, that his dead wife, Agnes, had appeared to him in the company of a bad-tempered French policeman and had told him it was time to lighten up and have fun and go with the flow and a whole lot of other hippie-speak and then the policeman had whacked him across the mouth with his nightstick.

Fraser and Pinkerton agreed with Mickey that they thought the policeman seemed to be a little keen on excessive force. Mickey was changed, though, the anger was gone.

Pinkerton announced that they must all take the camper van and travel to the convention in Alabama, that this was their calling, their destiny.

Mickey agreed and said he would be happy to drive, that he wanted to go with the flow.

As they stumbled aboard the camper, Fraser, who was being led by T-Bo, said that they should give the vehicle a name.

"It's got a name. It's a camper," said T-Bo.

"No, he means a name like *Titanic* or *Queen Mary,*" said Cherry.

"How 'bout *Queen T-Bo*?" said Vermont. T-Bo glared at him and he apologized.

"I've always thought of her as taking the name of my wife, Agnes," said Mickey.

They all agreed that it was only right that Mickey choose the name of their craft, given that he owned it, so Potter grabbed some red paint from his little shed and painted on the front of the RV, just above the radiator grille:

AGNES DAY

They had to wait for a moment while Potter explained to the graves of his family that he was going on a little trip and would be back soon. Then Mickey started up *Agnes* and the big bus rattled slowly out of the woods, through the little dead town past the Gupta gas station, and toward the turnpike.

They had been traveling for about an hour when they saw a minivan parked at the side of the road. Half a dozen large black ladies seemed to be fussing around something, and the sight looked comical to Mickey, who tried to describe it to Fraser.

Fraser said that they should stop and the Reverend Pinkerton said that Fraser spoke with the tongues of angels and was blind, so they stopped.

The ladies were the Salome Henderson Gospel Sextet from Miami. They had been headed to the convention in Alabama in a minivan because Salome herself was afraid to fly. In the minivan she had fainted and the others feared she'd had a stroke or heart attack. There had been a great deal of panic and hysteria in the little van and the result was that Magdalene Brightwell (a distant cousin of the unfortunate Lashanda Brightwell, Tootsiepop Ted's fourth victim), who was driving, had pulled to a stop rather too suddenly. The vehicle had gone into a skid and they had hit the crash barrier. The van was badly damaged on the front end and Salome had still not regained consciousness. The ladies were in a panic and begged the Reverend Pinkerton for a cell phone to call an ambulance when he went over to them to inquire if he could help.

Pinkerton said that they had no need of an ambulance, that he had a holyman with him who could heal the unfortunate Salome.

Fraser was led out of the truck and the ladies looked dubious as the battered blind man in the orange dress was taken over to the unfortunate Salome, who was lying prostrate at the side of the highway.

Fraser put his hands on Salome's forehead, then ran his fingers over her ample body. The ladies clucked and shuffled a little at this but Reverend Pinkerton shushed them.

Fraser felt the side of Salome's head, then he bent over and whispered into her ear, "Come back. Please come back."

Suddenly, Salome sat bolt upright at the side of the road and inhaled deeply, as if she had just surfaced from a deep dive.

The ladies of the gospel sextet and Fraser's little troop whooped and hollered and clapped and high-fived and a miracle was declared.

Fraser said that he wasn't sure if it really was a miracle, that maybe it was a bit hot and airless in the van and perhaps Salome, who had to be close to three hundred pounds, had overheated and just fainted. But no one wanted to hear any of that nonsense. They were pilgrims on their way to a gathering and a holyman had delivered them a miracle. This was what they had been waiting for.

That the minivan was trashed was of little consequence to the Salome Henderson Gospel Sextet because Pinkerton said that they should travel in the *Agnes Day.* The ladies were delighted to accept, although Magdalene said that they should get in touch with her brother, Thomas, who owned the van so that he could send a tow truck. The Reverend and Salome, who seemed to have formed an attraction almost instantly, assured Magdalene that everything would be all right.

So Fraser, blind and battered, sat in the back of the *Agnes Day* as it rumbled toward Birmingham, Alabama. The ladies of the Salome Henderson Gospel Sextet sang devotional hymns in their beautiful, clear voices and the rest of Fraser's disciples joined in.

Fraser thought about what the guys in the Press Bar in Glasgow would think of him now. He wondered what jokes they would come up with. He smiled to himself. They weren't bad men, just afraid. Afraid of change, afraid of everything. That's probably why they drank so much. For Dutch courage.

He thought about Gus, his old boss. Fraser wondered if he could have his job back. He could wear his orange dress and do a little preaching as Salome and the girls made beautiful music. He chuckled to himself. Probably not. Maybe Margaret, his agent, could book them a little tour of the Highlands. He thought about Margaret. He wondered why she had never asked him if the allegations against him were true. He supposed she probably knew more about him than he knew himself at that point.

He thought about George, his old school friend he hadn't seen in years. He wondered about that strange experience in the trench. He wondered if George was dead, like Brinsley and Carl and H.P. Lovecraft and Virgil and Corporal McLachlan.

It felt stuffy and he asked T-Bo to open a window.

The big camper was getting a little crowded.

They now had a baker's dozen.

The holyman plus twelve.

In the firmament high above the turnpike, the regularly scheduled Delta Airlines flight from Fort Lauderdale to Atlanta and a small Federal Express cargo plane rushing a fresh donor heart from a car crash victim in Savannah to a hopeful patient who was already being prepped for surgery in a hospital in New Orleans passed within fifteen hundred feet of each other.

This is a perfectly acceptable distance and neither of the planes was in any danger at any time. The pilots had acknowledged each other by radio and exchanged a few pleasantries.

Because of the atmospheric conditions, both aircraft were leaving brilliant white vapor trails behind them, and given the trajectory of their respective routes, the trails formed a perfect saltire in the heavens.

A white cross on a clear blue sky. The banner of Saint Andrew.

The flag of Scotland.

THE ROAD TO GOD: TWELVE

THE CONSTRUCTION OF THE NEW FAITH was Saul's salvation. It gave him something to be interested in, something to be enthusiastic about, and also, given that he had received his instructions from on high, something that placed him in complete control even though he was a motionless fat man in a hospital bed. He actually began to think that his condition helped people buy his story, so he hammed it up a little with the holyman shtick. He said "unto" and "thy" a lot. It seemed to do the trick.

He told Leon that the Holy Visitor (who appeared every other night for a while) had told him it was time for a New Way, a New Church that was to be headed by both of them. In the way that Rome had been built by Romulus and Remus, Leon and Saul were to build the Holy United Church of America.

At first Saul played the L.A. card. He had Leon bring some of his flakiest friends into the hospital and he recounted his experience. He elaborated a bit on his Holy Visitor—he stopped short at calling him Jesus, since he knew that for maximum impact he needed to be as nondenominational as possible while still adhering to the look and feel of the established churches, and he didn't want to rule out any disaffected Jews.

Saul collected a little group of spiritual VIPs around him. He knew how to play Los Angeles—basically, just tell people there is a room they can't get into. A room that contains successful people in the entertainment industry.

Saul was surprised to see Meg Roberts show up. It turned out that after he had his stroke, she had been very kind to Leon, and although their romance had not rekindled—she was now living with her counselor from the Malibu treatment center that she had attended for her addiction to hypnoyoga—they had become friends again.

She was actually a very sweet woman, gullible, well meaning, and open. Perfect for Saul's design.

The Church grew slowly at first. Saul was visited three times a week by his chosen disciples. They sat around his bed and he told them what information he had received from the Holy Visitor, how they should raise money, how they should spread the word.

He found (and paid) a friendly doctor who said his partial recovery could only have occurred by divine intervention. It was in fact a miracle.

More cynical doctors said that the reasons for Saul's recovery were inconclusive—which helped his case for a miracle even more than the paid doctor.

He told his little congregation that they were as the first apostles in the New Order, the Holy United Church of America. Then after about a month, he tipped off a paparazzo he knew and made sure that Meg and Leon and the others (who included the former child star Jonathon Daimler-Thomason, who at seventeen had been thrown out of three rehabs and was tabloid gold) were photographed as they left the hospital.

He fed a line to a syndicated gossip columnist and sat back, although he really did nothing but sit back these days anyway. The woolly-headed public's disappointment at not being involved in showbiz would take care of the rest. He was dead on.

Within three years, the Holy United Church had bought their first property, an old movie theater in the San Fernando Valley. They had the place renovated and had services three times a week.

Leon would sing quasi-devotional easy-listening songs like "Feeling Groovy About God" or "My Soul Is Open," and Saul had himself wheeled onto the stage, where he would thank the congregation and say that the Universe was happy that they had come. His bed was draped in purple robes not unlike the ones he had seen the Reverend Pinkerton wear but he didn't talk too much; he wasn't much of a public speaker before and the massive stroke had not improved his technique.

Leon would sing some more and a movie star or comedian would testify as to how they were lost until the power of the Holy United Church had saved them—emotionally, financially, professionally, artistically, the usual crap.

There was nothing really different in the doctrine they were spouting, it was basic stuff: Be good, help others, try not to lose your temper, and of course, the big-time perennial favorite—forgiveness of sins.

Saul had come up with two ideas, the two strokes of genius that he felt were their big money spinners. They were: (1) The Holy United Church of America told the people that God only wanted them to be happy in any way that they could, and if that meant committing sin, then they should go ahead and commit sin and then atone by doing good in the community, but if they didn't have time for that, they could pay for someone else to do it. The Holy United Church would be happy to make the arrangements, just sign here. (This is not new, of course. Some people are happy to let another person die for their sins.) And (2) you could join the Holy United Church of America without renouncing any of your other beliefs. The Holy United Church said that people of all beliefs were welcome—Catholics, Protestants, Hindus, Muslims, Jews, atheists, anybody. They were nondenominational worshippers of God without prejudice. Tithe only 5—yes, only *five*—percent of your earnings (tax deductible) and you were saved. Guaranteed!

They were off to the races.

Two years after they bought the property in the Valley, they had raised enough money for what Saul really wanted.

Saul knew that that if they stayed in Los Angeles, the Church would eventually fall from grace and be replaced by some other fashionable movement. Already Meg Roberts had stopped wearing her green handkerchief.

They had to reach the Great American Public: Once you hooked this bunch, you were in. These were people who were loyal to a fault. It had taken them three years after the scripts turned to shit before they stopped watching *Oh Leon!*

This was the audience/congregation Saul wanted.

Plus he noticed that most of the competition in the evangelism field wasn't that strong. A bunch of pudgy white guys with very bad hair, or Negroes who yelled too much. He had Leon, the freaky power of his own obvious infirmity, and Hollywood kudos behind him.

And Saul wanted out of town. He kept thinking Roscoe might come back, he could hardly sleep for worrying about it. He wondered why the thought of the fat man's return terrified him so much. He took extra drugs to sleep, on top of the ones he took for his condition.

So the Holy United Church of America—Saul and Leon, the joint heads, or pastors as they now called themselves—bought TEN, The Evangelical Network based in Atlanta, for eighty million dollars (they raised and borrowed money at extraordinary rates from converts to the faith) and moved back home to the South.

IN THE GARDEN

CLAUDETTE RETURNED TO THE GARDEN OF GETHSEMANE. She waved across to the ugly English composer Anthony Boyd-Webster, who was still sitting at a harpsichord under the twisted branches of one of the olive trees. Boyd-Webster smiled back at her but did not stop playing his tinkling, medieval-sounding rendition of the Velvet Underground classic "All Tomorrow's Parties."

The garden was bathed in moonlight and Claudette felt the warm summer night's breeze on her skin. She was wearing a light linen dress that somehow was a wedding gown even though it was cut a little like the habit she had worn as an apprentice nun. She had an overwhelming feeling of well-being.

Jesus looked fabulous.

He was barefoot but wearing a dark-blue Donna Karan single-breasted suit and white open-necked shirt. He walked across the grass to meet her.

He took her hands in his and he smiled at her.

"You're fired," He said and kissed her lightly on the forehead.

She awoke smiling and felt the bed for George before she opened her eyes. He was gone. She read the note he left her, her heart suddenly pounding. She dressed quickly and ran outside but she had no idea where to go. In a panic she ran down Rue Madame and headed toward the river.

She turned and bumped into an officer who was just leaving the big police station across the square from the cathedral of Saint-Sulpice.

"Hey!" snapped the cop. "Take it easy."

"Sorry!" she said and hurried across the square past the big theatrical fountain.

The cop yelled at her to stop.

She turned around and looked at him. He was weird. She was desperate to get away but had no idea where to.

"Pont-Neuf," said the gendarme.

She looked at him for a second, puzzled.

"Pont-Neuf," he said again.

She turned and ran in the direction of the famous bridge.

THIRTEEN

THE CONVENTION OF TELEVISION EVANGELISTS had been Saul's idea. It was his way of absorbing the competition into his own church. He brought in TV and radio preachers from all over the country. He let them rant and rave their particular brand of devotion in front of a large gathered congregation who had paid up to sixty bucks a head (tax deductible) for the pleasure of seeing them. He televised these guys and sold the shows at home and overseas and used their performances on his own network, which was anchored most of the time by Leon, of course.

The first two conventions had been hugely successful and had brought thousands of pilgrims and converts to Atlanta. Saul chose to hold the third convention in Birmingham, Alabama, because they had a massive new hotel and conference center there and were providing huge cash incentives to anyone who would use it. Plus, Alabama had a lot of good God-fearing poor folks who had been enthusiastic supporters of the Church, and it wasn't too far for him to travel. He could have his air-conditioned ambulance take him there with the minimum of discomfort.

He also decided that for the third year they would send invitations out to television evangelists overseas—you never know, they might get a few bites from there too.

* * *

Saul was having his afternoon massage when he first saw Fraser. Dolores was working his lower back. She was an attractive physiotherapist with a drug problem, who had to work with the hideous Saul to support her habit. He made her stick her finger in his anus every time—he couldn't feel it but he wanted to know she had done it. He checked by smelling her hand.

He was watching the local television news coverage of the pilgrims who were flocking into town for the big roundup. The place was packed, this would be the best yet. There was more money pouring into Birmingham than they had seen since the slave trade.

A young reporter had gotten some footage of the *Agnes Day* parked outside the convention center. Salome and the girls had started singing and a little crowd had gathered.

There was a little impromptu interview with Salome, who told of the miracle on the turnpike and the blind Scottish holyman. There was an interview with the Reverend Pinkerton, who waxed lyrical on how Fraser was sent by God Himself to speak His word to the convention.

Saul was horrified to see Pinkerton.

He told Dolores to get her fucking clumsy hands off him and turn up the volume on the TV.

Saul hadn't seen the old buzzard since he'd brained him and his bitch wife with the clothes iron. He looked much older and crazier but it was definitely him.

Then there was an interview with T-Bo and Vermont, just quick sound bites about how they had seen the light through the miracles of Fraser, and then there was an interview with Fraser himself.

Saul was baffled by him.

Most of his preachers were immaculate strutting peacocks, while this one looked like he'd had the shit kicked out of him, and what the fuck was he wearing? Was that a dress? And he's blind! Shit, what is this? Why didn't he know about this one, what list was he on? He listened to Fraser speak in that strange Bravehearty/Shrecky accent.

Fraser said that everyone was a beautiful and flawed child of God, he said he was glad to be here and that everyone had been very kind, and he looked forward to the moment during the convention when all the money was handed to the poor.

Saul almost choked. What the fuck was this clown smoking?

The reporter wound up the piece with a little wry remark about how it takes all sorts to seek the Lord.

Saul swore at Dolores and told her to go and get Leon.

The little crowd that had gathered to hear Salome and her girls sing had grown to almost a thousand. The big black women were extraordinary singers and wonderful to watch. They swayed and rocked and danced and invested each song with a passion and enthusiasm that most people don't even have for sex.

They sang for free and this also helped swell the crowd, given that it cost money to see the rest of the entertainment, never mind to enter the convention center to hear the preachers.

The afternoon was hot, though, and after an hour or so the girls needed a rest. The Reverend Pinkerton took advantage of the sweaty, happy audience. He climbed on the roof of the *Agnes Day* and yelled, "Sinners all!"

This was what the people had come for. Old-timey religion. Sparky hell and damnation from a boggle-eyed, crazy-looking, rabid-dog Southerner. The local news cameras turned on him and the people fell quiet.

Even more pilgrims drifted into the parking lot.

The Reverend launched into a furious diatribe on the state of the modern world, on abortion and liberals and terrorists, the very things that the audience was afraid of. They listened in rapture.

T-Bo watched the performance in awe. He hadn't really warmed to the psychotic old coot but he was impressed by the performance.

How amazing to have people pay attention to you like this. To hang on your every word. What power.

Pinkerton told of how he believed that all the answers to all the questions he'd ever had were in the Bible, and certainly he got Amen'd for that.

Then he said that they were lucky to live in this time, to be here in this moment. He said that God had sent a healer, a holyman, among them. An angel.

Then he had T-Bo and Vermont lift Fraser up onto the roof of the *Agnes Day.* Fraser, who had been sitting in a deck chair while Cherry the anorexic stripper gave him a foot rub, tried to protest but to no avail.

The large audience was hushed as Fraser stood before them on the roof of the camper. That he was blind was a help to him. He wasn't intimidated by the size of the crowd. The people looked on aghast at the sight of this strange man.

Pinkerton rode the mood.

"Do not judge a man by the cloth of his robes. For surely even Our Lord was naked on the cross!"

A few Amens. People relaxed a little.

"This blind beggar has seen a vision of a Holy Messenger. As I have myself. But he has been chosen to heal the sick. He must be the one we listen to. He is the Chosen One."

Fraser tried to speak but Pinkerton put his hand on him and whispered, "Not yet."

Pinkerton continued, "This man healed me of my chronic depression." He pointed at Vermont. "He cured this boy of his addiction to the crack cocaine."

Vermont, who was fast getting caught up in the feel of the event, smiled and waved and yelled, "S'all true. I was a nasty, cracky little dipshit. Now I am saved, Praise Jesus."

The audience applauded.

Pinkerton indicated Cherry. "This girl was starving to death with the crippling demonic possession of anorexia. She was saved by the blind man in the orange summer dress who is filled with the Holy Spirit!"

Cherry took a little bow. The applause was building, the Reverend really had to yell now to be heard. He pointed at T-Bo. "He cured this young man of ho-mo-sex-uality!"

T-Bo didn't feel it was the right time to correct the preacher.

Fraser tried to protest but the Reverend was on a roll.

"And if that were not enough"—he pointed toward Salome, who was fanning herself with a hymn sheet—"he brought this beautiful lady back from the dead!"

Salome sang a powerful "Amen" and the crowd went wild.

Pinkerton spoke to Fraser above the noise. "Your people," he said.

Fraser had a headache. The crowd fell silent and waited for him to speak. There was an uncomfortably long silence and then he said, "Help others."

The audience applauded.

Fraser thought about all the phony hypocritical garbage he had spouted on his God spot on late-night television. He thought about Carl telling him he was interesting. He thought how much he had disliked the man he had become before his walk across the desert of his soul with the long-dead poet.

He came to a decision.

"That's all I have to say," he said.

The people laughed and clapped and waited for more.

When Pinkerton saw that there was no more, he announced to the crowd that the holyman was tired and had to rest and he would appear before them later.

He hustled Fraser back inside the camper and closed the door.

Saul and Leon watched the video footage of the performance that had been taken by one of their cameramen on the scene. They had chosen not to broadcast it.

Leon was scared that Pinkerton had turned up. They hadn't heard a peep out of him all the years they were in Hollywood and now this, like a bolt out of the blue.

Saul wasn't too happy about Pinkerton being around either. It was an ugly story that he'd rather not have get out in the open. Getting your jollies by crapping on the face of a hooker in California is one thing, you can beg forgiveness and blame the devil, but smacking a man of God with a kitchen appliance while your brother is fucking his wife is quite another.

"Who will rid us of this turbulent priest?" he muttered.

As concerned as he was about Pinkerton—and he was very concerned—Saul was bothered more by the weird rogue healer in the frock. There was something compelling and unstaged and strangely familiar about him.

"We have to get rid of his vagrant friend as well."

"What'll we do?" asked Leon.

Saul didn't even have to think about it.

"Find them."

Pinkerton had been living as a mad recluse with his cretin roommate in a broken-down church next to a swamp for nearly twenty years. He had neglected to have television installed, preferring the entertainment provided by his pathology and the home-made whisky. Consequently he had no idea that the pastors who ran the Holy United Church were the demons he had battled with so long ago. Not until Mickey Day connected the little portable in the trailer and he saw Leon on TV.

When Salome explained to him that Saul and Leon were the heads of the Church, he knew that he was part of a bigger battle. He insisted that they leave the parking lot in the *Agnes Day* and drive to a quiet spot where nobody could find them. He said it was very important but he didn't say why. He was a very forceful man, as most preachers are.

The *Agnes Day* nudged through the crowd of parking-lot pilgrims, Pinkerton standing at the door insisting that they would return to heal the already growing band of hopeful cripples who waited to see Fraser. He told them that the holyman had to go to a place of solitude for a time of prayer and meditation.

They drove a little ways out of town, then off of the main road and through a run-down industrial neighborhood until they found a deserted, derelict building. It was a dilapidated olive-oil-pressing plant that had been shut down years ago. There were no dogs, no security men, no cameras, nothing but the pungent odor of rusty old machines and the billions of olives that had been squeezed for their precious residue.

"This is perfect!" cried Pinkerton. "They'll never find us here." He ushered them all inside.

Once Mickey had parked the *Agnes Day* around the back of the building and everyone was settled, Pinkerton explained the reason for his cloak-and-dagger tactics, that the very demons he had fought were now heads of the Church. The devil himself was at the reins. Salome and her girls were appalled and skeptical until Pinkerton told them the whole story of the day he found his wife with Leon on the tumble dryer.

Salome had read *Hot Lunch/Cold Hearts* a few years ago and had been titillated by the stories of Saul's debaucheries but he had repented publicly and declared himself reborn. Surely a man must be forgiven his past.

Pinkerton persisted that this was no ordinary man. This was an agent of the dark one and would say anything to gain power and an edge over the Lord's children. They must protect Fraser, whom he would seek to destroy.

Salome believed him because she wanted to. She had fallen hard for this fiery preacher and he in turn had lost his head over her.

T-Bo sighed.

He was beginning to realize that he was the only one among this group who was not delusional and probably suffering from some kind of brain damage. Actually, he'd been pretty aware of it before but it had been much less fun since crazy Pinkerton had shown up.

He was getting bored listening to the mad old bastard.

Fraser was being a pain in the ass too. He seemed totally detached from the craziness that was going on around him. He hardly said anything. If he spoke at all, it was just to ask for more chocolate biscuits. Vermont was also driving him crazy. He had thrown himself into the God thing in the way that only a recovering addict can.

T-Bo suggested that he take the camper and go and get them some food. He'd go on his own so as not to attract attention. He really wanted a break from his new dysfunctional family.

Fraser championed the idea because he'd get more biscuits, so Pinkerton had to agree, but he warned T-Bo to be careful.

"Don't worry. I won' take any candy from strangers," said T-Bo.

"See that you don't," said Pinkerton.

T-Bo just needed some time to himself. He wasn't looking for trouble. He thought it might be a blast to drive by the convention center, see if the crowd was still there.

They were, and had grown.

There were now people camped on the sidewalks. News of the healer had spread fast and there were some pretty desperate people in Alabama. They rushed the *Agnes Day* and blocked its path. No one would believe T-Bo that Fraser wasn't there until he let a few of them inside to see and report back to the crowd.

Leon had been reluctant to tell Saul that he couldn't find the holyman and Pinkerton, so he was delighted when he caught sight of T-Bo. He had been about to give up.

From the backseat of the town car with the tinted windows, Leon watched the *Agnes Day* push through the crowd. Donal, the tubby red-headed chauffeur, had been delighted to follow the camper from the parking lot. He was a huge fan of spy movies and had always dreamed of one day being told to "follow that car," especially with the delicious codicil "Don't let them know we're tailing them."

Leon had even said it the right way, of course—he had been in movies.

T-Bo pulled into a gas station to fill up and to get Fraser his Oreos. Donal asked Leon what they should do now. Leon didn't know, so he called Saul.

Saul knew; he was a predator.

Go after the one that breaks from the herd.

T-Bo was standing at the pump when he saw Leon walk over to him. He recognized him immediately. The singing guy from TV. Leon held out his hand in true celebrity fashion and permitted T-Bo to shake it.

"Hi, I'm Leon Martini. You're with the Reverend Pinkerton's party, right?"

T-Bo nodded. Suspicious.

"I have a proposition for you I think you might be interested in."

Leon loved talking like this. It made him feel like he was back in Hollywood.

THE BRIDGE

THE BOOK OF REVELATION DESCRIBES A HEAVENLY CITY with a river running through it. A place for God's children after the pain. Pont-Neuf (New Bridge) is the oldest bridge left standing in Paris. Construction was started by Henri III but had to be halted for yet another war over religion.

The project was finished by Henri IV—well, not by him personally, he was an aristocratic milquetoast who never did an honest day's work in his life. Laborers and craftsmen in the king's employ, many of whom who were veterans of the religious wars, finished the job.

Henri IV gets the credit because the study of history had been forbidden to the common folk until comparatively recently. The bridge is in two parts, split by the Île de la Cité, the chic and picturesque little haven in the middle of the river.

George stood in one of the little semicircular projections that Henri IV's experts had added to the structure and gazed down at the water below. The drop wasn't enough to kill a man on a fall, not convincingly. It was only about fifty or sixty feet to the surface.

George wasn't too concerned by that. If he was not rendered unconscious by the violent impact on the surface of the water, which he probably would be, all he had to do was get below and take a deep breath—or so he had read somewhere. Death would be swift and painless. But even if he couldn't manage that, he had his guilty secret.

All of his life he had told himself that the day he had refused to drink from the bottle of Eldorado and had protected Fraser from the gross ministrations of Willie Elmslie, he had been acting as a good egg. A loyal pal. He had done the right thing but he knew in his heart that this was not true. The reason he had whipped the older boy with the fishing rod, the reason he had not joined in the cheap wine communion, was that he was afraid. He could not be out of control or have events get out of his control so close to a body of water.

He couldn't swim.

He had never learned. He had had a fear of water as a little boy, and by the time he reached adolescence, he was too embarrassed to admit his failing to his friends. Then the moment had passed and he had plunged into a dry life that had not required him to do much swimming. He had played with his daughter in the water when she was little but he had never gotten out of his depth.

Actually, Nancy had been taught to swim by Barry Symington at the leisure center. George still couldn't believe he wasn't gay. Sheila must have gotten it wrong.

He had never really been out of his depth in anything until the test results. Since the diagnosis, he had been drowning. Claudette had waded in to his rescue but he was dragging her down. The right thing to do was jump, push off, and let her swim to safety.

Claudette had told him the previous evening that she wanted to go with him when he went. There was too much death in the world, her heart had been shattered too many times, and she wanted to leave with him.

He had been appalled and put the conversation down to too much wine and enthusiastic, romantic pillow talk, but he couldn't take the chance of being around her anymore. He was pulling her under.

It was still reasonably quiet. The big department store nearby, Samaritain, had not yet opened its doors, and the only people about were a few late revelers who had pulled all-nighters, a couple of jet-lagged tourists, and some people on their way to work.

One or two of the ubiquitous coal barges puttered up the river on their way to or from the north coast ports. George took a deep breath; he looked all around him at the heavenly city, then climbed onto the parapet.

Claudette screamed his name as she came running down the street to the bridge, her voice echoing off the buildings. She was running as fast as she could, tears streaming down her face.

George knew that he would not be able to resist her if she got to him. He had to go now and make it quick, or hang on for a world of agony and despair—and then go anyway.

He looked at her. He mouthed, *"Je suis désolé."*

He thumped his chest and threw out his hand toward her as if tossing her his heart. He sent up a quick and silent prayer to anything that might be there asking for help for Claudette.

Then he jumped.

LIFE ON EARTH

IT HAD BEEN A CHALLENGE for Saul to deal with T-Bo. He wanted to tell him he was a dim-witted, grubby nigger and have him whipped but he knew he had to be a bit more canny in the world these days. Instead he promised the young man wealth and fame. He promised him a place in the Holy United Church seminary, and when he graduated (which he also had to guarantee), he would be taken into the Church as a pastor and—this was the clincher—given his own spot on the religious network.

T-Bo also made him promise that no harm would come to Fraser or any of his friends.

Saul had promised unreservedly, he had no intention of making a martyr. He remembered the story that Roscoe had told him years ago. Only tyrants and fools made martyrs.

He was certainly no fool.

And he was no tyrant either—how could he be, he had suffered a hideous stroke. He was a victim. The victim excuse, where evil is born.

T-Bo had given them the location of the disused olive-oil plant but none of Saul's security guys could find it; they were all imports from Atlanta and didn't have a clue how to get around Birmingham.

Finally, Saul made him guide them to the site and T-Bo was deeply embarrassed when Fraser and the others saw him in the company of the Holy United Churchmen, who demanded that Fraser come with them.

Pinkerton, Potter, Mickey, and Vermont had wanted to fight, as did Cherry and Salome and the rest of the girls, but Fraser had broken his silence and said that to fight would not be helping others, it would only be helping themselves, and he would not endorse it.

He allowed himself to be taken away but before he did he spoke to Pinkerton.

"You must not fight this Church. It doesn't matter if demons are at its head. It doesn't matter if it is founded on wickedness and deceit. It helps some people. All that matters is that you help others. Before yourself. Go back and repair your own church in the woods. Have Potter and Vermont and Mickey and the others help you. Leave the snakes alone. Ask Salome and the girls to sing for you, that'll bring the people in."

Pinkerton cried, said that he would do as he was told, then kissed the hem of Fraser's orange dress. As Fraser was taken out by the church security men, even though he was still as blind as a bat, he seemed to sense T-Bo. He stopped and put out his hand until he touched the young man's face. He felt the cheeks and the eyes and the mouth to make sure, then he leaned in and kissed T-Bo lightly on the forehead.

Leon had wanted to know why they hadn't taken in the Reverend Pinkerton, surely he was where the real trouble was, but Saul said no.

After his discussions with T-Bo, Saul had reached the conclusion that Fraser was the head of the monster, and that without the holyman, Pinkerton would retreat back into the shadows. Leon had assented.

Saul was always right.

Fraser stood sightless at the feet of the motionless fat man propped up in the hospital bed. Saul had insisted that he speak to Fraser alone, and now that he looked at this filthy, blind cripple he felt sick. Sicker than usual.

"You smell nice," said Fraser.

Saul was wary. He was trying to determine if Fraser was fooling with him or was genuine. He thought back to the day he had met

Potter Templeton and had told him he and Leon had been thrown out of the orphanage for being good Christians. He remembered Potter's suspicion.

"What do you want here?" Saul asked.

"Nothing," said Fraser.

"Then why did you come?

Fraser shrugged. "I just kind of drifted along and ended up here. I suppose God brought me."

Saul asked Fraser if he knew a fat man named Roscoe. Fraser said that no he didn't but that he knew a French policeman who was a bit quick with his nightstick.

"Can you really heal people?" asked Saul.

"I don't think so," said Fraser. "They think I can heal them and that's what does it. I think it just helps them feel better if they know there are miracles in the world."

"What about the woman you brought back from the dead?"

"She wasn't dead, she fainted."

"Could you heal yourself?"

"There's nothing wrong with me."

"You can't see."

"Oh, that. That'll clear up. Or it won't."

"You're insane."

"Yes, probably."

Saul paused, moved his left hand slightly, the only motion allowed him below the neck. "Could you heal me?"

Fraser said he didn't know but he'd give it a shot, if Saul wanted.

Saul whispered a tiny yes, that he would, then Fraser stepped forward hesitantly and felt the bed.

Saul watched Fraser's hands dance lightly along the covers, over his purple robes, until he had his dirty hands on Saul's head. The two men were very close. Saul closed his eyes and tried not to breathe, unable to stand the sight or smell of this disgusting tramp close up.

"I don't think I can heal you," mused Fraser sadly.

Saul asked why.

Fraser said, "Because this is who you are."

Saul thought for a moment. Then said, "You're a phony."

Fraser agreed that, yes, he was a phony, and also asked that Saul not forget that he was also a hypocrite and a drunk and was wearing a stolen frock.

Saul, for the first time since Candy Chambers had blown him in a stall at the Foxy nightclub, started to cry. Big, fat, helpless tears poured down his cheeks. Fraser put his hand out to touch the man's face.

But Saul turned his head away.

Fraser said, "I once got so afraid that I lay in a ditch with my hands over my ears until my friend fell on me. I hated myself and I had to change, and he helped me. I had to let him but I had also to participate in my metamorphosis. Misery is a choice. I got help from a brave soldier. If you want to feel better, help others."

Saul whimpered, "How can I help others? Look at me!"

"I'm blind," Fraser reminded him.

Saul wasn't listening. He wept openly for a time, then he yelled for Leon and had Fraser removed.

Before he left Fraser told Saul that it was nice to meet him and wished him luck and courage.

Leon felt a deep melancholy as he watched Fraser be taken away. He couldn't put his finger on it but he somehow knew that something very valuable was going with the mad blind cleric.

He shook off the thought. Saul would take care of it. Saul would take care of him. Saul would take care of everything.

After Fraser left, Saul fell into a deep sleep.

He dreamed he was young and fit and free. The dream terrified him.

Over the next few weeks and months he began to have terrible dreams. Dreams of health and well-being that only compounded his misery when he was awake. He could not throw himself into the relief of his unconsciousness, he had to stay in the temporal world, or what felt like the temporal world, at all costs. He was afraid that in another dimension he would be held accountable for who he had become, not for a moment considering that accountability was already upon him.

He began taking amphetamines in order to avoid sleep, and that is how he lived out the rest of his long, long life at the head of the giant, profitable organized religion he had created.

Motionless, terrified, completely awake, and dreamless.

THE RIVER

AS HE FELL, George's life did not flash in front of his eyes. He supposed that was because it had been slowly unfurling since the diagnosis.

He felt the fun-fair thrill of the quickening as gravity grabbed him, and then he thought about Father Kenny. Father Kenny was a young hippie-type Jesuit priest who had taught religious instruction when he was in high school.

His first name was Kenny. Kenny McCann. Older churchgoers insisted on calling him Father McCann even though he said he preferred the use of his Christian name. He was, after all, a Christian. This was his wee joke.

Father Kenny was one of a new breed of Catholic clergy who had started to appear around that time, just after the Second Vatican Council. Priests who wanted to be friendly with the kids. Not in a disgusting, altar-boy-abuse sort of way, but in a genuine and earnest fashion.

Father Kenny had talked to the teenagers in his class about all manner of things. Love, sex, death, the weather, drugs, contraception—anything. He had always declared that no subject was off limits, and he would be happy to discuss and defend the Church on whatever topic his pupils desired.

At first the kids were wary, they had a long history of teachers lulling them into a false sense of security, but Father Kenny kept his word. He never admonished a student for a belief or a stance, even in the case of Maxine Harrison, who at the time claimed to be a practicing Satanist. She wasn't really, of course, but sometimes she listened to Black Sabbath with the lights out.

During one of his class discussions, George had asked Father Kenny if it was true that all suicides went to hell.

Father Kenny hemmed and hawed a little bit. Finally he said that probably most suicides were in hell before they even attempted the act. The earnest teens would not let him get away with that, so Kenny was forced to admit that given that suicide was a mortal sin with no chance of repentance, yes, he supposed it would be inevitable that they would go to hell. But he added a codicil.

If, for example, a person had jumped off of a bridge to take his own life and genuinely repented before he hit the river, then he would enter the kingdom of the Lord.

The children had asked what constituted repentance in this case.

Father Kenny told them a true regret for having committed the act in the first place.

George figured this must mean he was going to hell because he remained certain that this course of action was the only right one for him.

Father Kenny would have had no trouble explaining what happened next but it puzzled George, Claudette, Alain Pantelic, Yves Bunuel, and a few others for many years to come.

Father Kenny would have said that, because the last thing that George had done before stepping into the void was to offer a prayer for someone else, he brought upon himself an act of divine intervention.

Alain Pantelic said that the results were inconclusive.

Claudette said that Love is stronger than death.

Yves Bunuel said Parisians were getting crazier.

M. Bunuel had been running a coal barge from Calais down to Paris for over thirty years and things had changed a great deal in that time. The river was busier but not with commercial traffic, with pleasure boats and speedboats and Jet Skis and all manner of nonsense. The city of Paris was by far the worst part of the journey. The place was crawling with Bateaux Mouches, the huge sightseeing boats that ferried Japanese and American tourists past all the sights, and then there were the restaurant boats. Yves could never understand why anyone would eat in a restaurant that you couldn't leave if you didn't like the food or the service.

Also, he hardly carried coal anymore. There was too much competition from road and rail haulage. It seemed that the world was burning fewer fossils. He took any cargo the agency could get for him.

On this day, he was carrying a huge consignment of new, extra-comfortable mattresses to a luxury spa that was being built on the coast. Most times, they would be carried by road, but thankfully, the truck drivers were on strike again and the trains were overstretched.

The resort was set to open in three weeks and they still had no beds. The mattresses were in the open hold but were hermetically sealed in plastic sheeting to avoid picking up any moisture.

George hit them at approximately fifty miles per hour, and no matter how comfortable the mattresses were, the thump was pretty bone jarring. But not as jarring as the surprise he felt. He looked up just in time to see Claudette smiling down at him.

"It's not time yet," she yelled.

Something else had happened.

The pain in his back was gone.

The following day, after Yves had pulled into the quay and angrily thrown George off his boat, and Claudette had immediately ran to him, and after they had gone home and made love, George went to see Alain Pantelic, who reluctantly agreed to retest him.

The French doctor found that George was cancer free. He could not explain it.

This is what happened.

There were two large tumors on George's lungs and an additional smaller malignant growth attached to his lymph nodes when he hit the extra-comfortable mattresses. The violence of the impact had knocked all three aliens into George's bloodstream, where they had floated, confused and angry, until they found themselves in his liver, being hit with all manner of poisons.

They tried splitting, multiplying, diversifying, all the tricks of their loathsome breed, but they were thwarted at every turn. George's immune system had become as tough and fearless as a combat-trained Glaswegian soldier. Everywhere they tried to go there was another wall of fierce white corpuscles herding them like sheep. From his liver they were transported and shunted roughly back along his intestinal tract and at about two o'clock that morning, when George left Claudette sleeping in the big warm bed, padded across the wooden floor, and sat down sleepily on the toilet, they were thrown rudely into a white porcelain hell with a partially digested lobster thermidore and what was left of some very expensive Chablis.

Hallelujah.

This, of course, is impossible.

Just like when Fraser's invitation was delivered on a Sunday, or when the moon shines underground, or when an ugly woman turns into a cat, or when an all-powerful ancient regime topples, or when a holyman is brutalized and horribly murdered by a mob of thugs but comes back from the dead three days later to tell everyone they should be nice to each other. Or when a bumblebee flies.

OMEGA MEN

THE SECURITY GUARDS from the Holy United Church of America had driven Fraser out of town in the back of Leon's town car. They hadn't been rough with him; they were big, good-natured American white boys, they didn't really want to be mean to anybody except leftists, atheists, and al-Qaeda.

They left Fraser by the roadside in the middle of some farmland miles from anywhere. They gave him a bottle of water and some Oreo cookies and wished him luck. He thanked them for their kindness and waved in what he hoped was the direction of the departing car.

Fraser thought that walking would be a bit dangerous, given that he had no idea where he was. His feet were still bare, so he moved a little till he felt grass rather than tarmac under his feet and then he sat down. He drank some water, ate some cookies, and lay back to have a little think.

A week earlier he had been a (somewhat) respected famous TV preacher in his home country. Now he was an outcast and a bum in a foreign land, he had nothing—no woman to fuss over him and have sex with, no money, no stuff, no job, no clothes, no shoes, no sight.

What a relief, he thought.

He drifted off and Carl appeared next to him. No one is blind in their dreams.

"I thought I wasn't going to see you again," said Fraser.

Carl smiled. "Well, I thought about it and I surmised that perhaps I am just a figment of your imagination, and if I am, then it's not really up to me, is it?"

Fraser laughed. "You're a weird guy, Carl," he said.

"Takes one to know one," chuckled the great, dead psychologist.

THANKS TO

John Naismith, Philip McGrade, and Alan Darby for patience and hilarity and friendship and valued counsel.

Brinsley Sheridan for the laughs and the lesson about time.

Andi O'Reilly for faith and encouragement.

Andrea Brandt, Sascha Ferguson, Lisa Gallant, Melanie Greene, David Harte, Judy Johnson, Peter and Alice Lassally, Cheryl Maisel, Peter Morris, Richard Murphy, Michael Naidus, Catherine Olim, Mimi Rogers, Sarah Stitt, Megan Wallace-Cunningham, Amy Yasbeck, and everyone else who read early unedited drafts and made the right noises.

Heather Taekman for pushing me uphill.

BJ Robbins for commitment and belief.

Jay Schaefer and Micaela Heekin for being so damn smart.

David Leventhal and Haydee Campos for making sure I didn't blow everything on candy.

The waiters in Les Deux Magots for the time to think.

The Fergusons and Ingrams of Glasgow for love and childhood.

Bill Wilson and Robert Smith and all of their friends.

Adam McLachlan for the past.

Milo Ferguson for the present and the future.

READER'S GUIDE

Dear Readers,

If your group has decided to discuss my book then let me first of all thank you for your attention and time.

Here are a few random thoughts that may stimulate your discussions.

I began the book with five statements. Apologia, History, Confession, Time, and Science. Why are these statements made so early? Are they rules for the world you are about to enter? If they are, are the rules followed? Are the statements truthful or accurate? Does this matter?

The first chapter of the book is entitled Alpha Wolves, the last chapter is called Omega Men. This is obviously a biblical reference. Do you think I'm drawing any conclusions about God in the book? Is this a religious work? What constitutes a religious work or act? Can writing, even if it contains dissention and doubt, be an act of worship?

Is all art an act of worship?

There are some sexual acts described in graphic detail. Is this salacious? Why is photographed sex "pornography" but written sex "literature"? Is that true? Is fictional sex better than the real thing?

Someone who read the book early on said that Carl Jung was my father figure. I thought Jung might be an imagining of the Deity, or maybe just the ghost of Carl Jung. What do you think?

A few characters in the book are already dead but this doesn't seem to slow them down much. Does the continuance of life after death prove the existence of God? If it does, then does the existence of life before death prove the existence of God? Is it a good idea to prove the existence of God? What happens to faith if you have proof? Do you need faith if you have proof? Is the existence of faith an admission that there is some doubt as to the existence of God?

Claudette believes that evil is born in the victim excuse. Do people really use injustices committed on them in their past to justify their actions? Do you do this? Does your country? Your family? Your ethnic group?

Is it valid to use aggression or antisocial behavior on the descendants of those who persecuted your ancestors? If not, how are the wrongs of the past dealt with? Should they be dealt with at all? Is it enough to simply apologize? On a personal or even international level?

George attempts suicide. Is he morally wrong to do so?

The church founded by Saul and Leon is built on lies and deceit, yet Fraser thinks that this ultimately doesn't matter because it helps some people. Is he right?

There are many hidden literary references in the text. For example, the old Icelandic boatman who ferries Fraser across the underground sea is called Arne Saknussem, a lesser character in Jules Verne's *Journey to the Center of the Earth.* Why do you think I did this? Was I just showing off or is there a reason for it?

What do you know of Jung's theory of the collective unconscious? Does it seem valid to you?

My heart was broken when I wrote this book. Is that kind of thing necessary to stimulate creativity? Can a person be happy and creative?

I know the answers to maybe two or three of these questions.

I wish you better luck figuring things out.

Peace and Love,
Craig
x